I0823410

Very Slowly All at Once

Very Slowly All at Once

A Novel

Lauren Schott

An *Imprint of* HarperCollins*Publishers*

HarperCollins books may be purchased for educational, business, or sales promotional use. For information, please email the Special Markets Department at SPsales@harpercollins.com.

hc.com

FIRST EDITION

Designed by Elina Cohen
Title illustration © tetiana_u / Shutterstock

Library of Congress Cataloging-in-Publication Data has been applied for.

ISBN 978-0-06-343271-0

25 26 27 28 29 LBC 5 4 3 2 1

For Chris

1.

They spent just over a million on that house, which seems like a lot for two people with pretty ordinary jobs. A big chunk of that price tag was for the lot—on the corner, close to the lake, best one in the Magpie Court development. Not a huge piece of land, not the rolling hills that the mansions on the shoreline have, but theirs is the only spot on the street that gets you views of the lake and the sailboats lined up outside the Shoreby Club.

The whole street is brand-new, with only five houses on it, all variations on the same style: sharp angles to the roofs, and exteriors in local stone and wood so dark that when it rains the surface gleams like metal. In summer, the landscaping is fat with green hydrangea and bushy rows of lavender, and in the winter the place looks like a little pioneer town. Two rows of (seven-figure) cabins lined up cozy in the snow, the glowing windows like paintings: *Emptying Miele Dishwasher*, oil on canvas, 2022.

Even the neighbors farther away in the mansions, your plastic surgeons and your tech magnates and your battle-scarred bankers who have taken on the upkeep of the estates built by the great Cleveland industrialists, even some of those guys must sit in their train-station houses with leaky roofs and outdated paneling and envy these sleek new builds. Most people would take a custom kitchen and a first-floor master over a chilly ballroom and a cracked swimming pool any day of the week.

The downside to the houses in Magpie Court is the name: The developers insist on referring to them as "cluster homes," on account of the smaller parcels of land. This is a terrible piece of marketing if you ask me. Only bad things come in clusters: headaches, viruses, bombs.

Fucks too, and not the good kind.

2.

Mack

The mail, always a highlight of Mack's day in the summer months, was mostly of a financial nature.

There was a letter from Duke University's Annual Fund, begging him to make a difference and donate now, and helpfully pointing him in the direction of an app that would make doing this easier. Mack read that he was the missing piece of the alumni puzzle, which was a shame, because he would have to remain a hole in the thousand-piece collegiate landscape: he was (unfortunately) living in every cent of his disposable income, having blown a small fortune on marble countertops, luxury bathroom fixtures, and hand-painted wallpaper. He took the identical letter addressed to Hailey and balled them up together.

There was also an invoice for the Wakefields' window, $4,789.25 from PaneLess Glass Repair, with a note attached on Betsy's initialed, plaid-bordered stationery: *Mack, please pay them directly. ASAP please and thanks. Thanks, ESW.*

Mack had been expecting this. Betsy Wakefield had been pretty gracious when he sliced his golf ball through her great room window, all things considered, even though she'd been hosting a party when he sheepishly presented himself at her front door, still holding his five iron. One of her guests, a woman Mack vaguely recognized from the Shoreby Club pool, had an angry red oval blooming right between her eyes, and for a second Mack feared the worst—Hailey was right, he never should have been hitting golf balls in such close proximity to the neighbors. He could've killed this woman. Then he noticed red swelling down the side of another lady's jawline, and, in the living room, an ice pack being held to a forehead. This surely must have been the most powerful drive he'd ever hit, to go through a window and still ricochet like that. He could've made the PGA tour after all.

"It's a Botox party," Betsy had whispered, her finger to her lips. "Shhh, don't tell anyone."

"Your secret is safe with me," Mack told her, and it had been. He hadn't even told his wife, who, Mack thought as he surveyed the freshly Botoxed faces more carefully, must've been the only neighbor not invited. Not that he was surprised.

He tucked Betsy's expensive note under his armpit.

The final piece of mail was a brown envelope with one of those clear plastic windows for the address, and it must have come straight from the golf gods, because it more than made up for the damage to next door's window: It was a check for $5,000, from a company called Sunshine Enterprises, Ltd., and it was made out to him, Malcolm P. Evans.

Mack turned the thin paper—pretty much a relic in this day and age—over in his hands. There was only the machine-generated check, with a bar code and some serial numbers. No statement, no return address. The postmark was from Newark, New Jersey.

As he ran through the list of their pensions and investments in his head—and unfortunately for Duke University, it was a very short list—Mack felt the tightening of something deep in his ribs. He had no idea what kind of business Sunshine Enterprises was in, but already, in the brief seconds that had passed since he opened the envelope, Mack had formed his suspicions about its provenance.

He had also decided that he was damn well going to deposit this check, if, given how long it had been since he'd dealt in anything but Venmo and direct deposits, he could even remember how to do it. He had a vague notion that Hailey kept the checkbook and deposit slips in the desk drawer in the kitchen.

He stuffed the check in his back pocket and padded through the cavernous front hall in his socks. In the kitchen he bypassed the $2,000 coffee maker—it had been broken since their second morning in the house—and made himself a giant travel mug of instant. He took two quick finger scoops of peanut butter, polished off half a tub of blueberry yogurt using Mabel's dirty spoon from breakfast, and made his way downstairs. He had three hours before he had to pick up the girls from camp and a lot of ground to cover. As an assistant professor of English at a college that was famous for science and technology, for Mack summer breaks meant occasionally checking his emails to remind himself that the mothership did in fact still exist. But this summer was not like other summers. This summer Mack was going to be conscientious. He was going to polish his lesson plans and lectures until they shone, like the serious academic that he was. That would show them, those doubters at Cleveland Tech. That would shut them up once and for all.

Down in the basement he passed through the lushly carpeted playroom, stepping over Lego and Hailey's vintage My Little Ponies, now among his daughters' most prized possessions. He closed the door to civilization behind him as he passed into the underbelly of the new house, through the exposed, still-gleaming pipes and the giant hot water tanks. On the far side of the boiler room was the raw wooden door to his office.

The big inhale for the sigh Mack was about to give brought three scents to his nostrils as he stepped into his lair. First, the routine skunk of the marijuana that he was growing on the sill of the high, narrow window (just a single sickly plant, not enough to land him in prison but sufficient to allow him to cling to the last vestiges of his adolescence). Next came the not-unpleasant odor of sunbaked dachshund. He'd left Gulliver snoozing in here earlier this morning, shut the door on him, and forgotten about him entirely. Which explained the third smell: on the concrete floor under Mack's desk there was a big puddle of fresh dog piss.

He had neither the time nor the materials to clean it up with; he was already six minutes late for his Zoom. Carefully placing a foot on either side of Gulliver's urine, Mack sat down and logged on.

"There he is!" An unnaturally white set of teeth filled his screen, then sticky pink lipstick, a mouth encased in deep lines. "I said to myself, I said, he's a good boy. Mack Evans wouldn't forget about lunch with his mommy, no sir. He never forgets. You got a sandwich?"

"I ate already," Mack said, as the lips were replaced with an extreme close-up of a sun-leathered bosom bursting out of white polyester. Mack shifted in his chair and felt dog pee seep into the inside edges of his socks.

"Okay, well, we're having Subway over here today," the bosom said, and was swiftly replaced on the screen by a turkey sub wrapped in logoed paper, thrust toward the camera. "You look so handsome, Mackie. You got some sun on ya. You been playin' a lot of golf?"

"Only in the backyard."

"And how's the house?"

"Still good."

"And Hailey and the girls? I was thinking the other day, Mabel and Gigi must be getting so big. I'd love to see them sometime."

"Yeah, we could do that. It's just a little tricky . . ."

"I know." The sandwich disappeared from view as Mack's screen flashed with industrial ceiling lights. "Look Leonora, there's your boy. Look how handsome he looks today! You're a lucky lady, to have a good-lookin' kid like this one."

The camera came to rest on his mother's thin figure, propped up in her adjustable bed. Her hair was immaculately styled as always, her face empty as a swimming pool in deepest winter.

"Hey Mom," Mack said, as Tilda settled down with her sandwich on the edge of the frame. "You're looking well. That yellow housecoat really suits you. Mabel chose it, did I tell you that? She likes yellow too."

Leonora Evans said nothing, and Mack went quiet for a minute too. He was thinking about the color yellow and how, the last time he'd seen his mother alive and well, she'd been wearing a yellow sundress and even he—even her own teenage son who took her for granted every single day of her life and basically thought of her as part of the furniture—even Mack had noticed how beautiful she was in that yellow dress that day. Now he knew it had been a premonition: early the next morning, home from college on spring break, he'd found Leonora bent over double with a headache. Another day after that and his mother was gone, in everything but the most basic, biological sense—an aneurism had stolen everything but her ability to breathe on her own. She had been forty-nine years old.

"She smiled today." Tilda was a good nurse; she had a sixth sense about when to break Mack's silences. "I noticed she really likes the Everly Brothers. You know, 'Wake Up Little Susie'? We've been listening to it during our exercises, and it's twice now that she's smiled. She's a big fan."

Mack very much doubted it. His mother had liked the Who and Led Zeppelin, had been at Woodstock and then at Studio 54, before she'd followed Mack's father down south to Florida. But Mack wasn't about to burst Tilda's bubble; she was too important to him. She gave up her lunch hours so Mack could talk into the air, sent him updates peppered with nursing-home gossip. Leonora was her favorite patient, she'd told Mack, and he hoped like hell that it was the truth, since his mother lived thirteen hundred miles away from him, in the Sandy Hollow nursing home in Jupiter, Florida. (*We can't talk to my one grandma*, Mabel had told another child once, *because she lives on another planet.*)

Tilda was also discreet. She'd never asked him why, as the only living relative of a woman in a permanent near-vegetative state, he didn't move his mother closer to where he lived.

Mack leaned sideways to pull the check from his back pocket and in doing so placed the ball of his right foot squarely in the middle of the dog pee. "This is a weird question," he said to Tilda, while making a silent vow to take Gulliver to the pound, "but has she had any visitors?"

"Only Mrs. Weigand," said Tilda. "Every Tuesday, like clockwork."

"Mmm." Irene Weigand had been part of his mother's bridge group, all of whom were much, much older than his mom. Irene must be pushing ninety by now; the rest of them were presumably all dead. His mother had kept herself to herself down there in Florida, but she had loved bridge and apparently elderly retirees too, even if she never got to be one. Irene Weigand didn't interest him, though. Not now and not ever. "No one else, huh?"

"Nope," said Tilda. "Same time on Friday, Mack?"

"Only if it works for you."

"You know it does. Have a good week, Mackie."

"You too, Tilda," Mack said without thinking, and then, "Goodbye, Mom."

He ended the call, set the check from Sunshine Enterprises on his desk, and then reached down with one hand to peel the wet socks off his feet.

"You little asshole," Mack said to Gulliver, who had wandered over to inspect his handiwork. "You can't hold it in for like two hours?" Mack's coffee was empty, so he took a can of Dr Pepper from his mini-fridge and clicked through his emails while Gulliver sniffed at the discarded socks in disgust.

Seven fresh emails since this morning: one from a former student, two from Mabel's new school with forms to fill out, two from Hailey with dates for his diary (as if he kept one, as if he wanted a trip into the ninth circle of corporate hell). And finally, two emails from the English department, though neither of those was the one he was looking for, the one he needed. Mack was waiting for the email assigning his tutor group, the email that would give him the names of the six students he would guide through the highs and lows of their English major experience at the Cleveland Institute of Technology. The one that meant the department had made up their minds to trust him again.

3.

Hailey

It was the surprise in the man's eyes that caught Hailey's attention. They were like a cartoon character's, the whites bulging so violently that she thought they might pop right out of his head. Her mind made quick work of the input it was receiving from the next table over: a charged silence spiraling outward from his general direction, those eyes, the strange, raspy squeak coming from his lips, the hands gesturing madly at his own throat.

Definitely choking.

A quick glance at her fellow diners, and Hailey's assessment was confirmed. So was the bystander effect: everyone stared, and everyone waited for someone else to do something. Hailey's lunch partner, a potential associate hire with an impressive track record in personal injury, blinked at her blankly. He'd never get a job out of her now.

Hailey stood, took three quick strides to reach the man's chair. He was already turning blue.

"I'm going to perform the Heimlich now," she told him as she swung his legs sideways. He shook his head, and Hailey ignored him. He was big and clearly reluctant; better to keep him seated. She reached her forearms around him, feeling the starchy roughness of his shirt through the thin fabric of her silk sleeves. He was as wide as a fridge; her hands barely met on his chest even though her body was pressed tightly against his back. Still, her fist found the sweet spot under his ribs, her thumb bone angled for maximum leverage. Lucky for him she worked out, at least occasionally, so the difference in their sizes didn't matter. Her first thrust cracked two of his ribs.

The pain roused him. The man struggled to stand, with Hailey still attached to his back, her biceps unwilling or unable to release their hold. He flapped around like a marlin on a boat deck, and she saw the half-eaten T-bone on his plate recede farther and farther below her. He was lifting her off her feet, and still she couldn't feel him breathe. Her legs scrambled, found chair and then floor. Too late she saw the man's eyes roll back in his head, felt his backward momentum. In a panicked misfire, her arms pulled him even closer toward her, her hands trying again for the target at the base of his sternum. She found it just as the heel of her Chanel pump gave way beneath her, sliding across the floor and leading the way down for the rest of her body, and his too. Blackness closed in as the full weight of him landed smack on top of her.

When she opened her eyes, the man's sweaty face was inches from her own. He was conscious and extremely, extremely concerned.

"Don't move," he said to her, and from far away she could hear paramedics parting the crowd. "Don't move, hon, something could be broken. You could have internal injuries. You've been unconscious." The color was back in his face. His cheeks were flushed with embarrassment.

Hailey sat up, fought the cartoon stars in the corner of her vision. The back of her head hurt, but not as badly as her ribs. The man watched as she pressed a hand to her side and gasped in pain.

"I think you broke a couple of mine as well," he said. "I could sue you, you know?" But his eyes were grateful.

"I'm okay, really," Hailey told him, gripping the hand he extended. "And I wouldn't try that. I'm a lawyer."

"Me too." He held her arm as she got to her feet, and before she could stop him, he pressed her to his chest in a massive bear hug, right there in front of an entire restaurant full of Cleveland's white-collar workforce. They clapped and cheered, and for a wild minute, Hailey wished that Mack had been there to see it.

✦

By 3:00 p.m. Hailey was all patched up, with fresh makeup and a spritz of perfume to hide the sweaty, steak-y smell that clung to her blouse. She took her place in the conference room across from Rebekah Rainier, who was, in a manner of speaking, their small firm's biggest client. Rebekah was closing in on a divorce settlement of almost $7 million, although she was doing her best to screw it up. Today's meeting was a strategy session to get her back on track, and Rebekah had brought her business manager (whatever that meant; she had no income and didn't work), her mother, and, for some completely unknown reason, a man she had matter-of-factly introduced as her hairdresser.

"I just don't know that I can fight David anymore," Rebekah was saying to Hailey and two junior associates. "You can't do battle with a sociopathic narcissist. My personal stress levels are unsustainable. I can hardly function. I'm not living my life, I'm just *existing*. While he's over there in Europe fucking everything that moves."

"We don't have any proof of that," Hailey told her. "And for our purposes it doesn't really matter anyway. What concerns me here is the change in custody arrangements—"

Rebekah's phone rang. As she answered it, she held up a finger for silence, and Hailey came to the sudden realization that she had never hated anyone as much as she hated this woman. She watched as the silicone blobs that stood in for Rebekah's lips gave instructions to someone who was obviously packing up her house, a Crystal Lake McMansion worth less now than when the Rainiers bought it thanks to the "improvements" Rebekah had overseen. "Don't damage the shoeboxes," Hailey's client was barking. "And I want the clothes packed hanging. And don't crush them."

The pain in Hailey's ribs made tolerating this almost impossible. "I don't recall being told that you are vacating the marital home?" Hailey said as Rebekah hung up the phone. "That has big implications. That's abandonment. That's what we're trying to hit David with."

"How could I abandon him when he hardly even lives here?"

It was a fair point. Rebekah's husband had indeed spent many a night away from Cleveland in the past six months—Hailey's team had tracked his movements—and yet the man's presence couldn't have loomed larger in his adopted city. Rainier had swooped in two years back with big plans to revitalize Cleveland's eyesore of a lakefront. He had sunk many millions into a deal to buy the old chemical plant that ate up acres of valuable shoreline, and local columnists fizzed with anticipation about what Cleveland's white knight had in mind for the land, how he was working on a new stadium, condominiums, a shopping pavilion, a marina.

Right then, though, Hailey happened to know that Rebekah was right: the man was in Europe. On vacation. Hailey had seen Rainier's social media, had stalked him moving through Paris with his and Rebekah's young twins. She had seen snaps of them outside the Louvre and rowing along the Seine in a little boat—the three of them smiling the squinty, happy smiles of those who had time and money for adventure. And Hailey, with the ball and chain of the new house and the looming outcome of this settlement keeping her firmly planted in northeastern Ohio for the summer, had been insanely jealous of this man even as she plotted to carve out a chunk of his net worth. *Yes*, some of it was probably staged for the courts, and *yes*, maybe David Rainier was committing a little adultery in between family outings, but the fact remained that Rebekah hadn't seen her children in months and had never thought to complain about it.

Until today.

"I just don't think I can fight him anymore," Rebekah was saying again. "He always wins. I just want to have my babies with me and move on. If I take the place in Short Hills, I'll get the kids sometimes, he'll give me an allowance . . . it's not like I ever want to get married again anyway, not after what I've been through—"

"Wait, what?" Hailey's cool professionalism, honed by a decade of watching couples humiliate themselves, bolted from the room like it was on fire. "What are you talking about?"

"I'm saying I want to move on. I want to put this behind me."

"That part comes after the actual divorce, Rebekah."

"My mental health can't wait that long. I've got to handle this another way." Rebekah's mother was nodding in agreement, and Hailey's heart began smashing against her tender ribs. She had to have this wrong.

"Are you saying you're no longer going to divorce him?"

"No." Rebekah tilted her head and flashed her Chiclet veneers in a way that made Hailey want to reach across the table and strangle her. "I mean, *of course* I'm going to divorce him." But just as the air returned to Hailey's lungs, Rebekah came out with a doozy: "I'm just going to divorce him mentally and spiritually, as opposed to legally."

It took Hailey a beat or two to comprehend the Rainiers' plan: Rebekah would stay married to David. David would let Rebekah live in their *other* McMansion back in New Jersey, give her an allowance, let her see the kids, though they'd live with him in Manhattan. There would be two very separate lives, but no divorce.

And no divorce settlement.

"I'm sorry to bring this up in front of your . . . *companions*"—Hailey threw a grim smile in the direction of her client's entourage—"but you already owe this firm a quarter million in fees. Does David know that he'll be absorbing this debt?"

"You'll have to talk to him about that," Rebekah said, getting to her feet. "He'll just stonewall me, and I'm not in any state to cope with this."

Hailey fought the urge to drag her back down to the table. "Rebekah, this firm made an exception for you when we extended you a line of credit. *I* made an exception for you, as a woman and as a mother, because I knew David had all the assets and all the power. But this outstanding legal bill is your responsibility. If there's going to be no divorce settlement to take our payment out of, it will have to be paid outright. As soon as possible. This is a business, and we did a tremendous amount of work on your behalf." Almost eight hundred hours of work, the last time Hailey checked. Not to mention that they had paid outside experts and asset tracers to try to find David's money. Even the firm's *bank* knew about this pending settlement, was actively waiting for it.

"You're so full of crap," said Rebekah, and Hailey noted that her client's mother didn't so much as raise an eyebrow as the tone went nuclear: "I was in no state to make any arrangement with you. You didn't give two shits about me. You just saw the dollar signs and went for it, so now you can take it up with David. Good fucking luck."

The associates fled the room almost as fast as Rebekah and her flotsam did. Hailey stayed. She put her head down on the cool surface of the marble table and visualized Rebekah Rainier getting hit by a high-speed train, then dying in a fiery plane crash, and finally getting torn apart—slowly, lips saved for last—by a rabid dog.

Even then, though, Hailey still wouldn't see any money. Rebekah had nothing in her own name, and David Rainier had huge pockets, probably even deeper than they knew about. His wealth was spread all over the world. All Hailey had been after, all she had stuck her neck out for, was a little piece of it for Rebekah. But now, without the looming threat of the family court system and the bargaining chip of his children, the firm would have to go after David using its own resources. They might be successful in some small way, eventually, but it would take years. It would cost millions. It was all Hailey's fault.

Hailey vomited into a trash can. Her head was throbbing, and even though she knew that Mack (who because of his mother still suffered from extreme paranoia about headaches) would never forgive her for it, she prayed this was a brain hemorrhage from hitting her head earlier. That had to be an easier road forward than the one she had just veered onto.

4.

Bratenahl, Ohio, is a strange little suburb. In the space of just over one square mile, there is a real mixed bag of property offerings. You've got your newer developments like Magpie Court, for the trendy millennials and the smug early retirees with huge savings pots who think they are millennials. Then there are those big mansions I told you about—truly spectacular by any standard, at least from a distance. Even the scruffy ones that the old fogies don't maintain properly.

You've got a few super-modern houses, mostly built by basketball and football stars that are hardly ever in them, and on the edges of the township, tucked away behind the fire station, there are some streets of more modest homes from the postwar housing boom. I always imagine that the people who live there—a mix of normal retirees and young, less affluent families—must get sick of having to look out across the untended back lots of the lakefront behemoths every time they leave their houses.

Most citizens of Bratenahl do make an effort, though. Even the poorest of the rich folks put a flag up for the Fourth of July, spring for a cheap plastic basket of begonias beside the door. In the clustered world of Magpie Court all the heavy upkeep is done for you, and the unspoken understanding is that if you *must* do more, then your Halloween scarecrow will be a tasteful chappie, and your Christmas lights will be virginal white.

Which is why the Evans house stands out. Granted, Hailey Evans does manage to grow pots of red geraniums that tone nicely with the lavender, and the souped-up Jeep Cherokee they sometimes leave out in the driveway is unusually clean for a family car. But there are cracks in the facade. Hideous, gaping cracks: cheap plastic pinwheels stuck in front of the hedges, bird sculptures of reclaimed metal on the lawn, wind chimes swinging from the corner of the garage. And the shoes. Oh my God the shoes.

I can only surmise that they went for some kind of rare flooring option. Expensive, elegant, and utterly impractical. The delicate nature of bamboo, maybe, is the only possible explanation for the piles of footwear that I have seen amassed on the Evans's front porch: tiny Crocs and muddied running shoes, stilettos and snow boots, flip-flops and sneakers and fur-lined slippers and Wellingtons. Golf spikes and ski boots and roller skates and . . . it's a miracle they can still access their own front door, the absolute hillbillies.

Let me tell you, growing up in my house, you kept your shoes in the closet or on your feet. Otherwise, you got hit with one right across your backside.

5.

Mack

"What the hell is this?"

Mack's stomach did a little flip. Hailey had snuck up on him in the kitchen, a letter in her hands. It would be the one from the English department, telling him that he was on probation, that he was under investigation for inappropriate interactions with his students, during and after the Covid lockdown. The department administrator had warned him this was coming, and Mack had been patrolling the mail even more religiously than usual. Except today Hailey beat him to it. He had not given her even the tiniest warning about the shit-storm that was blowing in, and this was not the way he wanted her to find out. He braced himself for impact, until he realized that what she was actually holding was another check from Sunshine Enterprises. He snatched it from her.

"Why do you insist on opening mail addressed to me? That's a felony, you know."

"Why is someone paying you seven thousand dollars?"

Mack pushed his glasses down from his forehead. She was right about the amount. This was the third check in six weeks, and each time the amount had increased by $1,000.

Hailey stood staring at him. He sighed. Maybe this would be good practice for the rest of the truths he had to deliver.

"I think they're coming from my dad."

"*They*?"

Interesting that she had seized on the pronoun. "Yep. He's been sending money."

"Your *dad*? The dad you hardly know? How much money?"

Mack was an English professor; it took him a long minute to do the math. "This makes eighteen grand. There were two other checks."

"How could you not . . . You *cashed* them?"

"I *deposited* them. I'm surprised you didn't notice." *Turn it around on her*, he told himself. *The best defense is a good offense.*

"Don't try to turn this around on me. You didn't think to mention that your father—the father that you hate, the father that you haven't spoken to in twenty-five years—has been in touch? Have I just entered the Twilight Zone?"

"He didn't get in touch. I mean, not other than to send these."

She took the check back from him. "But how do you even know it's him? There's no name on it. What's Sunshine Enterprises?"

Mack sighed again. This was but a drop in the ocean of what he had been keeping from her. "He's tried to send me money before, back when I was starting college. I thought I'd told you about it before. I sent it back."

Hailey's face softened. He had to give her credit; she had always trodden lightly around the topic of his father, had sensed not to poke that bear. "I didn't know that. I didn't know you ever knew where he lived."

"He lives in Daytona. Or at least he did then."

"How would he get our address?"

"Google?"

Gulliver's nails clicked across the kitchen floor. His ears were tied up like pigtails with two purple hair scrunchies, and he was wearing a pink-and-blue bathrobe commandeered from Mabel's American Girl doll. The pained expression in his eyes almost made Mack feel sorry for him, especially when Hailey laughed. The betrayal must've broken Gulliver's momma's-boy heart; he fled the kitchen immediately.

"I can't believe I didn't know this about your dad. Maybe he's trying to—"

"Who cares what he's trying to do," Mack interrupted her. "But I will take his money. It's not like he doesn't owe me."

Something that looked like sadness flashed across Hailey's face, and it irritated him.

"Listen to me, this is not a big deal. If my father wants to get in touch because I accept this money, let him. There are a few things I'd like to say to him." Mack had always imagined that he'd start with a nice little anecdote about how hard his mom had worked to fill the void his father's sudden departure had left. Mack was seven years old, and Leonora tried to take him to a Dolphins game. She'd gotten lost, got a flat tire, forgotten the tickets, and eventually they'd ended up listening to the end of the game in the car while she sobbed.

Yeah, now that he thought about it, Mack hoped his dad would get in touch. But until he did, Mack would sit back and take his money.

"But you can't just take this money. There are tax implications too, Mack. Do you even know what this company is? Did you google it?"

"Obviously. There are about a billion Sunshine Enterprises, though."

"Did you google it with his name?"

"Of course. Nothing comes up." Why did she think he was so stupid?

"But then how can you be sure—"

Gigi saved him. "Mabel won't share Gulliver," she announced, tearing into the kitchen. "She's got him in the doll buggy and she won't let him out and he's sad and she won't listen to me about any of it and it's very upsetting to me." Gigi at three was more eloquent than most adults; she was like living with a tiny version of one of Mack's more erudite colleagues. *Former* colleagues, soon.

Mack normally wouldn't have jumped so quickly on the chance to rescue Gulliver, but this was enough truth for Hailey's first helping.

He found the dog down in the playroom, where Mabel had strapped him, upright with his belly exposed, into a doll stroller using the belt from Hailey's fancy trench coat. He couldn't have been there long, but Gulliver's hips were wedged in deeply, and his short legs stuck out helplessly in front of him. The worst thing though, the thing that was making Gulliver howl like a banshee, was that the poor dog's hairy little penis was all in a twist, squeezed by the belt and folded at a terrible angle. Mack knew exactly how he felt.

✦

That night, after the girls were tucked in and the painkillers the emergency vet had prescribed Gulliver had rendered him unconscious, Mack treated Hailey to a little more of the story of his father. They were in bed, and she was wearing a silk nightie that he liked, and he thought that if he laid the groundwork properly, he might even get some sex out of his terrible childhood.

He brought her a glass of red, though it was August and hot as hell outside, and he told her everything he knew. (Everything about Warner Thomas Evans, that is.) Mack's dad had been shady, *really* shady. Maybe even Mafia shady, though Leonora had only ever hinted at this once, after they'd watched *The Godfather* on VHS. But Mack's mom had been clear on the fact that Warner was in construction, and that he was a criminal. In the 1970s, he'd been involved in the building of three massive high-rise condominium complexes down in the Florida Keys. Hundreds of apartments were pre-sold for 300K a pop, a lot in those days. Mack's dad's company finished off the construction, moved all the retirees and snowbirds in, and everyone was happy. Until the ceilings began to crumble on the new owners. The cement used to make the building had been mixed with untreated seawater to cut costs, and his mother's legend had it that within six months the walls literally came tumbling down when the saltwater corroded the steel reinforcements. By which point Warner Evans had vanished into thin air, taking the money and leaving behind his wife and young son. Leonora had told Mack later that throughout most of his childhood, she wasn't even sure whether her husband was dead or alive.

Hailey was speechless. "I see what you mean," she said finally. "*Sunshine Enterprises*. As in, the Sunshine State." Then she said something that surprised him: "You know, I almost feel sorry for your dad."

"Why? I've just told you; the man was a criminal."

"I know, but I mean, is anyone sure he *meant* to do it? What if it was just a mistake?"

"Mixing concrete with saltwater is a pretty big mistake."

"I'm just saying," Hailey said. "You might want to hear the man out. Plus, think of all the money he's spent on your mom's care all these years. He couldn't be *all* bad. I mean, I get why you hate him so much, but think about it—it must be hundreds of thousands of dollars by now, your mom's been in that home so long. I'd always wondered where he got that much money from."

"Yeah, well, the stress he caused probably put her in that place."

When it had become clear that Mack's mother wasn't ever going to recover from the aneurism, nor would she be lucky enough to die anytime soon, there was a brief and terrible interval when her insurance company refused to pay for a decent nursing home. And then in a matter of weeks, Leonora's lawyer had come to see Mack and delivered the news that from this point on his mother's care was being handled by a trust, set up by an anonymous benefactor. There was enough money that Mack didn't have to worry about it going forward, and this benefactor wanted Leonora's son to go on and live his life as best he could, and here also was a very small nest egg to get Mack started. Mack knew exactly who this mystery benefactor was: the very same one who had tried to give him a thousand bucks the year before, when he'd gone off to Duke on a whole lot of financial aid and a partial golf scholarship. Then, Mack had told that "benefactor" that he could go fuck himself, even though he could have used the money. But getting his mother taken care of was too big for Mack to take a stand over. An exception to the embargo on his father was made, and now Mack's thinking was that he would take the same approach toward these new payments. Especially if he was about to lose his job and his entire career and thus have no salary for the remainder of his life.

"But then couldn't this be like Mafia money you're taking? Or homeless old people's money?"

Mack could sense that Hailey was still in the foreplay phase of this conversation, whereas he was already smoking his metaphorical cigarette.

"Who even cares anymore? My mom and I were his victims too. Nah, I'm going to take it and spend it and not feel even the slightest bit bad about it. I will look into the tax implications though, don't worry." He only added the last bit because it made him sound capable. The IRS wasn't going to come after an English professor, for fuck's sake. Especially an ex-English professor on unemployment . . . he had to stop thinking like this.

"But I mean, *God*, Mack," Hailey said, stretching out her smooth, tanned legs in a way that filled him with hope. "This is pretty big to keep from me. I feel like I don't even know you anymore."

That must've been a positive thing in her eyes, though, because he did get sex.

Afterward, he was just drifting off when Hailey prodded him awake.

"I can't stop thinking about the fact that he knows where we live."

"Who?"

"Your father. If he is some big criminal, he has our address. He could be keeping tabs on us, watching us, anything. Do you even know what he looks like?"

Mack did not; he had no photos of his dad. But the idea of his father spying on them didn't bother him so much. If he was really honest with himself, in his mind Warner Evans had been watching him his whole life. His father had been the invisible, internal audience throughout all of Mack's triumphs, and especially during his defeats.

"I wouldn't lose any sleep over it," he said to Hailey. "If he's that big of a criminal still, he'll have more interesting things to worry about than us."

6.

Hailey

Why did everything always have to happen all at once?

Thursday, August 29. Mabel and Gigi's camp had finished for the summer. But (of course) school and preschool didn't start until the following week, so neither did the after-school babysitter. Mack had promised the girls one last trip to the pool at the Shoreby Club, and then inevitably swanned off to some mysterious department meeting. Yesterday, Hailey's mother had selfishly decided to break her ankle in what must have been the only jazzercise class still running in the twenty-first century. Gulliver was only now starting to recover from a near-death experience; the incident with Mabel's doll stroller had resulted in a strangulated hernia and an infection that cost $2,000 and nearly killed him, and now he couldn't be left unattended, lest he try to chew at his freshly stitched-up manhood. And the grand finale: the firm's best paralegal, the ballbuster rock star who worked all hours and rose to every challenge Hailey set for her, had chosen today of all days to arrange a call between Hailey and the impossible-to-get-hold-of David Rainier. Rebekah's estranged husband was basically Batman, as far as Hailey could tell, so this wasn't something that could be rescheduled for a more convenient time.

No matter: Hailey would dial in from the pool. She would put Gulliver into her big canvas bag and smuggle him past the club attendant. She'd blow up the swim floaties, wipe the chlorinated snot from Gigi's face, and coax Mabel off the diving board a few times.

She'd order the girls grilled cheese sandwiches and reapply their sunscream, as Mabel still called it. Then, after she'd squeezed in delivering the news to David Rainier about the two hundred and fifty grand he owed her, she would put the kids and the invalid sausage in the car and drive down to Akron to check on her mal-coordinated mom.

(A thousand dollars said Mack had been told about this meeting months and months ago, and just hadn't bothered to write it down. Any sympathy Hailey felt over his *Goodfellas* childhood had evaporated.)

Gulliver hated riding in any kind of anything, especially now, which meant that Hailey knew ahead of time that she'd have to cover his head with towels and sneak past the zitty teenage pool attendant with a writhing, jumping beach bag on her arm. This had been her focus during the preparations, and so she hadn't supervised Mabel's final swimsuit choice. Which was why Mabel, who had just removed her cover-up, was now prancing around the very exclusive Shoreby Club in a tiny sequined bikini from Walmart and jelly plastic platform sandals, both gifted by Hailey's mother. She looked like a six-year-old stripper.

Hailey took a deep breath, and a bit of luck came her way: there were three chaises free on the far corner closest to the lake. She could tuck Gulliver behind one of them and he could snooze undetected in the shade. She had even remembered to bring the leftover painkillers from the vet in case he had trouble falling asleep. She waved to Allison Murdoch as she passed, she of the six boys in seven years (and all in private school!), and then smiled at the old guy with the weird mustache who lived in one of the big houses on the shore. He was always around, walking the neighborhood, swimming laps in the pool, checking his perimeter. Oh, to be retired! Hailey was more than ready.

Too late she recognized the occupants of the chaises next to the ones she was aiming for: their next-door neighbor Betsy Wakefield and her two daughters. The eldest, Arabella, was wearing the exact same strawberry-print (one-piece) Crewcuts swimsuit that Hailey had laid out for Mabel that morning, and also the matching hair bow and the coordinating flip-flops. She and her equally well-turned-out sister, whose name Hailey couldn't remember, were both reading books that looked very advanced for their ages. Hailey made a mental note to get Mabel brushed up on her phonics. Mabel was always a little behind in everything: she had been born at twenty-two weeks and, having fought like hell for six months to stay alive, now seemed to have only placid happiness left in her. No matter; Hailey would clear a path around Mabel for the rest of her life if she had to. Mabel had kept up her end of the bargain by not dying.

Neither of the Wakefield kids acknowledged Mabel or Gigi, and the snub was roundly reciprocated, even though the girls had all played together a few times. Hailey wished adults could indulge the same instincts; she and Betsy hadn't even been able to get past vague pleasantries and empty discussions of meeting for coffee. Hailey said hello to the Wakefield females and made a comment on the beautiful day.

"We brought our dog Gulliver swimming," Gigi immediately said to Betsy. "He has an infection in his privates and so we can't leave him so now we're going to take him in the pool so he can swim. Have you met Gulliver?"

"I certainly *hear* Gulliver all the time," said Betsy, with a disgusted glance at the verboten four-legged pool guest. "But I don't believe we've met formally, no."

Hailey's phone buzzed. It was a 212 number that flashed up; it had to be David Rainier. A full two hours ahead of schedule. Of course she took the call, directing Mabel and Gigi, who still hadn't taken her T-shirt and shorts off, toward the baby pool. Fortunately, Mabel knew the drill, and Hailey's voice came out calm and even when she spoke: "Mr. Rainier. Thank you so much for agreeing to this call today."

"Yep."

"I felt sure that if we could just connect and speak candidly, we could come to an arrangement."

"You mean you're sure you can talk me into paying you?" He laughed. "Rebekah told me you want two hundred and fifty grand?" He laughed again.

So this was how it was going to go.

"You think you shouldn't pay me? You'd rather that I tell all the people that work for me that the hundreds of hours they spent fighting in your wife's corner in good faith was just for fun?"

Rainier didn't say anything, but he didn't hang up, either.

"Then I'll have to fire a few of those people, of course, because of the bank breathing down my neck, but I'm sure they'll register for unemployment cozy in the knowledge that you and your wife have decided to rekindle your romance, at least for now."

More silence. Hailey saw that Mabel had tugged up her bikini bottom so that it was basically a thong, and Gigi was sitting in the shallow water fully clothed. Any minute now they would be thrown out of here.

"Look, Ms. Evans. Hailey. I dislike my wife even more than you probably do. Off the record, she's a nasty, narcissistic cokehead that I wouldn't leave my children alone with for five minutes. We both know the family courts would try to make me do just that, and that she'd use custody as leverage. So Rebekah and I have come to an arrangement, as distasteful to me as that may be."

"Then your arrangement needs to include settling her legal bills."

"I don't think so. I'm really sorry." He sounded *genuinely* sorry, which threw Hailey off. "I really am, but I don't have two fifty to throw around just because your firm was dumb enough to give a crazy woman a huge line of credit. It's the principle, is the way I see it.

"People change their minds about getting divorced all the time. Surely your policy should be to make your clients pay you up front, or at least as they go."

"We extended credit in Rebekah's case because— "

Gulliver had escaped Hailey's bag and was sprinting toward the baby pool. He was going to pull the stitches right out of his dick.

She pressed on. "We made an exception because . . . because— "

"Because you knew I had a lot of money to go after. I'm sorry, Ms. Evans. You took a gamble, and it didn't work out this time. But I'm not covering for this stupidity."

It was unclear whether he meant her own stupidity or Rebekah's.

Gulliver briefly tested the water in the baby pool, deemed it unsuitable, and was now running back toward Hailey, with hordes of excited children in pursuit. She had to get off the phone before their shouts got loud enough for Rainier to hear.

"You'll hear from our counsel, then. We're going to get our money, and that's all there is to it. HaveanicedayMisterRainier."

As she hung up, the pool manager was approaching, in his Shoreby polo shirt and logoed blazer. They'd called in the big guns. He reached her just as Gulliver cocked his leg over Betsy Wakefield's espadrille.

"Ewww," screeched Arabella. "Gross, Mommy look! He's doing a wee wee in your shoe!"

"He's always doing that," said Mabel casually as the pool manager dove to snatch the sandal out from underneath Gulliver. "Peeing in shoes is like his most favoritest thing in the world."

✦

Hailey's mother's foot was not broken, just badly sprained. She'd therefore ignored the medical advice to keep the weight off it, and she hobbled out into her driveway to help Hailey unload the girls. In her hands she dangled a pair of jelly plastic shoes identical to Mabel's, but smaller. Gigi was ecstatic (her size had been previously unavailable), and Hailey sighed. She didn't have the heart to tell Pamela Byers that the shoes were the ugliest things she'd ever seen and that the buckle on Mabel's was already broken; her mother had been as excited about them as her granddaughters. And Pammy Byers was just warming up.

She led Hailey immediately to a pair of twisted metal chickens by the front steps. They were new since Hailey had come by the week before, though had her mother not pointed them out she might not have noticed them among the other wildlife: flamingos and porcupines and foxes and deer, in stone and wire and wicker. The chickens were especially hideous though, up close. They looked sinister somehow.

"Wow."

"You like them? They're yours. Marc's has a deal going on the farm animals."

"Oh no, you keep them. They're in the perfect spot right there."

"Mine are in the back, I got these for you. Ten bucks a pair, can you believe that?" Hailey lived in fear of the bargain treasures her mother would force on her; Pammy's biweekly trips to Marc's discount superstore yielded anything from giant boxes of goldfish crackers to a fly swatter in the shape of a freight train. Still, Pammy had already planned next week's excursion with Mabel to buy her granddaughter her *second* round of school supplies, and Hailey knew that Grammie, as the girls called her, would hop there on one foot—backward—if she had to. Pammy did anything and everything for Hailey and her girls, and for Mack too, so Hailey had never breathed an honest word about the junk Pam bought her, and displayed it faithfully. She suspected Pammy's lawn ornaments in particular had a very specific purpose: though she'd never said it out loud, Hailey knew that her mother found the new house, and indeed Bratenahl itself, stuffy and soulless. Which was ironic, because it was Pammy who had first sparked her daughter's ambition to live there.

When Hailey was still a very little girl, they'd gone to Bratenahl to hit up an estate sale. (It certainly wasn't called a garage sale in Bratenahl.) Hailey had little memory of the house they went to, but the specter of the giant estates with their yards running right down into Lake Erie was like nothing she'd ever seen before.

"I'm gonna have one of those when I grow up," Hailey had told her parents, her nose pressed against the rear window of her dad's Cutlass Supreme.

"You can clean it then," Pammy said. "Just think of all those bathrooms."

The moment had stuck in Hailey's brain forever. Her obsession with the neighborhood had endured, and the very first phone call she made from her brand-new house in the new Magpie Court subdivision of Bratenahl, Ohio, was to Molly Maids. The $200 they charged for a biweekly visit was worth every penny.

Hailey set up the sprinkler in her parents' small front yard for the girls to run through. Pammy poured out purple Kool-Aid (also from Marc's and served in plastic cups so old they had to be shedding BPA by the bucketful) and then finally sat down to put her foot up.

"Dad fishing?"

Pammy nodded. "You said Mack had some meeting? Sorry we couldn't help this morning, Dad was already gone and I—"

"It was fine." Hailey had only been a little bit distracted, had only failed in her attempt to save her firm from bankruptcy. No big deal.

"And what's this I hear about Mack going to see his mom?"

"When did he tell you that?" He'd only told Hailey last night.

"When he called to ask me to handle school on Tuesday. You'll have to tell me how the drop-off works, but I should be fine to drive by then—"

"He's such a—" Hailey stopped herself; her mother hated to hear a bad word uttered about Mack, it was infuriating. "I can't believe he's going to miss Mabel's first day. I can't take any more time off, and he should—"

"I wouldn't sweat it, honey. I don't remember anything about your first day of school, and I doubt you do either. It's only your generation that insists on all these ridiculous milestones. Anyway, you'll both be able to come to the six-week anniversary of her starting kindergarten ceremony. That won't be too far away."

Hailey laughed in spite of herself. Maybe the Kool-Aid had vodka in it. It wouldn't have been the first time.

"Is his mom worse? Poor Mack."

"No, she's the same. It's more like an admin thing."

"Maybe he can finally move her up here. I couldn't stand to be that far away from you, it's hard enough with you all the way in Cleveland and your sister leaving us behind—"

Hailey's sister Lyndsey had moved to Dayton, which was, to Pammy, like moving to Siberia. It took three hours and half a tank of gas to get there.

"Mack's mother doesn't *know* she's far away, Mom. She doesn't know anything."

"That's a little harsh, sweetheart."

Hailey let it go. She was eager to change the subject. Her mother was a bloodhound when it came to secrets, and Mack was really going to Florida to try to find out about his father. Eighteen thousand dollars was a lot of money, when you thought about it, and it had been gnawing at Hailey even as it flew out of their bank account. Mabel's school bill would have made a big dent in their savings if it hadn't been for this present from the Father Fairy, but Hailey didn't like the idea of being beholden to a Mafia don, even if he was technically family. She was a member of the Ohio bar, for God's sake, and she wanted reassurance that Mack's dad was just a harmless old con man trying to settle his affairs before he croaked. That way she could spend his money in peace and guiltlessly use it to replace the bonus that there was probably no chance of this year.

Finally, *finally*, after hours of chipping away at him, Mack had caved and agreed to investigate further. Then he'd gone too far in the other direction, and now he was taking himself off to Florida. Why he couldn't just make a phone call, why he had to buy a plane ticket and fly all the way to Jupiter just to ask a couple of people a few questions, was absolutely beyond her. Maybe it was his last hurrah before his classes started again.

It was then, sitting on her mother's porch getting drunk on Kool-Aid, that Hailey realized that for the first time in the history of their relationship, she didn't actually know *when* Mack was going back to school. He'd always made a big deal of counting down the last days of summer, and in the week before all the students came back to campus, he would insist Hailey take a day off. He'd buy Cedar Point tickets so they could spend a day riding roller coasters and eating crap, then maybe he'd take her to a concert at Nautica. But this year he seemed to have abandoned tradition.

Maybe, Hailey thought, he was finally starting to grow up.

7.

In 1965 the Bratenahl Development Corporation began the construction of two fifteen-story apartment blocks, the first high-rise residential buildings in the state of Ohio. Bratenahl Place was to be a mecca for modern city living: one tower would house not just condominiums but also shops, a restaurant, a hairdresser—amenities that meant Bratenahl residents would no longer have to venture into the mean streets of Cleveland proper for their basic needs. The second tower would consist entirely of rental apartments, making the Bratenahl brand accessible to the (almost) common man.

In the heart of a country still newly enamored with the suburban lifestyle, the towers were not an immediate success. They sat, mostly unsold and vacant, for years. Everyone panicked: the architects sued the contractors and vice versa, the BDC imploded, the shopkeepers went bust.

There's only one reason those towers are thriving today: the selfless effort of a wealthy widow and Bratenahl lifer named Gertrude Britton. Gertie had lived at 10316 Brighton Road, then upgraded to the colossal 11801 Lake Shore Boulevard until that house burned to the ground in 1950, and then, finally, settled in the eleven-thousand-square-foot "Carriage House" at 11 Hanna Lane. Her philanthropy and contribution to the community knew no bounds, and for decades she bailed out the failed Bratenahl Place complex, even, so I've read, going so far as to pay for the lights to be left on in the empty apartments at night so that no one would know just how empty they were. Her deep pockets bought the towers time until the world caught up with this vision of the good life.

You might argue that a donation to the Salvation Army would have been more charitable, or maybe the sponsorship of an inner-city school, but I disagree. If you can get past the god-awful exteriors of the Bratenahl Place towers and focus on the majestic lobbies and the airy apartments looking down over tennis courts and landscaped grounds, you will appreciate the true nobility of Gertrude Britton's contribution. She was nurturing that most American of sensibilities: Dream it, build it, worry later about how much it costs. Or, from Gertie's perspective: Keep the money flowing, and eventually they will come.

That's my plan too.

8.

Mack

Irene Weigand had lived a hundred yards from the beach for forty-odd years, but sitting in her living room, you'd never have guessed it. There were no boat paintings or mounted starfish or carefully preserved conch shells, just dark, heavy damask curtains, thick rugs, black lacquered furniture, and gold-trimmed everything. Mack tried to picture his mother here; it would have been almost twenty years ago now since Leonora had last sat at the card table in the corner, playing bridge with her friends and drinking martinis. Irene was drinking one now, even though it was nine on a Tuesday morning, and so Mack had allowed himself the beer she offered him. From the other room, he could hear the hiss of Irene's husband's oxygen machine.

"She was gorgeous, your mother," Irene was saying to him in a raspy smoker's voice. "Really a light in my life; my Ron's been sick for so many years, and she was a tonic. We loved her, my friends too—all us old biddies. Don't know why she put up with us." She laughed, and so Mack did too.

"It broke my heart, what happened to her," Irene continued. "But it's so good to see you looking so well, Malcolm. I hope you don't mind me saying, but she'd be proud of you. I hope seeing her wasn't too hard."

"Well, I kind of see her every week," Mack said. "On Zoom . . . On the computer." But it *had* been hard yesterday, harder than he'd thought it would be. His visits had gotten fewer and farther between over the years, and seeing up close his mom's papery skin, her thinning mouth, the lines that had set in around her eyes, had left him nearly choking on the unfairness of it all, at how his mother could still be aging, could still be inching toward death without even getting to be alive. And the urge he had, primal and juvenile, to shake her, to scream at her to *just wake the fuck up*, was as strong as it had been in the days after her stroke. He chugged half his beer at the memory of it and wondered whether Irene would offer him another one.

"Well, thanks for letting me come by. I won't take up too much of your time—"

"Don't be stupid, kiddo," Irene said, hoisting herself from her chair and wobbling across the huge room—her condo took up an entire floor of the building—toward the kitchen. "I love seeing you. I hear you're a professor now? Tilda told me you've been very successful. You've built yourself a big new house? I wish Leonora could see it."

"Yes, things are going well." Mack sat in silence with his lie until Irene returned with the beer. "I'm writing a book too, actually," he told her. Another lie, but *someone* might as well think he was a success. Maybe Irene would tell his mom about it; maybe it would reach Leonora somehow, deep in the recesses of her broken mind, and make her proud. Neither woman would ever have to know he wasn't really writing anything, that it had taken him nine years to dribble out two thousand words.

"So, Mrs. Weigand—"

"Irene, please."

"Irene. The nice folks at Sandy Hollow told me that you are the executor of Mom's trust. I'm sorry you've been saddled with this all these years, I had no idea. I would've taken over if I'd known it needed monitoring . . ."

"That's probably not a bad idea, you know, Malcolm. I may not look it, but I'm getting up there. I mean, I'm almost fifty." This time Mack laughed in earnest, and he stopped himself from making a joke about the strong Florida sun just in time. The beer was going straight to his head.

"So ah, are you in direct contact with him," he asked her, "or does the home do that?" Sandy Hollow had flat-out refused to share Mack's father's contact information. They'd had to get the trustee's approval before they would even tell him who handled his own mother's bills. He had been shocked to hear Irene Weigand's name.

"Direct contact with who?"

"My father."

"Uh . . ." Mack watched as Irene took a big slug of her martini. "Uh, I haven't . . . Oh dear. I was under the impression that you were in touch with him over the years."

"No."

"I see." She topped up her glass with a long pour from the gin bottle on the side table next to her. "Malcolm, I'm sorry to be the one to tell you this, but your father is deceased."

"What?"

"He's dead. About five years ago. No, that's not right—more like seven now. Heart attack, I believe. I only heard through a mutual acquaintance. I thought you would have known; just before she got sick, Leonora told me he'd reached out to you, so I assumed . . . well, I shouldn't have assumed. I'm sorry."

"He tried to make contact when I went off to college, but we weren't ever really in touch." Mack took another long chug of his beer. "It's just—I never found an obituary. I mean, I searched for him online a few times." What did it matter if one old lady knew he was a sad, fatherless snoop?

"He went by Warner Evers after everything that happened, you know; try that, and you'll find it. He changed his name. Who can blame him? He was the most hated man in Florida for a good long while. I know people that lost a lot of money because of him. I've had calls from journalists and relatives asking about him over the years, and I only knew him casually."

"I just don't . . . Wow." Mack was having trouble catching his breath. "So he left you to handle his estate? To deal with the money for my mom?"

The considerable wrinkles in Irene's forehead deepened further. "What money? He ended up more broke than the Ten Commandments, far as I know. You did know that your father was a criminal, Malcolm? That he spent time in prison? That life caught up with him eventually, it always does. Leonora must have told you—"

"Yes, she did, but I thought . . . I always thought he must've kept some funds hidden, you know? Put something aside?" Mack was way past feeling any shame at the idea of his father squirreling away a few stolen millions. "I mean, how else could he have paid for Mom's care? How did he set up this trust?"

And how in the hell did he just send me $18,000? Mack only just stopped himself from adding.

Irene set her empty glass on the marble tabletop; she was more than keeping pace with him. "Ah. I see how we have our wires crossed here, Malcolm. My fault. Your father had nothing to do with your mom's trust. He was a penniless ex-con, if you'll excuse me for saying it. No, I set up the trust. In fact, I *am* the trust."

This couldn't be right. Mack's brain grasped desperately for the rope that it had clung to for years and years: this idea that his father, even though he was 100 percent grade-A asshole, had at least been their savior at the end.

Now Mack saw that this narrative had been entirely his own fabrication. A thousand dollars offered to a poor college freshman was not the same as two decades of medical care. Mack's lifeline was no more substantial than a piece of string, and he could feel himself hurling down a cliff face with nothing to grab onto to break his fall. "Let me make sure I understand," he said. "Are you saying that you've been the one paying for my mother all these years?"

"Well, yes. Me and the other bridge gals. But they've been gone a long time now, so it's mostly been me. And Ronnie too," she said, gesturing toward the room where her husband was presumably in a state not unlike Mack's mother's.

"Oh my God." Mack leaned back in his chair, stared up at the pebble-dash ceiling, and fought like hell to recover himself. "I mean, *thank you*. I had no idea."

"No, well, I wanted it that way. It was my great pleasure. Like I said, I loved your mother. And I was lucky enough to be in a position to do it. It was a gift to be able to pass it on."

They sat quietly for a long minute, Mack's mind still spinning. Was Irene Weigand Sunshine Enterprises then? Twenty years ago, it had been Irene that had given Mack his nest egg and sent him on his way, Irene that had paid for his mom, and now that she was getting up there, was it Irene slowly siphoning off her riches to him via those checks? She must have had a LOT of money not to miss hundreds of thousands on Sandy Hollow. Should he ask her point-blank? He had no choice, really, not if he was going to face Hailey. But Irene was on her way across the room again and Mack didn't trust himself to stand, so he waited for an eternity while she got him another beer. (Surely the woman could afford someone to help her around the house?) By the time she got back, he wasn't really thinking about her anymore, or about his mother or Sunshine Enterprises. As he accepted his third drink of the morning, Mack had become stuck on the fact that, once again, his father had utterly and completely let him down.

✦

Hailey had gone quiet, but Mack knew this was only temporary, that she was formulating a plan of attack. They were in Lakewood, their old neighborhood, the girls and Gulliver racing ahead of them on the lakefront path. His wife had been so nice to him since he'd returned from Florida—she rubbed his back, she brought Starbucks down to his office in the basement, she even came home from work early a few times—and Mack had almost convinced himself that via his death his father had finally contributed something to his life after all. Then, after putting it off for as long as he dared, he'd had to tell Hailey about Irene's request.

Hailey stopped by the steps down to the lake and squinted into the horizon, still silent. She would let this tension build and build until he broke open like a goddamn water balloon at a Fourth of July picnic, Mack knew she would. But he wasn't some hysterical gold digger, he was an academic. He would focus on the issue at hand, one crisis at a time, alligator nearest the boat, etc. etc. etc. There were any number of metaphors that could save him now.

"We've just got to look at this the right way, is all," Mack said to Hailey. "I got twenty-plus years of world-class care for Mom, for free. That was a good thing, but all good things come to an end."

"This isn't like summer camp or a honeymoon in the Bahamas, Mack. This is ten grand a month. How are we going to come up with ten thousand dollars a month? Do you have ten thousand dollars a month?"

He did not. His entire salary wouldn't have covered Leonora's nursing home, but he hadn't had the heart to tell Irene Weigand that. He was doing so well, Irene had said to him after they had drunk most of the morning away and Mack still hadn't worked up the nerve to ask her about Sunshine Enterprises. Mack was doing so well that Irene wondered, was it now possible for him to take over his mother's care? Only because she was pushing fifty—that time Mack didn't even crack a smile—and she needed to think about having enough to cover the rest of her life, maybe have a little something to leave to charity. As soon as he'd realized that she was serious about pulling her funds, Mack should have spilled his guts and told her he was losing his job and that it was his hotshot wife who paid for his fancy new house and he would soon have two kids in private school and there was no way, NO WAY, that he could afford to pay ten grand a month for his mother, but he couldn't quite bring himself to do it. It was partly the six beers he'd had by that point, and partly because he was focused on the realization that, if she was talking about cutting back on expenses, Irene couldn't possibly have anything to do with Sunshine Enterprises. She was giving him less money (none), not *extra*.

He watched as Hailey worked this out now: Mack's father was dead, Irene Weigand was off the list even before Hailey had known she was on it, and so—

"Who the hell has been sending us these checks, then? You've deposited eighteen grand, and we don't have any idea where it's from." Even though it was ninety degrees, he saw Hailey shiver in the wind coming off the lake. "Girls, come back this way! Let's go see Tai and Etta and the boys!" Hailey and Mack both took a sharp intake of breath as Gulliver passed within inches of Mabel's scooter wheels. Hailey snatched him up as the girls flew back past them and tucked him under her arm.

"I don't know. I'll do some investigating—"

Hailey actually *snorted*, and Mack found he resented her standing there in her designer sunglasses and crazy expensive cutoffs, her Cartier bracelet digging into poor Gulliver's side, thinking she was so much better than him. But he didn't take the bait.

"Look, we can cover my mom for a few months, and then I can move her up here, somewhere cheaper—"

"Cheaper? She needs around-the-clock medical care. Did you even try to talk to this Irene woman and find out why—"

"My mom is not her responsibility, Hailey. She's *my* mom." Mack was surprised at how strongly he meant this.

"I know that, and I totally get how you must feel. But this woman took on the responsibility when she set up the arrangement; otherwise you would've worked something else out."

"Like what? Put my mother in some state-funded hellhole? Dropped out of school to try to take care of her myself? You and I would never have even met then."

He had backed them into a dangerous corner and was relieved when she led them out, however roughly: "You don't know that every state-funded care home is a hellhole. So help me God, Mack Evans, you are going to be the one to take care of this. This is not going to be another thing that I have to deal with. And in case you are completely delusional, we do not have ten thousand dollars a month. Not even close. This is not a great time for the firm."

In silence, they trailed the girls around the dusty Lakewood Park baseball diamond and past the picnic pavilion smoky with afternoon barbecues, then alongside the adventure playground and the teeming community pool. They followed the familiar sidewalks until they reached their old house, and Mack felt a pang of longing for its shadowy porch, the kitchen with its uncomplicated, working appliances, and his office in the third bedroom where he looked out at clouds and treetops. Hailey didn't give the place so much as a sideways glance, and the girls had already sped past it and were banging on their former neighbor's front door. Mack could smell the grill and hear his friend's voice coming from the backyard; salvation was near. He swallowed his remark about hoping more couples would start hating each other in time for the last quarter of her financial year, and instead leaned in and pecked Hailey on the lips. "It's gonna be okay."

And he felt sure that it would be, at least until he was finally forced to tell her about his tutor group, and especially about Mackenzie Ewing. Then it might not be okay at all, though that would be entirely up to his wife and whether she believed his side of the story.

9.

Hailey

Something was wrong. September was well underway and yet Mack was not going back to school. He was *thinking of taking the semester off.* His mental health was not good, he'd said, like he was reading a public service announcement. This thing with his mom was preying on his mind, it was impossible to concentrate, he would be doing his students a disservice. He felt he needed a leave of absence, and the department had agreed to it.

No one had asked Hailey if she agreed to it.

For three mornings in a row, she watched Mack get the girls up for school. She said goodbye to him as he made their waffles, watched him through the glass in the front door sip his cheap instant coffee as she dug around the porch for her Prada wedges. He was crouched over his phone in his sweatpants and his smelly old Duke T-shirt, and he looked sneaky and anxious, Hailey thought, like one of her clients whose explicit texts with his mistress were about to be read out by opposing counsel.

As she was pulling out of the driveway, Mack came sprinting out.

"Babysitter," he shouted through the closed car window. "Did you call her?"

They went three rounds—again—on why Hailey couldn't just cancel the babysitter indefinitely, on said babysitter's contract, and on what would happen when Mack went back to work, because he *was* going back to work. Hailey couldn't help feeling disgusted at his ten-day-old stubble and his glorified pajamas, and she burned with shame when she realized that she wasn't the only one checking out the state of him: Betsy Wakefield stood on the strip of lawn between their houses as her two beribboned daughters climbed into the back of her Mercedes.

"Morning!" she called out to Mack and Hailey, and Mack replied with the same. "Have a great day at school, girls," he added, turning back to Hailey.

"You too, Mack!" Betsy shouted back. Though it was impossible, Hailey felt sure from the tone of Betsy's voice that their neighbor knew just what a freeloader Mack had suddenly become. How could she not? He was the picture of failure this morning, rumpled and whiskery and sour. Were there to be no more button-downs with rolled-up sleeves, no more stories about his Gen Z students being offended? He was really going to stand here and beg for the babysitter's job? If Mack didn't snap out of this, he might never need his sexy reading glasses again, and then Hailey really would leave him. Already three days had felt an eternity.

She waited until Betsy had driven off down the street. Her daughters were at the same school as Mabel, though no one had yet broached the subject of a carpool. It really was a waste of time and gas for both households to drive to the same place every morning, though, so Hailey would have to sort it out when she got a free half minute. She turned her attention back to Mack. "How long are you thinking this leave of absence is going to last exactly? The whole semester?"

Across the street, Grady and Deborah Sinclair emerged from their house in matching golf attire. Though they looked way too young for it, Hailey had heard they were retired, and they certainly seemed to do everything together. They waved a curt good morning in unison. Neither of them ever smiled; maybe that was what marriage did to you. Especially when you stopped working.

Mack bowed his head and backed away from the car. "Hailey, just . . . *please*. Just give me some time to deal with everything."

Even with the sneaky shadow that flashed across his eyes again, even with his vague mutterings and his refusal to give her any concrete details, Hailey was still suddenly overcome with the urge to get out of the car and give him a hug. He looked so diminished standing there, a little boy who'd lost his father and then his mother and was all alone in the world except for Hailey. And despite everything he had been through, Mack was *never* diminished. He never seemed to find life too much, and he was never too far the other way, either, never inflamed with unrealized ambition. Mack had always cruised happily through the middle of his existence, and whenever he'd needed to, he'd reached out and pulled Hailey along beside him, away from the spiky ups and downs she was prone to. His unflappability was like a drug, and Hailey felt its withdrawal acutely.

Which made her even madder. What right did Mack have to choose this moment to finally let something get to him? Something that was his own damn fault? He had sleepwalked right into this situation with his mother, and now he was going to neglect Hailey too?

"As long as they keep paying you, I guess you know what you need," Hailey called out to him as she rolled her eyes and rolled up the window. The way Mack fled toward the house didn't exactly fill her with confidence.

✦

Marla, their rock-star paralegal, jumped on her as soon as she got to the office.

"I tried to call you," the woman said in a breathless tone Hailey had never heard her use before. "He's here. I don't know why he's here, but he's here. David Rainier."

Hailey's hand shook, and her Starbucks splashed across her dress. Panic gripped her insides: Had she set up a meeting with David Rainier and forgotten? Was Rebekah about to descend on them too? Marla the paralegal would never have allowed such a slipup, and she rushed to reassure Hailey: "There's nothing in the schedule. He says he just wants to talk, to meet you. I put him in the big conference room."

"Okay." Hailey had kept a freshly dry-cleaned blouse in the cupboard behind her desk ever since the Feldman divorce; Bruce Feldman's now ex-wife had had a penchant for throwing cups of coffee at him in the heat of the moment, and though it had cost her dearly in the end, more than once Hailey had been caught in the crossfire and had to spend half a day drenched in French roast. Forever after she was prepared, except that today she was wearing a dress and there was no skirt or pair of pants in that closet. Instead, she attempted some creative folding to hide the stain as she made her way to the conference room, passing the perplexed faces of two senior partners lurking in the hallway. They'd want a full report; David Rainier and his bill-dodging wife were now the whole firm's problem.

He was a big problem, too, bigger than she'd pictured—at least six foot four when he stood up to shake her hand, wide shoulders and arms bulging at the sleeves of his crisp white shirt. She took in his flawless smile, an expensive watch, a gold wedding band, of all things. Brown eyes framed by a thick head of dark hair. His LinkedIn photo and the selfies Hailey had seen from the social media research did not do him justice, so even though her brain was already tying itself in knots over all the things he could possibly say to cheat her out of a quarter million, Hailey did not have to force her own smile as she shook his hand: he looked like a worthy opponent.

He did not apologize for coming unannounced, and Hailey had no idea how long he had been waiting for her. She decided to let him speak first, but Rainier had the same plan; after accepting Marla's offer of coffee (he took it black), he fixed Hailey with a look that bordered on the intense, and then he *waited*. Hailey took the seat on the corner next to him—across the table was too adversarial—and they battled out the silence until Hailey cracked.

"So. Here you are." She wasn't about to indulge him with a *Thanks for coming in today*, or an *I hope you weren't waiting long*.

"Yep. Here I am."

He was good at this; he hadn't made his millions being an idiot. Two fifty was chump change to him.

Hailey jumped on this thought.

"Did you come to settle your bill in person?" If he laughed, so help her God, she would tear him limb from muscly limb.

He didn't laugh. He sighed. "No. I came to explain."

"I'm not sure how that's going to work, Mr. Rainier. Legally, you owe what you owe—what Rebekah owes—so unless I can convince you two to make good on that, I think it's probably best if we speak through counsel."

"Call me David, please. Listen, Hailey, I know what you're thinking. You're thinking, *This asshole can afford to pay me, he just won't because he's an asshole*."

She hadn't told him to call her Hailey, and wild horses could not have dragged a sound from her at this moment.

They both watched as his phone on the table lit up twice with incoming calls—Ben/Assistant and John McRory/JP Morgan. He ignored both.

"Hear me out," he said finally. "I just can't let Rebekah do this. I have to take a moral stand. If I pay you, if I take care of this, Rebekah will expect me to clean up every mess she makes, and our *arrangement*"—he spat out the word—"won't work."

Another incoming call: Glenn Paul/Blackrock. If Hailey had ever doubted this guy was a serious player, she didn't now.

But he wasn't going to play *her*. "So you're teaching the little wife a lesson? Is that what this is?"

David looked down at his hands in what could have been shame when Hailey spoke; his eyelashes were impossibly long against his cheek.

"Or is it, Mr. Rainier, that you're going to lure Rebekah back east, get the kids settled and reside in New York City, and then file for divorce there, where there's no community property? And then, what with this huge outstanding legal bill in Rebekah's name making its way through the court system, no decent Manhattan divorce attorney will touch her? That would be a great plan, if maybe a little obvious."

His face gave nothing away. She could see tiny blue specks in his dark eyes as he leaned forward in his chair. "You know, I read your interview in *Cleveland Social*," he told her.

"Okay."

"And I'm not sure what you said is right."

"Oh?" He had a lot of nerve; she would say that for him.

"You said divorce happens very slowly and then all at once. I don't think that's true."

"I didn't actually say that," Hailey told him. "The author Tom Wolfe did, and I was quoting him. And in my experience that *is* what happens. Couples pick at each other, little things build, then all of a sudden they're here in this room. And then after I clean up their mess, they pay me." The *Cleveland Social* piece had been a puff profile of Hailey the divorce guru and her happy family, concluding with her thoughts on how to avoid needing her services. "People pay me, and then I feed my kids," she added, hoping David had seen the family photos the magazine ran, her and Mack with the children in their yard. He obviously doted on his own kids; maybe she could find a soft spot.

"It wasn't like that with Rebekah. There was nothing slow about it ever." He frowned. "Or maybe the slow part came before we met. She was like a goddamn crocodile, lying in wait for me. We literally laid eyes on each other, and then *boom*! She was pregnant, we got married, and she turned into a total psychopath. *That* was all at once. So I guess you are right, in a way."

"And presumably you were unconscious throughout this entire process?"

"No. I was stupid, I admit it. And distracted. But now the woman has completely abandoned our children, which would be a great thing except they love her. Do you know how heartbreaking that is? She forgets to pick them up from school, lets the nanny raise them when I can't be there, and they still love her. And so—completely off the record—I've got to find some way to keep her under control, keep everyone happy, keep my children safe."

He did sound wounded, but who really knew. Hailey found herself trying to picture him flirting with Rebekah, asking her out. Where would they have met? Wherever it was, Hailey's worst client of all time must have thought she'd died and gone to heaven. Rebekah had been a restaurant hostess; Rainier had a fifty-foot sailboat and a house in the Caymans. (Hailey had seen the floor plans of both.)

"If that's true, I'm sorry for the way things have turned out for your family." She meant this, which made what followed work so well: "But if I don't get paid, I'm not going to be able to keep everyone on *my* end happy and safe. You seem like a really nice guy who's just found himself in a bad situation, so please, make this easy on all of us and do the right thing here. The legally obligated thing."

He leaned forward in his chair and bit his lower lip. The skin on his face looked impossibly soft for someone so masculine. Hailey was annoyed with herself for noticing it.

"I've got to tell you again," he said finally, "the idea that you extended her credit—well, I hope I'm not being patronizing when I say it's just bad business. And all right, you got me. I do like the idea of Rebekah having shit like this hanging over her, of getting her ass dragged through court, even if it means I am too, eventually. But what you said about your people working for free makes me pissed off for you. I'm going to see what I can do. Maybe we can come to an arrangement."

"I would really, *really* appreciate that," Hailey told him, even though she wasn't sure what exactly it was he needed to see about. It was pretty simple: he needed to pay her. But at least this was progress, and this was a marathon, not a sprint. She would pace herself. "I'm glad you came in, David. Thank you."

"I wanted to meet you." As he said this, his phone rang again, and the screen lit up with a photo of a little boy grinning wide enough to show his missing two front teeth. Hailey wasn't trying to look, but the name over the picture came up as Doodlebug. "Excuse me," he said, "but I have to take this." He shook her hand. "I'll be in touch." His grip had just the right amount of pressure, and to her surprise, Hailey was sorry when he let go.

10.

So one morning I'm at the dentist, waiting for my turn in the hot seat, and I'm thumbing through a limp copy of *Cleveland Social* and there she is, smiling up at me: Hailey Evans, divorce lawyer extraordinaire. They've got her whole Fam Damn-ily there too. Reckless, I think, having photos of your children showcased like that.

She looks good in the pictures. So does Malcolm "Mack" Evans, assistant professor of English at the Cleveland Institute of Technology. Before I have to face getting my wobbly veneer repaired, I get a little five-hundred-word peek into their lives, and I feel like I've struck gold without even digging.

(And I have dug, I admit it. I'm a little obsessed with them: I've found his name on old track and field score sheets from the late nineties, seen the two of them posing at a Heart Foundation fundraiser at the Chagrin Valley Hunt Club. Then it's click, click, click and before I know it, the corner of my screen says 4:00 a.m., my eyeballs look like the surface of Mars, and I've spent another whole night on Mack and Hailey Evans.)

So anyway, there was Hailey Evans on page 7 of *Cleveland Social*, talking about how not to get divorced. She dropped this Tom Wolfe quote, which at first I thought was pretty damn impressive—she's not even the literary one. Then later when I looked it up, it turns out it was Hemingway who said it, not Wolfe, and he was talking about bankruptcy and not divorce, and even that was a loose interpretation of what he'd actually said. Hailey should really have checked with that husband of hers before she started spouting stuff like this.

Her point, I guess, was not to let the little troubles of married life build up, lest they suddenly explode on you. I myself like a little explosion every now and then, but it's a wholesome thought, this idea that diligent couples would take time to air tiny grievances each day: You call that loading a dishwasher, snookums? Might I suggest an alternative placement for some of the silverware, dearest, if it wouldn't offend you too much?

Somehow I doubt that Mr. and Mrs. Evans really practice what she preaches. I mean, far be it from me to contradict the expert, but who could live like that? Such relentless diplomacy would be exhausting.

(Then again, so is divorce. When you're ready to throw in the towel on your marriage, hire a hit man. It's definitely an easier way out.)

11.

Mack

The dean of humanities was stuck on the fact that Mackenzie Ewing, an eighteen-year-old rising sophomore and a member of Mack's tutor group from last year, had regularly referred to him in emails and text messages as "Big Mack."

"It's just a reference to McDonald's," Mack told Ernest Favre. "And to both our first names."

"But you concede that it was a nickname?"

"I guess you could call it that. I have a friendly relationship with all of my students, and we just thought it was funny that we were both called . . ." Mack gave up. He had lost Favre at "relationship," could see him shut down. Neeta Tulley, head of the English department, had fallen even earlier, at the first meeting a few weeks back, when Mack had had to admit that he had sent and received multiple text messages from Mackenzie, some at unsociable hours.

"So you deny the suggestion of the anonymous student mentioned previously that 'big' is a reference to the size of your . . . manhood?" Favre's specialty was Renaissance prose and poetry. He had written an inexplicably successful nonfiction book called *The Tragedie of Grand Theft Auto*, some garbage that Mack hadn't read about how poetic virtual carjacking could be. Favre would probably leave soon, head for somewhere with a proper big-boy English department, and Mack simmered with jealousy every time he saw him, which made the current situation even worse, if such a thing was possible.

"Yes, I deny it. It's ridiculous."

"This student is lying?"

"Or mistaken. I can't really speak to a rumor I know nothing about."

"But you don't deny hosting these get-togethers at your home, at least some of which were during a pandemic?"

Mack sat still as a Michelangelo as he explained for the thousandth time: "During the pandemic we sat outside. Some of my group—a lot of them actually—were having mental health issues, and I—"

Favre leaned forward and straightened the stacked copies of his own book on the corner of his desk. "I'm going to be straight with you, Mack. Everyone in the department has heard talk of these little parties, and we turned a blind eye to them because you're a good professor. A very good professor. But what I'm hearing now is extremely disturbing. Booze, drugs, underage students . . ."

Mack could only stare down at the floor.

"Did you ever meet with Mackenzie Ewing alone?"

"No, never alone. Always with at least one other student." This was a *tiny* bit of a lie, because sometimes the students who were supposed to be with Mackenzie came late or left early. That wasn't Mack's fault, though, and it certainly didn't need mentioning now.

"Mack, listen. I don't want to believe anything happened with this girl." Favre leaned forward again, lowered his voice. "But this looks bad. We've got all these text messages back and forth, with *nicknames* . . ."

"*Nicknames*? It's not like I called her Sugar Tits, Ernie," Mack said, and watched Favre recoil in horror. "I care about my students. She was a *friend*."

"She's twenty years younger than you. A student can't be your friend. And for your sake, I hope to God she wasn't more than that. No—don't say anything, I don't want to know. Just be aware that if there was anything sexual involved, the university will come down on you like a ton of bricks and there's nothing I can do to stop it."

"Did someone say that there was sex involved?" Even Mack could hear the panic creep into his own voice.

"It's been insinuated, is all I can say. It's pending investigation."

"What does that mean, *insinuated*? What is this, Kafka? As far as I can tell there isn't even an accusation, so why am I being pressured into time off? Maybe I need a lawyer."

"Maybe you do; I can't advise you on that. Talk to your wife about it." Favre had met Hailey and must have been aware of her profession, but this was not the only reason he was bringing her up. "This isn't going away, Mack," the dean told him. "It'll be on the minutes of the Board of Trustees meeting next week, and possibly in the public domain. And I'm afraid that because of the alcohol and substance charges involved, and the accusations of grade inflation and fraud, we have to refer the matter to the police. It's just standard procedure these days. You must understand; the college has to protect itself."

"I don't know what to say to that, except that this is beyond crazy." Mack stood too quickly, almost knocking over a potted plant on the table next to him. "I have to pick up my kids."

✦

Sitting in the car outside Gigi's day care, Mack let his mind wander to places he had banned it from going. It sprinted straight for Mackenzie Ewing, on the porch swing of his old house in Lakewood, saucerlike eyes blinking up at him from underneath a bobble hat, small hands in fingerless gloves clutching a red wineglass. God, he'd loved that house, how his students congregated there, how it made them see him as one of their own, how they felt relaxed and safe, hugged in the smoke of his homegrown marijuana.

Yes, Mack had broken a few rules. But he'd done it for their sake, for his students, to show them that being an adult didn't have to mean selling out and turning into some corporate dick. You might not get rich, but you could spend your life smoking weed and teaching

Hemingway and discussing the meaning of it all on a winter's night, if you were brave enough to make that choice. (The only flaw in Mack's own personal version of that plan had been when he married someone who insisted on living in Bratenahl.)

Once Gigi was safely buckled in her car seat, Mack picked his way toward Shaker Heights, where he joined a long line of cars that cost as much as his annual salary. A ridiculously young-looking teacher nodded Mabel toward him, and she collapsed into her booster seat with a sigh.

"How was school today, Mabie?" There was no answer she could give that would bring him joy: If she loved it, it only meant that someday he'd have to break it to her that they couldn't afford it, and that they'd have to move away because Daddy was a pariah. If she hated it, he would be equally devastated that they'd paid $24,000 for her to be miserable.

"Fine," Mabel said.

"What did you do?"

"Some stuff."

"Okay." He knew Hailey would push enough for the both of them, make Mabel recount every single second at Shaker School for Girls before she was allowed to eat her dinner.

"I did Play-Doh," said Gigi, though no one had asked. "What did you do today, Daddy?"

"Some stuff," Mack said, and he turned up the radio, let an inane preschool song paralyze his brain cells. The drive home passed in a blur, so much so that he almost rear-ended Betsy Wakefield as she made the right-hand turn into Magpie Court. She noticed; she waved her hand at Mack in a not altogether friendly gesture. He had maybe been tailgating. They pulled in their respective driveways, and she rolled her window down.

"We meet again!"

"We do," said Mack, though to him the morning was a thousand years ago.

"I keep meaning to talk to you and Hailey," she said. "We should carpool. Silly to both drive, now that the girls are settled in."

Mack looked at Mabel in the rearview mirror. She was sucking her thumb, hair disheveled, eyes drooping. He couldn't abandon her to some strange lady's car, not when everything was still so new and daunting. He felt an overwhelming instinct to draw his family in close—even Hailey, who would require a careful grip.

Besides, give it another week and Betsy Wakefield wouldn't let her daughters anywhere near him.

"Uh, yeah. You probably should text Hailey. I just go where she tells me to." Mercifully, they were interrupted by the babysitter pulling up behind him, here to fulfil her goddamn contracted hours. Mack waved and pulled the rest of the way into his driveway.

The babysitter's arrival was now the low point of Mack's day. He wondered what Hailey had told Chenise about reducing her hours, about him being home when she was there. He hated the overlap; it made him feel the way he had when he was a scruffy teenager in a dollar-store hoodie, and the manager of the local 7–Eleven would stare him down like the theft of a Twix might crumble his entire convenience-store empire. Mack did not steal candy, and he didn't give a shit what Chenise got up to with his kids, either, as long as they were happy. Chenise hadn't picked up on his apathy; even all the way down in his office, Mack could hear her singsong voice, and he always had the sense that she was performing for him.

He said an awkward hello, and then numbly let her take over. He heard talk of fruit snacks and playing in the yard and then the three of them disappeared into the kitchen, leaving Mack in the front hall. He picked up the mail from the floor, saw the thin brown envelope, recognized what it was at once, and tore it open: Sunshine Enterprises again, $25,000. But it wasn't the climbing amount that sent Mack's heart rate soaring, it was the payee: Hailey J. Evans, Esq.

12.

Hailey

"I just thought we were on track to sort this thing out," David Rainier was telling her. "And I said to myself, let's get it done. Keep the momentum going."

Hailey had been googling him again when he called to ask her for a drink, not three hours after their meeting. He was on a hot streak, to be sure: she read about recent deals in St. Louis, in Orlando, in Barcelona—the guy must never sleep, and yet he was making time for her. This was a good sign, and besides, how could she turn down a drink with him, and miss a chance to get to know the enemy? He'd chosen a cocktail bar in Tremont and insisted on picking her up at her office and driving her there. When they were seated, Hailey ordered something called the To Kill a Tiger; it tasted strong and tropical, and it hit her like a tsunami.

"So I—"

"I don't usually—"

Hailey laughed, and he blushed, and . . . *What was she doing here?* "I was about to say that I don't do a lot of drinks meetings," she managed to say. "I've got little ones, younger than yours even."

"How old?"

"Three and six."

"Sex?"

Hailey choked on a piece of ice, which was a good thing because it gave her brain a little time to catch up. "Two girls. Gigi and Mabel." Why was she telling him their names?

"Ah yes, I remember. From the magazine article. Three is a magical age," he said. "And actually, so is six. Nothing sweeter than a kindergartner."

"Eight isn't sweet?"

"It's still pretty sweet. Ask me again when the twins are thirteen, though." He laughed, and Hailey felt Rebekah's presence looming over them like a specter.

He must have sensed it. "They're in New York now, with my family."

She tried not to make a mental note of this for the custody battle. It was just habit; there *was* no custody battle anymore. She could be a human being. "You must miss them."

He nodded. "I don't like being away from them. They've had a hard time."

Hailey and David Rainier were walking a fine line. As pleasant as he was to talk to, as nice as he was to look at, as much as Hailey sympathized with *anyone* who had to spend even five minutes in a room with Rebekah, he wasn't worth getting disbarred over. She couldn't sit here and trash-talk her own client. This was still a divorce, even if it was delayed, and in two weeks he might be screaming at Rebekah about how even her own lawyer had called her a rapacious bitch and—worse—a terrible mother. She steered the chat into neutral waters.

They ordered a second round. He went for whiskey; something called a Midnight Haiku. Hailey ordered the Royal Highness, tropical again, but this one promised to be "smoky and spicy." He was talking about spending two months traveling, trying to distract his kids from the divorce, trying to work at the same time. Telling her how he'd found some amazing places in Europe, out-of-the-way gems. How sexy the French countryside was, how he'd loved traveling with his children but sometimes you wanted a grown-up, especially one that wasn't his ex-wife, which made them both laugh. Hailey countered, told him about her time in Europe as an undergrad, three months in Paris, but when she found herself cutting Mack out of the narrative, she realized that this could be edging toward inappropriate. She listened to a story about how David's daughter was a pro at hailing a New York taxi, and then she took control.

"I might order some food. I didn't have much lunch." As soon as the waitress approached, Hailey asked for the most substantial thing she could find on the menu: a pulled pork sandwich that came with a pile of fries. Greasy, messy, stick-in-your-teeth food that would form a barrier against this strange flirtation. Then it was David Rainier's turn to counter; he ordered a bottle of obscenely expensive red and a plate of meat and cheese. Hopefully he wasn't trying to change the mood—probably he ate like a European playboy all the time. He certainly had the money for it. All she needed to do was to stay on track, to remember why she was here.

"So, David, now that we've had a few drinks, gotten to know each other a little, indulge me with a question." The rum held her hand, made her bold.

"Shoot."

"Are you planning to pay us, or is this just a long, slow fuck-you?"

He gave her a sheepish smile; there were those long lashes again, curling down on his face, something sweet and babylike about them. When he looked up, his eyes locked on Hailey's.

"There's nothing I'm better at than a long, slow fuck . . ." He smiled, wide and wicked, and then finally said, "*you.*"

Then he laughed and looked away. "Too much?"

Hailey took a sip of her fresh drink; it tasted like Tabasco and suntan lotion. "Just a touch. And you didn't answer my question."

"Okay then. Yes, I do intend to pay you, Hailey Evans. It will break my cold dead heart to bail my wife out of this, but I will pay you. Please don't spend any more time worrying about it. I'm sorry for the stress my hellhole of a marriage has caused. I never thought I'd be here, honestly. I'm a careful guy."

Hailey felt the permanent painful tangle in her stomach loosen, felt oxygen reach muscle fibers that had been starved for weeks. It was going to be okay. He would pay. She could relax.

"I understand," she told him. "No one gets married looking forward to the divorce. Or the—the breakdown of the relationship, in your case." She couldn't help rolling her eyes.

"I'll bet you've seen some things. It must wear on you, all that hatred people can have for each other."

"You must've been in some difficult negotiations too. Those are some pretty epic real estate deals on your résumé." Hailey had read about people being pushed out of their homes as David's developments went in, about objections over wildlife and local character and an outsider swooping in, and yet it sounded like the man was unstoppable.

"You've done your research," he said.

"It's my job."

"Right. Of course."

He had been inspired, he told her, by time spent working as a contractor in war zones. He talked about entire cities destroyed, and how he had passed the time thinking about exactly how he would rebuild them, if he could, and how that had led to his career. His plans for the Cleveland lakefront could not have been more ambitious.

"This could be a great town," he was saying. "It *will* be great. It gets a bad rap, but the lakefront, the river—"

"You mean the river that caught on fire?"

"Hey," he said, palms in the air. "It's your city, I'm not going to try to sell it to you. But I like the place, genuinely. It's a workingman's town, and to me that's a good thing. New York, London,

Paris—they're so far removed now from actual industry. From *grit*. But Cleveland's still working its ass off—or trying to—and for me, that gives it character. Besides, the river on fire makes for a great comeback story."

"And you're going to single-handedly orchestrate that comeback?"

"Yes, ma'am. This is strictly confidential"—he leaned forward to whisper in her ear—"but we're calling the development on the old Cargill site 'Burning River.' I've pulled in half a billion in investment so far. Cleveland's going to be one hell of a metropolis when I'm through with her."

"Wow," Hailey said, and she meant it. "To Cleveland." They clinked glasses and moved on to other topics: children and marriage and divorce.

Hailey tried to stay professional as she listened to the intricacies of his heartache, and she tried to keep her private life private while still getting him onside, but she was riding a wave of Bacardi, and before she knew it, a scale had tipped, a pendulum swung, and then she was taking her turn too, telling him about Mack, and how she didn't know what to do with him lately, and about the pressure she was under to hold their family together, how it made her fearless and fierce and more than a little *crazy*. David Rainier felt this pressure too—with the added live grenade in the mix that was Rebekah—and so when he asked if she wanted to take the bottle of wine to go, to get out of there and see a spectacular sunset, Hailey thought, Why not? It was like she was back in high school, when she'd peeled off from the prom with a shaggy-haired boy she'd never spoken to before, simply because they could both see the wood right in the thickest part of the teenage trees. She'd sit and get drunk with David Rainier too, on pinot this time instead of Boone's Farm, and that would be it. She had already betrayed Mack in the worst way possible, complaining about him to a man like this.

They'd only been on I-90 for a few minutes when she had a terrible realization that tore through her bravado: David was heading toward Bratenahl. They'd left the too-intimate conversation in the bar, she was sitting in some strange man's very nice car, speeding toward her own neighborhood, toward her husband and children. Did this guy know what he was doing? The *Cleveland Social* article hadn't printed their address; she'd made sure of it. But it would be easy enough to find out.

"I live here," she finally said as he turned off Lake Shore.

"Bratenahl? You're kidding. Then my view will be old news for you, I guess."

But it wasn't. She'd figured he'd joined the Shoreby Club, that he was going to show her the view from the terrace, which, even though Hailey had seen it dozens of times, was pretty spectacular. She was trying to decide whether she was too drunk to be seen in public with a man who wasn't Mack, especially at her own club, and then David pulled into the parking garage for Two Bratenahl Place. This must be where he was living now when he was in town; did the firm know this? Did he own this place too, a missed asset? Hailey the lawyer would not surrender quietly, and nor would Hailey the wife: the notion that Mack might be out walking Gulliver, might see her here in this fishbowl lobby, did skitter across Hailey's gray matter. But all these thoughts tangled together and fell right out of her head, and nothing, legal or marital or otherwise, stuck to the sides once the lobby door shut behind her. And so it was just Hailey, stripped down to her most fundamental self, who followed David between wood-paneled pillars and across the ice-white floor; it was this Hailey who waited as he pushed the button to call the elevator.

The silence as they began to ascend was unbearable; there was no way that David Rainier couldn't see the rise and fall of Hailey's chest as she fought to slow her breathing. Somewhere around the sixth floor he turned toward her, took her face roughly in his hands, and kissed her.

"I didn't plan this," he said. "I swear it." His mouth was strong on her own, the force of it powerful enough to press Hailey up against the back wall of the elevator. Someone else's arms—not hers, surely—reached for his chest, pulled on his shoulders to bring him closer, slid up the back of his neck into his hair, which was surprisingly soft. Softer than Mack's, and curly around the edges. She could feel his hands on her shoulder blades, smell starch and cologne instead of dog and peanut butter.

When the doors opened, he pulled her into the hall. As he turned away and fumbled for his keys, there was a brief moment of awkwardness when Hailey could have escaped. She could have straightened herself up, laughed, made a joke about that last drink—*what the hell was in it?*—and fled.

She did not do that.

After, as she lay naked under gray linen sheets in his bed in an apartment that was nondescript except for its vista over the dark lake—they had missed the sunset—all she could think about was his *otherness*: how solid he was, thighs like tree trunks, his arms curving in all the places Mack's didn't. At close range this man breathed differently, spoke less, smiled not at all—he had too much intensity for that. He was not some college kid playing at adulting; here lying next to her was the real thing. And perhaps now at last, Hailey was a grown-up too. In a matter of ten minutes (David would have said more like twenty), she had left Mack behind, entered some strange country she'd heard stories of but had never planned to visit. Is this how her clients felt, or their soon-to-be-exes? How *did* she feel? She needed to get out of here to decide.

David didn't seem thrown by her swift exit, or that she wouldn't let him drive her anywhere, although he did make an earnest attempt. Before he opened the apartment door, he kissed her again. This time felt the most foreign of all, and not necessarily in a pleasant way. "I'm not sure what happened here," he said to her, "but you should know that it isn't something I do all the time."

"No?" said a voice that must have been Hailey's. "Gosh, I do. This is pretty much your standard Wednesday night, for me." He laughed, finally, and she was proud of herself. Her years of experience in extricating people from difficult situations had finally paid off.

✦

The lobby was deserted, and for a brief moment Hailey feared she was locked in, but with a second push one of the heavy glass doors opened into a night that was fresh and cool; the lake smelled as much like the ocean as it ever did. She took off her shoes, made her way across the grounds and through the iron gate that separated Two Bratenahl Place from the rest of the neighborhood. When she reached the sidewalk, she picked up her pace; Bratenahl was safe, mostly, but most people did not make a habit of walking around in the dark. This was still Cleveland, and Hailey had seen photographs on the Bratenahl Police Facebook page of all the guns seized from the cars pulled over on the interstate, just up the street. There was no main Bratenahl gate, only an unspoken understanding: turn left off I-90 and have a cocktail at the Shoreby and a swim in the pool. Turn right and—well, that's where the violence was supposed to stay, one of the most dangerous areas of the country, according to the statistics. Hailey did not make the rules, but she counted on them being followed.

A figure appeared up ahead. Her heart threw off its exhausted stupor and jumped to attention. This was a man, tall and lanky. A split second later, and the adrenaline was for nothing—a streetlight revealed that he was holding a leash, with a small white dog attached to it. Mack would have called it frouffy; this creature made even Gulliver look like a pit bull. As she got closer, she realized it was just the old guy she saw all the time, the one with the twisty mustache who loved his perimeter. He was only a few yards away from it now, if he lived where she thought he did.

"Evening," he said.

"Hello. Nice out, isn't it? Feels like fall."

This was perfectly normal, what Hailey was doing. She was heading back from a drink at the Shoreby Club, maybe. Much less weird than taking your ankle-biter for a walk late at night in the dark, when you had acres of private land for it to do its business in. He must be very lonely.

He ran a hand through his graying hair and pointed to a Save Our Beachfront sign on the edge of his estate. "Shame what they've done to the beach access, isn't it? It's only going to get worse, with this new Huron Landing development. Have you signed the petition?"

She hadn't; she couldn't have cared less about the petition or the beach or the new development. She only smiled, nodded, floated past him around the corner, through the unmanned Magpie Court gate.

The house was dark. Gulliver made a stealth entrance impossible, and it wasn't just the incessant barking. He knew she'd been up to no good. He sniffed at her feet, stood up on his hind legs for a whiff of her thighs, savoring all the strange and foreign smells. She pushed him down and went to the kitchen to get a drink; her mouth felt dry and swollen. She stood at the sink, washing her hands. She couldn't just throw herself in the shower—Mack might be awake and think she wanted sex—but maybe she could disguise the smell of David Rainier with Mrs. Meyer's hand soap. She was scrubbing in like a surgeon when she saw Mack sitting in the Eames in the corner of the family room. In the dark. Watching her.

He knew. They had been together too long; he could sense it, he could smell it like Gulliver could.

"Jesus. You made me jump. Why are you still up?"

"How was your night?"

"Fine. Boring. What's wrong?" She would deny it until her last breath, Hailey decided in that moment. Like all the husbands did, even in the face of photographic evidence. The balls on them used to blow her mind, but now she understood.

"Are you drunk?"

"No." Hailey caught sight of the little cardigan she had laid out for Gigi that morning, hung over one of the chairs at the breakfast counter. The thought of what was at stake flushed any last vestige of drunkenness from her body. "I left the car at the office, just to be safe, but I'm fine."

"Good, because we need to talk."

She turned on the light. He did not blink. His eyes were still focused on her, right at her chest.

"Whoa," he said. "What happened to you?"

Hailey froze, following his gaze. The coffee stain. From her Starbucks. It was worse than she'd realized. It had been there all day.

"Feldmans back at it?"

"No, I was just . . . clumsy. What's going on?" But before he could answer, she saw the check in his hand, recognized the color of the paper and the font of the serial numbers.

13.

There used to be this unwritten understanding in Bratenahl that everyone would share the main path down to the waterfront, even though technically it runs through private land. It had been this way—a gentlemen's agreement—since the dawn of the twentieth century. In recent years, though, the families in the abutting estates got together and decided that the clock had run down on free beach access for every slob in the neighborhood.

One look at the local papers will tell you that this has not been a popular decision, and it was only aggravated when new development began to cut off other, lesser-used paths to the lake. But I get it: Why should these homeowners let people trespass on their private property? Who wants some random in a banana hammock and flip-flops peeking in the windows at your art collection, or watching your kids play Marco Polo in your pool? The Beach Lords maintained they didn't have a problem with their freeloading fellow Bratenahlers per se; their focus was on a potential outsider, they said, some serial killer who happened to be passing through this part of Cleveland, waiting for just the right ungated path to go down, who would no doubt snatch any privileged offspring right out of their $20,000 tree houses. It was their right! one Mrs. Martin Leland told *The Plain Dealer*. It was their prerogative to protect their babies from strangers!

I'm all for a man's home being his castle, but I will venture that this is bad parenting on the part of this Leland woman. I mean, sure, you can manage like that for a while, in a suburb. You can make your advances on Whole Foods in Rocky River and Crate & Barrel in Beachwood in your souped-up SUV tank, with maybe a concealed-carry in your glove box for good measure. But sooner or later, real life is going to hit your little brats like a load of artisanally crafted bricks, the way this world is going.

My own father, God rest his soul, was a big believer in getting young persons ready for the harsh environment we live in. He sent me off through Central Park late at night on my shiny new bike (goodbye, bike!) and let me ride the subway alone as soon as I could see over the turnstile (hello, pickpockets and muggers!). There was no greater badge of honor than when I was thirteen and some guy in a ski mask held a gun to the back of my head right in the middle of Fifth Avenue. And you survived to tell the tale, was what my father said afterward. Good for you kid!

I did survive (goodbye, wallet!), and so I can tell you, based on all of my years of practical experience in the field, that stranger danger is not what you should be worrying about. It's the people you know who will really fuck you over.

Someone should tell Mrs. Martin Leland this, before one of her landlocked neighbors finally loses it and burns down her house because of a three-foot gate across a cobblestone path that leads to a beach that's too cold to sit on for ten months of the year. Stranger things have happened.

14.

Mack

He had never known Hailey to be this reckless.

She was flying down I-95, going at least thirty miles per hour over the limit, overtaking even the boy-racers in their ricers. She hadn't said much since they passed through the edge of Virginia, where they'd stopped for lunch at a Cracker Barrel. Mack had driven the first seven hours or so, and under normal circumstances he would have polished off his Sunrise Sampler, laid back the passenger seat, and fallen asleep, especially since they'd left home at 4:00 a.m. He should have been drifting off gangsta-style, safe in the knowledge that Hailey drove like a little old lady, but today she was scaring him half to death. He tried to suppress his gasps—he hated when she got dramatic about *his* driving—but it wasn't easy, especially when she was inches from the rear bumper of a Honda CRX that was itself doing ninety-five.

The check had thrown her, that he could tell. It was all well and good to spend Sunshine Enterprises's money when it was in *Mack*'s name, but now that she'd been officially dragged into it, Hailey had gone into panic mode. She'd stood there in the family room two nights before, staring at her name on the payee line, and then at Mack. She'd acted like he'd tricked her, so much so that he began to wonder if he had. They'd agreed not to cash this one—that part was easy—but she still seemed off . . . stiff somehow. Even stiffer than usual. And then she'd gone and agreed way too quickly to this fool's errand to Jupiter. It had been so easy to convince her to leave the kids with her parents and to take time off work that it felt to Mack as if he'd blinked in Cleveland and ended up south of the Mason-Dixon with a complete stranger.

What Mack was doing here was taking charge; *of course* they were not going to cash that check, and so he needed a plan for his mother before they faced down those $10,000 monthly bills. Inviting Hailey to come along with him had been an afterthought, a courtesy, and he'd expected a firm *no* instead of the "Okay" that came from her lips. Maybe she saw this as a way to hurry his return to work, or maybe she just wanted to get as far away from the temptation of that check as possible, because it was fucking tempting. She'd left it pinned to the corkboard that hung next to the refrigerator, among the birthday party invites and a flyer for the Halloween parade. More recklessness on her part—who sticks $25,000 to the wall of their kitchen? She was trying to make a point, Mack knew; it was as if she'd taped his bad report card to the fridge door.

"What will your parents think?" he'd wondered aloud. Twenty-five grand might as well have been a million to the Byers, who were staying at the house with the girls so the school run would be easier.

"They'll think it's a mistake, which it is," Hailey had barked at him. "We'll figure it out when we get back, return the money to whoever sent it. I don't want to talk about it now."

She still didn't want to talk about it, or anything else. They sped past billboards advertising fireworks and strip clubs and tracked their progress on the signs for South of the Border—YOU NEVER SAUSAGE A PLACE! YOU'RE ALWAYS A WEINER AT PEDRO'S! JUST TEN MORE MILES!

"Should we stop for a quickie?" Mack asked Hailey, gripping the door handle as they weaved around an ancient Ford Probe.

Hailey managed the ghost of a smile, but otherwise gave no sign of fondness at the memory he was referring to: in the spring of their senior year at Duke, they'd been on their way to Myrtle Beach with a carload of friends. On a dare, and with enough beers in them to make it seem like a good idea, they'd had sex in the disabled bathroom of the giant tourist-trap service station, exiting to the claps and cheers of half a dozen truck drivers. He'd known then that Hailey was his soulmate: smart, beautiful, and more than a little rough . . . not around the edges, but way deep in the cracks where no one could see it but him. He still had the faded Sombrero mug he'd bought that day in his office. He shifted in his seat at the memory, but Hailey stared straight ahead, expressionless.

When the SOTB mileage signs finally reached zero, they did not stop for a quickie, but pressed on for nine more hours, barely pausing to eat and pee. They slept a little in a Best Western on the edge of Jupiter, in side-by-side double beds. Mack dreamed that he'd accidentally let Gulliver loose in a parking lot, and he was trying to dodge cars and giant sombreros to catch him before Hailey noticed. When he woke, covered in sweat and freezing in the air-conditioning, he wondered what would have happened if his dream self had simply asked for Hailey's help, instead of hiding from her like a bad little kid.

✦

Sandy Hollow felt different with his wife there. Or maybe it was that he'd visited twice in a single month. He'd been coming here (more or less) annually for fifteen years, and yet had hardly noticed the ocean views before, or how cushy the furniture in the lobby was. He'd always entered the place with his head down, his jaw clenched. Now he saw it as if for the first time, this luxurious God's waiting room by the sea. It probably *was* worth ten grand a month. He hoped his wife thought so too, since it was her money they'd have to spend, at least until they could make a change or work something out. Hailey had never been to Sandy Hollow, had never met his mother even after all this time, and Mack stumbled at the introductions.

"Well, here she is," he said as he rounded the final corner to Leonora's room, his throat closing up with the smell of old age and disinfectant. He wasn't quite sure whether he was presenting his mom to Hailey or vice versa, but the stakes felt high. His stomach churned with watery orange juice and coffee, his back throbbed from the hotel mattress, and his eyes were dry and stinging from the stale air of various climate-controlled environs. What if Hailey went all *Hailey* on his mom, and rushed through this encounter like it was some kind of sidebar? Or she might continue this judgy, quiet thing she'd been doing lately, and just shrug her shoulders at the sight of his mother—after all, Leonora was a disappointment to her too. Their daughters were down two grandparents right from the word go, and Hailey had been denied the basic human right to complain about your mother-in-law. The prospect of a disappointed silence from both Mrs. Evanses, of such a terrible combination of emptiness and resentment, brought forth a verbal diarrhea like Mack had never experienced.

"Looks like they're doing breakfast now, maybe we should come back. It's going to be hard to top the food here, if we have to move her. They're limited as to what she can eat, of course, but Tilda says they do a pretty good job of offering variety, and even though it's hard to know exactly how much she's aware of, it's a good sign that she can still digest real food. She has to be fed, of course, but—"

He stopped because Hailey had reached his mother's bedside, had stepped around the untouched breakfast tray and moved in close.

"Hello," Hailey said softly, and Mack heard himself exhale. His mom returned his wife's gaze, but only by coincidence. And yet Hailey took his mother's hand in both of her own and gently uncurled Leonora's fingers. "I've been waiting such a long time to meet you."

Mack could not think of when she might have come across anyone else in this state, so how was Hailey so sure of herself? He never had been.

"In person she looks so much like Gigi," Hailey whispered, as if it were a secret. "I never realized."

Mack had. The soft angles of his mother's nose, the fullness of her lips, the set of her gray-blue eyes—it was unmistakable. He had always tried not to think of Leonora as Mabel and Gigi's grandmother, had resisted categorizing her with the sixty- and seventy-something women he'd watched dipping a baby's toes into the Shoreby pool or holding chubby hands as they walked along the dock. Or cramming little feet into crappy plastic shoes, the way Pammy Byers did. Better not to dwell on what Leonora might have been or done . . . probably she would have just taught Gigi to swear, or corrupted Mabel's fledgling musical sensibilities with "Le Freak."

"Mack? Are you okay?"

"Yeah. Fine." His voice cracked. "I'm just going to go talk to the manager and see what's what. Are you all right to stay with her? I don't know where Tilda is, but she's always around. I told her we were coming."

"It's fine. We're fine."

It took Mack ten minutes of wandering up and down washed-out-pastel hallways to find the Sandy Hollow business office, where a woman named Marilyn Murphy was expecting him. He took a seat behind a coffee table covered in binders and brochures; Sandy Hollow had quite the marketing budget. He wondered whether Leonora would ever have chosen the place for herself if she'd been given the option. He guessed Irene Weigand had made the decision; he had no recollection of any of it.

"It's so nice to finally meet you, Mr. Evans," Marilyn said. "I'm sorry our paths haven't crossed before. I've been here almost five years now, but I guess our timings have never matched up. I've heard so much about you from Tilda and Irene . . . Mrs. Weigand."

Mack nodded. He was aware of being somewhat of a celebrity at Sandy Hollow. Tilda had told him about how the staff still asked after Leonora's handsome son, even the ones hired in more recent years for whom he was only folklore, the teenager whose mother had suffered a fate worse than death while he was in the middle of rushing fraternities and playing beer pong.

"We'd be so sorry to see Mrs. Evans go," Marilyn was telling Mack in a hushed voice. "Though I understand if you want her closer to you."

"Yeah, well, like I said on the phone, it seems I'm taking over her care from the trust—from Mrs. Weigand." He suddenly felt embarrassed, a cheapskate whose free cable trial had long since run out.

"Yes, she's informed us of the changes. I've got a lot of your details on the emergency contact sheet, so we can set up the billing today, if that works for you."

"The thing is," Mack told her, "You see, *the thing is*, I hadn't really been aware of the situation."

"The situation?"

"With my mother's finances. I didn't know Irene Weigand was paying for her. Or that she might stop paying for her."

"I see. That must have come as quite a shock."

"Shock doesn't cover it. I'm just wondering if there is federal funding we can access—Medicaid or Medicare, or something we can apply for? I really don't want to move her from here, but I'm not sure quite what to do."

Mack had secretly hoped that doing this in person might make his plea more convincing, but he could not find much comfort in Marilyn's face.

"We can get the ball rolling to try to get some supplementary funds, certainly," she said after a minute. "Though I must tell you that most of our residents are self-paying; we're not really a Medicaid-type facility. In the meantime, why don't we set up a meeting with Mrs. Weigand, and let her know your concerns?"

"Umm, yeah, if we have time." Mack felt coldly ruthless toward

Irene Weigand, if he was being honest with himself. It felt like she was punishing him for not being a mind reader, and he kind of hated her for it.

"Are the two of you close?"

"Not really. She just did me—did us—a huge kindness. I mean, beyond huge. Colossal."

"Well, I'm sure she'll want to work this out too, so let's don't go and panic. Let's not make any rash decisions about your mother's care just yet."

Mack wondered whether Marilyn would still be saying this when there was a stack of unpaid bills in front of her. Could Sandy Hollow just throw his mother out? Call the state to come get her? Was he even legally responsible for Leonora? Hailey would know. But hopefully—somehow—it wouldn't come to that.

"I wonder," Mack said carefully, "whether my mother may have received any correspondence from a company called Sunshine Enterprises?"

"I'm not sure." Marilyn frowned. "What kind of company is it?"

How could Mack explain that he had no idea what kind of company Sunshine Enterprises was? Or whether it was a real company at all? But Marilyn didn't wait for an answer.

"I don't think your mom gets very much mail, Mr. Evans. She's been here so very long, you know . . ."

"Right, of course," Mack said. "And this trust that took care of my mom's bills, did it have, like, an official name?"

"It's in your mother's name." Marilyn got to her feet. "And as I mentioned on the phone, I do have some paperwork that belongs to Leonora. I've taken the liberty of getting it out of storage, and I can give this to you to take now, if you want? The files passed from her lawyer when he retired . . . tax forms, I think mostly. I don't recall any recent mail being in there, but you never know."

"Okay, sure." Mack watched as she lugged a substantial cardboard box from the corner of the room. He took it from her, and stood holding it while she went over some details of his mother's care—medicines and trips to the specialist dentist and, *Oh, Mrs. Evans also has her hair done by the visiting beautician twice a week, and Mrs. Weigand has offered to keep that up, so that's good news, isn't it?*

Mack tried his best to look grateful.

"I'll let you get back to your mom now, Mr. Evans," Marilyn said finally, "and we'll just stay in touch over the next few weeks. Ah, and one last formality: I *am* required to tell you that your mother is categorized as an extremely vulnerable adult. What that means is that we do need to have information about where she's being transferred to, if you indeed decide that Mrs. Evans is going to leave us. We need to make sure it's an appropriate facility that can meet her care needs."

"Right." Mack hugged the box of papers to his stomach; he looked and felt like he'd just been fired from something.

As he bade Marilyn goodbye and started down the empty hallway, Mack realized that he was being watched. An elderly woman stood in one of the doorways he passed, and with surprising swiftness she stepped into the elevator with him just as the doors were closing. As Mack pushed the button for his mother's floor with his elbow, the old lady reached out and gripped his arm with such force that he almost dropped his box.

"Help me," she begged, clutching at him with both hands. "They're watching. Get me out of here." Her cloudy eyes were full of desperation; her fingernails dug into his skin.

"I—" The box pitched sideways. He righted it with his knee and used the opposite hand to frantically push for the button to open the doors.

"You have to help me," she said again. "I'm trapped, and they're watching. I want to go home."

Salt poured into Mack's every wound. His heart fluttered, and his mind went utterly blank. All he could think about was the painful pressure being applied to his wrist by this small, wrinkled woman.

"Please," he said to her. "Please, just hold on a sec, and we'll call someone—" The elevator was moving.

"No! Don't tell them! Just get me out of here!"

The doors pinged, then what felt like a thousand years passed while they shuddered open.

"Tilda!" yelled Mack, and the sight of the nurse's puzzled face appearing from Leonora's room was like the second coming to him. "Tilda, I think this lady needs some help."

As Tilda took her arm—*Ah, Miss Angela, on the move again, are we?*—the old woman shook her head and bared her teeth at Mack. "You—"

He didn't hear the rest because he fled to Leonora's room and shut the door behind him. He stood by the side of his mother's bed, next to his wife, and made no move to stop the tears running down his face. He was grateful when Hailey didn't speak, and when she reached out for his hand.

"I had this crazy idea," he finally managed. "That we'd take Mom home with us today. Don't laugh. I mean, I didn't *really* think that, but it crossed my mind in some way, you know? Not being able to pay for this place seemed like a great excuse to just . . . I've always wondered if I could just get her out of here and . . . maybe, maybe take her out for a beer or something, or a drive, then she'd want to wake up and be alive again. *Fuck!*"

He saw Hailey jump as the huge sob escaped from him. She dropped his hand, took a step back, and Mack felt like he might just burst apart. But then Hailey's arms were around his shoulders, and even though he was rocking back and forth and sobbing and shuddering like mad, she was so damn strong that he couldn't break free of her. After a while, he stopped trying to.

15.

Hailey

The price tag on the red bathing suit was $495. It was not a brand Hailey had heard of before, but the color was striking, just a touch of a *Baywatch* vibe while still classy enough for the pool at the Breakers Hotel in Palm Beach. She bought it, and a pair of nearly-as-pricey trunks for Mack too. She declined the offer of a shopping bag and returned to her husband's side at the check-in desk.

They had possibly collectively lost their minds. The Breakers was almost a thousand dollars a night. Hailey was still in deep shit at work, Mack seemed to be in deep shit at life in general, and they had no real savings left apart from the untouchable check from Sunshine Enterprises. Yet here they were, checking into one of the most luxurious hotels in the country, choosing the *New York Times* as their morning paper option, asking about breakfast.

"Tell me where you'd take her," Hailey had said to Mack as she'd held him by Leonora's bedside. "One place your mom always wanted to go."

Mack's mother had apparently aspired way beyond her means, and so, in a flurry of emotion and rash decision, here they were—though, of course, without Mack's mother. Sunlight streamed into the giant lobby of the Breakers, its beams bathing the furniture, the rugs, and the endless flower displays in an otherworldly and dust-particle-free glow. Hailey searched the edges of her consciousness for the first hints of panic but couldn't find any. Bad thoughts were banned from here, best left outside with the poor people.

Mack took the room key from the receptionist, and they made their way to the elevator. A bellboy wheeled the trolley of their embarrassing luggage—L.L.Bean duffel bags, the cardboard box with Leonora's papers that Mack had refused to leave in the car—on its own discrete journey, freeing Hailey to pretend that they belonged in this place. She wondered, fleetingly, if David Rainier had ever stayed here, and then slapped him from her mind. Mack needed her; what was done was done, and now she had to press ahead without overthinking.

The hotel room was not a room, but a suite, with two Juliet balconies overlooking the ocean.

"Did you ask for a—"

"It was all they had," Mack said, sinking onto a pristine white sofa. She could not bring herself to ask him how much. The bellboy knocked, and Mack didn't move, so it was Hailey who let him in, watched him place their bags on the luggage racks, awkwardly gave him a twenty-dollar bill. (Five hardly seemed enough, given the pile on the carpet and the exotic fruit basket on the dining table.) Once the man was dispatched with, Hailey stretched out on the bed, closed her eyes, and breathed in the scent of unattainable wealth. No matter how many coffee stains she had had laundered, no matter how many broken hearts she had achieved revenge for or Cartier love bracelets she bought herself, she would never be immune to this kind of luxury. Too much blue-collar water had passed under the bridge for her to take even a lesser five-star hotel for granted. Maybe they should bring the girls here, whet their sense of entitlement, acclimatize them early.

When she opened her eyes, Mack had not moved from the sofa. Hailey sat up.

"How about we try the pool?"

He didn't respond. Hailey had the distinct feeling that twenty years' worth of denying his traumatic past may have come to an abrupt end. Which was just great. She really needed him to keep it buried for a while longer; this was not a good year for digging up a nervous breakdown.

She checked her phone. One email, from Marla the paralegal. Straus and Clarke, the two most senior partners, had been looking for her, had been "surprised" to hear she was out of the office.

Any update on Rainier payment? Hailey sent off with a prayer. The negative reply was instant, and still Hailey couldn't bring herself to text David. She dragged herself from the bed, grabbed the $250 Vilebrequin swim shorts she had bought for Mack, and tossed them onto the coffee table in front of him. She saw him grimace at the print.

"These are some very expensive turtles," she said to him, leaning down to pop the tags. "Come on, they want an outing."

The long hallways were empty, and Hailey was glad no one was around; she had not sprung for additional beachwear, and they were both in sneakers and T-shirts, looking for all the world like they'd just wandered in from Marc's. But poolside it was another story: even in his delirium she saw Mack gape at the red bathing suit as she undressed. He and his turtles followed her unprompted into the water and to the far side of the empty pool. He still wasn't saying much, but that was fine with Hailey, and long after the sun dipped down into the ocean the two of them floated there on the edge of the infinity, only their elbows touching.

✦

Hailey came out of the shower the color of a lobster; her every pore had been opened to maximum capacity, and the mirror above the mini bar in the living room area steamed up as she opened the bathroom door.

"You okay?" Mack wanted to know. "Better?"

"I think it must have been the chlorine. Chlorine and exhaustion." Mack had rallied, had pounced on her like a tiger when they'd come back from the pool, but Hailey had panicked, found herself unable to breathe as the room spun around her. She couldn't explain it, not even to herself. Nor did she want to try.

Mack was back on the sofa, and Hailey saw that he had opened Leonora's box. She knelt over him in her towel to inspect the documents he'd laid out on the coffee table. One was a marriage license, dated 1977.

"Oh wow, look. Both your parents' signatures are there."

"I was just thinking she should have run a mile."

Hailey thought so too, but said in her best divorce lawyer voice, "You can't ever know that when you start out." She examined the whisper-thin sheet of paper, tried to picture them in some New York registry office, completely oblivious of what lay before them. The document felt cursed; she put it back down on the table.

Mack was already moving on. He had found an old black-and-white photograph of two small children and presumably their parents, scowling out at the camera from the steps of a partially built house. It could have been almost Civil War–era, based on their clothing and the state of the paper. The background behind them was one of desolation, all barren fields and dust Hailey could almost feel on her tongue.

"That looks like *Little House on the Prairie*," she said to Mack. "Who are they?"

"I have no idea, how sad is that? No names on the back, so I guess that info dies with Mom."

Hailey could feel him teetering on some kind of precipice. She held up the room service menu. "Are we ordering in or going out somewhere? I don't think we have the right clothes for any of the restaurants in the hotel . . . except maybe the staff kitchen."

"Definitely in. I'm never leaving this room again."

"You'd better win the lottery then."

Mack did not answer, and the air was heavy with a question: Had they already? They were getting free money in the mail . . . wasn't that the same thing? A Publishers Clearing House of sorts?

Hailey slipped into a logoed bathrobe and continued her examination of the in-room dining offering. An order of chicken fingers was $45. For a minute she thought Mack shared her indignation; he gasped just as her eyes landed on the $32 piece of flourless chocolate cake. But his attention was still on his mother's box, and a handwritten letter he had found within it.

Dear Leonora,

He won't take my money. You probably already know that.

You'll say it's his decision, and I guess you're right. But he's just a kid. A smart one—you did good. I went up to Duke, just to lay eyes on him there. He's gotten so tall.

Maybe you're happy that he hates me. Maybe you told him to. But I'm here, like always. We both know I'll never, ever stop being his father. I'll always look after him, I promise you that. And I will love you forever, and always wish I'd taken you both with me.

Yours,
Tommy

"I thought your father's name was Warner?" Hailey said when she had finished reading.

"Warner Thomas. I don't remember what she called him. I was so little when he left; I don't remember her calling him anything but 'your father.'" Mack leaned back and closed his eyes; she was losing him again.

"It must be some comfort to know that he was still looking out for you. Even after you told him to go away. Which he deserved," she added hastily.

It took Mack a minute to reply. "I guess. Except I thought he had been looking out for me all along. I thought he paid for my mom, and then I thought he was Sunshine Enterprises . . . I mean, how could I just assume that?"

"It makes sense." Hailey studied the dark, desperate scratches under *never, ever*. "Or it did before you knew he'd passed away. It made as much sense as anything." She handed Mack the room service menu, and once he'd chosen, she called in their order. Mack was on his phone by the time she'd hung up.

"What are you doing?"

He turned his screen around to show her. He had pulled up his father's obituary in the *Daytona Beach News-Journal*. It was a bare-bones write-up of the life of Warner T Evers and gave no hint of the man's background apart from "he is survived by one son."

"I looked for that and couldn't find it," Hailey admitted.

"I found it last week. It was way down in the Google search results."

"Right."

"There's no photo with the obit though."

"So?"

"So what if he's not really dead?"

"Oh, Mack." Hailey felt as sorry for him then as she had by his mother's bedside.

"Just hear me out. What if he's not dead, what if he faked it? What if he faked his own death so he could start over?"

"He's like eighty, Mack," Hailey said gently. "That's a little late in life for that kind of thing, isn't it?"

"Or okay, if he *is* dead, what if he set up some kind of thing where somebody else pays us for him? On his behalf, I mean? I know it sounds crazy, but I just don't know anyone else rich enough to be sending us money out of nowhere, do you?"

"No."

"And I don't know, maybe Irene Weigand *is* overseeing it. Maybe she's not telling me the whole truth—"

"Why would she change up how she pays for things? She could just keep paying for your mom the way she always does."

"I don't know, I don't *know*! A way to hand off the money maybe, since she's getting old. But those checks *have* to be tied to my dad somehow. Why would anyone else just send us a bunch of money?"

Hailey couldn't think of an answer, at least not one that she was ready to voice out loud. David Rainier *was* there, though, sipping his whiskey cocktail in the dark corners of her almost-subconscious. Was it possible? Had the timing been right? That first check that Mack had deposited, when exactly had it come? She would ask him, later. Because David Rainier did owe her, no matter how much he hated his wife, and he was very, *very* rich. Though she suspected that even he might have been shocked at the bill for their room service order.

16.

Feel free to disagree with me, but I think that most people find comfort in having big decisions taken out of their hands, even if they wouldn't admit to it.

Take my mother, for example. The woman who could never decide on anything. Not where she wanted to live, not whether to leave my father, not could-she-or-couldn't-she face sending her sweet baby off to boarding school. (She could, it turned out.) This indecision was written into her very person—the hand-wringing, the shallow breathing, the inability to get herself dressed for a night on the town. Even the small things like whether or not she felt up to eating dinner with us—whether she could bear the company of her own family on any given day—were best left for someone else to decide.

And it can be awfully hard work being that someone else. It's a thankless job being responsible for someone so listless and ephemeral, and so I really sympathized with my father the time I caught him standing over Mother's dressing table with his hands on her neck, telling her to start acting like a living, breathing human being or, by God, he would make sure she wasn't one. Maybe he was a little rough about it, maybe his methods were a little heavy-handed (get it?!), but he got her attention. Sometimes people need that kind of intervention, is all I'm saying. It keeps life moving forward.

I've solved the mystery of the Evanses' lawn ornaments, by the way. Mack and Hailey haven't been around this week, and in their absence three goats have appeared at their house: one new one, made out of cheap plastic, on the lawn by the side gate, and two old ones, inside taking care of the grandkids.

17.

Mack

Somehow Hailey had fixated on the figure of $12,000. Mack had no idea what she was basing this on, whether she remembered that obscure detail from when they'd built the house, or whether it was just a nice shocking number. Pammy and Eddie Byers looked pretty shocked.

"Now, Hailey, let's not get carried away. I could refinish that floor myself—"

"It's sandalwood, Dad. You can't just slap a coat of paint down. Oh my God, *oh my God*, this is just bare wood now. What did you use on it?"

"Just Mr. Clean." Hailey's mother was on the verge of tears. "And a few drops of bleach, to take away the urine smell. You have to do that so they don't piddle in the same place again—"

"Why the hell was he peeing in the house? Did you let him out?"

"We did. We walked him, we took him out in the yard about a million times. I don't know what got into him."

Mack knew exactly what had gotten into Gulliver. This was revenge pissing, because his beloved mommy had gone away and left him for five whole days. Each of the irregular patches of newly stripped wood that dotted the front hall and the family room was a pointed *fuck you* in response to Gulliver's abandonment. Although, as usual, it wasn't the dog that Hailey blamed.

"I can't believe you put bleach on a wood floor," she was telling her mother. “The whole downstairs is going to have to be sanded down and refinished. And I’m not exaggerating, it’ll cost twelve grand if we’re *lucky*.”

“I’m so sorry.” Pammy was crying now, actual tears, and Mack was desperate to get out of the room. He was edging toward the basement door when things took a turn for the worse.

“I also had a little issue with the girls’ laundry,” Pammy went on, obviously no expert in self-preservation. “I put some of their things in the dryer, and the little sweaters just shrank right up. I’ve never seen that happen before— ”

“Which sweaters?” Hailey’s voice was now monotone, and Mack wondered if her parents knew what that meant, whether they knew that now was the time to run for the hills. “How many sweaters?”

“Well . . . quite a few. I thought I would get them ready for the colder weather, and— ”

“You shrank all their knitwear?” Pammy’s flow of tears indicated that this was the case. “Oh my God, Mom— ” Hailey closed her eyes and clamped her mouth shut in exactly the same way she had when Mack had backed into the corner of the garage the day they’d moved into the house. He felt for Pammy, he really did, but he wasn’t about to open his mouth.

“Your mother was just trying to help.” It was Eddie who finally asserted his status as the paterfamilias. “Now you listen, young lady, we won’t be talked to that way. We’ve been busting our butts looking after the girls and that damn dog, cleaning up this house, runnin’ around all over God’s green earth doing errands for you, organizing your mess. You show a little respect.”

Mack was fascinated to see shame spread across his wife’s features. This reaction had never been his experience when it came to calling Hailey out. He felt a strange surge of protectiveness; her obsession with the house and the sweaters and everything else in their daughters’ little world wasn’t *quite* as selfish as it seemed right then. . . .

Surely Eddie must understand that his daughter just wanted her own daughters' lives to be perfect, even if most of her priorities were all wrong? Surely Eddie too must feel some pity at the way Hailey was mourning each teeny, tiny sweater that Pammy was now setting down in front of her in a kind of twisted self-flagellation?

Still, this wasn't Mack's fight . . . or maybe it was. He had just taken another step toward freedom when Eddie turned on him too: "And you've got plenty of goddamn money to fix that floor. It's disgraceful, the pair of you. Leaving big checks lying around. Careless."

Mack's eyes went to the pinboard above the kitchen desk. There was an empty tack next to a picture of the girls from the Fourth of July.

"Where's the check that was here?" Hailey had clocked the bare spot on the wall too, and she didn't sound angry anymore. She sounded something else entirely.

"I deposited it for you." Eddie shook his head. "And I get that you've been successful, but that's disgusting, Hailey. I don't care how rich you are, you put your money in the goddamn bank."

✦

There was no way that Mack was going to walk into National City Bank and start a big thing. "It's your name on the check anyway," he told Hailey as they sat at one end of the kitchen island, eating greasy Chinese takeout. He waited for an explosion, something that would at least end the conversation—Pammy and Eddie had fled for home and left him in the hotseat—but that didn't happen.

"It was your name on the first three checks."

Monotone. Mack was in dangerous waters. "If we go into the bank," he said carefully, "it'll flag it to them. They'll start asking questions we can't answer, when probably no one would have ever paid attention. Why go looking for trouble?"

"Looking for trouble? Have you lost your mind? This is a lot of money. We can't just sit back and do nothing and spend money that we have no idea—"

"Fine, you do it!" Maybe Mack would explode this time! "Do whatever you want. I've got other things to worry about. I *am* about to lose my fucking mind—"

"Shut up!" Hailey got up and swung the kitchen door shut, nearly crushing Gulliver in the process. "You'll wake up the girls. Obviously I'm sorry about your mother—how many times can I say it—but we have got to figure this Sunshine Enterprises thing out. *Now.*"

"It's not just my mom. I've got shit at work—"

"You've got shit at work? *You've* got shit? You're not even at work. You're home in your sweats all day doing God knows what, because giving a few lectures and hanging out with twenty-year-olds is *sooo* fucking stressful."

Mack stared at Hailey's mouth as it yelled, at the thin line of her lips. He didn't pity her at all now, and she looked old when she screamed at him like this—how could he be married to a woman so old? It was hard to believe this was the same person that had been with him in the pool two days ago, in that red swimsuit. That was the problem with Hailey; she could morph in front of his eyes. Lately there was something about her that made Mack think of a racehorse: from afar, she was fierce and capable and beautiful, and he was increasingly in awe of her. But up close, he saw way too much of the whites of her eyes and the flash of her teeth, and he spent a lot of time worrying about when she might suddenly decide to kick him.

Mackenzie Ewing was not like this. None of his students were. To a man (and a woman), they were *constant.* Always wanting to hear what Mack thought, always patient while he worked out just the right way to say it. And Mackenzie had been the best of them, the brightest spark. When Mackenzie smiled, Mack smiled, and when she called him Big Mack, or waved across the quad, when she brought him flat whites before his lectures, when her papers shone with his own ideas reshaped and perfected, when she sought him out at his home and marveled at all of his books and his house and his kids who were *so, so cute!*, all of this made Mack's life and career feel like exactly what he'd dreamed they could be, back when he was the one who was fresh and new in the world. He might not be rich, he might not be powerful, but by God did Mack Evans's tutor group worship him. He was a god, he was a guru, he was the Hunter S. Thompson to a gaggle of baby Johnny Depps.

"I'm in trouble at work," Mack told Hailey flatly, and felt a medium-sized thrill as that took the wind from her sails.

"What kind of trouble?"

"The department thinks I've been inappropriate with the students."

Hailey waited until he had no choice but to carry on.

"It's the gatherings," Mack said, and it went without saying that Hailey had told him so. Years before, she had railed against Mack's clandestine Covid meetups in their backyard, had asked him and then begged him and finally commanded him not to assemble a bunch of teenagers in a pandemic for something as unessential as reading Shakespeare around a fire pit, but Mack had fought his corner and he had won. He had seen his students' gray skin and dead eyes staring back at him over Zoom, had watched them grow quieter and a little bit less young each day, and he would have risked almost anything to reassure them that the rest of their only-just-beginning lives wouldn't be (couldn't be!) confined to the dismal walls of a dorm room. (And that was when they were lucky enough to be allowed on campus.) All those kids needed was a little taste of what lay in store for them when this was all over, and Mack had made his best offering: weed, wine, words. Repeated every six weeks or so. Hailey had stayed away.

The parties could've stopped when the world opened back up, except the kids that came along *after* the pandemic seemed a touch deadened too, like POWs returning home from some willfully forgotten conflict. By then Mack had a rep to protect: these new tutor groups had heard rumors about how he was the tutor everyone wanted, the one who really cared about them, and who was he to let them down? So Mack continued the gatherings in the old tradition, and in his heyday there were dinner parties too. Even Hailey had come to some of those, though she'd stayed on the periphery, always at arm's length, until she could disappear upstairs to work on a brief or some kind of motion to dismiss something. It was always clear that she'd been indulging him, that she thought all his fun and camaraderie was a terrible thing, even when it wasn't technically illegal. She must have been over the moon when they'd moved to Bratenahl, when the parties had stopped because he couldn't bear to bring his students to this temple of yuppie mundanity.

"How were the dinners inappropriate? What exactly are they saying?"

"That I served alcohol. That I was too close to one of the students. That some of them smoked weed."

"Which student?"

Of course Hailey would know the exact spot to dig in, but Mack was beyond caring. He felt as raw as their floorboards.

"Mackenzie. That freshman from last year. You met her."

Mack waited for her to start interrogating him. He braced himself for the crash of her stool on the floor as she jumped to her feet, for accusation and storming out of the room. It caught him off guard when she simply hung her head and slumped her shoulders forward over the counter. She put her face in her hands and, after what felt like an eternity passed while Mack stared at his wife's scalp, Hailey mumbled to him through her fingers.

"How did this happen to us?"

It was a bottomless question that Mack wanted nothing to do with. "Listen, you have to believe me: I never laid a finger on Mackenzie Ewing."

And that, even though he knew that Hailey certainly did *not* have to believe him and probably wouldn't, was God's honest truth. Mackenzie Ewing was a kid, and Mack was not some kind of pervert. Besides, he loved his wife—even right in that moment, when he felt more afraid of her than ever before.

18.

Hailey

There was an envelope peeking out from under the doormat; Hailey noticed it as she came down the stairs the next morning, after she took in the fact that the pee-damaged patches in the floor had been covered over with doll blankets and little mountains of toys. Mabel's or Gigi's solution to yesterday's catastrophe brought a lump to Hailey's throat, and she stepped carefully around their efforts as she reached for the dropped piece of mail. The specific brown shade of the envelope brought a flash flood of perspiration to her skin.

When she tore it open, Hailey found that there was not a check inside. It *was* from Sunshine Enterprises, but this time it was a sort of invoice. It gave the dates and the amounts of all of the checks they had received—four grand, then five, then six, then seven, then twenty-five—in a neat column. Forty-seven thousand dollars paid out, the paper shouted at her, though a lot of that—more than half—could only just have hit their bank account. They could still pay most of it back. All of it, if they scraped into their overdraft. (Private school was *so* damn expensive!)

Mack was in the kitchen making the girls pancakes on a weekday, trying to prove he was Father of the Year instead of a useless, soon-to-be-unemployed lech. Hailey kissed the top of Gigi's head as she handed him the document.

She watched his eyes run down the length of the paper, then dart back to the top. He set the spatula down in the frying pan.

"I don't get it. It looks like a bill, but for what? What is this minus forty-seven thousand?"

"Uh, maybe because we took forty-seven thousand?" This was worth abandoning the silent treatment for, Hailey decided. After she'd gotten over the initial shock of her husband's stupidity and betrayal, she'd boarded up her mouth like the derelict houses that peppered the not-distant-enough streets that surrounded Bratenahl. Last night she hadn't trusted herself to speak as she put clean sheets on the bed in the guest room; she had been too afraid of matching Mack strike-for-strike. The impact of David Rainier would plow over his glorified teenage groupie, would destroy what was left of their marriage in a single nuclear explosion.

"Forty-seven thousand whats?" Mabel wanted to know.

"Eat your pancake," Mack told her.

"We didn't *take* it," he said to Hailey. "It was paid out to us. That's what this is saying. Look, right here. It says, 'Statement of your Account.' "

"The account is negative. They obviously want the money back."

"You don't know that. We don't even know who *they* are. We don't even *have* an account." Mack turned the document over, just as Hailey had done two minutes earlier. "There's no address, no bank details." Hailey already knew this; there was only the familiar logo in orange and yellow ink, of a sun rising (or setting?) over the horizon, above the date. "I mean, how would we even be supposed to pay it?"

"I don't know. I didn't think this could get any weirder." Hailey watched Gigi dump half a bottle of syrup onto her plate. Then she reached over Mack and took the spatula out of the frying pan; there was a black mark where it had melted onto the nonstick surface. "I'm late. I'm taking this with me." Hailey grabbed the paper from his hand. "I'm going to see if one of our researchers can find this company." She left the kitchen so fast that she was in the car before she realized that she hadn't said goodbye to her daughters.

✦

Though it wasn't even October yet and it was almost sixty degrees outside, there was a woman in a garish mink coat getting out of a Mercedes across from Hailey's parking space. Hailey had one foot out of her own car before she realized that this woman was Rebekah Rainier.

"Now that's what I call perfect timing." Something in Rebekah's voice was off; it grated even more than usual.

"Good morning, Rebekah." This was just about the last thing Hailey needed; she had to force civility into her syllables. "Do we have a meeting? Come on up to the office, and you'll have to give me a minute. I haven't really looked at my schedule because I've been away—"

"Away fucking my husband?"

It felt like a semi had been driven straight through Hailey's chest.

"What?"

"You heard me. You. Fucked. My. Husband."

Hailey's lungs seemed to collapse in on themselves. She felt as if she was flying backward through the garage, even as she was frozen in place. "Rebekah, I have no idea what you're talking about." Fighting the paralysis in her legs, she backed toward the door that led to the elevators. Rebekah followed her.

"He called me, you know. David called me just to tell me that he'd fucked my lawyer. *My* lawyer, the one who's supposed to be on my side. How could you be so stupid?"

"Listen to me, I—"

"I *told* you. I told you *exactly* what he was. You're such a snot, sitting up there in your fancy office, thinking you know everything. Are you going to tell the other lawyers that you screwed the guy who's screwing all of them? Was that your plan to get your money back?" As Rebekah's laugh echoed around the concrete, Hailey heard a car pull into the parking garage. Someone was going to see them.

Anyone could be listening. She was torn between getting back in her car and running into the building. Could she lock the stairwell door behind her? Rebekah Rainier loose in the halls of Arthur, Clarke & Straus was the only thing that could be worse than this.

"He's never going to pay you, you stupid bitch," Rebekah said, with an expression that looked almost like joy. "It's a game to him, don't you see that?"

Hailey said a silent prayer to all the unfaithful spouses who'd parked in this very garage, and she followed their lead: "Rebekah, I honestly don't know what you are talking about. I certainly didn't sleep with your husband—or your estranged husband or whatever he is—no matter what he may have told you. You can't go around making crazy accusations without anything to back them up."

Hailey hoped to God that Rebekah didn't have anything to back them up.

"Uh-huh," said Rebekah. "You just keep right on lying and see where it gets you." She was close to Hailey now, and very tall. Her face was threatening to bust free of its Botox shell; Hailey could see faint frown lines and an angry almost-wrinkle slashing its way down the center of her forehead. "He set you up, and you played right into his hands," Rebekah went on. "And you go ahead, keep right on lying till you're blue in the face, but I wouldn't be surprised if David has proof. I'd watch that back of yours, and maybe in the future stay off it."

Hailey turned away and ducked into the musty stairwell. The heavy door swung shut of its own accord, and like a child, Hailey pushed her body weight against it. No resistance came from Rebekah, though after a minute a man Hailey recognized from the insurance agency on the top floor appeared through the glass panel in the door. Hailey had no choice but to let him in. If he'd heard the angry exchange, he didn't let on.

Hailey felt she might suffocate on the elevator ride. David had never called her. He hadn't emailed or texted a single word since that night. She'd been so wrapped up in Mack, so busy telling herself that she'd deal with David *later*, that she hadn't considered what his own silence might mean. Surely he was just being a gentleman, just waiting for her to set the tone of what had occurred between them? Because Rebekah had to be wrong; there was no way that he had set her up. Hailey was much too smart to have misread him, much too clever to let herself become a pawn in some millionaire's divorce battle.

It was simply not a possibility.

By the time Hailey reached her office, she had decided to send him a text. It was safer than email somehow, less official: *Hello David, can we speak today? Give me a call when you can.* It was the first message between them—she only had his number in her phone from the day he'd called her at the pool—so should she sign her name?

She did not.

She took the statement from Sunshine Enterprises out of her bag and, taking a Sharpie from her desk, blacked out hers and Mack's names and their address from the top of the page. Then, casting a glance down the hallway to make sure Rebekah wasn't in the reception area, she made her way past rock-star paralegal Marla's desk, past Straus's and Clarke's offices, to the L-shaped corridor that housed the firm's two researchers-for-hire. Dennis—the one she was looking for, the only one who would do for this task—was hunched over a Dunkin' Donuts mug, glasses fogged from the steam coming out of it. He straightened at the sight of her, mumbled something that must have been hello. If she'd met him on the street, Hailey would have put his age at no more than sixteen.

"I need you to do something for me, Dennis." Hailey didn't trust her voice with pleasantries; the shock of Rebekah's assault was still ricocheting through her nervous system. She set the statement from Sunshine Enterprises in front of him. "Can you please find out everything you can about this company?"

Dennis frowned—God, he really was almost prepubescent—and Hailey nearly lost it as he googled the company right in front of her. There were fifteen million results.

They locked eyes. On some fundamental level Hailey needed him to be afraid of her, and, wrapped in the warm blanket of self-preservation that was his generation's instinct, Dennis was not about to oblige.

"I need more to go on if you want me to narrow this down at all," he said with a shrug.

"I'm aware of that," Hailey snapped. "I was about to tell you—in strict confidence—that I need you to find out if there is a connection between a company by this name and David Rainier." She put her hand out to stop him as he went to amend his google search. "And let me be clear: I really need you to keep this line of investigation between us."

He seemed to perk up a little at the subterfuge. "I don't remember seeing this company name when we analyzed his financials."

"No, I know. I'm just wondering about the amounts—can you match them up with money flowing through his accounts?"

"I can't access a third party's statements," said Dennis flatly, but they both knew this was not true. In the thick of Rebekah's divorce proceedings, the kid had submitted two files of research on David Rainier to Marla and Hailey: one contained legally obtained material that was usable in court, the other was only to be used for reference purposes and never shared outside the firm. Dennis, Marla had told Hailey back then, was a bona fide hacker. At the time, Hailey had been unimpressed—what researcher his age wasn't? But now she really needed him to be something special.

"Maybe if you give me the account these were paid into," he

was saying, looking down at the statement. "If I had that, I could possibly—and I'm speaking sort of like hypothetically here—get the details on the payer."

"They were checks," said Hailey. "Does that matter?"

"Checks?"

"Yes, like paper checks." She had a sudden recollection of an Instagram reel about teenagers struggling to dial rotary phones. "Checks that come in the mail and you deposit in your bank account."

"Right. No, I don't think it would matter. Although a check would have account numbers on it that we could trace, maybe a bank address—"

"I don't have that. The checks were already deposited." Thanks to Hailey's greedy husband and her busybody father, those serial numbers were now the property of National City Bank. And as much as she hated to admit it, she just wasn't sure that Mack was wrong to be wary of red-flagging the strange payments.

"And you say you don't have the payee account details? Knowing who's getting the money would help too."

Hailey sighed. She took in Dennis's unbrushed hair, his vegan Vans, and the Chipotle loyalty card tucked alongside his ergonomic keyboard.

"I have them," she said, and wrote down hers and Mack's full names and bank account number. Dennis's eyes widened, but he said nothing.

"I don't think I need to tell you what will happen if this gets around the office." Hailey almost laughed at her own ridiculousness, but he only nodded. "And one more thing. There's no way that whoever the sender is—whoever runs Sunshine Enterprises—will know you are looking into this, right?" She lowered her voice. "They can't see whatever it is you do to search through these accounts, right?"

"There's no way," Dennis said. "That would basically be, like, impossible." She saw that his eyes had come to rest on the –$47,000 at the bottom of the page. "Just a thought—What does it say on your bank account statements? It might give the bank this money comes from on there?"

"It doesn't, I checked. It just says Sunshine Enterprises. No other information. It's like the money is coming from nowhere."

"That's impossible too," said Dennis. "I just need a little time."

19.

When I was almost twenty, I suffered what they called a "catastrophic dental incident." In layman's terms, I fell headfirst down the concrete stairs that led from one level of our terrace to another. I landed on my chin, my top teeth crashed into the bottom ones, and the result was like someone had taken a baseball bat to a china cabinet. Even now, decades later, I'm still constantly at the dentist. Root canals, veneers, bridges, crowns, implants—I've had them all. I've been through five dentists in as many years, dozens in my lifetime, but no matter who's doing the drilling, it always hurts like hell, even with a boatload of Novocaine.

What really makes me crazy, though, worse than the pain, is the waiting: I wait to get called in to the chair, I wait while they get all their instruments of torture ready, I wait while they take X-rays and harden their tooth-making materials with little UV lamps, and I wait while the dentist talks to the hygienist about the weather and football and—let me tell you—it's enough to drive someone completely nuts.

It does give me that chance to keep up with my reading, however. And today, another tasty tidbit: who would have thought, there in the pages of *Cleveland Social*, rivaling his wife for the media spotlight, would be Malcolm Evans, assistant professor of English at the Cleveland Institute of Technology? It seems Professor Evans, who lives in Bratenahl—gasp!—with his young family, has been playing naughty with the students—inappropriate gatherings, rumors of impropriety.

Wine, marijuana, really juicy stuff. Now he's gone and gotten himself suspended, pending an investigation.

Suspended without pay, is what it said, and I didn't think they could do something like this in America. I thought "innocent until proven guilty" and all that.

Not that I'm complaining.

20.

Mack

Mack still had Mackenzie Ewing's number in his phone. He had every one of his tutor group's details, and he could have called any one of those kids, could have asked any of those students what the hell they'd said that had the English Department so sure that Mack was a drug-pushing pedophile . . . Or maybe it was what they hadn't said. Why hadn't Mackenzie stuck up for him? Why hadn't she told the department that Mack had done nothing wrong?

This limbo was the worst part. If only the *Plain Dealer* or the six o'clock news or the Associated Press had picked up the sorry story. A major outlet would have brought shock and scandal in one big wave, and then Mack would know where he stood. Maybe someone would have investigated a little and uncovered just how ridiculous and unfounded this whole thing was. But now, with just an odd little mention of his impropriety in *Cleveland Social*, three mortifying posts on a website called Rate My Professors, and one probing phone call from a local paper in University Heights, the shame was trickling in like Chinese water torture. That young teacher at Mabel's pickup hadn't smiled yesterday. Betsy Wakefield from next door had ceased her insufferable good mornings—did that mean anything? Chenise had sounded borderline belligerent when Mack suggested ravioli for the girls' dinner last night, and was he being paranoid, or had he felt eyes on him at his second-favorite Starbucks? (He didn't dare visit the one on campus, so he went all the way to Lakewood instead. What the hell else did he have to do?)

The whole world had it in for him. Irene Weigand had really and truly handed over the baton, as she put it, and cut him and his mother loose. Marilyn from Sandy Hollow had already sent Mack the bill for the month of November. If they paid it, and Hailey really did get no bonus this year, then they—a college professor and a highly regarded attorney—would be broke by Christmas. The hardwood floor specialists had more or less confirmed Hailey's estimate for the damage caused by Gulliver's tantrum, and the English Department had told Mack that they would contact him "in good time" when they were ready to proceed. Which would be great—he looked forward to the chance to clear his name, if he didn't die first of a heart attack brought on by stress.

Mack had given up running when he went to college, but now felt like as good a time as any to get back into it. In high school he'd made the cross-country team, before golf had completely taken over, and with any luck being fit was like riding a bike. He dug out an old pair of Adidas sneakers, the kind that were good for looking like an 1980s skater kid but not for actual jogging. He would make do. He put on some shorts and his not-very-clean Duke T-shirt. He sized up Gulliver and decided there was no way the little shit could keep up, so he left the dog in the kitchen, where he would pee again in protest, but what did it matter now?

The cold autumn air coming off the lake gave Mack the last bit of incentive he needed to plow through his inertia. He focused on the scuff-scuff of his shoes on the pavement as his heart began to thump in his chest. He scuff-scuffed down the smooth road surface of Magpie Court gate to the main drag, which was uneven and badly patched in some places, and predictably had nothing on it but a few parked cars that belonged to groundskeepers and cleaners. He stopped briefly to drop the incriminating issue of *Cleveland Social* into a public trash can. (He had only barely scanned the article about himself, and he could only pray that Hailey would never see it.) Then his feet scuff-squished into the wet grass as he cut across the grounds of the Bratenahl Place towers. He lost his depth perception for a minute as he turned his head to look up at Two Bratenahl Place. It was weird to think that people were living stacked up like this in the middle of his suburban nightmare.

He'd always been fond of the apartment blocks in Lakewood, buzzing with life as people came and went. They'd reassured him that he still lived in a big city, provided him with some of the flavor of the years he and Hailey had spent in New York while he did his PhD and she worked ninety hours a week for a firm nicknamed "the Death Star." But in Bratenahl, tall buildings and people in close proximity felt wrong. Part of the Bratenahl pitch was the privacy, and you paid a premium for all that distance from other humans, especially the not-rich ones. Did anyone even *live* in those Bratenahl towers? Some mysterious urban energy was missing here, some comradery . . . not that Mack really knew. Neither he nor Hailey had ever even set foot—

As he made it to the lakefront path a sudden sting hit his left ankle, and then he kicked something with his shoe. A white blur went airborne off to his left side, and Mack heard a yelp as he stumbled and hit the ground.

"Colman!" a raspy voice called. "Colman, get back here!"

Mack saw driving loafers in the grass and baggy corduroy pants, then above them a face with a meticulously groomed mustache. It bent close to reach for a leash attached to a frouffy white dog of the kind Mack detested.

"He got away from me," the man said. "Damn dog. Did you break anything?"

Mack got to his feet, shook out his legs. "No, I'm fine."

"Don't see many joggers out at this time of day. That's why we walk; Colman hates joggers. You live in Magpie Court?" Mack saw that the dog had a brown patch on its side where it had connected with the sole of his foot, and also that there was blood trickling from his left ankle, turning his sock red. The wound started to hurt as soon as he looked at it.

"I think he bit me," Mack said.

The man gave a cursory glance at Mack's ankle. "It's not a bad one. Just a scratch. I think you caught his tooth when you fell." He did not apologize. "I've seen you around—Two Magpie, right? On the corner. I've come across your wife a few times."

"Uh, okay." Mack couldn't keep the irritation from his face; it was taking all of his self-control not to yell at this guy.

"They're expensive, those new houses," the man continued. "But nice inside, I'm told. Have to say I'm glad I bought my pile of bricks when I did. Been here quite a few years now."

So he was going to rub real estate prices in Mack's face. Mack was about to jog off, but he'd just realized that the guy was pointing toward the wall that surrounded the Eliot estate, one of the biggest properties in Bratenahl. No wonder the man was so entitled.

He was looking at Mack's feet in disgust. "You shouldn't be jogging in flat shoes like that, you know. Bad for the arches."

"So is getting attacked by a dog."

They both turned toward Colman, who was listening intently to the conversation. "See? He doesn't mind you now that you're not running." The man nodded as if Mack had finally got the hang of something. "Listen, I'm in the shoe business, or I was. One of the first investors in Saucony. Made a fortune. I've got running shoes coming out of my ears. Come and I'll give you a pair."

"Thanks," Mack said, "but I'm okay. I'd better get going." There was no urgency in his voice, though; his fit of good intention was over, and he was staring down the barrel of a long, depressing afternoon. His brain itched just thinking about it.

"I insist. Follow me. They're great shoes, and by the looks of it you need them."

Mack thought about suggesting that the man drop the shoes by his house, but the lure of the Eliot estate was too great. He'd seen it from the lake a few times when he was out on the water, and the only word that could describe the house was *colossal*. It was the same size as the Shoreby Club, bigger even; a handful of mansions had been built at the same time, but only this one was still a private residence. Mack's first thought was how excited Hailey would be when he told her he'd been in the place, and then he remembered she wasn't speaking to him. He followed the man anyway.

"You been here about six months?" the guy said as Mack fell into step beside him, careful not to trip over his dog again.

"Yeah, thereabouts."

"I watched them build that development, of course. Followed the sales. Always risky, investing in new construction." He studied Mack carefully. "You're Mack Evans, right?"

Mack nodded.

"And your wife, she's Hailey Evans, the lawyer?"

"Yes."

"Saw a piece on her in *Cleveland Social*."

"Oh right." The thought of this guy thumbing through the magazine that had just shamed him made Mack's heart sink, and to make matters worse, for about a hundred yards he thought this was a wasted trip; they'd reached the wall of the Eliot estate and turned away from the house, and now he was going to have to go back to some run-of-the-mill split-level in a far-flung corner of Bratenahl just to get a pair of running shoes he'd never use again for fear of bumping into this guy. Then a gate appeared, almost totally obscured by ivy, the man punched in 00000 on a rusty keypad, and they stepped inside.

Immediately Mack thought, *Golf course*: the grass was greener than felt naturally possible, and the yard was huge and hilly. He saw a fountain and a sundial and topiaries—none of the brown-patched bareness of the other big houses he could see from the street. The overhang on the front of this house reminded him of the Breakers hotel; God, would it blow Hailey's mind that this was right here on her doorstep.

"Sorry, what did you say your name was?"

"I didn't. It's Gerry, Gerry Baptista."

Mack racked his brain; it seemed impossible that someone with this kind of wealth wouldn't be known around town, but then again Bratenahl was not Mack's town, not really. If this guy was anything to go by it might hold all kinds of secret characters, a thought that cheered Mack up a little.

"Quite a place you've got here, Gerry."

"Eliot was a steel man," Gerry said. "But then an academic like you probably knows that."

"I'm an English professor. I know Hemingway and Kerouac, mostly. Not much local history, I'm afraid."

"The steel barons were *national* history, I should think. They built a lot of this country."

They'd walked the length of the house, under the overhang and past a five-car garage around to the back. As they climbed one side of a pair of steep curving staircases toward a shady back terrace, Mack panicked that he might not get a proper look inside—he'd already decided that this adventure was his inroad with Hailey. "Boy, those barons sure knew how to build houses. What a spot you've got here."

"Yes," Gerry Baptista agreed. "They don't build them like they used to. No offense, of course."

Mack was too taken with the view to let this dig get to him. The semicircular terrace on the back of the house curved in reverse of the shoreline, so it almost felt like you could step off into the steely lake and carry on walking through the sky beyond it. Even in bleak

November it was vast and breathtaking. Beneath him, tucked among some trees, Mack could see a greenhouse. Farther down toward the gray water, which was crashing onto the stone barricade at the edge of the lawn in angry waves, there was a dock and a boathouse with a decent-sized powerboat still in the water.

"You better get that out soon," Mack said. He knew next to nothing about boats, but he had seen Lake Erie good and frozen in November before.

Gerry had already turned to go into the house, and so Mack (and Colman) trotted along behind him. The house had a warm, floral scent, and right away Mack saw heavy curtains and copious chandeliers.

"Are you married?" he asked Gerry as he followed him along a narrow hallway resplendent with crown moldings and elaborate wallpaper.

"Not anymore. Tried four times, and I figure that's enough trying."

"Ah."

They emerged into a huge wood-paneled office with a window overlooking the lake. An oak desk the size of a pool table stood opposite an actual pool table, and every surface was loaded with technology—laptops, desktops, speakers of all shapes and sizes, at least half a dozen screens alight and tracking financial markets. This guy was no sleepy retiree.

Gerry opened one of a dozen large cupboards; it revealed itself to be full of shoeboxes. "Size?"

"Eight and a half."

He selected a box, opened it, and presented it to Mack; the shoes were bright orange and blue and about half the weight of the ones on his feet.

"This is great," Mack told him. "Worth getting nipped for."

"Best business decision I ever made," Gerry said, nodding down at Mack's feet.

Some petty inner voice stopped Mack from saying a direct thank-you for the sneakers, but Gerry took as good as he gave and didn't seem to expect one.

"You want a pair for your wife? I don't have as many women's sizes."

"No, really, that's okay. She's got more shoes than she knows what to do with. She doesn't run much these days, anyway."

"You should tell her not to be out on the lakefront at night. It's not safe."

"At night? No, I don't think she goes out at night—"

"I saw her . . . a month or so ago now. Maybe she was on her way back from the club. I wouldn't let a wife of mine walk around here after dark, is all I'm saying. Even the fourth wife, and I hated her the most."

"Right, no," Mack said. Maybe this guy had Mack linked up with the wrong Bratenahl female. When had Hailey ever gone for a walk at night? He made a mental note to ask her about it once they were speaking again.

"You'll be at the Christmas party, I take it?"

"At the Shoreby? Uh, probably. Hailey always organizes that kind of thing, but I'm sure she won't want to miss it."

"Everyone goes," Gerry said. "It's a good party. I'm glad they're letting people from the newer developments join the club. It needed fresh blood."

Mack was not going to bite; whether or not he should be allowed into the Shoreby Club was not a hill he was prepared to die on. "Yeah, well, we love the pool."

"I'm sure you'll get a lot of use out of it. Probably best not to bring your dog again though," Gerry told Mack, who once more had no idea what he was talking about. He was tired of humoring this old man, and he felt strangely claustrophobic in this giant place.

"Well, I better be getting back," he said, and Gerry led him out a door on the far side of the study and through the rooms along the front of the house. The largest was as big as a hotel lobby, with huge bay windows and an elaborate ceiling. Its proportions dwarfed the sparse furnishings, and Mack felt his annoyance abate again. This guy rattled around in here all alone?

"You can let yourself out the side gate, right?" Gerry said to Mack. "It's been nice to meet you, son. Although I still say it's a damn shame they blocked up the lakefront with that Magpie development of yours. I hope your house is worth it."

"I sure think so," said Mack, lying through his teeth.

✦

Back home, Mack squished his way through the landscaping on the side of his house looking for the garden hose. His shoes were muddy, and he figured a blast of cold water might feel good on his sore ankle. It was a stupid place to install a hose, he realized; the bushes that grew in front of his basement office window had been trampled by people trying to get to the faucet, and there were footprints all through the soil. As he bent over to rest the box with his new shoes on one of the less-damaged shrubs, something in the sandy-colored stone on the wall caught his eye: a crack. A deep crack, rising up from ground level. It didn't keep to the lines of the mortar; it sliced right through the middle of at least a dozen of the bricks on the exterior wall of the house. Mack took a step backward, letting the hose spray at his side. A foot or so farther along, he found another crack. This one didn't stretch quite as high, but it was deep too, deeper than the first.

Mack could hear Gulliver howling at him from inside as he squished his way around toward the backyard and counted a dozen cracks of varying sizes in three different walls. He was no Mr. Fixit (he'd had no one to teach him), but even he could see that the stonework around the base of the house was fucked. The bricks were mostly decorative, though, from what he could tell, and he made the decision that he was more than okay with leaving them to crumble for now. This didn't need mentioning to Hailey; it would be summer before she noticed, and everything might be better then. Or it might be worse.

When he'd finished his survey and thoroughly flooded the flower beds, he turned off the hose and backed away onto the lawn, at which point he almost broke his neck on—of all goddamn things—a tacky plastic goat. Betsy Wakefield was just pulling into her driveway as Mack, bleeding, barefoot, and still swearing, dug his house key out of the flowerpot by the front door. She did not wave hello.

21.

Hailey

She had no business googling this Mackenzie Ewing. Why exactly was she sitting here in the car with the engine switched off, freezing her ass off, outside her own house? Why was Hailey looking through this girl's sorority photos, and at the pictures of her in some debutante ball, in a low-cut white dress? Why was Hailey sitting here wondering whether Mack had burrowed his face into this girl's practically adolescent breasts? Would he? Was he capable of it, and the lying that would have had to follow?

Hailey was. How could she expect Mack to behave any better? Mack had looked her straight in the face and denied everything, but now she knew up close and personal how essential this tactic could become, when you were desperate enough.

Hailey could be—should be—at Mabel's gymnastics lesson, taking over from Chenise. Instead, she'd asked Chenise to stay late and drop the girls home, and then Hailey had left work for no real reason, and now here she was. Squandering precious family time on a trampy Delta-Something with a penchant for posting Hemingway quotes to her Instagram. This nineteen-year-old and Mack were a match made in heaven.

Hailey got out of the car and shut the garage. Halfway to the front door she spotted a dark shape in one of the barren bushes on the side of the house. She went to investigate and found a pair of running shoes, brand-new, in the box. They looked expensive.

Where had these come from? She tucked them under her arm and went inside.

There were muddy socks scattered around the front hall, and the mail was all over the floor at her feet. Gulliver blinked up at her guiltily; next to him was a sizable puddle of pee. It had run along the floorboards to one of the piles of toys that covered the patches in the floor, seeping into a My Little Pony's tail and pooling around some Lego.

"Didn't anybody let you out today, you poor thing?" Hailey said as loudly as she could. "I hope that person is planning to clean this up!" There was no response from Mack; he was too busy down in his office not working.

Hailey set the mysterious shoes on the hall table and started in on the mail. There was an envelope from Sandy Hollow that had to be a bill. She felt her irritation with Mack reach nuclear levels. There were a bunch of catalogues (CHRISTMAS IS COMING! they all shouted at her) and a rather insulting flyer about the beach access issue: ACCESS FOR ALL! HURON LANDING! COLDHARBOR CLOSE! MAGPIE COURT! STOP STRANGLING OUR SHORELINE! NO MORE NEW DEVELOPMENT! She was opening the last piece of mail, a large envelope addressed to Mr. and Mrs. Malcolm Evans, when the return address on the back caught her eye: Gray Skies Road. The logo on the letter inside confirmed a hunch that had sprouted: Sunshine Enterprises.

There was a heading at the top of the first page she pulled out, under the logo, "Payment now due," and it was addressed to "Dear Malcolm and Hailey Evans." Beneath this, it read, "Kindly commence with demolition of outbuilding located near 411 Fullerton Close, Bratenahl." There was no sign-off and no signature.

Hailey reached again into the envelope and pulled out two glossy photographs of what appeared to be a large shed, and then a folded printout of a map showing its location. Hailey vaguely knew it; the spot couldn't have been more than a fifteen-minute walk away. In the white space below the map, someone had handwritten an instruction in thick black ink: *I want you to burn it to the ground.*

"Mack!" Hailey shouted, as something squeezed inside her chest. "Mack!" Gulliver began to bark and run in furious circles at her feet. After a minute the sound of Mack bounding up the basement stairs rose over the click of the dog's toenails. The sun had set all at once, and she could hardly see Mack as he entered the dark hallway.

"Jesus, Hailey, you scared the shit out of me," he said, and she felt something almost like hatred for him.

"Look at *this*!" She thrust the paper out in his direction, and the photographs slipped through her fingers to the floor.

Mack gathered them up at an infuriatingly slow rate, and then he crossed the room to switch on the overhead light. Hailey could have hit him; she didn't deserve to be alone in this panic.

"I don't get it," he said finally, *calmly*, when he'd looked the stuff over. "I guess it's a prank?"

"It's not a prank. This company is telling us to burn down a goddamn building."

She watched as Mack shook his head, could see him physically reject the notion that something might actually be serious. "It's got to be someone just being weird. I mean, why would we burn down a garage? Because this company wrote a letter and told us to?"

"Because they *paid* us to, you idiot." Her contempt sucked the air from the room, but Hailey was okay with that. "This person might just be some weirdo, but they've also paid us forty-seven thousand dollars. Which we've taken."

"You're missing the point—" Mack was headed for the kitchen with the papers, and his path took him straight through the puddle of Gulliver's pee. His bare foot slipped on the wet wood, and Hailey felt a fleeting flash of joy.

"God damn it, that fucking, fucking dog!" Mack hopped, dripping, the rest of the way to the kitchen on one leg as Gulliver fled the scene. Mack put the envelope and its contents on the countertop and swiped angrily at the sole of his foot with a paper towel.

"That fucking dog," Mack growled again. "If I step in one more—"

"This is not about the dog," Hailey said. "This is about *crazy*. Some totally wacko . . . *arsonist* has given us money and we've taken it. This is serious, Mack. It's time to call the police." They both studied the letter and the photos, and after a minute Hailey said in a softer voice. "And it's here. In Bratenahl. I mean, this person is *close by*."

"The postmark is in Kentucky." Mack turned the envelope over. "It says Lexington here."

She'd overlooked that somehow, had been too distracted by Gray Skies Road, by being instructed to commit a felony. "But then how do they even know about this shed? Why are they having us burn down something in Bratenahl if they're not here?"

"I guess because *we* live here."

Hailey looked from the photographs to the map. "It's not an address you could find on a map. I mean, it's a *shed*—"

"It looks more like a garage, actually."

"It's a shed. I'm pretty sure I've been past it before. Anyway, it doesn't matter, the point is, we—"

"The point is, we're not going to 'burn it to the ground.'" Mack made quotation marks in the air with his index fingers as he said this. "We're not, like, drunken teenagers with nothing better to do on a Friday night, Hailey."

How stupid could he be, she wondered then, not to see a threat like this for what it was? Why was she always the one who had to know better?

"Look," she told him. "I'm not going to argue with you about it. I put our researcher on Sunshine Enterprises today, but I really think now we have to at least go to the bank. Both of us. We'll say there has been a mistake; they can trace the payments and wire the money back. Then we'll call the police about these letters. Or maybe the bank will."

"Fine. Okay." He sounded willing, like he agreed with her. He had to, she supposed, because he was in the doghouse. But then he said, "There's something I need to show you."

✦

"This can't be good." Hailey was on her hands and knees, peering at the concrete floor in the basement. "Look, this one is like two inches wide."

"They're outside too," Mack said. "I noticed them this morning on the back walls. The bricks are actually splitting. I thought it might not be a big deal, that it might be only a surface thing, but then I figured I'd better check the inside—"

"We'll just have to call the builder," Hailey decided, leaning back on her heels. "I mean, the house isn't even a year old. It's not like it's anything we did. Simeon will just have to deal with it. He probably gets stuff like this all the time."

Mack was silent, and Hailey knew he wouldn't be volunteering to make the call. Mack *hated* builders, especially Simeon, whom even Hailey had to admit was kind of a know-it-all. After a few contentious snags in the construction process—some ill-fitting patio doors, a kitchen island that was the wrong height—Mack had cut off all contact with Simeon's team and had refused to make any decisions about the house whatsoever. It was around that time that Hailey realized—too late—that Mack hadn't wanted to build the house at all, that he had zero interest in moving on from Lakewood. And now, because of the standoff between Mack and Simeon, the interior door from the kitchen to the garage had been stuck for three months, and so, even though they'd paid for an attached garage with a heated floor and custom cabinetry, they still had to brave the elements every time they wanted to get in the car.

Hailey left Mack there on his knees and went into the furnace room. She flipped on the bare overhead bulb and peered at the walls.

The cracks were smaller in here, but they spread out along the concrete block like a massive spider's web. There was also, she saw now, a huge split in the floor near a drain that was supposed to prevent damage in the event of a water tank leak. The concrete had moved so much that the still-shiny drain cover had come loose. She looked at the door to Mack's office and felt another blast of rage.

"How could you not have noticed this in here?"

"What?" He appeared in the doorway, cowering like a little kid.

"You walk through here every single day, multiple times. How could you not notice this?" She pointed (manically, even she would have admitted) at the drain. "This isn't like a small thing. You didn't see this?"

"Oh, so this is my fault too? It must be so hard for you to go through life dragging an asshole like me behind you. You just can't wait to—"

Hailey pushed past him and ran up the stairs. Both sets, all the way to their bedroom. She slammed the door and locked it, then stood in the big bay window looking out into the darkness over Lake Erie.

When the builders had first laid the floor in this room, before the staircase had even gone in and you had to climb a ladder to get up here, this view had made the house feel like a fortress. A precarious one at first—this was all their money; would these piles of bricks and wood actually turn into a real-life, grown-up house? But the view saw her through any doubt. The idea that people out on the lake—on dinner cruises or sailboat charters—would look up and see the light in this bedroom at night and think, *Wow, what a spot. Can you imagine living there?* just as Hailey herself had once done from her father's back seat, kept her going through financial freak-outs and Mack's indifference. It was this room that she thought of while she hunched over briefs at midnight in her office downtown, surrounded by an ocean of dark offices and deserted parking lots, and this spot she aimed for on the long, traffic-congested drive back from her parents'.

On the day Simeon's team had formally handed the keys over, Hailey and Mack had made love in this window, and then on the built-in ottoman in the middle of the dressing room, among the custom cabinetry that would soon be home to shoes and clothing that had only ever known overcrowded closets and plastic IKEA crates. They'd moved on to the master bathroom and run a bath to see if they both fit in the tub (they did!) and, giddy with new homeownership, forgotten there would be no towels. They pulled their clothes back on over damp skin gritty with construction dust, but it had been worth it. It was still worth it, Hailey thought. She loved this house. It would never let her down.

Hailey sank onto the bed and pulled her phone from her blazer pocket. For the thousandth time that day she checked her messages for David Rainier's name. When there wasn't anything from him, she felt nothing. She knew his neglect of her own message (long ago confirmed delivered and read) was binary. He had used her and then ghosted her, and all she could do was hope that this was the worst of what he had in mind.

22.

You don't hear much about it, but at the time of the Great Chicago Fire in 1871, other cities around the Great Lakes were burning too: Holland, Michigan, and Peshtigo, Wisconsin, also fell prey to dry conditions at the end of a long, hot summer. Cleveland was not so lucky.

Hear me out: Those Chicagoans—the same mix of scrappy immigrants and wayward *Mayflower* descendants and budding industrialists that existed in Cleveland at that time—got a do-over thanks to Mrs. O'Leary's cow. One collision of hoof and lantern, so the story goes, and all the crappy little houses and businesses that were clogging up the shores of Lake Michigan back then burned up like kindling. Then, ka-zaam! A snazzy plan for rebuilding, some creative zoning laws, and Chicago would be called, just a few decades later, Paris on the Prairie.

Cleveland, as you'll probably have gathered, got no such reboot, having had to make do with smaller, isolated disasters and a river with a penchant for flammability—and is thus now known as the Mistake on the Lake.

Moral of the story: fire can be a good thing, children, if it's used correctly. Sometimes you need to burn things to the ground to get them right where you want them.

23.

Mack

It was obvious that Gulliver couldn't believe his luck. They'd been walking for fifteen whole minutes, on a route they'd never taken, with lots of exciting new places to pee. The dog's little mouth was open, and even from his higher vantage point—higher than usual thanks to the thick, cushy soles of his swish new shoes—Mack could see tongue and teeth; it looked for all the world like Gulliver was grinning as he strode along the pavement. Maybe, Mack realized, if the little shit had more variety in his life he wouldn't feel the need to—

There it was. It *was* more of a shed than a garage, Mack had to admit. It was built of plywood, with a roof that looked like peeling sandpaper; it resembled some old military outpost. There was a narrow boarded-up door, and the windows had been covered over too. The grass around the structure was brown and dry, and Mack was sure the whole place would go up like a Christmas tree in February if you put a match to it.

Not that he was going to.

They strolled a wide circle around the little hut—there was broken glass everywhere—and though he tried, Mack couldn't figure out which property the thing was part of. The houses were spread out back here; this land could easily have been owned by the township itself. There was a serious-looking power station box a few hundred yards away, with some dramatically illustrated DANGER! RISK OF DEATH BY ELECTROCUTION! notices pasted on it, but basically the area was a no-man's-land. This shed blocked no one's view, it wasn't anywhere near the contentious beachfront, and there was absolutely no reason Mack could think of for anyone to want to burn it down. Someone was fucking with them, was all.

It was working, too. Hailey might be persecuting Mack and freezing him out and treating him like an imbecile, but the one thing he didn't begrudge her was being freaked out. Who was this person that thought he could tell Mack Evans what to do just because he'd sent some money?

Even if it was kind of a lot of money.

He and Gulliver rounded their circle for home, both reluctantly. Mack was supposed to meet Simeon and show him the cracks in the house. The goddamn builder went by a single moniker, like he was the Cher of overpriced, Sims-inspired architecture. Mack had already run through the conversation they would have in his mind, in which Simeon would insinuate that this too was something any real man would be able to fix himself. A few months before, when one of Hailey's closet doors had broken, Simeon had actually had the balls to ask why Mack couldn't just replace the hinge himself and save Simeon a trip out to Bratenahl. "Sure," Mack told him, "as long as you can cover my class on the foundations of American poetry this morning."

Now Mack was going to have to play nice. Hailey was not interested in taking over; after their fight over the furnace room floor, she had sunk into some unidentifiable state of gloominess. It made Mack nervous; he could tell that she didn't believe him when he said that nothing had happened with Mackenzie, but he also got the sense that she didn't really *care*. He'd felt that there should have been more drama, more shouting, more accusations that he could deny, but instead they'd spent days in the kind of quiet that happens after a child takes a nasty fall and doesn't cry, that vacuum of sound that signals the situation is serious.

Mack had found a way to break through though. That very morning, he had done something that he and Hailey had neither agreed upon nor even discussed: he paid his mother's nursing home bills for November and December. Their bank balance was now minus $67.13.

They did have a $12,000 overdraft and room on the American Express, though, so it wasn't as serious as it sounded.

Had he done it to buy himself another month in case Hailey left him and took her salary with her? Or had he done it just for the reaction, *any* reaction? Mack couldn't say for sure.

Gulliver stopped to sniff at a streetlight that was supposed to look like the old gas lamps from Victorian England, its false flame flickering like a jet-lagged firefly in the ten a.m. daylight. Mack stood looking across at their house and trying to figure out whether he really minded if it all came crumbling down. Boy, would Simeon look stupid then.

As Gulliver cocked his stubby leg for the thousandth time, Mack emerged from the fantasy of Simeon beneath a pile of rubble and saw that their garage door was open, and that the Cherokee was inside it, next to his ancient Audi. He tugged Gulliver on.

Inside the house, he found Hailey sitting on the steps, still in her high heels. The first thing Mack noticed was the pallor of her skin; it looked like his mother's, and like the faces of his students during the pandemic. Mack's and Hailey's eyes met in a fresh kind of souped-up wordlessness, and he waited for her to tell him she was leaving him. It took an eternity for her voice to reach him, and when it did, her volume was so low that Mack had to crouch down to hear her:

"That money originated in Liberia. It was sent from an unregulated Liberian bank."

Mack let out his breath as Gulliver sniffed at Hailey's feet. "Jesus," he said, careful not to expose himself with any hint of analysis. Except Hailey was looking at him, for once, like he should know what to do. "That can't be right."

"It's right. Our researcher found it."

Mack took a stab in the dark: "Could it be a banking thing then? Like maybe how money gets routed through different banks as it's moved around—" Mack was blowing smoke; he had no idea how money moved, except that it tended to flow away from him a lot faster than it came toward him.

"I don't think so. It's a real account, if that's what you mean. This researcher—Dennis—he can . . . I don't know the specifics, but somehow he can monitor other people's banking activity. He's like a hacker, that's why we hired him. He says this account is all transactions with *other* shady banks and foreign individuals. He said he can't believe the payments haven't been flagged, that it's only because they are small amounts." She scooped up Gulliver and pressed him to her. "I just—I can't believe someone like this would bother with us. This is crazy."

Mack tried to identify the most immediate threat. "So this hacker—does he know we got the money? Does he know you're personally involved?"

"He's a kid, Mack. He needs his job. He's not interested in getting us in trouble."

Mack turned to follow Hailey's gaze; Simeon's van had pulled into the driveway. Gulliver squirmed until he fell to the floor and then ran like a madman toward the front door.

"I think we just go to the bank now, like we said." Mack fought to be heard over the sound of Gulliver's yapping. "I tried to call that personal banker who gave us his card when we did the mortgage, Colin something, but I didn't leave a message. I'll try him again." This was not technically the truth; Mack had *thought* about looking for Colin's card. He hadn't actually done anything yet.

"I don't know . . . the account is overdrawn." Hailey's expression told Mack she 1,000 percent already knew he'd made the Sandy Hollow payments. "And now that we know this money is . . . oh God, I don't even know what the hell this money is! I mean, *Liberia*? National City will be all over us."

This was not right. He, Mack, was supposed to be the irresponsible one, the one who fucked around and played loose with the rules. (Dreamy, is how he liked to characterize it.) Now Hailey, the straight arrow, the one with a goddamn JD, was suggesting they not do the obviously by-the-book right thing?

Even though he could see Mack and Hailey through the glass in the front door, Simeon went right ahead and rang the doorbell. Twice.

"Then I guess we call the police," Mack said as softly as he could, though just the word put him back in Favre's office, back to when he'd had his first little taste of feeling on the wrong side of the law. He realized in that moment that he'd been waiting weeks for the cops to ring his doorbell, and now he was going to have to invite them over. How exactly would he explain taking $47,000 of random money from Liberia? His bit of homegrown weed might start to look more like a drug cartel when you threw 47K into the mix.

Hailey was shaking her head. "No. The thing is, Mack, I think I know who might be—" She went silent as Mack turned the door handle and Simeon stepped across the threshold. Entirely by accident, of course, Mack had forgotten about Gulliver. The dog launched himself on the builder, snarling and snapping, and in that moment, Mack forgave him for every errant drop of piss he'd ever squeezed out.

✦

Simeon stood, shifting his weight from one foot to the other, sucking air between his teeth, shaking his head. "Now this I haven't seen." They were all three outside in the flower bed, shivering in the cold. Simeon's dimples wilted as he frowned. He ran a finger over one particularly deep crack and flicked a chunk of loose brick onto the ground.

"Huh," he said, and Mack could have hit him.

"It can't be good that it's downstairs and out here too," Hailey pressed him. "The whole bottom half of the house could be full of cracks, right?"

Simeon shook his head again. He had already *huh*'d and *yeah*'d over the cracks in the basement. "It's a puzzler, this one."

He stood there for an eternity, until Mack finally said, "Well, then, what do we *do* about it?"

Simeon turned to walk back toward his van. "Let me talk to my concrete guy," he said over his shoulder. Mack would have just let him go, but Hailey slipped around the hedge and got to the van before Simeon did.

"So that's the next step? And then you'll get back to us? Because I'm sure you can appreciate that this is really stressful. I mean, this is a brand-new house, and it looks like it's about to fall down." Hailey sounded on the edge of hysteria, Mack thought, and he wondered whether this would work for them or against them.

"Now don't let's all panic," Simeon said, calm as could be. "This is just one of those joys of the construction business. I'm sure it looks scary to you, but this is the sort of thing that gets blown out of proportion. The cracks might be the house settling on the lot, might be the time of year . . . Biggest thing is, you folks don't panic and ruin the enjoyment of your new home. Keep your heads, I'll get my concrete specialist out and we'll get you all fixed up. Okay?"

"Right," said Mack. "Like the garage door?"

Simeon pretended not to hear. As he drove off, Hailey watched Mack struggling to untie his new running shoes. "Where'd those come from?"

"Oh, it's a crazy story. You know that guy with a weird moustache that walks around here all the time? His dog like jumped out of nowhere and bit me, and he gave me these shoes, I guess so I wouldn't sue him. He lives in the Eliot estate, you should see it. It's like something out of a movie—"

"You went to that guy's house?"

"Yeah. He showed me around, and you wouldn't believe this place, like something out of *Gatsby*."

"That's just great, Mack. I'm glad you're chilling with retirees while our lives fall apart around us. Don't worry about it, though, I'll take care of *everything*, okay?"

It felt like the sting that hit Mack originated from somewhere inside him, instead of from Hailey. The two of them stood, not looking at each other, while Mack tried her own trick against her and waited to see if she would say anything else.

Eventually she did: "I'm late. I've got a meeting. I don't even know why I came home."

Hailey went to get her bag from inside. As Mack dove to grab Gulliver before he ran into the street, she brushed past him again on her way to the car, shaking him off when he tried to ask her about calling the police. "I told you, I'll take care of it." She sped off and left Mack standing beside an eggshell of a house that he had never wanted, holding a dog that had never loved him.

Fine.

Mack would focus on Simeon; if that prick had messed up their house, maybe he'd messed up the whole damn street of them. Maybe there was even some money to be had from his ineptitude. Mack dropped Gulliver back inside, retied his shoelaces, and made his way to the Wakefields' front door. The layout of the porch, a mirror image of his own, gave Mack a slight sense of vertigo. Their doorbells were identical; he listened as the Wakefields' echoed through their house. Betsy came to the door.

"Well hello neighbor," she said dryly. She was wearing tennis whites and K-Swiss sneakers. Her bare legs were a similar shape to Hailey's, but longer.

"Hey. Sorry to bother you. I just wanted to ask you something about the house . . . your house, I mean. Have you guys had any trouble with cracks?"

"You mean like in the windows?" She stared at him.

Mack looked at her blankly.

The golf ball! She was talking about Mack's golf ball. "No, sorry, I uh—"

"I'm only kidding." She opened the door wider, and Mack could see through into her big living room with its double-story windows. "See? All better now."

"Looks great," Mack said. "Those guys did a good job. And again, I'm really sorry. I hope your tennis game is better than my golf game."

She laughed a little then, and Mack felt rehabilitated. This woman liked him, maybe, even if his own wife didn't. He had to admit Betsy was attractive, in a prissy kind of way. He peeped into the house—he saw lots of pink and green and tassels, nothing like Hailey's slick grays and whites—and Betsy caught him looking.

"Do you want to come in? It's a little cold out to have the door wide open." Her tennis skirt was short, and there were indeed goose bumps on her skin, Mack noticed.

"Nah, sorry, I'll be quick. It's just we've just got some cracks that have come out in the concrete in the house, and I thought I'd check to see if you'd had the same kind of trouble."

"Cracks? No. No cracks here."

"I just thought since the houses were built at the same time . . . well, anyway, be sure to check your basement. We've got bad ones in the floor and the walls. And then some outside too." He glanced toward her brickwork. It looked fine from where he was standing.

"I'll keep an eye out, thanks. Not teaching today?"

"No. I'm on leave."

"I thought I'd seen more of you around lately." Something in her voice let Mack know she was in on his secret, and he felt his confidence shrink. Betsy's own husband worked so much that Mack had never even laid eyes on the guy.

"Yeah, well, anyway . . . thanks," he said to her, though he wasn't sure for what. He turned to face the street. He'd knock on the Sinclairs' next—their house was across from the Wakefields'—but he wanted to be thorough. "I just realized I don't know . . . Who owns the lot next to you on the other side here?"

"I don't know," Betsy told him. "The people who bought it got into a fight over their view, or lack thereof. I think they're still trying to get their money back from Cletus."

"From who?"

"Cletus. Cletus Simeon, *your builder*? You know, the one who built all of our houses?"

"His first name is *Cletus*?"

"Yes." She looked at Mack with something like pity. "I'm going to close the door now, okay?"

"Yes, yeah. Sorry. Just let me know if you find any damage, okay?"

"Will do."

Mack knocked on a few more doors, but no one was around. He knew the couple on the far opposite side of the street were lawyers too, and were hardly ever home. He had caught only glimpses of their children; most of the kids in Bratenahl he had only seen staring out at him from the back seats of giant Escalades, like miniature presidents being driven by motorcade from one activity to the next. The guy in the middle house was a snowbird and probably in Florida, and the Sinclairs would be golfing or tennis-ing or bridge-ing . . . Even though the houses were close together, Magpie Court always felt empty; it was what he hated most about the place. He checked his watch and made his way home. He ditched his shoes, now pretty much ruined by the mud, and polished off a stale bag of pretzels and half a tub of Häagen-Dazs. Then he went down to his office and called his mom.

"There he is," said Tilda, after the usual shuffling of the camera. She was having Chick-fil-A. Mack's mother was in the yellow robe again, and, like always, Mack could see the Florida sunshine streaming in through the window in her room. Thank God he had at least gotten her through the end of the year.

(Or Hailey had.)

"Hey, Mom. Hi, Tilda."

"How are all your girls, Mackie? They good?"

"We're fine. Everything's fine."

"Good. I said to Irene this week, I said they'll have such a nice time decorating their big new house for Christmas. You started yet?"

It occurred to Mack then that Tilda's bragging about him might have been what led Irene Weigand to pull the plug on their arrangement. "Nah. It's not *that* big of a house, you know, Tilda. Don't forget I'm on a teacher's salary." *Or I was*, thought Mack gloomily. At least his mother would never have to hear the name Mackenzie Ewing or read about her son the drug-dealing booze hound. Every cloud and all that.

"So Irene's still coming to visit her?" Mack asked Tilda.

"Of course. Ten a.m. on Tuesdays, same as always."

"Right." He knew it was irrational, he knew it was unfair, but Mack hated that Irene Weigand was still showing up there. His mom needed Irene's money, not her time. What use did his mother have for friends now?

"She was asking me about your book. How's the writing going?"

"It's going great." Mack watched as his mom shifted a little in her bed. He knew better than to think she'd understood him.

"Irene was really sorry not to meet Hailey," Tilda went on. "I told her how nice and down-to-earth she is, even though she's a hotshot lawyer and all. Course, Irene's heard so much about her over the years. Where you're living, what you're doing." The nurse laughed. "Ah, there's nothing like us old ladies gossiping."

Jesus Christ. Tilda had probably single-handedly caused the greatest financial crisis of Mack's life. Wasn't there some sort of patient confidentiality nurses were supposed to abide by?

"Irene said she's real proud of you, too. For stepping up."

"What? *Stepping up?* What does that mean?"

"Oh now, I didn't mean to speak out of turn. Watch me put my foot in it. She's just glad you can be there for your mother now, that's all."

Irene was just an old woman gossiping, Mack reminded himself. A lonely old lady who had paid out hundreds of thousands of dollars for his mother. He had to let her commentary go.

"How's Mom been this week? You been playing her some good tunes?"

"Oh yes! We've had some Everly Brothers and— "

"I'd ask Tilda for some Hendrix, if I were you, Mom," Mack said. "I know you used to love him."

"I'll do that for her, Mackie." Tilda looked at her watch. "It's rounds time, so we've got to keep it short today. You have a great weekend, okay?"

After he'd clicked off the call, Mack stared up through his tiny window. There was a recess there to increase the light, and he could see the chunk of brick that Simeon had knocked from the house; part of it had turned to powder when it hit the mud. Mack thought of concrete, and then of his father's crumbling towers down in the Florida Keys.

Forty-seven thousand dollars. From Liberia.

Did the Mafia operate in Liberia? These days they probably did.

Mack clicked around on his laptop until he found a website for the Florida Department of Health. For $8, he ordered a copy of the death certificate for Warner Thomas Evers. What exactly that would prove, he didn't know, but there was nothing else to reach for. Only the barest traces of his father existed online; there was no one left to ask about him except for rickety, judgy Irene Weigand, so what could Mack do? Drive down there *again*, interview some coroner from seven years ago? Start digging into the records of those shitty towers he'd built?

Mack grabbed the last Dr Pepper from his fridge. Even if his father *was* alive, even if he *was* their sunny benefactor—and way deep down, Mack still thought he probably was—why on earth would he ask Mack to burn down an old shed?

The box of his mom's papers was next to Mack's desk, and he took his dad's letter from it. He studied the desperation in the words *never, ever*. Desperation never got you anywhere, Mack knew. He felt pretty desperate right now, yet all he was doing was treading water, winding himself up. He took out the photograph of the old-time prairie family, presumably some of his relatives. They looked like all pioneers did: dusty and miserable. But also stoic, resolute, watchful. Mack propped the picture up on his desk.

There was no use in panicking now, he told himself. Unless Hailey dragged him—which was looking unlikely—he wasn't going to the police. And he wasn't going to the bank. And he sure as hell wasn't going to burn down any old buildings or take orders from some strange company. He would stay the course, and it would all shake out: his job, the house, this money.

Even, with a bit of luck and a lot of patience, his marriage.

24.

Hailey

Hailey had overordered on the turkey. It took up most of the trunk of the Cherokee and it would never fit in the oven, but that was a *later* problem. The *now* problem was that it was almost sixty-five degrees outside, and she had no choice but to leave this bird in the car while she met Rebekah. The Whole Foods parking lot had already been a logjam at 9:00 a.m.; to go on the way home was unthinkable. All she could do was pray that this act of desperation didn't give her entire family food poisoning.

It had taken a lot to get Rebekah to agree to see her. Hailey had promised to remove her name from the litigation the firm was starting against her husband, something she had yet to run by the other partners. She'd also lured her former client there with the carrot of a plan about how Rebekah might move forward out of her situation, how she might untangle herself from David. In actuality, that plan was just about as solid as the walls in Hailey's basement.

Hailey had admitted to nothing, and if Rebekah had proof of her night with David, she hadn't revealed it yet. The café Rebekah had chosen, Milk & Honey on Superior, was bright and eerily empty on the Wednesday morning before Thanksgiving: half of Cleveland was home opening up cans of Libby's, and the other half were on the road or in an airport.

Rebekah sat alone at a table in the corner. She had calmed down considerably since their last meeting and kept a faint smile on her face while Hailey put her order in. Anyone might have mistaken them for friends, Hailey realized, until the barista was safely out of earshot.

"So what do you want?"

Hailey was grateful for this slash straight through the bullshit. "I need some information. About your ex-husband."

"I'd say you know all about my ex-husband."

There was real droop to Rebekah's face now; her eyes were dull and tired, and yet somehow still jumpy with the restlessness that Hailey had always found so irritating. Still, in Hailey's expert opinion this did not look like a woman reveling in the certainty of her convictions.

"I think it's important that you know I never slept with him." This felt so *true* as it came out of Hailey's mouth. "He's just trying to use that accusation to get at you, and we need to figure out a way through it."

"I thought we had figured out a way through it," Rebekah said, her eyes fixed on Hailey. "*Me and David* had figured out a way through it. But he fucks me over every time. You too, apparently." She took a deep breath and blew it out across the frothy coffee that had just been put down in front of her. "I know you never believed me about how bad he is. I know what you think: I'm a gold digger, I trapped some rich guy, why can't I just shut up and get divorced like a nice little girl so you can make your money?"

She didn't seem to want a response. After a long sip of her coffee, she continued.

"You know he did have affairs. Even if you all didn't find any evidence. He left me at home with two little kids, all alone in this crappy city where I don't know anyone and where he didn't even want to live. I mean, he's in New York, in Paris—everywhere, and I'm here!"

Hailey tried her best to look sympathetic, but she was mostly focused on not remembering David's eyes over the rim of his fancy cocktail glass, or the feel of his hands on her back in the elevator, or the weight of him on top of her.

"And I could have lived with that, you know?" Rebekah went on. "Except I couldn't pay for anything. David controlled every fucking cent. I had more money working front of house at Houston's than I ever did as his wife. He wanted receipts for everything I bought, and he told me how I should look, where I should buy groceries, what color I should paint my fucking fingernails. My fingernails! As if he didn't already have control over half this city!" This time Rebekah sloshed her coffee onto the table. Hailey passed her a napkin, but she used it to wipe her eyes instead.

"He also told our children—from the age of two, by the way—that Mommy was a bimbo. He told our friends that I was psychotic, that I did drugs. He put video cameras everywhere—for safety, he said—and then he'd call me at night and tell me what I'd done wrong that day. It *did* make me psychotic, so eventually he was right."

Rebekah folded the napkin into smaller and smaller squares. The shiny puffiness of her face looked different in this light—swollen and tender.

"Why didn't you tell me this before?"

"I did tell you. You just didn't listen."

Hailey felt blood rush to her cheeks. She had heard Rebekah complaining about not having enough money. She had heard Rebekah complaining that her husband was sneaky and domineering. But Rebekah was right: she had not listened. Instead, she had jumped right into the hands, literally and figuratively, of someone who got a thrill out of controlling people with his money. Who was now, she was certain, trying to control her.

It was too late for apologies. "Listen, the only way we're going to get at David—and I've always thought this—is through his finances. Have you ever heard of a company called Sunshine Enterprises?"

"No."

"Think really carefully. Ever seen any statements with a sun logo on it? Ever heard him mention it?"

"No." Rebekah's irritation was obvious. "This is why you asked me here?"

"We've been getting payments from a bank in Liberia that I think could be from him. And some threatening letters." *Threatening* might have been a stretch, but *weird* didn't feel like a strong enough word.

Rebekah laughed. "You've got to hand it to him. Only David would go threatening a bunch of lawyers. But I seriously doubt he'd send money."

"It feels like he is after me personally. My family."

"Well, if you fucked him, that sort of makes it personal, right?"

Hailey sighed. "Rebekah, I really need your help. My researcher can't find a link between David and this company. But there's a lot of money in its accounts, and I know in my gut it's him. If I can prove it, I can show he was hiding assets, maybe that he is involved in criminal activity. I might be able to get you your kids back. You could have a real divorce and freedom from him."

Rebekah stared Hailey down for an uncomfortably long time. "You know he won't even let me see them on Thanksgiving? I think they're in Tahoe or somewhere. He told me I could see the twins after I'm settled in the house in Short Hills. In fucking January." Tears had worn paths through Rebekah's foundation, revealing the raw skin underneath. "And so like a good girl I'll finish packing things up and go where I'm told."

"Is there any way you can get access to his computers? His papers? Or can you think of anyone who could help you?"

Rebekah's laugh was different this time. "You sound as desperate as I do. Your money is gone. Just tell the other lawyers to forget about it, and maybe David will leave you alone. You do not want to take him on, trust me. He'll ruin your goddamn life and enjoy doing it."

"But will you at least try?"

"There's no point," said Rebekah, rising to go. "You don't have a clue what you are up against, do you? The man is a control freak with a God complex and a billion dollars. It's not a good combination."

As she reached the door she turned back and called out: "Have a great Thanksgiving with your family." It sounded almost menacing, but then again everything sounded like a threat to Hailey these days.

✦

Though it was not a strategy they'd talked about directly—they weren't talking about much of anything directly—Mack and Hailey were extra careful that her parents did not get so much as a whiff of how stressed out they were. Thanksgiving Day was to be a break from it all, and Hailey was determined to host it like a grown-up—a true-life grown-up, as Mabel would have put it. It was Pammy Byers's tradition to kick off the cooking with a few Bloody Marys, and so when the turkey really didn't fit in the oven, there was much debate among the generations over what to do about it. Finally, Mack had picked up the giant bird on his hip like an infant and disappeared. A minute or so later Hailey, Pam, and Eddie had startled at the sound of his chain saw (his bought-for-the-new-house-and-never-before-even-used-yet chain saw) revving to life. They arrived in the garage just in time to see flecks of poultry flesh and bone whirling through the air like snow. Mack had set the turkey on his workbench and was sawing away at the raw meat.

"How will we put the stuffing in?" Hailey wondered aloud.

"You two are as nuts as each other," Eddie Byers said, draining his cocktail, but Hailey heard approval in his tone. She fetched Mack the roasting tin, and together they plunked most of the pasty, goose-bumped turkey parts into it.

"Nobody likes the leg meat anyway," Mack said, tossing the drumsticks into the big garage trash can. "Who wants a beer?"

"I bought the pies," Hailey confessed to her mother, "So we've got those even if everything else is terrible."

But it wasn't terrible. The turkey turned out fine—better than normal, maybe. Hailey's sister Lyndsey arrived from the faraway land of Dayton with her husband, three kids, and some overcooked baked goods, the Macy's parade was watched by all, and the new house was duly toasted, with only the quickest side-eye between Hailey and Mack. Those with double-digit ages were just polishing off the last of another bottle of wine when the doorbell rang. Hailey felt the house sway slightly as she made her way through the hall; at this rate the dishes might have to wait until tomorrow morning. She set her wineglass down on the hall table and didn't bother to look through the peephole. Luckily it was only Betsy from next door.

"Happy Thanksgiving," Betsy said, and Hailey was struck by the dramatic arches of her perfect eyebrows. "Sorry to bother you."

"No problem." Even in her current state, even with her fixation on Betsy's facial grooming, Hailey was able to reach down for Gulliver in one smooth swoop as he came charging down the stairs. It wasn't like him to be late for a front-door frenzy. He must have been passed out on tryptophan from his share of the Frankenstein turkey.

"I just wanted to bring you this," Betsy said, stepping back slightly. "It got misdelivered yesterday. It looks urgent." She held out an envelope, and the feast in Hailey's stomach did a dangerous churn. This was classic Sunshine Enterprises font and stationery, and stamped in red above their address were the words FINAL NOTICE. Hailey felt her cheeks grow hot.

"I just didn't want them turning off your electricity or something," Betsy continued in a hushed tone, glancing toward the voices coming from deeper within the house. "I didn't notice it yesterday, and when I saw the envelope just now, I thought, oh no, what if they can't cook din—"

"I don't think it's that kind of bill, but thanks for bringing it over." The back of the envelope had the same red stamp, Hailey noticed as she took it from her neighbor.

"I brought you some banana bread too," Betsy said, and then she continued the tradition they had kept up for six months: "And we really should have that coffee sometime."

"Definitely," Hailey said. "Let's find a date after the holidays." She did not invite Betsy in; she could barely bring herself to say goodbye. The delight in their neighbor's eyes at this tasty tidbit of Bratenahl gossip—*it seems like the husband is out of work, and they can't even pay their bills!*—was evident, and what a bonus for Betsy that it had arrived just in time for Christmas! Hailey thought of the upcoming Shoreby party and felt the dread sink into her soul.

She shut the door, plopped Gulliver down, and opened the letter. Her first thought was that she really was drunk off her face; angry red letters jumped off the page at her. But this was not wine goggles: in her hands was the same *Payment now due* letter they had received a week ago, but with the FINAL NOTICE stamp all over it, repeated at least a hundred times. The back was covered too; it looked like a small child had been playing office, except that someone had written in the same terrifying scrawl, in the same black marker as before: *A deal is a deal.*

Hailey felt something akin to a tantrum rise in her. There had been no deal! But she was raging at someone—no, some*thing*, some faceless entity—that she didn't understand the first thing about. It felt like Gigi's hysteria when they'd tried to explain to her that, no matter how many birthdays she had, she would never be older than Mabel.

"Hailey?" Her mother, swaying slightly, had come to look for her. "Who's here?"

"Just the neighbor, dropping something off."

But her mother had spotted the letter, with its red stamps and angry marker.

"What's this, honey?"

"Nothing! It's nothing—"

"Mommy, we need you." Mabel appeared in the doorway, with Hailey's father behind her, holding part of a Playmobil house.

"What's that?" Eddie was an aficionado of poking his nose in, and in that moment Hailey longed to hand the letter over, to let him take charge and have him tell her it was not as bad as it seemed.

She did not do that.

"For Christ's sake just give me a minute, all of you!" She thrust the banana bread—Hailey *hated* banana bread—at her bewildered mother, fled upstairs, and slammed the bedroom door behind her. The letter looked even more frightening in here, like it was worming its way deeper into their lives. Who would send this? She looked out over the lake and knew that there could only be one answer. All of this had started with the deterioration of Rebekah Rainier's divorce.

Hailey pulled her phone from the back pocket of her jeans. The wine was really hitting her now, and it took her a minute to scroll through her messages and find his number. It went straight to voicemail, which was pretty much what she had been expecting.

"Fucking stop this right now!" she screamed into the phone. "I know it's you, David! You got what you wanted. You win, okay? You screwed your wife's lawyer. Now leave me alone. *I mean it*, you total psychopath! Leave us alone before I call the police!"

Hailey ended the call and fought to slow the air being sucked into her lungs. She leaned back on her pillow and closed her eyes. It was only when she opened them again that she noticed Mack standing there in the doorway.

25.

My father was a newspaper man. Or a paperboy, as he liked to call himself. He started on a local desk covering dime-store openings and dog shows, and he worked his way up. Way up—you would recognize his name. He was known for convincing his sources to reveal everything, and then later, as an editor, for convincing his reporters to risk everything. He used to tell great stories around the dinner table, of journos tapping phones, hiding in bathrooms, posing as policemen. His foot soldiers, he called them, and the content war was a game to him: What could he make them do today in the pursuit of news? (My mother was long gone by then, thank God—she could never have countenanced such excitement!)

My father said that some of his bosses called him ruthless, that some of them professed to be horrified when they heard whispers of reporters stalking crime victims or shadowing celebrity children. They didn't fire him, though, did they? And I'm sure they wished they had, because by the time I reached puberty he had bought the paper and relieved them of their jobs. Then he ran his empire the same way he'd conquered it. He lured the best writers away from the competition, swallowed smaller outfits whole, and invested in expansion with every penny he could get his hands on . . . including a few pennies that weren't his own.

He taught me everything I know, and for a long time, I would have proudly called myself his protégé, though admittedly the apprenticeship was a difficult one. Being family, I was used to his quirks and his exacting standards, but when his underlings—secretaries, accountants, lawyers—started coming to me with reservations about his managerial style, things got tricky. "He's using 401(k)s!" they cried, and "The world is changing, he can't run a business like this anymore!"

I was an eager little beaver back then—still wet behind the ears and living in my childhood bedroom—so I was determined to make myself a useful intermediary. I sat my father down one night and presented him with several suggestions for modernizing the company. I gave him the names of some reputable and discreet consultants who might be able to help us to straighten things out. My father seemed to be taking it all in.

Then he said to me: "I had no idea you were such a pussy."

I don't remember much of what happened after that, only that my entanglement with the dental industry began immediately afterward.

The point is, my dad really didn't appreciate people questioning the way he conducted his business, and neither do I. I wish those Evanses would just get on with it; it's way too early in the game for things to get ugly.

26.

Mack

It was the irony that Mack couldn't get over. He had never touched Mackenzie Ewing or anyone else, and here he was, about to swing for it, while this whole time Hailey had been the one playing around.

(Hailey!)

The betrayal hit him like a punch to the throat. His wife—his difficult, cranky, hard-to-manage wife—had been at it with another man. And he knew she'd done it, no matter how she tried to squirm her way out of that word he'd overheard. Mack had not been born yesterday; there was no way that "screwed" was meant in the metaphorical sense. He could tell from the tone of her voice, from the intimacy of her desperation.

From the guilt on her face.

"Let me make sure I understand this right. You screwed him, and now this guy's paying us? Must've been good." Mack wasn't shouting yet, but he was close. "So what, you're like a fancy prostitute now?"

He regretted this as soon as it left his lips. Hailey was silent but hysterical, gasping for breath, and his outrage melted. Really and truly melted—to his surprise, Mack found that he was crying. Then he caught sight of the letter, and the dark cloud that threatened to swallow him whole became a tornado again, external and violent.

"What the hell—who is this asshole? What's his name?"

Hailey shook her head, and the person shouting at her became not Mack but some stranger who had taken over his body: "I said what the fuck is his name! Tell me. Tell me, or I walk out of here right now and never come back. David something, isn't it?"

He was surprised by how quickly Hailey caved in: "David Rainier." Her voice was quiet and even in a way that did not match her eyes. "He's Rebekah Rainier's husband. He'll stop now, Mack. I think . . . I think Sunshine Enterprises must be his fucked-up way of paying his bill. Please, let's—"

There were footsteps on the landing, and then Hailey's father called her name, and it was like a bucket of cold water had been poured over them. Mack took the letter from the bed and brushed past Eddie. Let Hailey try to explain the state of herself to him.

Down in his office, Mack took a pouch of tobacco and the jar of buds he'd been drying from the top shelf of his bookcase, and he rolled himself two fat joints. He lit one while he searched the internet for David Rainer.

(No, *Rainier.*)

Boy, could Hailey pick 'em. The guy had a real estate empire, a private jet, and a yacht. He looked like a total prick, and he had screwed Mack's wife. Possibly multiple times.

With one joint between his lips and the other tucked into his front shirt pocket next to his Zippo, Mack grabbed his five-iron from the corner. He pilfered a bottle of wine as he passed through the kitchen, briefly registered the shock on his sister-in-law's face at the sight of him, and stomped toward the eternally jammed side door to the garage. He kicked it twice with his socked foot, which hurt like hell, and then—with ash an inch long dangling on the end of his joint—he began to bash at the doorknob with his golf club. He only stopped when the bottle of wine started to slip from the crook of his elbow.

He abandoned the side door then and veered toward the front hall. He could hear splashing in the bathtub upstairs and Pammy's low murmur in the background, but Mabel was still out on the landing.

She gaped at him, pressing her cheeks through the banister. "Daddy, are you smok—"

"I'll be back in a minute, baby," he said through the side of his mouth. "You go get a bath." He almost dropped the wine again as he closed the front door behind him. He stuffed his feet in the muddy Sauconys and fumbled in the dark garage for his bucket of golf balls.

The temperature had plummeted. The freezing air mixed with the smoke in his lungs, and Mack had never felt more ferociously alive as he stood on the frozen grass in his backyard. He whiffed his first shot completely, but on his second swing the ball disappeared into the black, starless night. He strained his ears for a splash, but no sound came.

Hailey had let this prick into their lives. She had kissed him and had sex with him and then she had lied. About him, about the money.

Hailey knew exactly where that money came from! His throat threatened to collapse from all the punches it was taking.

Mack snuffed out his joint and sliced a shot into the fence between their yard and the Wakefields'. He heard the wooden panel crack.

Good.

Who did this? Who fucked someone's wife and then sent them money and weird letters and—he glanced down at the light in his underground office window. He'd left the letter out on his desk.

And why all the goddamn red stamps? FINAL NOTICE? The guy was taunting Mack, that's why.

Mack hit another shot out into the lake; this time he did hear the splash.

This guy thought he could tell Mack what to do. He'd sent Mack money, as if Mack were some needy college kid, like Mack was eighteen again and all on his fucking own. Had Hailey told this guy Mack was broke? What else had she told him?

His next ball went left, over the fence on the other side and probably onto the road. Fortunately, there was no scream, no smack of breaking glass. On his backswing though, Mack had seen Eddie and Pammy Byers in Mabel's bedroom window. What a show he was giving them!

The real kicker was that this prick Hailey was screwing was just like every frat boy Mack had ever known: loaded, entitled, smug in the knowledge that life was just a good time when you had money to back you up. When you had your own brand-new Toyota Forerunner at sixteen and your parents' ski lodge in Jackson Hole and as many private golf lessons at the country club as you could ever fucking dream of . . .

Mack's next swing sent the ball rolling along the ground like he was playing croquet, and then somehow his bucket was empty.

He leaned his club against his fucked-up house and chugged at the wine bottle. He was freezing, but he couldn't go back inside now, not while everyone was still here.

He decided to go for a walk. Who cared if it was nighttime? Who cared if it was November? Who cared if nobody went for walks around Bratenahl except geriatric sneaker magnates?

Mack knew what this David guy was, he realized as he got to the end of the driveway. Mack had cut his teeth observing David Moneybags's type of privilege. West Palm Beach High School had been a melting pot of mega-wealthy kids and the offspring of masseuses and cleaners, and people like himself, who fell somewhere in between. Mack had worked his ass off to get into Duke, had had a four-point-something GPA, had founded a literary society, and by sixteen had a poem published in *The Paris Review*. For his last two years of high school he had single-handedly run the school newspaper and founded a reading program at a nearby homeless shelter. And in between all this, Mack dragged rich people's golf bags around Bear Creek Country Club and refreshed off-season water glasses and bread baskets so that he wouldn't have to live completely off Leonora's hard-won salary. With all of that effort, he had just about managed to squeak in Duke's door, begging and pleading for financial aid, for federal loans, for a last-minute golf scholarship. He had elbowed his way into a banquet of debt, among the engineers and the future neurosurgeons with 1600s on their SATs.

Then there was Nicholas Flack. Nick Flack's house looked a lot like Mar-a-Lago, Mack knew. He drove a Porsche 911 to school and he sat in non-AP classes in his rolled-up $75 Abercrombie khakis earning mostly Bs, from what Mack could tell. His grandfather had founded one of the biggest insurance companies in the country; his uncle was a senator.

Nick Flack got into Duke too, even though he hadn't even graduated with honors, and even though five other more qualified kids in their graduating class had been rejected.

Mack stumbled past the Magpie Court gate. What good was a damn gate if there was no one there to man it? He tossed his wine bottle at the useless guard hut, heard it smash on the pavement.

Good!

Yep, Nick Flack had bought his way into Duke—perfectly legally, with school buildings and Mommy and Daddy's tax write-offs—and now Hailey had screwed him.

(Okay, not Nick himself, but someone just like him.)

Hailey was supposed to know better than this. She was supposed to *be* better. But all along, she'd just been waiting for her chance with a Nick Flack. Mack hated her then, and yet somehow ached for her too, like he had never ached before. He had to fight the urge to run home and shake her until she could tell him that it wasn't true, that it hadn't happened, that of course he had misunderstood, that she was still who she had always been.

Instead, Mack staggered left out of his development, away from the lake. There were no cars, and out here the streetlights were just the plain old kind, instead of the new, very-old-looking kind.

He wandered, past leafless November trees and houses with light peeking through drawn curtains. Occasionally he saw headlights in the distance, but only until he turned off the main road. His head had started to hurt, so he took out the other joint and watched the end of it spark to life beneath his nose.

Always, *always* Mack had tried to do the opposite of what people like Nick Flack and David Whatever-the-Fuck-His-Name-Was had told him to.

They said: *Be a banker, dude, you'll make a shit ton of cash*, and Mack had not done it.

They said: *Go ahead and play around on your wife, dude, everyone does*, and Mack had not done it. (Even though apparently everyone thought he had!)

And now, in more direct language than ever before, those pricks were talking in his ear. Now they were writing him *letters*.

Mack stopped in front of the old shed. There were no streetlights at all now, and pretty much all he could see was the outline of the building and the glow of his cigarette. The night was silent, though Mack swore he could hear a chorus of prick voices from all around the world, laughing at him. His head began to swim, and he felt rage sloshing around with the wine in his stomach.

He couldn't even complain. His whole life, he'd had enough food and a decent place to live. He'd had his own opportunity and privilege bestowed upon him just by being born into the skin he was, he knew this. And even though he'd lost her so cruelly, he'd had his mother too, with her excellent soundtrack and her relentless drive to make sure her son had everything he could want. So yes, Mack was very aware that most people on the planet had it so much worse.

The thing was though, some had it *better*. And it was one of these better people who was screwing his wife.

He wished for his golf club then. He yearned to smack it against the dry, ramshackle wood, to feel the splintering of old boards as he beat the thing to death. But his iron was at home, and all Mack had now was the shirt on his back and the joint in his mouth.

You win, pricks.

In a single motion he flicked the joint from his lips into the tangle of weeds at the base of the small structure. He saw its red tip land and surge slightly, and then it went dark. He swayed on his feet, backward and forward, laughing at himself, at how ridiculous he was. How inept even at this. Nick Flack and David Whateverhisnamewas would be so disappointed in him; he couldn't even play their prick game right.

The wind picked up, and the sharp blast of winter air made Mack think of Christmas, of pine trees and eggnog and log fires.

How would they do Christmas now? In their miserable gray identikit house, in this isolated neighborhood among all this damage Hailey had inflicted?

Mack had barely registered the thin curl of smoke snaking up from the weeds when an angry lick of flame appeared. He managed to stamp it out—he felt its heat through the sole of his sneaker—but then another burst of orange popped up, and another. Mack stood frozen as the fire spread along the vegetation at the base of the little building, but by the time the first board had ignited, he had turned and run for home.

27.

When I said that Cleveland had never burned, that wasn't entirely accurate. What I meant was, Cleveland has never burned *to the ground*, not in the transformational way that Chi-town did. The Mistake on the Lake has had its fair share of fire, to be sure. There's the Cuyahoga River, of course, and, less than a ten-minute drive from Bratenahl, the Hough neighborhood exploded into six days of riots in the summer of 1966. Whole blocks went up in smoke, businesses were destroyed, four people were killed, scores injured.

It happened like this: tenants in the mostly Black neighborhood lived in overcrowded properties that were neglected by their mostly white landlords. The streets were filthy with uncollected trash, kids played with rats, there were building violations wherever you turned—you get the picture. It was 1966, and the city was a powder keg of police brutality, inequality, and racial tension that those of us who live in these gentler times would struggle to recognize. Even back then, civil rights experts saw what was coming and tried to get the situation addressed, but—shocker—nobody would listen.

No one knows for sure exactly what set the whole thing off, but most historians agree that the Hough riots had something to do with the Seventy-Niners bar on East Seventy-Ninth and Hough Avenue. In one account, a Black woman was denied the right to leave a collection box for her deceased friend's children; another involved a sign on the door that read "No Water for N******." Whatever went down, somebody in

Hough had finally had enough. Somebody was the first person to convince a friend to head on down there, and once a crowd of three hundred or so friends had gathered outside the Seventy-Niners, somebody threw that first rock. And then somebody (maybe even the same somebody) lit that bar full of racist drunks on fire. Everything that burned after—the diners, the dry cleaners, the Chevys, and the converted multifamily houses—started with a single spark of rage.

Now you'll get mad at me for saying this—madder at me for saying this than for anything that might happen later, I'll bet—but it is not race that interests me about the story of the Hough riots. It is humanity, and that single moment when something ignites inside and coaxes from us—any of us—acts that we never before dreamed possible.

I'm not big on religion, but I am a believer in Free Will, and I'm fairly certain that God—or Karma or the Universe or whoever is pulling the strings—can never tell precisely when this fire will be lit, or what will draw it forth. All we can do is wait and watch for the smoke.

In other words, I never know exactly why they do it. But they almost always do.

28.

Hailey

Hailey was woken by the hollow feeling in her still-overstuffed stomach. She lay there, alone in bed, as the previous day played through her mind: raw turkey parts, the shock on her father's face as she ran to him like a little kid, her drunk sister telling her that she'd always thought Mack was a jerk, that this kind of behavior after they'd driven three whole hours to spend Thanksgiving with him just proved it.

Eventually she got to the worst part, and Mack's discovery of her night with David Rainier settled over Hailey like the flu. She would've stayed there in the brushed-cotton sheets forever, except that the four thousand calories she'd eaten and drunk yesterday were not sitting well. She leaped from bed and made it to the bathroom just in time. She was still retching when she heard Mabel's voice behind her.

"Are you okay, Mommy? Mommy? Should I get Daddy?"

Hailey sat back and leaned against the side of the toilet cubicle. The library-themed wallpaper that had seemed so clever when she'd chosen it now made her feel like she was about to be crushed to death by the sepia-washed spines of a thousand books with no titles.

"Can you just get me a wet washcloth, baby?" Hailey said, and Nurse Mabel raced to fulfill this duty. "Is Daddy here?"

"He was sleeping in the playroom," Mabel said. "I brunged him a blanket."

"Brought. Thanks, Mabs, I feel so much better." She pressed the cool terry cloth to her face, and she did feel better. Especially since it sounded like Mack was in a safe location: downstairs and far enough away that she had a minute to think about what to do, but not gone forever, which felt entirely possible and filled Hailey with a fear so great that she could really only sense the edges of it. She had fantasized about leaving Mack more than she would ever admit, even to herself, but never in her deepest, darkest thoughts did the end of their twenty-year relationship look like this.

"Can I try on my dress now?"

Hailey sighed. Mabel was obsessed with the Christmas dress Hailey had bought her. It was navy taffeta with a white velvet collar (both fabrics being impossible to get stains out of, Hailey's mom had warned), and the skirt was printed with a forest of snow-covered pine trees. It had come from Italy, by way of an obscenely expensive children's boutique in Chagrin Falls. Gigi had a similar number in pink and navy plaid; Hailey had spent almost five hundred dollars on the dresses and two pairs of black patent leather Mary Janes. It was a ludicrous amount, but she'd told herself it was for the Christmas card photos, and for the Shoreby party.

The party. Why would anyone schedule a Christmas party two days after Thanksgiving? Hailey's stomach lurched again at the thought of it. She pressed the washcloth to her forehead.

"Please, Mommy?"

"Okay, okay. You get it out, and I'll come help you."

Sweat had plastered Hailey's hair to her forehead, and in the bathroom mirror she could already see tiny flecks of red on her cheeks like freckles, burst blood vessels from being so violently sick. Her eyes were rimmed with dark smudges that the makeup remover she reached for didn't wipe away.

She splashed her face and wobbled into the hallway, keeping an ear out for Mack. The gentle pink of Mabel's bedroom walls felt like a hug, and Hailey let herself crumple onto the soft carpet. Mabel and Gigi were in their underpants, struggling into their dresses. Hailey didn't have the energy to remind them to be careful, but she did think to wish for her phone as Mabel buttoned up the back of her sister's collar.

"Do I look pretty, Mommy?"

"So pretty," Hailey told Gigi. "Pretty as a picture. You're both going to be the most beautiful ones there, but more importantly the smartest and the nicest too." How could such normal parent-speak come from the mouth of someone who had done what Hailey had done? She had let some sort of monster into their lives and didn't deserve to be here among the stuffed bunnies and the snow globes and the glow-in-the-dark star stickers on the ceiling.

Mabel frowned as she struggled to tie Gigi's sash. "But no one can see nice and smart, so that doesn't matter for the party."

"It always matters," Hailey told her, and she sat watching them until they were ready to show Mack the dresses and went off to find him. Then she hauled herself up and took Gigi's discarded nightgown to her bedroom. From the dormer window in there, she spotted Mack and Gulliver coming up the driveway. Mack was wearing a coat over his flannel pajama bottoms and carrying something down at his side, away from the dog. It was a broken wine bottle; Hailey could just make out the pieces in his hand. She stood behind the floral curtain and watched him drop them into the recycling bin. His simple movements gave no hint as to his state of mind. She needed to catch him in front of Mabel and Gigi when he would have to engage with her like a sane person. Hopefully.

It happened in the kitchen, with the girls crowding around him as he fixed them cereal. Even Gulliver stuck close by his ankles, which probably had to do with proximity to food but made Hailey feel even more alone. Mack's eyes flicked up from the milk he was pouring and stared into Hailey's with a look that was unmistakable. She had seen it too many times before not to know what it meant: her husband hated her now, and nothing between them would ever be the same. His thing with his student had put them in choppy, dangerous waters; this was a giant, unmissable iceberg, and their marriage was the *Titanic*. And yet . . . there was something appealing about him. Something uncharacteristically decisive in his cruelty.

They both stood in silence as the girls crunched their Rice Krispies. Too late Hailey realized that they were sitting there dribbling milk down their chins in half a grand's worth of children's couture, but she wasn't about to kick up a fuss now and make herself the bad guy.

Instead, she inhaled deeply. "What are we going to do?"

There was more crunching, three pairs of eyes watched her—four, counting Gulliver's—and then, when Mack didn't speak, Hailey added, "Today, I mean. What are we going to do today?"

"Playmobil," said Mabel ceremoniously. "All day." Gigi nodded, and Hailey saw that she'd already bagged the favorite and most contested Playmobil figure and tucked it under her cereal bowl. A fight was coming over that blond piece of plastic with the red-and-white-striped dress and the tiny purse that was always going missing.

Another fight was coming too, but what would kick it off? Hailey sank down onto the stool at the kitchen island.

"Did you and Grandpa fix the townhouse?" Hailey thought longingly of her father wandering around with the half-assembled "City Life" house yesterday.

"I fixed it this morning," said Mack, with menace.

"It's only *sort of* fixed, though. Gigi broke it for good," Mabel said with her mouth full. "She stepped right in the kitchen—she did it on purpose, Mommy, she did—and now there's a crack. Now it's like *our* kitchen." When Hailey looked at her in bewilderment, Mabel jumped down from her chair and half closed the door to the back hall that was always left open. "See?"

Hailey did see, and out of the corner of her eye she saw Mack see too: another crack, about an inch wide at its worst, rose up from the floorboards.

"Jesus." Hailey felt something like relief at this new point of focus, until Gigi added her two cents:

"That's not as bad as what Daddy did to the door." She got down too, and led Hailey through the back hall to the side door to the garage. The aluminum was full of deep dents, and the doorknob was missing.

"What the—" Gigi's big gray eyes stared up at her, and Hailey stopped herself. "I'm sure it was an accident." She said it loudly in case Mack was listening. But when they went back through, he had moved into the front hall, and she could hear him on the phone. All three of them could hear him on the phone:

"The thing is, *Cletus*, I don't care if it's a holiday. My goddamn house is falling down, and all you keep talking about is maybe sending this concrete guy. Where the hell is he? Get somebody out here to fix this, or I'm calling a lawyer in and, so help me God, I will sue the shit out of you. Hope you had a nice Thanksgiving. We're lucky the ceiling didn't fall in on ours."

Even though her back was to them, Hailey could *feel* Mabel's and Gigi's jaws drop. "I know Daddy's saying some bad words," she started, "but—"

"And he smokes," said Mabel. "Did you know that, Mommy? Daddy smokes."

✦

Despite everything, Hailey still felt a shot of pride at what they looked like: Mack in a sports coat and his trademark Christmas bow tie, and for no apparent reason his glasses too, as if he knew how much she loved them, as if he knew that those crooked tortoiseshell frames would be what finally shattered her heart. The girls in their new dresses and Mary Janes, velvet ribbons in their freshly washed hair. Even Mabel's clip-on diamond Disney Princess earrings (a present from Grammie) were mostly hidden by her soft, shiny curls.

Hailey's own dress was black velvet, with ivory silk bows in a neat row across her back. Mack had wordlessly tied them for her; Mabel wasn't quite up to the task, and so she'd had no choice but to ask him. Afterward, she'd twisted her hair up so tightly it hurt her scalp and applied makeup like war paint—angry slashes of red blush, crimson lips, three coats of jet-black mascara.

Mack did not look twice. He'd made an obvious point of not even looking once.

They drove the five hundred yards to the Shoreby, because everyone did. The entire front of the grand estate had been spectacularly outlined in Christmas lights, but Hailey did not experience the usual thrill when the valet parking attendant bade her good evening. Instead, she felt dread; dread that this thing between her and Mack would crawl out from underneath the white tablecloths and slither along the silver and the china into the warm candlelight to reveal itself to everyone in the room. And that everyone included Santa Claus himself, Hailey saw. As soon as they'd checked their coats, Mabel and Gigi ran off to join the throngs of children waiting to visit him, leaving her and Mack awkwardly, horribly alone.

Then Mack said, "I'm going to the bar," and he abandoned her there to the crowd of friends and neighbors, none of whom she really knew. She was about to make her way toward the Santa line too when Allison Murdoch—six boys in seven years—appeared beside her.

"Don't you look pretty, Hailey," Allison said, but it came out more like an accusation than a greeting. Hailey felt the bareness of her shoulders and the redness of her lips and was conscious of Allison running her hands through her own short, wash-and-wear hair. Allison had on an ill-fitting navy shift dress with penny loafers and no makeup, even here at this ritzy party deep in plastic-surgery land. Maybe being surrounded by all that testosterone did things to you.

"You too," Hailey said weakly, and then came up blank as to what to say next.

Fortunately, Allison knew right where she wanted the small talk to go: "I was so sorry to hear about your husband's trouble at Tech," she said. "What a terrible thing for you all."

Hailey's cheeks caught fire beneath all of her makeup. "Oh, yes . . . thanks. It's actually just a misunderstanding—"

"You don't have to explain it to me. World's gone crazy." Allison's teeth were stained with red wine.

"Mmmm," Hailey shoveled desperately through her brain for something to fill the gaping hole that was threatening to open in the conversation. "Isn't this nice? This is our first Shoreby Christmas party. It's really something."

Allison nodded. "Although it's too bad they're not doing the carriage rides this year. My kids love that. They're so disappointed." Hailey wasn't sure which of the dozens of boys tearing around the party belonged to this woman, but none of them were exactly crying in the corner. She stepped awkwardly toward a buffet table full of desserts and was unpleasantly surprised when Allison moved with her. Then, as she was looking for Mabel and Gigi in the crowd, Hailey realized that one of the Wakefield daughters—Arabella it was—had on the exact same dress that she had bought Mabel. Of course she did.

"Are you having a good time?"

Hailey drew a sharp breath as a specter appeared in front of her: the man she had seen in the street after her night with David Rainier. Panic pulsed through her as it dawned on her that it wouldn't be a million miles from possible that David himself could be here tonight; he had enough cash and cache to have joined the Shoreby, or he might come as the guest of a neighbor . . . What would she do? Blank him? Corner him? And Jesus, what would *Mack* do, if he found out who he was?

She had forgotten about the man in front of her. "Yes, great party," she said quickly. "It's our first one." She glanced at Allison, who should by now have tired of Hailey's loop and moved on, but no,

Allison stood planted beside the giant gingerbread house that loomed over the buffet and sipped her wine. The man took no interest in her, and he and Hailey both spoke at the same time.

"I heard you met my—"

"I met your other half." He took over from there. "I hope he likes his new shoes."

"He does, thank you so much. He's already worn them a lot." Talking about Mack this casually felt more like a lie than anything Hailey had said to Rebekah. She could see Mack now, across the room, talking to Betsy Wakefield. He must have been desperate to escape her. Hailey watched him make his excuses and head toward their little trio. But Betsy, clad in a plaid cocktail dress that Hailey wanted to hate but couldn't quite do it, followed him.

"I thought I'd come say hi," Betsy said to Hailey. "And tell you what excellent taste you have in children's clothing."

"Same," said Hailey. "And I love your shoes too." Betsy's plaid pumps, with little plaid bows on them, matched her dress. She was the complete opposite of Allison, fashionwise: everything about the woman belonged in a country club. It was a cold truth, but Hailey knew that she would never find a friend in either of these two extremes. Where were the rest of the in-betweeners in Bratenahl? The nice, normal professional women who maybe *occasionally* got it wrong and overdressed for something like this, as Hailey had clearly done, but hadn't quite embraced the complete club aesthetic, or abandoned any attempt at fashion? They had to exist. Once upon a time, back when the invitations went out, Hailey had hoped to find some today, but the small groups of women clustered around holding "Candy Cane Cosmopolitans" looked impenetrable.

"So how does it feel to be famous?" Betsy said to her. "You're just all over *Cleveland Social* these days!"

Allison nodded sloppily, and Hailey saw Mack go very still.

"Our local hero!" Allison declared into her wineglass.

Hailey reddened. "Oh God, that divorce article feels like a lifetime ago. I don't know why I even agreed to it."

"It made for fascinating reading," said Gerry, who had reminded Mack of his name loudly enough for Hailey to overhear it. "I wish I'd come across that advice three marriages ago."

"Not *that* article," Betsy chided him. "I mean the one about how Hailey saved the man from choking." She took in Hailey's expression. "Have you not seen it? This month's issue?"

"I guess I missed it."

"Oh, you have to see it! I'll drop my copy by," Betsy continued. "It's just a little paragraph in the back with the photo off your firm website, but it mentions Bratenahl. You've done us proud!" When she finished speaking, Hailey watched everyone's eyes land on Mack. Did they *all* know about the scandal at Tech, or was she just paranoid?

Suddenly Hailey felt naked standing there in her cocktail dress. *Exposed.* She'd written some dumb advice column for publicity, for the firm's benefit, but she hadn't taken the time to think about who might read it. Who might be *watching*. And no one had asked her if she wanted to be in that magazine again, or whether she'd wanted people to know where she lived. How had they known, if they hadn't bothered to call her? Had someone researched her? Googled her?

The thought made her feel sick.

Gerry did not help matters when he laid a hand on her bare shoulder. As Hailey flinched, he put his other hand on Mack's shoulder, and then he said, "You two are all over that rag. Why, you're the talk of this town."

This time there was no mistaking the nervous expressions that flickered over the group and deliberately *avoided* Mack this time; they all knew what they knew. It made Hailey want to run and hide, but Gerry moved on to extolling the virtues of the club building itself, how it had been built just for parties like this even when it was a private home. He pointed out the huge back windows facing out at the darkness. "And of course, during Prohibition they brought the booze right up to the dock back here. Erie had her own pirates back then."

Allison was visibly struggling to keep up with his history lesson, and went back to her favorite subject: "It's a shame about the carriage rides this year, though. My kids are devastated."

"What's happened to the carriage rides?" They all turned to Mack; it was the first time he had opened his mouth.

"They said the horses are not in the mood."

Allison was getting through her wine pretty quickly, Hailey noticed, and she longed for some of her own. "I know how they feel," she said wearily. "Not ready for the holidays yet, I guess."

"No, it's because of the fire," Allison said. "The stables are near there, and the horses are all really unsettled. The police said it wouldn't be safe to bring them out around the kids."

"Terrible thing that," Gerry said. "I've been saying for years those outbuildings were unsafe. Not to mention a terrible eyesore."

"What fire?" As Mack spoke again, Hailey saw that the veins in the side of his face were visible, as if her betrayal had worn a layer of skin off him.

"Don't you two follow local news?" Betsy chided them. "Some old shack burned down, just up the road. Right in Bratenahl. They said it was just teenagers messing around, but one of them got hurt."

It could have been Hailey's imagination, but it felt like the warm, boozy atmosphere that surrounded them had frozen over as quickly as the late November air outside. She watched this information spread over Mack's features, and a terrible feeling came over her.

"That's awful," Hailey managed. "I hope everyone is all right now."

The answer took forever to reach her ears.

"No, I don't think so." Gerry shook his head with grandfatherly solemnity. "Third-degree burns, is what they said. Fire marshal told me some youths were inside smoking marijuana or what have you and the place went up like a haystack. I knew it would happen. I pick up beer bottles from all around the neighborhood; you wouldn't believe the delinquents that run around here at night." Was it Hailey's imagination, or was he looking right into her soul as he said this?

"They didn't say whether these were neighborhood kids or, well, *you know* . . ." The three of them waited for Allison to finish her sentence, and when she didn't, Mack seemed to come alive again.

"We know *what*?" There was such an edge to his voice that for a moment Hailey felt relief: he wouldn't be picking a fight if he'd had anything to do with the fire. She was crazy even to entertain it. But the coincidence was shocking . . . *impossible* even.

"What is it that we know?" Mack said again, and his words were shrill and dangerous.

Even with as much wine as Hailey had just watched Allison drink, the woman knew enough to be defensive. "I just meant that it could be outsiders who came in to make trouble, that's all."

"And so they deserved to be . . ." Mack choked on his words. "Burned up? Just because they aren't rich Bratenahl bra—" He stopped himself and clenched his jaw, and Hailey knew again without having to think about it that he was guilty, and also that she had to save him before he made a scene.

"I'm so sorry," she said to the little circle. "That's just such an upsetting story, and my husband's been under a lot of stress recently." She smiled knowingly at the little group and prayed that the acknowledgment of one secret would bury the trail of another. "We'd better go find the girls, Mack, and leave these nice people to their drinks."

Fortunately, Mabel and Gigi were nowhere to be seen in the main ballroom, so Hailey was able to follow Mack as he fled through the foyer and out the main front door. She faced him as he bent double in the bushes.

"Mack, stop it. Whatever's going on you can't do this here—"

"Are you okay, sir?" One of the parking valets had started toward them.

"He's fine," said Hailey, blocking his view of Mack with her body. "He just needs a little air."

The kid nodded and headed back toward his cohorts; discretion was everything at the Shoreby.

Mack mumbled something incoherent.

"What?"

"I can't breathe. I just . . . I really can't breathe."

A Cadillac pulled up in front of them, and a family they had pushed past to get out the door piled toward it—parents, grandparents, and children. The sound of their laughter was obscene.

"Will you look at that!" cried the grandmother, and Hailey noticed for the first time that snow was falling around them. "It was sixty-five degrees on Wednesday. Winter's hit us all at once!"

Their waiting Cadillac gave Hailey an idea. She took the valet ticket from her purse and flagged down the same attendant. "I'm going to go get the girls," she told Mack. "Just get in the car when he brings it back, okay? Just wait in there. I'll drive. Don't talk to anyone."

As she pressed back through the crowd, she weighed up the best way to lure her daughters away; they'd been here in this winter wonderland for less than an hour. She was prepared to pull them out kicking and screaming, but when she found Mabel at a glitter-covered art table, she was teary and miserable. As her daughter rose from her child-sized chair, Hailey saw why: the beautiful white-tipped forest on the Christmas dress was no more. All of the hand-painted snow-covered trees had been colored in with a fat green marker; Hailey could still see it there, lying capless at Mabel's place. It was the scented kind—this dark-green color, Hailey knew, smelled ironically like pine—and now Mabel was left with a plain blue dress with irregular dark blobs on it. Thanks to her mother, Hailey knew the stains would never come out.

"Arabella made me do it," said Mabel, tears pooling in her eyes. "She said she got her dress first, and I copied."

"That's just silly. It'll wash out, Mabs," Hailey lied. "Don't worry. Where's your sister?"

"Dunno." Mabel put her thumb in her mouth and kept it there while Hailey picked her way through endless rooms overflowing with Christmas trees and wooden reindeer and human-sized snowmen and giant sleighs full of stacks and stacks of brightly wrapped presents. After fifteen minutes of circling and just as real panic was setting in, they found Gigi in some sort of library room. Hailey arrived in the arched doorway just in time to see her youngest sneeze all over an untouched tray of intricately decorated Christmas cookies, much to the horror of a group of nearby parents. Hailey swooped in with the waitress, who removed the contaminated baked goods almost as quickly as Hailey made off with Gigi.

When they finally made it outside, the car was in the front turning circle. The driver door was open, and the engine was running, but Mack was nowhere to be found.

29.

At the height of his power, my father had a sailboat—a hundred-foot Hallberg-Rassy—that he named *Chasing Sunshine*. I still have some of the detritus from it: personalized paper cocktail napkins, a deck chair with my name on it, an orange-and-yellow-striped life preserver.

My father was never happier than when he was at the helm of that ship. I think he knew that it helped people to overlook those personality quirks of his that I've mentioned previously; he was a man who saw what he wanted and took it, and if you could get over his methods, there was a lot of fun to be had in sharing the spoils. We cracked open many a lobster tail on *Sunshine*'s deck, floating in bright-blue Caribbean waters and romancing various twentysomethings. The setting more than made up for my father's favorite joke: Watch the boom doesn't knock out those new pearly whites, kiddo, they cost me a fortune!

We set sail on *Sunshine* to enjoy the best of what life has to offer, and so it struck me as particularly tragic that that's where my father died.

It was the pesky 401(k)s again, and the secretaries and the lawyers and now the federal agents who wouldn't shut up about them. The *Sunshine*'s crew had taken the dinghy to shore for the afternoon, and it was just the two of us left onboard when he finally lost his nerve. My father sat sweaty and wilting in his swim trunks, his fat stomach rolling down onto his thighs, and asked me—with a straight face—for the names of those consultants I'd mentioned way back when I still had all my own teeth.

I like to think that if I'd had more time to prepare, the ending might have been different. But he scared me, frankly, with all his talk about the angry mob of employees that would come for him, and for me too. At this eleventh hour he wanted to appease them, even if that meant backing down from all his plans and dreams with his tail between his legs. He wouldn't hear that it was too late to come clean, that it was better to keep this thing rolling forward, dishonest as it was, until it righted itself with new investment. No matter what I said, I knew that I was powerless to make him stay the course he'd set. (Not a mistake I've ever repeated.)

It was a disgusting thing to witness, this change of tack. You know what they say: In for a penny, in for a pound; the captain goes down with the ship! The captain of *Chasing Sunshine* went down without it, though, I'm sorry to report, and they never found his body.

30.

Mack

As soon as he opened the door to them, Mack knew that he was going to prison. He could easily picture the iron bars slamming in his face; the sloppy beige food he would eat; that bar of soap forever out of reach in the treacherous communal shower. For all his procrastinating on his novel, Mack had been blessed with a writer's imagination, and so by the time the two police officers stepped into his front hall, he had already worked his way through to how his daughters would grow to hate him, just as he had hated his own incarcerated father. Mabs and Gigi would callously reject his attempts to help them (ha—as if he'd have any money to send them!), and then the circle of life would be complete.

The cops were a man and a woman, and underneath their navy winter jackets they had guns and handcuffs. Mack saw officers like these two every day—on campus, around town, in traffic, in Starbucks—but this was the first time he'd ever been sickened at the sight of them, afraid enough to really consider his answer when the female asked if they could come inside for a minute to talk.

She did all the talking. As Mack perched on the sofa, trying to ignore Hailey lurking in the basement stairwell, the cop broke it to him:

"Mr. Evans, it's always tricky to make a visit like this," she said, and Mack felt vomit rise in the back of his throat. "I can tell I'm missing a lot of information. Maybe you can fill in some of the blanks for me."

She was baiting him, playing dumb. This was just like *Law & Order*, and Mack saw that he was doomed. He had never meant to hurt anyone, had he? He had been out for a walk and thought his cigarette—his *joint*, ugh—was out. Obviously, it wasn't, but he was pretty sure, if he remembered rightly, that he'd had *no idea* that it wasn't. Now he would spend the rest of his life making restitution.

This is what he was going to say to her, and he almost believed it was the truth.

Except what if the teenager, whose name Mack now knew, what if fifteen-year-old Kyle Cavenaugh had actually *died*? What if these two cops were here to accuse Mack of *murder*? For the life of him, he hadn't been able to work out how badly the kid had been injured. He couldn't find anything about those third-degree burns that Gerry Baptista had mentioned, though for the past few days Mack had thought of little else. He had been woken over and over by dreams of melting skin.

Now he couldn't think of a single word to say, and the female officer looked very disappointed with him. Mack couldn't even remember what she'd told him her name was, not two minutes ago.

She tried again. "What I mean is, Mr. Evans, is that it's really only you who knows what happened. From the information I've been given and the statements we've taken—"

Statements. Mack imagined these two at fifteen-year-old Kyle Cavenaugh's bedside as he choked out his last words in front of his devastated parents. The living room went fuzzy, until all at once everything came back into focus: "I can't see that there's been an actual crime here," the female cop was saying. "At least not one that we are interested in pursuing, believe me. Misconduct maybe, but we don't deal in that."

"Oh," said Mack. "Okay."

The woman sighed heavily over the chatter coming through her partner's radio and gave Mack a long stare. She pushed her hair back with shiny fingernails. "Look, I'm gonna be honest with you: we don't have a ton of time for stuff like this. You probably know as well as I do that we're only here because the college wants to cover its ass."

"Yes," said Mack. *College, college, college* . . . His brain was pounding against the sides of his skull; his heart was pounding in his chest. How could these two not hear the drum of his nervous system?

"Now, I've interviewed Ms. Ewing, and she has told us that despite the rumors that have circulated, there was no sexual contact of any kind between the two of you, which I'm sure you'll say is correct, right?"

"Yes," said Mack. "Correct. Of course that's correct."

"But opening your home to students, plying them with alcohol—it's not a good look. It makes people think the worst of you, and then we get dragged in. That's how I get Ms. Ewing's father on the phone to me telling me you were partying with his teenager, and he doesn't think that's cool, even if she does. It's not cool, you understand what I'm saying?"

"Yes," said Mack.

"And then the rest of these kids get all riled up, and the dean is coming at me, telling me to charge you with improper fraternization. And you know what? There ain't no such thing. It's a waste of our time."

"I'm sorry," Mack said. "It's just I—" What he wanted to explain, finally, was that he, Mack, had had a professor once who'd taught him to toast Milton with whiskey, who'd sent words like rockets into Mack's brain at parties that lasted till five in the morning, who'd shown him and probably hundreds of other adoring undergrads that this life of knowledge was what they wanted, instead of huge houses and fancy cars.

"Well?"

"Never mind." The rules had changed; even Mack could see that now.

"Uh-huh." The cop filled her lungs and rolled her eyes, and then she set her card on the coffee table. It read *Maylee Briggs, Community Outreach, PCOS.* "You got lucky this time, Mr. Evans. Lucky for you we've got better things to do. But I know these students were drinking underage at your home and I also know they were smoking weed with you. Next time, don't give kids booze and drugs, okay? Let them get it for themselves."

Her partner chuckled. Mack did not.

"Consider yourself officially warned. This is on file, and I don't want to be back here again, you understand what I'm saying to you, Mr. Evans? *Professor* Evans?"

"Yes."

"Man of few words, I see." Officer Briggs and her partner stood up, and Mack led them numbly back to the front door. He felt like they'd just got there; he also felt like they'd been inside his house for a thousand years. There were so many things he wanted to ask them and to tell them that he was afraid to open his mouth at all, so he didn't. Especially once he saw that the mail had just been put through the slot. One large white envelope in particular caught his eye as the officers stepped right over it. He could just about read the return address without his glasses on: Gray Skies Road.

Mack hugged the envelope to his chest as he watched the cops walk to their patrol car. Their conversation was pretty much drowned out by the sound of that constantly crackling radio, but he did catch it when Officer Briggs said to her partner, "Creeps like that are exactly why I didn't waste my money on college."

✦

Relief had snuck up on Mack; even as he agonized over this injured boy, even as he held in his hands an envelope from Sunshine Enterprises with a PHOTOGRAPHS: DO NOT BEND stamp on the front, the abject fear that he was about to be led away in cuffs gave off an undeniable fizz as it left his body and was replaced with a strange feeling of lightness, at least until he slid his finger along the flap of that envelope.

He looked at the photographs first, and saw himself in the woods in black and white, his eyes glowing like a raccoon's, almost as bright as the reflective strips on his Sauconys. His khakis and his Thanksgiving-dinner-appropriate button-down were muted, but he could almost watch his arms and legs move as he flipped through the dozen or so images. In all of the pictures his cigarette glowed unmistakably, and then that dot of light grew larger and larger, until the final photo was just a ball of fire engulfing the dark void of the shed. Mack had to look twice before he noticed the shadowy figures in the background, fleeing the scene on the opposite side from the camera: it took his breath away to see the teenagers, how close to the fire they had been. One of them carried the flames away with him, his arm aglow in a brilliant cloud that Mack could almost feel the heat of even now.

"What is it?" Hailey asked him from the doorway. Her face was ashen; the cops had freaked her out too. So his wife did care if he got hauled off to prison—Mack still had that going for him.

He held the photographs out to her and turned his attention to the letter that had come with them. It read:

Dear Mack and Hailey Evans,

Thank you for your cooperation so far. Shame about the bystanders, but sometimes these things can't be helped.

Overleaf please find your revised statement. We'll be in touch again soon about settling your account.

Again there was no sign-off, and no mention of the photographs of Mack committing arson and . . . assault? Manslaughter? He flipped the paper over, eyeballed the account statement, and passed it to his wife.

"But there's no money off the total," was what Hailey said after a minute. "We still owe forty-seven grand, even though you . . . you did what they asked for."

Mack closed his eyes. He had seen it too.

"It actually says 'Demolition of outbuilding near 411 Fullerton Close' and then has zero as the value."

"I saw," Mack told her. "I guess burning down a building with someone in it doesn't bring in much bacon these days, you know?"

When he finally opened his eyes, Hailey was staring at him. It was maybe the first sustained eye contact they'd had in days, since he'd screamed at her after the Shoreby party. She's started in on him for running away—for running home—and so he'd given it right back to her: *Stay the fuck away from me!* is what he'd said, and she had listened. Charged silence had become their furniture, each of them afraid to ask the unthinkable questions that followed them everywhere. But the police visit had broken the spell, and the last of Mack's anger had left the building with those cops. Hailey must have felt the same.

"I really thought that was it," she said.

"Yeah, me too."

"But . . . *why*? Why on earth would you do it?" It didn't quite sound like an accusation, so Mack didn't take it that way.

"I don't know. I was so drunk. And so mad. I guess I wanted to see what would happen. And obviously I had no idea . . . I mean, that shed couldn't have looked more deserted. If I'd been sober, maybe I would've known it was a setup. This guy is going to ruin me."

The four feet or so between them felt more like four hundred.

"He must have known the kids were in there," he continued. "He knew. Sunshine Enterprises knew, I mean. Otherwise why the camera, for some old shed?" He took the photos back from Hailey. "Who *is* this guy? Why is he doing this to us?"

Hailey leaned against the banister, her face in her hands. "We don't know for sure it's him, Mack. But David Rainier hates me because I was trying to help his wife."

On the tip of Mack's tongue was *You helped her by screwing her husband?* He did not say it, but of course Hailey could read his mind.

"It was only once, you have to believe me. I was drunk too, and angry and—"

"Angry at what?"

Hailey shook her head. "Not angry. So, *so* stressed. I can't explain it. Rebekah—his wife—was trying to rip off the firm, and I . . . I know how it sounds, Mack. There's no excuse; I'm not trying to make excuses. It's crazy. But so is . . ."

Mack could fill in the rest: *So is burning down a building*. But Hailey had done it first, had set this chain of events in motion.

Sort of.

Not that Mack's own record had been spotless . . . but still.

Their thoughts ended up in the same place. "You didn't sleep with her, did you?" Hailey said now, softly.

"I told you I never touched her."

"I believe you. But then why weren't you outraged? Why didn't you tell me sooner, ask for my help? How could you just sit back and do nothing while she trashed your career and your reputation?"

"*She* didn't. Tech did. They completely overreacted. What was I—are we really talking about this now? That's the least of our problems. This guy could send me to prison, Hailey." He shoved the photographs back at her. "I might have killed someone, do you understand this? Maybe he wanted me to. Maybe that was the plan."

"We'd have heard about it if this boy died. It would be on the news."

Her coldness picked at the scabs of his rage. "Okay, *great*, so I've only maimed him for life, and your boyfriend can hang me for it whenever he wants to." But as he said this, instead of running from her, he went and threw himself down on the stairs next to her. *Beneath* her; it felt like a surrender. Someone had him by the balls, and for once it wasn't Hailey.

"I mean, why all these weird letters and . . . *statements*? This is someone pretty fucking crazy, Hailey, to do this. Is this guy crazy?"

"His ex-wife thinks so."

"So what am I supposed to do? Spend the rest of my life looking over my shoulder, waiting to go to prison? What the fuck am I supposed to do?" Mack's heart was racing; his chest was tight. He stood up to shake it off, and for one fleeting second he glimpsed a final and terrible way out of this nightmare. The scariest thing was that imagining this brought him comfort, then, when he thought of his daughters, it brought tears. Great, he was crying again, in front of his wife, who hardly ever cried. At least not until recently.

Hailey put her hands on his shoulders; it was the first time she'd touched him in weeks. "There has to be a way out of this. If my job has taught me anything, it's that there's a way out of everything. If it's David doing this, we'll find something on him and head him off; or if the worst happens, we can say the photos were fake, we can say you acted under duress—there are so many things we can say." From below, Mack saw her straighten her back and harden her jaw, and it made him feel safe, it pushed away that dark thought that was trying to sneak its way back into his brain again.

"I'm going to call Dennis," Hailey said, "and I'll go after this guy head-on."

Mack felt so grateful for her resolve that the dirty and damning retort that popped into his head never found its way to his lips.

31.

I'm not going to lie: this situation has really turned itself around. We're almost at the good part now, with hardly any arm-twisting at all. It could be quick from here. The pace is up to them, though: if there's one thing I've learned from my father, it's that it's no good slowing things down at the eleventh hour.

It all worked out in the end, in case you are wondering. Yes, my father's personal fortune was seized, his reputation ruined, his empire disbanded. Yes, he lost the penthouse and the Hamptons house and the Paris apartment and—this one hurt the most—the *Chasing Sunshine*, but my father must have seen the gray skies gathering on the horizon, because he had his affairs in order. In our family safety deposit box, tucked among my mother's jewelry (she hadn't needed it, he'd said once, where she was going), there was a note to me in my father's handwriting. It contained a short, uncharacteristic kindness, and also some bank details that have gone a long way toward erasing his failures as a businessman. Twenty-five million will buy you a lot of forgiveness, and so even though I've had to endure decades of dental work, and I had to change my name and uproot (get it?) my entire life, I do regret my last words to him as I watched him struggle to stay afloat, drowning in the disbelief that his own offspring had pushed him overboard: "Who's the pussy now?"

32.

Hailey

I don't understand." Hailey thought if maybe she shook her head long enough, Dennis would change his opinion. "How can you be so sure?"

"It just doesn't feel like his financial signature." He had come into Hailey's office holding a baseball, and he stood before her tossing it from one hand to the other, which was making her want to kill him. "Look, I've been through all Rainier's accounts, so I can see if he's tied to these funds or Sunshine Enterprises in any way at all. His money's spread out, some in trusts, some in bonds and crypto, but it's all legit. He's got no unexplained assets; apart from the boat he's got no money-laundering red flags, and I can literally see exactly how he's paid for everything."

"How can you see?"

Dennis crossed his arms, and the baseball disappeared into his armpit. He pressed his lips into a straight line.

"What about the Bratenahl apartment?" Hailey thought of its rumpled gray bedsheets and stark surfaces and felt nauseous. "Rainier's got an apartment in Cleveland that I don't remember seeing in your original report on him."

"Rented in September. Short term, no deposit, two thousand a month. I've seen the lease."

"Could he be running money through his wife? What about something in Rebekah's name?"

"That's what we *started out* looking for, remember? There is literally nothing on this earth in Rebekah's name except a yoga studio membership in Pepper Pike. You can be one thousand percent sure of that."

Hailey could feel sweat on her forehead, on her palms. "What else can we do?"

Dennis's eyebrows met in the middle as he frowned. "Look, if his money is findable, if he has any contact to it, then I know about it."

"But again, *how*? I need to be sure. This goes beyond the firm. This guy . . . I told you before, this man is going after me personally."

"Have you told any of the board this? Clarke or Straus?"

"No. It's more complicated than that." Hailey rubbed her temples for so long she almost forgot Dennis was in her office.

"It's called Pegasus," he said finally.

"What is?"

"The program I use. It's spyware. It moves through phones, computers. I can see anything on them—his bank accounts, messages, everything. It's, umm, not really legal, so . . . just trust me, it does the job. So, could Rainier have gotten a bunch of cash from nowhere and physically dropped it off in this Liberian account? I guess so, but the money that you got never touched anything he's ever touched, and he's never mentioned Bank Nacional Liberia or Sunshine Enterprises in anything I've scanned through. And he's never been to Liberia, either."

"You're that sure?"

"Yeah. I'm sure."

"Why doesn't that make me feel any better?"

"I'm sorry."

A thought slotted into place in Hailey's brain. "You can read all of his messages? WhatsApp and texts and everything?"

Dennis set the baseball down on the edge of Hailey's desk and sank into a chair. "Yeah."

"Did he . . . did you come across anything at all about me?"

"Some. Not too much. Nothing very flattering."

"I see."

Had this kid listened to the voice message she had left for David? Could he have read, say, a message from David to Rebekah referring to how he'd slept with her lawyer? Did it even matter now, what some twenty-two-year-old IT geek knew? Hailey kept her eyes focused on the baseball. For once she was unsure of the next move.

"You should probably know that he's thinking of filing an injunction against you." Dennis picked at the rubber on the bottom of his shoe with extreme focus. "For harassment."

"I yelled at him," Hailey said quickly. "I lost my temper."

"Ah." If Dennis had heard her voice message, he gave nothing away.

Hailey picked up the baseball; the last time she'd held one in her hand had to be ten years ago. She and her dad used to play catch after dinner in the summer, until she'd left for college.

"Does Rainier have any proof that I yelled at him?"

"He does," said Dennis, finally reddening. "Sorry."

It was strange, but Hailey thought of Mack then, of how it must have been for him when the trouble with his student had started. *So this is how an entire career goes up in smoke*. Mack hadn't even been guilty, but Hailey was! Suddenly the whole thing felt like one big, terrible joke.

"So this Liberian bank," she said. "If it isn't David Rainier sending me this money, if it really isn't him, then what are the clients like? Shady rich people?"

"Rich offshore corporations," said Dennis. "No names, just account numbers. The account these payments came from had eight figures attached."

"Well, that's good news." Hailey allowed herself a hint of a smile at Dennis's response. "I mean, I wouldn't want to take weird money from some average rich person, would I?"

Dennis reached out and took his ball back. "Listen, like I told you: this is not some nice forgotten relative. You don't run your cash through a bank like this unless you have to." He stood up, but Hailey couldn't quite bring herself to end the meeting.

"So what do I do?"

"You're asking me?"

"I guess I am. What would you do about this money?"

He took his time, then he said, "Get your bank to wire it back. Tell them it was a mistake, that you just didn't notice it. That's what I'd do." He nodded goodbye, and then he stopped in the doorway and turned back to Hailey. "Actually, I probably wouldn't. I'd probably just keep it and hope no one ever came looking for it . . . But that's just me."

✦

The concrete guy was late. He hadn't called, and Hailey had left work early to be home for him, having spent the rest of the morning researching Bank Nacional and also "walls cracking new houses." Now she was down in the playroom studying those cracks up close. Mabel's purple My Little Pony was drinking from a magic stream that flowed two inches wide and a lot deeper than it had last week. The cracks were spreading fast. If she sat here long enough, Hailey might actually be able to see the floor fall apart in front of her.

"No!" Mabel's shout tore through Hailey's tender nerve endings. "You know you aren't allowed to have those!"

Gigi had emerged from the walk-in toy cupboard with a plastic box almost as big as she was. It contained Hailey's old collection of Polly Pockets.

Hailey sighed. "Gig, you know the pieces are too small. We have to save those until you are a little bigger. Even Mabel doesn't play with those."

Gigi studied the tantalizing pastel toys through the clear plastic.

"Please, Mommy, can we just see them? Just to look? You're here now, and you're *never* here."

Gigi knew just the right button, and Hailey caved immediately. "Just until the concrete guy comes, okay? Then we put the Pollys away."

By the time she'd finished her sentence, Gigi had torn the dusty lid from the box and was opening a blue heart-shaped plastic case to reveal the tiny dollhouse inside—the perfect size for the redheaded Polly, no bigger than a toddler's thumb, that Mabel held up to inspect. The redhead had always been Hailey's favorite Polly doll.

Mabel and Gigi took turns opening each of the small cases: a princess castle, a park with a merry-go-round and a slide, a pet store, a café that still had its tiny milkshakes. The sets had been carefully preserved as new by Pammy Byers and passed to Hailey when Mabel was born.

"Look, the kitchen floor in this one is just like our old floor!" cried Mabel. " 'Member, we used to do hopscotch on there?"

Gigi stared down at the inch-long checkerboard sticker. "I don't remember that at all," she said, and Hailey was struck for the thousandth time how odd it was that she sounded so much older than her big sister. But they'd lived in Bratenahl for more than a sixth of Gigi's life; no wonder she had no memory of the Lakewood house.

They had started lining up the open cases on the carpet to make a city when the concrete guy finally arrived. He was not at all what Hailey had pictured—he was young and wiry and drove a Lexus SUV instead of a mixer truck. He was unfazed by Gulliver's barking and bent down to scratch the dog's ears.

"I took a quick look outside," he said to Hailey. "But Simeon said the worst damage is in the basement?"

"I guess so." That word *damage* didn't sit well. "It seems to be spreading."

"Okay, let's take a look-see. Do you want shoes off?" He was dressed in crisp khakis and a bomber jacket, but he did have huge work boots with splashes of paint and crusty concrete on them. Still, she didn't feel up to explaining to him why he'd have to leave them outside the door in the cold (Gulliver was already sniffing around them hungrily), and besides, the floor was already permanently trashed, so what did it matter?

"It's fine."

"Cool place you got here," he said as they made their way to the basement. "I like the high ceilings."

He bid a friendly hello to the girls, but his eyes were already on the cracks in the drywall when Gigi asked him, "Are you the concrete guy?"

"Most people call me Ben," he said. "But yeah, I pretty much am. Mind if I pull up the carpet?"

They watched as he took photos of the floor and the walls with his phone, and then the girls went back to the Pollys while he worked his way around to the furnace room. The crack along the drain had grown even deeper, and the ones in the walls had splintered and fanned out in new directions.

The guy gestured toward the raw wood door in the corner. "Can I go in there?"

"Sure. It's my husband's office. He's not home right now," she added, when the guy went to knock. Then as he opened the door, she had a panicked moment: What if Mack had left the Sunshine Enterprise photographs of himself out on his desk?

But when they stepped inside, apart from all the weird things Mack collected—mugs and shot glasses and bobbleheads, dozens of Dr Pepper cans and Starbucks cups, a few wilted plants—there was nothing of interest, not even any cracks. At least not that Hailey could see. But then Ben the Concrete Guy moved aside the box of Mack's mother's papers and a stack of old comic books to reveal another sizable crack in the floor.

"They're just *everywhere*," said Hailey. "There's one in the kitchen wall too. I forgot. I'll show you on the way back up."

"The drywall cracks are nothing to worry about." Something in his manner reminded Hailey of the girls' pediatrician, capable and reassuring, but this only lasted for a second or two. "These cracks in the concrete itself though, they're pretty unusual," he continued. "We'd expect to see this if the ground under the house was unstable—like if it was silt or sand—but that's not the case. This is hard clay around here, solid. But look—" He measured the width of the crack in Mack's concrete floor with his thumb and forefinger and held up the inch of empty space for Hailey to see. "This here tells me the house is moving. The steel foundation beams are shifting in the ground, for some reason."

Hailey stared at him. "What reason?"

He chuckled. "Like an earthquake would do it," he said, and Hailey did not think this was at all funny. "Although it's obviously *not* an earthquake."

"Could it be erosion? From the lake?"

"Not this far back from the water. I'm going to take some samples away with me, but I'd also like to get down under there and get access to the S beams. Are you okay if I get someone in here to take up the floor?"

"The *concrete* floor?"

"Yeah, we'll blast it, check everything out, and then repour it."

"The *whole* floor?"

"Just the part near the beams to start with."

"Oh my god," said Hailey, reeling at the image of a construction crew with sledgehammers descending on her house. "I do *not* need this right now. I really don't, I—wait, could this be dangerous? I mean, are we safe to stay here?"

"I think for now—"

"Oh God," Hailey said again. "I just don't believe this. How can this be happening? The house is brand-new!" She could hear the whining in her voice but had no way of stopping it.

"Ain't that always the way," Ben said. "But you're in luck, timing-wise. I can get my boys in Monday, and we'll get it over with quick as we can."

"And Simeon pays for it?"

"I don't handle that part," he said, backing away from her. "You'll have to work it out with him."

"But generally speaking, is this something insurance should cover, either Simeon's or ours?"

"I would guess so, but I couldn't say for sure. Depends on the cause, really. Simeon said you're a lawyer?"

"Did he?" Would that have been in passing conversation, or in the context of a lawsuit? Judging by the way this guy was watching her now, it had to be the latter. "Yes, I'm a divorce lawyer."

"I see." He headed for the stairs. "Well, Divorce Lawyer Girl, your kids will want to play somewhere else next week probably. There's gonna be a lot of dust down here."

Mack's Audi was pulling in just as the Concrete Guy's Lexus was pulling out. Mack had been at Tech for a meeting, and he headed straight for the fridge and gulped down a beer. From the other side of the counter, Hailey took in his sharp cheekbones and the way his pants drooped at the back and around his waist. He was disappearing in front of her; soon he would be nothing but black circles and ashen skin.

"They want me to come back," he said when the beer must have been almost empty, and even though this is what Hailey had wanted, she didn't see how this person in front of her could possibly cope with a job, even a cushy one like his.

"They basically want to forget that anything happened. The dean called it 'this unfortunate incident.'" There was not a trace of life in Mack's voice.

"We could sue them, you know."

He did not acknowledge this, but Hailey kept trying, mostly to fill the silence: "For not protecting you better. We could sue them for not investigating before they hung you out to dry."

Mack set the beer can down and leaned on the counter, cocked his head sideways, and began to bob his chin up and down, something between a tic and a nod. "What difference does it make?"

"What do you mean? Do you *want* to go back to work?"

"I don't care really at all," said Mack, with a flatness that scared Hailey deep in her bones. She recognized at once the state he was in; she had been there herself a couple of times in her life. The first was when she—Hailey Byers, valedictorian of her high school class, summa cum laude graduate of Duke University, acer of the LSAT, and editor of the *NYU Law Review*—had (whisper it) failed the Ohio bar. Not by one silly little point, nor by the many, many points that would have signified a missed section, a small stroke, or some other such disaster, but by a margin that plainly demonstrated that this girl didn't know her stuff. Hailey was not descended from lawyers, she did not look like a lawyer, she did not feel grown-up enough to be a lawyer, and here was the numerical proof: the universe had caught her playing dress-up and it had put her back in her place, which turned out to be mostly in bed, staring at the wall. The Hailey Byers who never cracked under pressure had disintegrated in an instant, and no one around her had any idea what to do about it. Not her parents, not her sister, not the partners at the prestigious Cleveland law firm that had already hired her.

No one except for Mack.

It wasn't any grand gesture on his part. He mostly let Hailey mope, stared at the wall with her, told her stories about his new job teaching poetry and creative writing to teenage scientists who just wanted to know what the right answer was! He brought her Dr Peppers when she slept too long, played her Jimi Hendrix to put some fight back in her. All he wanted, he said, was to be with her. In any mental state she happened to be in that day.

And eventually it worked, as Mack had seemed sure it would, as he must've known from his own great disappointments, even though he never talked about them. When the numbness was over, when Hailey had faced her demons, retaken the bar, and passed, Mack had even admitted that he loved her more for having failed, that doing so had made her infinitely more interesting than she had been before. Hailey had briefly considered leaving him for that comment, but she decided to marry him instead.

The second time that Mack had saved her from oblivion wasn't anything nearly as frivolous. It had been when Mabel was born, which was also when Mabel had almost died. Without having to be told, Mack had shifted his watch, and while Hailey's body recovered, it was *Mabel* who got the poetry and the Hendrix, the student stories and the hole-by-hole commentary on the golf round that had won Mack his scholarship. Even when the nurses urged Mack to lay off the Dr Pepper, to go home and get some rest, he had never left their tiny daughter's side. What's more, whereas in those early days Hailey had been numb and mostly preoccupied by negotiations with God, Mack had been laser-focused on Mabel. Whenever Hailey joined the two of them in the NICU after they'd been alone for a while, it was as if Mack had been building a human out of the tiniest of beings: *She likes Salinger*, he'd say. *Her teenage years are gonna be rough.* Mabel's limbs were long (even though they weren't) and good for golf; her attitude toward the babies that cried too much and the resident who clicked his pen was poor at times. *She has musical sensibilities*, Mack explained. *She doesn't like all this discordant noise.*

What Mack had really done was to lead by example: *She's our person, and it's okay to start loving her.* And so Hailey had, even though it was the most frightening thing she had ever done.

"I don't seem to care about anything," Mack was saying now. "I just sat there today in the dean's office; you know? I couldn't think of anything to say to the department head. And then I went to the hospital— "

"What? *Why*? Why would you do that?"

"I have to find out what happened to the kid, Hailey, I— "

"I told you, we'll see something in the news if it is serious. I've been checking. Did you speak to anyone?"

"*The Plain Dealer* said they took him to Metro, so I thought maybe if I— "

"Did you speak to anyone there?" Hailey owed Mack, and she knew he needed her, but he sure wasn't making this easy.

"No. I chickened out. I— " He didn't seem to have enough breath left in him to get through his sentence. Hailey stood waiting until the silence was pierced by a scream from the basement, and then yelling:

"What did you do? Gigi, you stupid, stupid thing! I hate you!"

"Hey!" Mack jolted to life as if he'd been struck by lightning. "What's going on down there?" He turned toward the stairs, but Mabel was already in the doorway, eyes shiny with tears.

"Gigi drop-ded the Polly in the crack! She did it on purpose! It's Mommy's and it's lost and she always— "

"Okay, Mabs, don't worry, I'm sure we can get Polly back."

Mabel eyed Hailey warily; the marker had not washed out of her Christmas dress, and significant trust had been lost. Mabel put her thumb in her mouth and cried as Gigi appeared in the doorway, incandescent with rage.

"It was not my fault! She, she— "

Mack looked as if he might just keel over; Hailey had to get them out of his face. "Tweezers," she said. "I'll bet we can save Polly with tweezers."

But plastic Polly turned out to be too slippery for Hailey's eyebrow tweezers to get hold of, and the crack was too deep and narrow to allow for maximum leverage. Polly's hair, which might have been easier to snare, was angled away from them, wedged down into the deepest part of the split in the floor. "Mabs, we'll figure something else out, okay? But I really need to talk to Daddy for a minute first—"

Mabel stood, bottom lip quivering, as Hailey crouched, plucking at the basement floor. Gigi had slunk off at the first sign that Polly's rescue would not be straightforward.

Mabel was inhaling the beginning of a fresh sob when Mack appeared with the vacuum cleaner in his hand.

"No, Daddy!"

But Hailey saw what he was doing: a quick suck with the hose of the Dyson, and Polly was safely inside its clear cylinder, and then she was back in Mabel's palm, dusty but otherwise fine. Mabel threw herself at Mack's waist in gratitude, and for a second he looked like something more than a dead man walking. Then he looked worse than he had before.

"Let's put the Pollys away, okay, Mabs? You and I can play with them again soon, I promise. Where did Gigi run off to? She can help you clean up."

As Mabel dutifully began to close up the plastic houses and shops, Gigi reappeared at the top of the stairs.

"We saved Polly," Hailey told her, "in case you're wondering." But Gigi was engrossed in a tablet.

Hailey had had just about enough three-year-old for one day. "Where did you get that? You know you have to ask for screen time."

Gigi ignored her.

"Gigi!"

Mack moved to take the tablet from her, but Gigi turned her back to him, still gorging on the screen.

"Genevieve Pamela Evans, *now*!"

"Something's wrong with it, Mommy. Mabel changed it. Everything's different. Everything's wrong!"

Mack wrenched the tablet from her hands. "Enough!" His tone

snapped Gigi out of her stupor, but now Mabel too had grown concerned about their most prized (and fought over) possession. She took the tablet from Mack, and they watched her tear-stained face twist into a scowl. "What is this? What did you do, Gigi? Why is the picture—all the pictureses are different! You changed the games!"

Mack took the tablet back. "Enough of this! *Please*, girls. The tablet is fine—"

He glanced at it as he spoke, and then he frowned. Then he started scrolling.

"What's wrong, Daddy?" Mabel tried to take the tablet back from him, but he held it above her reach, still scrolling.

"When did you have this last?" he said to her through clenched teeth. "Tell me right now!"

Mabel looked to Hailey for help. "Yesterday?"

Mack still did not look up. "Did you take it out somewhere? Out of the house?" He turned to Hailey. "Did we?" His voice got louder, and Gulliver came bounding down the steps and began to bark at Mack's feet, but Mack kept scrolling, his face expressionless and terrifying.

"What's wrong with Daddy?" Mabel asked Hailey, as if Mack wasn't right there in front of them. Mack just wandered toward the stairs.

"Leave the Pollys, girls. Watch some TV for a minute. Daddy and I will be right back."

Hailey turned on *Peppa Pig*, and then she went after Mack. He had stopped by the busted side door, his face still inches from the screen.

"What is the matter with you?" Hailey snatched the thing from his hands. "You're scaring the girls to death." Right away she saw that the iPad's home screen, which had previously been a close-up of Mabel's and Gigi's smiling faces, had somehow been changed. Now it was a photograph of sunlight shining through a cloudy sky, and it only took another glance at Mack's horrified face for the significance of the image to register. Dotted over the top of this hellish skyscape were the icons for new apps, apps that there was no way Mabel or Gigi could have somehow installed.

"Did you—"

"No." Mack read her mind. "I haven't touched this thing in weeks."

With a shaking finger, he reached out and clicked on the new Facebook icon. When it opened to an account in the name of Sunshine Enterprises, Hailey felt like she might combust with fear.

33.

Bratenahl has always been home to fighters. At the turn of the twentieth century, when Cleveland was sinking into a pit of urbanization, this little strip of land fought to become its own separate village. Then for decades, Bratenahl fought to keep its school system separate—there's that word again—from the schools of the rest of the Cleveland masses. Then came civil war over those two ugly apartment blocks, and of course these days there are the brawls about beach access, all that snarling over property deeds and natural shorelines. It's a positive trait, I think: conflict like this keeps the mind sharp, when it otherwise might be pickled in privilege.

Once in a blue moon, though, an adversary comes along that's completely out of your league. A bomb gets dropped that you never saw coming; resistance is futile. This has happened in Bratenahl before too.

In the late 1940s, when the Cold War was just starting, Cleveland was one of this country's most important manufacturing hubs. In theory at least, it had become a prime target for a nuclear strike. The US Army's solution to this vulnerability was the Nike Ajax, a new antiaircraft missile system that would protect the Mistake on the Lake from assured destruction by the Russkies. (It was named Nike for the goddess of war, by the way, not the sneaker company.)

But where to keep this snazzy surface-to-air defense system? Nike had to be somewhere close to the target city, but somewhere separate too, somewhere discreet where no one would think to look for fifty thousand pounds of metal casing and rocket fuel . . . did such a place still exist in Cleveland at that time?

It did! We know it did! And once Uncle Sam set his sights on this particularly strategic stretch of Erie's southern coast, he didn't give two shits who lived there, or how rich they were. The battle for the western end of Bratenahl was literally nuclear, and it was over before it began.

Boom! The thirty-four-room Tudor manor house at 8907 Lakeshore Boulevard, built in 1899, was razed to the ground by the US military.

Blam! They took out 9913 Lakeshore the same year. That place was practically indestructible, they say. The army had to set fire to it—twice!—to finish the demolition.

Ka-bang! Down came "Orchards" at 489 East Eighty-Eighth. That was a hell of a house too, by all accounts, with a ninety-foot tower and views all the way to Canada.

Into this freshly cleared acreage, an entire military base was thrust upon Bratenahl's shell-shocked citizenry, complete with twenty missiles in underground storage, a launching area, and barracks for over a hundred military personnel. There was a mess hall too, and admin blocks and outbuildings.

You have to admire the ruthlessness of Uncle Sam here, this ability to plow through the bullshit and take what was needed. Pretty quickly, though, the whole Nike enterprise came to not much: by the 1970s the panic was over, and the site was decommissioned and disassembled. Some of the smaller buildings, however, are still standing today.

(And some aren't, but you knew that already.)

34.

Mack

Twice he got as far as the car, the terrible pink-cased iPad placed carefully on the front passenger seat, like a grenade that might explode. Both times he stopped short of starting the engine. He thought of Mabel and Gigi, and of Hailey too, all of them shamed and abandoned while Mack went to jail for arson. Shamed and abandoned, or worse.

Because that tablet had shown him there might be worse.

A predator had Mack in its sights, and he could feel its gaze sizzling through every cell in his body. Someone had hacked right into their daughters' budding electronic world, and left behind proof of an obsession that Mack couldn't begin to make sense of. As he clicked around the Sunshine Enterprises social media accounts for some scrap of information about who might be capable of doing this to them, all he found, in between infuriating photos of sunsets and sunrises over every landscape imaginable, was his own existence under a microscope. These accounts were about Mack, and Hailey too, and they were insidious. Sunshine Enterprises' first Instagram post was a link to Hailey's divorce article from *Cleveland Social*; the second was a screenshot of an old photo of the two of them at some fundraiser she'd dragged Mack to. Then there was a link to the piece about Hailey saving the man from choking. Mack was featured too, his own short but shameful magazine mention, and then—and this almost stopped his heart once and for all—there was the black-and-white photo of him in his Thanksgiving best and his glowing Saucony sneakers, a ball of fire exploding on the screen next to him.

Frantic, he clicked on some of Sunshine Enterprises' followers. They looked like dummy accounts, with names like Tornado Joe and Rainy Day. But how could he be sure? How private was this account? Would one link expose him to the media, to the police, to everyone he knew?

The social accounts were just the tip of the iPad iceberg. Hailey, ever thorough, had meticulously clicked open horror upon horror: there was a National City Bank app linked to their personal checking account, every transaction there in black and white, including the deposits from Sunshine Enterprises. This maybe—maybe—could have been some trickery of the Apple keychain, but there was no mistaking the text messages that had been loaded behind the innocuous little envelope icon. These had been . . . *curated*. There was no other word for it. There was one from Hailey to himself that Mack recognized from months ago: PLEASE can you call Simeon about the dressing room? I've asked you three times. There was another he'd sent to Hailey: I'm guessing you're home late again? Were you planning on telling me? One that made his blood boil: Hi David, Please can you give me a call when you get a minute? And his to Mackenzie Ewing: Don't worry if you're a few days late. Just hand it in whenever. I got your back, little Mack.

Sunshine Enterprises had found the worst of them and was reveling in it, but it knew all about the best of them, too: the iPad was also full of photos of Gigi and Mabel. There were the girls walking into school, in the playground, in their own driveway, on their grandparents' front porch—*recent* photos, and Mack had not taken these, and neither had Hailey.

"What the fuck," Hailey whispered to him. "Why would anyone do this to us? *Why*?"

Mack found at least a partial answer when Hailey—thorough to the very end—clicked on the weather app: the ten-day forecast for the Greater Cleveland metropolitan area in the middle of December was ninety-degree sunshine every day.

"Someone thinks this is *funny*," he said to her. "Some prick is out there somewhere laughing at how scared this will make us."

"But from how far away?" The dark had settled around them while they scrolled through the slings and arrows of their daily exchanges, and Mabel and Gigi had eaten dry cereal for dinner and fallen asleep on the carpet in front of the TV. Mack heard the fear in Hailey's voice, and as they scooped up the girls to take them to bed, it was all he could do not to press Mabel to his chest, to shout for Hailey to follow him and to run, screaming at the top of his lungs, out into the night.

Instead, once he had tucked Mabel in, he stood in between his daughters' bedroom doors and spent a long time thinking again about the car and the police. But it felt important that they stay together, so when he finally did force himself to move and found Hailey in the dressing room packing a bag, he panicked.

"Where are you going?"

"Not me, *we*."

"Where are we going?" As angry as he still was with her, as much as he had to believe that this whole thing was her fault, he prayed that he was still a part of her *we*.

"My parents'. We can't stay here."

He watched as she pulled a dozen pairs of underwear from a drawer.

"For how long?"

"I don't know! I don't know!" She crumpled onto the carpet, and Mack did not even think to try and catch her. "But that doesn't even help, does it? This person has been to my parents' house, Mack—those pictures! They . . . He could be listening to us now—" She gestured toward the hall, where Mack had left the iPad. "I don't . . . I don't even know where to start. It's *everywhere*! We can't go to a hotel because the bank account—what if they're tracking our phones?"

"I know. I still think the police are our only option. I think we have to tell them about Rainier, that he's doing this to you. To us."

Hailey closed her eyes, and it made Mack's heart beat even faster. "What?"

"We couldn't find anything in David Rainier's financials. He's clean. I'm sorry, you were so upset I didn't know how to tell you. It doesn't mean he can't be involved, but I don't know how we'd prove it."

Mack dug his fingernails into his palms. "Just call him. Call the prick and tell him you're even, tell him to cut this the hell out, and let the firm write off the loss. Lose your job, so what. You can start over."

"I tried that. I *tried* to call him off! I'm going to lose my job anyway. He has proof that I—that I—"

Mack turned away from her. "What kind of proof?"

"I don't know. Dennis at work got into his phone—"

"What do you mean, got into his phone? *How?*"

"I told you, he's our IT. He's a hacker. I'm—"

"And you don't think Dennis the hacker might have something to do with the fact that EVERY SINGLE PART OF OUR LIVES has been hacked?"

"*Dennis*? Why would Dennis, who works for *me* . . ." She kept going, but Mack wasn't listening. Hailey was speaking to him in that way that he hated most of all, like he was an imbecile, like he didn't have a master's and a PhD and—

"Mack? Are you even hearing me right now?"

He was fighting with everything he had not to scream her down. If he said what he was thinking, she might leave without him. She might leave without him *anyway*, and he realized that more than anything he didn't want that. He let her finish. He nodded in all the right places. Of course it wasn't Dennis the hacker who was hacking into their lives, how could Mack be so stupid as to think it might be?

And actually, he realized, even if it *were* Dennis, or if it were David Rainier, or Mack's dead father, or his favorite Starbucks barista, even if he could figure out exactly who it was doing this to them, what *then*? Mack had no answer, and so, when Hailey had finished talking at him, he took out his tattered duffel bag and began to pack.

Then he *un*packed, when Hailey decided that, thinking it over, they shouldn't go anywhere. That it wasn't safe to be out in the dead of night with two tiny kids on icy roads with probably a lunatic in hot pursuit.

They turned off the router and the Bluetooth on their phones, and then, when that didn't feel like enough, they switched off the phones themselves. Mack kept the landline cordless in his pocket, comforted by the old-fashioned heft of it, and then—feeling a lot more scared than he ever would have admitted to—he checked the locks on all the windows and the doors. The inch-long gap he always left in his tiny office window to combat the heat of the furnace room felt like an open drawbridge, and as he tugged it closed, he knocked his marijuana plant from the windowsill. The pot smashed on the concrete, and dirt went everywhere. With the cold, judgment-filled eyes of his pioneer ancestors looking on, he grabbed the withered plant by its stem and closed the door on the mess.

Back up in the bedroom, he flicked on the fireplace and tossed the plant into it. Hailey, who was sitting on the end of the bed with Gulliver next to her, looked on wordlessly as Mack's minuscule cannabis crop was lost to the flames. It was just about the least of his problems, but it still felt like he'd escaped from something; cultivation of controlled substances would not be on his rap sheet.

"We have to take back control of this." Mack took in a deep breath that he hoped contained some trace of narcotic. "I know you think I shouldn't have gone to the hospital, but I've got to find out what happened to that boy. It's driving me crazy. How can I make any decisions about getting the police involved unless I know how bad it is? That kid is all I can think about."

"But you *can't* just think about that kid. He's part of a bigger picture that we're already too much a part of. We took the money, and you did what they wanted, and if anyone starts looking into *any* of this, we're implicated up to our eyeballs."

A thought slipped into Mack's head then, like a rat into a sewer: What if Hailey knew more about that forty-seven grand than she was letting on? She'd had an affair. What else had she done? He studied her face; her skin was sallow, and there was makeup smudged beneath her eyes that gave her a witchy appearance that was entirely new to him. He thought of someone else's hands on the buttons of her shirt, of some guy's lips—he shook this off. The first check had come to him, hadn't it? To Malcolm P. Evans.

"Implicated in what, exactly?" he asked her.

"I have no idea. I just—I mean, what does this person want? To destroy our family?"

"He's not going to do that." Mack stood facing her as the room began to fill with tendrils of acrid smoke; the goddamn fireplace was not remotely functional.

"You checked the back door too?" Hailey asked him after a minute.

"I checked everywhere."

"I knew we should have gone for the security system. Everyone in Bratenahl has a security system. Everyone in *Cleveland*."

It was another dig at Mack, one more than he was prepared to take. "Even if we had one, Sunshine Enterprises would probably have the code. Anyway, breaking into our house would be a whole other level."

"Is it, though?" Hailey's voice cracked, and Mack steeled himself for the continuation of her here's-why-you're-a-moron lecture. Instead she whispered, "You don't understand. If it is somehow David

Rainier. . . . He's right here, Mack. Or at least he was. He *lives* in Bratenahl."

"Who does? David Rainier? David Rainier lives in Bratenahl?"

"Yes." He could barely hear her.

Mack's mind went back to the sewer. It flashed through graphic images of his wife and some shadowy figure in a fancy suit, and then it plunged into the depths of conspiracy.

"Did he move here for you?"

"No! It isn't like that. I told you—it was only once, and it was a *coincidence* that he was in Bratenahl. Or maybe he set me up. . . . I was drunk and upset about losing the firm's money and frustrated with . . . he could have set me up just like he set you up."

She was right about one thing: Mack had been set up. He turned away from her, grabbed a putter that had been resting against the wall, and used it to push the last remnants of his plant into the flames. He took another deep, toxic breath. They couldn't go on like this.

"Okay, listen to me, Hailey: I know things aren't great between us, but for right now we have to trust each other. I *trust* you, even though . . . even though what happened, happened. And you trust me, right? We have to plan what to do together, for Mabel and Gigi. Nothing happens without each other. We decide every move together. I won't go to the hospital again, I promise."

All he could read in her eyes was exhaustion, but she let him put his arms around her and pull her toward him, and he was hit by another slap of strangeness: when he hugged her, Hailey felt small and bony and *fluttery*, like a bird, not at all like someone who knew what she was doing. A single thought circled through Mack's head as he lay down next to her, on top of the covers, and stared at a new crack in the ceiling for six hours: he was completely alone in this.

Then again, he had always been alone. How stupid to ever think otherwise.

35.

Hailey

Hailey stood outside Jackson Clarke's thick office door, felt the reassuring weight of it as she pushed it open. Cocooned in the firm's dark wood paneling and pristine bookshelves, she felt better than she had last night, when Mack was burning up houseplants and spouting bullshit about being in this together. They weren't together, Hailey knew now, not in any sense, and the best Mack could do was to set things on fire. She hoped he would at least manage the conversation they'd planned that morning, about telling the girls' schools to keep a close eye on them and to release Mabel and Gigi to no one but their parents. Hailey doubted Mack would convey the seriousness of it like she would have, but she'd had no choice but to delegate: she had to be here. Clay Straus was already in Clarke's office, slouched in a big armchair. The two most senior partners fell silent as she entered. Their faces were tan and leathery; she had been lucky to catch them both in town. Under normal circumstances, Hailey would have called them snowbirds and asked about their golf handicaps, safe in the knowledge that she was their silver bullet. Hiring her had made them look good—apart from that unbearable six months between bar exams—and, once she had proven herself, promoting her to junior partner had made them look even better. Her ascent up the ranks of Cleveland divorce attorneys had made them *a lot* of money, which was the most important thing, and had more than redeemed her in everyone's eyes.

But today was not for office banter.

"So." Clarke gave a deep sigh, and his watery eyes met Straus's in a way that Hailey did not like. "Mr. and Mrs. Rainier."

This was the moment Hailey had been dreading for months, ever since Rebekah had announced her grand scheme to stiff them for a quarter of a million in advanced fees and expenses. Since then, Hailey had been hiding from these two men who had once been her mentors. More recently she had been hiding from *everyone*, and the feeling was mutual: the rock-star paralegal basically avoided Hailey like the plague, and even Dennis—Dennis who might unlock the secrets of the iPad, Dennis who Hailey still hoped could be the key to saving them—had started "working from home."

"Yes, the Rainiers." Hailey's voice came out stronger than she'd thought it might. "I don't even know where to start."

Straus did: "This can never happen again, for a start."

"No, of course not," said Hailey. "It was a huge mistake to advance the wife the credit."

Own it, Hailey thought to herself. *Don't try to explain. Own that you screwed up and then beg for their help. You need them.*

"Yes. What a delightful woman Mrs. Rainier is." Clarke rolled his eyes. "In all my years I've never had a phone call quite like that one."

Straus curled his lips in disgust and nodded: he had heard about this call, or received one of his own.

Hailey's chest tightened. It felt like ants were crawling down her arms.

"She made some pretty serious accusations about your relationship with her husband," Clarke went on. "And she claimed to have proof. Is she lying?"

Hailey didn't answer, and that was enough.

"I suppose I understand why you wanted to meet, but let me just say that I'm not inclined to get wrapped up in this," Clarke said, "unless Mrs. Rainier files an official complaint."

There it was. They knew Hailey had slept with a client's husband, and they were prepared to do nothing. All those late nights, the ferocious fights for and with her clients and their counsel, had paid off in loyalty. These two had taken her side over Rebekah's.

But it wasn't Rebekah that Hailey was afraid of.

"I just don't know how else to go after the money," she said. "I've tried everything. I don't think for a second that we should swallow the loss, but David Rainier—"

"Swallow the loss?"

This was good; Straus at least had no intention of giving up the fight. Once she'd told them David was messing with her family—or possibly messing with her family—they'd pull out the big guns: more IT sleuths like Dennis, maybe some security, definitely a truckload of legal reinforcements. Clarke was widely reputed to be the most aggressive attorney in Cleveland; he could take on David Rainier.

Hailey's voice gained strength. "Of course, I know we'd never walk away from an outstanding fee like that, it's just that Rainier is—"

Straus shook his head violently, and Hailey froze. "Walking away is *exactly* what we do," he said, his voice like steel. "The man has paid his bill, and that's the end of this discussion as far as I'm concerned."

"What?" Hailey's knees threatened to buckle.

"We've got our money back, so whatever personal entanglements you have are not this firm's business. I trust that whatever happened between you and your client's husband is now over—if indeed it happened," Straus added, ever the lawyer.

Hailey couldn't breathe, and she couldn't help herself: "Rainier paid . . . he paid in full?"

Now, finally, Straus lost it. "You didn't even know he paid us?" he roared. "Where the hell have you been? That should have been the most important thing on your plate!"

There was nothing to say. How could no one have told her? Where was Marla the rock-star paralegal? Where was Dennis?

Clarke couldn't even look at her. "I'm so disappointed in this, Hailey," he said to the wall opposite her. "To conduct yourself like this—letting Mrs. Rainier run up a huge balance to start with, but also publicly carrying on with this man—if this is true, what on earth were you *thinking*? You've obviously lost the respect of your colleagues, and . . . just stay well away from this man in the future, if you want to keep working for this firm."

At once Hailey was the teenager whose father had caught her making out with the quarterback right in her own bed. She was the tipsy college girl who had fled the South of the Border restroom in shame as truckers looked on and jeered. She was *worse* now, actually, because she should have been old enough to know better. Her face was hot enough to melt.

When Straus spoke again, he was calm. "Listen. It's almost Christmas. Take some time off, relax with your family. It's been a rough year for all of you."

Mack. He was talking about Mack's scandal. Hailey had brought shame on top of shame to Arthur, Clarke & Straus.

"We'll speak again in the new year," Straus went on. "But I've got to tell you, Hailey, your balance sheet is looking grim. This is not a bonus year for you, just so there are no surprises in January."

This news didn't even register; Hailey's mind was focused on a more pressing subject. Why would David suddenly pay? What was his move here? Was this whole thing about to be over, or was it about to get worse?

In the end, it was Marla the rock-star paralegal who told her what had happened, and it had nothing at all to do with Hailey, or with Rebekah. David Rainier's decision to settle his bill at Arthur, Clarke & Straus had just been a shrewd business move: Rainier was assembling a board of directors for his new Burning River superdevelopment, and the mayor of Cleveland himself had suggested that Jackson Clarke was the perfect choice to be on it. Rainier and Clarke had met for drinks, Marla told Hailey; they'd shot the shit and hit it off; and the rest, Hailey knew, would someday be Cleveland history. Rainier had agreed to pay his wife's legal bill before the ice in the empty Scotch glasses had melted because hey, what was two hundred and fifty grand between friends?

Although it sure had felt like a lot to Hailey.

✦

She hardly trusted herself to drive home. Her hands shook on the steering wheel—but was she afraid, or angry? Mostly she felt a void: there was a dark shadow that followed her everywhere now, and suddenly the person who cast it was less clear. Which, in a way, was more terrifying. The old boys' club had closed ranks like it always did, but who or what had it left her out in the cold with? A gray sky stretched over the interstate; the road was slushy and slippery from the drizzle that morning, but Hailey did not slow down. Normally all she would have wanted was the sanctuary of her bedroom, that view out over the lake reassuring her that she was somewhere safe and warm, but now the house felt like it was conspiring against them, crumbling under some unknown force and taking their investment with it. Two Magpie Court was in no shape to protect them from . . . whatever this was.

She was halfway to Akron before she really even knew where she was going, and then the yearning for her parents overcame her. To know they could never fix this, that they couldn't even provide a temporary shadow of relief from this terrible thing beating down on her life, filled Hailey with loneliness, and she wasn't sure she could face being in their presence.

She ended up in Marc's. She wandered the aisles, stacking a plastic shopping cart with out-of-date candy corn and lip smackers for the girls' Christmas stockings. She bought her mother an ice-skating penguin statue to go on her front steps, and her father a needlessly elaborate handheld sidewalk de-icer.

When Hailey got to the checkout, the bank card was declined. The checkout lady had seen it all before, but Hailey could sense the eyes of the other shoppers taking in her big diamond, her designer bag. Here was a different poverty—*fresh*—and they smelled it on her. The Visa was declined too, as a line built up behind her, and in the end only a tiny amount left on the Amex saved the day. Out in the parking lot she stood in the rain next to her plastic bags full of junk and scrolled the bank account: Had Sunshine Enterprises cleared them out? Why hadn't she thought of this, that if someone could get in, they could surely take money out? How could she be so stupid?

The truth was worse, the damage self-inflicted. There were no huge transfers to Liberia, only the last payments to Sandy Hollow, an advance to the Concrete Guy, and also the corresponding retainer to an attorney specializing in construction. (Simeon would be up for a fight over all those cracks, even if Hailey wasn't.) There were debits for groceries and Hailey's gym membership (neglected as of late) and the goddamn Christmas dresses and the Shoreby fees. And those charges were just the infantry: January would bring the heavy artillery, the next round of Sandy Hollow and the spring school fees, and lord knew what expenses for the stripped floors and the cracked walls . . .

The irony was not lost on Hailey; without Sunshine Enterprises, they'd have hit this low a lot sooner.

It was almost a blessing when her parents were not at home. The rain turned to snow as Hailey made her way back toward Cleveland, and this time she did have to concentrate on the road. Mack would be picking up the girls now, and whether it was that Hailey didn't want to be alone in the house or she didn't want *them* to be, the dread in the pit of her stomach had been replaced with something more urgent by the time she reached Bratenahl. It was just getting dark, and some of the Christmas lights had already come on; the fact that they had none of their own—no lights, no wreath, no tree yet—was barely a blip on Hailey's radar. Betsy had a wreath, of course; Hailey hadn't noticed before, but as she got closer to home, she could just about make out dried orange slices and cinnamon sticks; a rich velvet bow in sage green. It looked perfect, and expensive, and almost identical to the Sinclairs' across the street.

As she turned the wheel, Hailey glanced at her own naked front door and found it—open.

Wide open.

Mack. How could he be so careless, especially now? That thought lasted less than a second, before she saw that the study window was open too, with the sash pushed as high as it would go. The downstairs powder room window too, and the one in the dining room and—

Hailey stepped out of the car, leaving the door ajar.

"Oh my God," she half yelled into the empty street. And then, "Mack?

"Mack?!"

Keeping well back from the house, she circled the yard. The back patio doors were open, and the upstairs windows. She could hardly make contact with the buttons on her phone; it took her three tries to call Mack, and his "Hey" when they connected sounded like a voice from another world.

"The house is open!" she said to him. "All the windows! Someone's been here!"

"Huh? Hold on, I'm just up the street." He hung up on her, and not a minute later he was there, and she was screaming at him not to let the girls get out of the car.

"What the—"

"I came home, and everything was open like this! What the hell? This is insane! Someone could still be in there."

Mack opened the garage door—the sound was like thunder in the quiet street—and came out with a golf club.

"You can't go in," Hailey told him as he advanced toward the front door. "We have to call the police."

But he didn't listen, only shook his head. Then he disappeared inside the gloomy front hall, and Hailey held her breath as lights flicked on all over the house, and windows began to slam shut.

"Don't touch them!" she shouted. "Fingerprints!"

"Gulliver!" she heard Mack call, and then his face appeared in Mabel's window. "Is he out there?"

"No!" Hailey held nothing back now. "Gulliver!" she screamed. "Gulliver!" She scanned the bushes but was too afraid to leave the girls and check the backyard.

The slamming of windows and the shouting of the dog's name from inside the house continued, echoing through the cold air. For the first time, Hailey missed Lakewood—if this had happened at their old place, half the street would have been out within ten seconds, surrounding them, fussing over the girls, backing Mack up. Here in Bratenahl there was no one; the half dozen houses in the cul-de-sac were dark, except for the perfect white lines of the early Christmas lights.

It grew eerily quiet; maybe Mack was checking closets, or the basement. Or maybe he was lying dead in a pool of blood, and a murderer was about to charge out at them. Maybe only Hailey was left to protect her children.

She did what instinct told her to. Even though she knew the shit it might rain down on them, Hailey called the police.

36.

A few years before his demise, my father married for the second time on the deck of the *Chasing Sunshine*, and so the other thing he left behind for me when he died was his widow. Given the circumstances of his death, I was keen to settle his affairs quickly and get the hell out of Dodge, but during this time his wife was as indecisive and irritating as my own mother had been a decade earlier: Where should she go? What should she do? Where was all his money?

I was dealing with a question of my own: What to do with this albatross around my neck? I suppose I could have simply taken off and left her in the dust, but who knew what confidences this woman had been privy to, what details she could offer investigators? My warnings to back off went unheeded—hell hath no fury like a trophy wife denied her payout—and so when she started cozying up with the detectives looking into my father's financials, something had to be done.

They say that violence is never the answer, but there are exceptions to every rule. I know my father would have agreed with me on this. (His wives, maybe not so much, God rest their souls . . .)

37.

Mack

The older policeman was as irritated with Hailey as Mack was. Mack had just checked the last viable closet that could hide an intruder, had just about recovered from the biggest jolt of adrenaline he'd ever experienced, when he heard the sirens. He knew immediately that Hailey had done exactly what he'd told her not to; now the question was how much she was going to tell them.

"You're sure nothing is missing?" Even though they were inside, the policeman's breath was visible in the freezing family room. The house could have been wide open all day.

"I told you." Hailey sounded to Mack like she might cry. "The dog is missing."

"We've seen a real increase in pet theft ever since the pandemic," the younger cop said solemnly. "Was this a new puppy, by any chance? Had you posted anything about it on social—"

"No," said Mack. "We're talking about an aged dachshund. No one stole this dog, I assure you. This is not about the dog. Someone's trying to scare us."

"By opening all of your doors and windows and letting your dog out?" The older cop had somewhere else he wanted to be. "Look, I know you said you're sure you left the place closed up, but there's no sign of forced entry here. Check with your keyholders, and I'll file a report on the pet," he said gloomily. "But if the doors were open, it might just be out and about in the neighborhood. If it doesn't turn up tonight, if I were you, I'd put up some posters in the morning."

The girls were huddled on the sofa, crying for Gulliver. Hailey flitted between them and the two cops, winding herself up more and more as she circled.

"My parents are the only ones with a key," she said after she'd tucked a blanket around Mabel and Gigi. "But . . ." Hailey looked unsure of herself. "There is someone local, a client of mine—client's husband actually, I'm a divorce attorney. . . . Anyway, I think this guy's been harassing us, sending us threats."

"Sending threats how?" The younger cop's interest was piqued, and Mack was afraid of the silence that stretched out after his question.

"Letters, mostly," Hailey said finally. "We don't have them anymore. I threw them away."

This was a lie; the letters were in Mack's desk drawer.

Please not the iPad, Mack thought, glancing toward his daughters. *Please Hailey. Not until we know about the boy.*

"But it could be this man who broke in," Hailey finished. "Or someone he sent."

"Name?" The old guy took out a coffee-stained notepad; the younger cop took out his phone.

"David Rainier. He has an address here in Bratenahl, but he's a resident of New York. Listen, it's probably nothing, so if you could be discreet . . . I don't want to get in trouble at work, you know?"

She sounded so paranoid that Mack knew something had gone wrong in her meeting. Something very wrong, if she was suddenly so afraid to take on David Rainier. But really, could it get much worse than this?

"I get you," said the senior cop, taking David Rainier's contact information from Hailey. "I'll look into it—discreetly, as you put it—and see what he has to say for himself. In the meantime, get yourselves a security system."

Mack tried not to notice the way Hailey looked at him.

"Don't worry, ma'am," the younger cop said, mistaking Hailey's disgust for fear. "We're in the neighborhood all the time, and so are the local Bratenahl guys. We'll keep an eye on things for you."

There was the window of opportunity Mack had been hoping for ever since the cops had arrived, and he seized it: "Yeah, I gather it's been a pretty wild holiday season around here," he said.

Both sets of cop eyes landed squarely on his face.

"I mean, what with the fire on Thanksgiving and everything . . ."

"Yeah," said the old cop. "But we're mostly over here on traffic violations."

"Right."

Leave it. Leave it, Mack told himself, and then he couldn't: "But was the boy from that fire okay, do you know? I read that a kid got hurt."

"I heard smoke inhalation," said the younger cop. "Nasty business."

The older one kept his gaze on Mack, his expression unreadable.

Mack pressed on, avoiding Hailey's eyes: "Is he out of the hospital yet? I saw that he'd been taken to Metro . . . and then I never heard anything else about it, after that. I guess he wasn't a local, so it didn't make the papers . . ."

"Nah, they're keeping the details schtum." The senior cop was still staring at him, and Mack's pulse quickened with every word he spoke. "On account of they think it was arson. Now don't go blabbing that around the country club, okay? But they found some fancy-ass footprints around the ignition point, probably some rich brat smoking out the invading riffraff, know what I mean?"

Something dawned on Mack then that made him want to lean over and kiss the huge chip on this guy's shoulder: This cop's suspicious tone was because he thought Mack was *wealthy*, not because he had the slightest notion that the yuppie dad in front of him would burn down a building. It was hard not to laugh at the irony of it, though the thought of the incriminating Sauconys fifty feet away on the front porch helped a lot. He made a mental note to put them in the trash as soon as these two were gone.

Mack tried one more time: "Anyway, all I know is, I sure hope the kid is okay. As a parent, you know, you worry about these things."

"He'll be fine," said the cop at last, and Mack's weary conscience leaped to believe him. "You folks lock up tight now. We'll put out an APB on the sausage dog, so call us if it turns up."

"He," said Hailey. "Gulliver is a *he*."

✦

Hailey was still outside when the twenty-four-hour locksmith had finished with the downstairs windows and doors. She'd given up walking around calling Gulliver's name, and once Mack had coaxed the exhausted, hysterical girls to bed, he took her out a hot chocolate and sat down next to her on the front step. Underneath them, he knew, was a memento from one of the last days of construction before they moved into the house: four handprints and one pawprint, set into the cement with the date. Mabel had drawn a crooked heart around their offering, and then Simeon (blech) had laid a solid concrete slab on top, to finish off the step. Even Mack had felt a touch of excitement then, to be there at the beginning of something as significant and permanent as a whole house, though he would never have admitted it to Hailey.

"You're going to end up with hypothermia because of that dumb dog," he told her. He glanced over and saw that her eyes were red, and tiny ice crystals had formed on her lashes. "Oh, LeeLee, come on now."

He hadn't called her that in years; it must have been the sight of her tears that fired up some long-sleeping brain cell. She started to cry for real, her gasps heaving little puffs of frost in the air that twinkled in the porch light. Mack grew desperate for something to say. "He'll find his way back— "

"Remember when we got him?"

How could Mack forget? Gulliver had been an impulse purchase at a pet store in Akron, a gift for Hailey—an early Christmas gift, actually. He'd cost Mack $800 at a time when $800 was more than his monthly rent, and Gulliver had repaid this rescue from a life of cramped conditions in piss-soaked newspapers by pooping in Hailey's lap on the way home, and then with over a decade of urine-sodden shoes and bed pillows and hardwood floors. Mack was going to have to dig pretty deep to miss him.

"If he's out here somewhere, he might freeze to death," Hailey sobbed. "He's so old and— "

"His fur will keep him warm." Mack thought of the places on Gulliver's chest and belly where the hair came together from opposite directions, like the seams on a teddy bear. He thought of Gulliver's ridiculous wiry gray eyebrows, and how he liked to play hockey with a crushed-up Dr Pepper can.

"Gulliver!" he shouted, and at the same time, he reached for Hailey's hand. He was surprised to feel the weight of her head against his shoulder, and without meaning to, he inhaled the warm, familiar scent of her hair.

"Would someone really take him? Hurt him?"

Mack had no answer for her, but he laid his cheek against her head, and she let him. He felt her press closer, and after a minute he closed his eyes and tried to work up the courage to kiss her. She would probably push him away. She might even scream at him for trying this now, but something told him that equally, she might not . . .

There was a crunch, boots on snow, and Mack's eyes flew open. Betsy Wakefield was crossing the strip of snowy grass between her driveway and theirs, and, thrust awkwardly out in front of her, stubby legs flapping in the air like fish fins, was Gulliver. When the dog saw them, he yipped and squirmed harder, and Betsy rushed forward to hand him over. Hailey took him in her arms, and Gulliver got the kiss that Mack had been hoping for.

"I found him in the back, in my rhododendron," Betsy said. "He sure can whine. I thought someone had dumped a baby out there."

"Oh my God, I can't thank you enough," said Hailey, even though all Betsy had done was walk across her driveway. "I'm going to get him inside to warm up, I can't believe you found him. I owe you big time . . . we really have to have that coffee after Christmas. On me."

"Definitely," Betsy said, and Mack was left alone with her as Hailey went into the house.

"I'm really sorry for the commotion over here tonight," he told her. "We uh, we had a break-in. They didn't take anything, but still . . . I'd keep your house locked up. I think the police tried to knock to warn you or see if you heard anything, but— "

"We've been out most of the day." Betsy frowned, and Mack couldn't help but check for wrinkles; there were none. "Then I saw the police, but since they were parked on the corner, I assumed they were just trying to bust Allison again."

"Allison?"

"Allison Murdoch—I think you met at the Christmas party? She's the one with all the sons?"

Mack had no idea who Allison Murdoch was; he wanted to get back inside, back to stupid, stupid Gulliver, and to Hailey. He wanted to know if it was only fear that had thawed the ice between them or—

"They're after Allison because she's had two DUIs in the last couple of months," Betsy was saying. "She's not supposed to be driving, but I've seen her out tons of times. She's going to kill one of those children of hers, or someone else's. Honestly, you think you've moved into a nice neighborhood, and then— " She stopped as her eyes met Mack's, and he got the distinct feeling that she considered him part of the "and then."

I got my job back! He wanted to scream at her. *I didn't do anything wrong!*

"Damn," was all he said. "You guys be careful. And thanks so much again; the burglars left all the doors open, and Gulliver must have taken off. Some guard dog, eh?"

"Wasn't your security system on?" Betsy asked him, and Mack hoped to God that she'd never manage to schedule that coffee with Hailey.

38.

Hailey

There were about a half dozen Christmas trees left in the lot, a scraggly lineup of the crooked and needle-less. The lush ten-footer Hailey had envisioned for the family room was not going to happen, which might have been a good thing. The firm had moved up payday in advance of the holidays, but her salary wasn't going to go very far; they would still have all of January to get through. It was too late for Hailey to cancel the $150 garland she had ordered in August to put above the fireplace, and so during the chaos of the past few days, the pine roping with eucalyptus and white mistletoe berries had dried up in its shipping box next to the radiator, a neglected fire hazard too stiff with rigor mortis to put on the mantel.

Still, it was two days before Christmas, and she had the girls to think of. The four of them put on Santa hats and Christmas sweaters, and Hailey remembered to be grateful when Mack managed to spin the tree selection into something positive. There was a crooked, pathetic seven-footer, the ugliest of what remained, that had a half-moon shape sliced out of each side where the rope it was tied with had broken a lot of the branches. Only two thick ones remained, reaching out from the center of the tree like arms. Mack went with it: "Look at this poor tree," he said to Mabel and Gigi. "Left behind because he was skinny and scraggly. But see how he has no needles? That means the ornaments will show up better. The tree's a gem. I'm surprised it's still here."

Mabel was sold immediately, Gigi not so much. "That tree is horrible," she told Hailey. "It's naked."

"Think about it though, Gig. Santa Claus will be so proud of us for giving this tree a home," Hailey said, "that he'll probably leave you even more presents."

"And hey," said Mack, her coconspirator, "there's about three feet of bare trunk at the bottom, so plenty of room to stack them up."

He was doing okay today, looking brighter and less like he should be committed, but this was only because Hailey had a secret: in the rush to the tree farm, she had not told him about the phone call from the police detective bright and early this morning. The detective who had told her with much annoyance that David Rainier had been in Switzerland for the holidays, that he had expressed what seemed like genuine shock at being questioned about a robbery—or sort of a robbery—in Bratenahl, and that it was pretty likely that Hailey had pointed the finger at the wrong guy. Nor did this detective appreciate her trying to work out exactly how angry David had been at being accused; he was clearly not as worried about Hailey's job security as she was.

As if that weren't enough, about a half hour later, while Mack was searching for the bungee cords to tie the tree to the car, the man himself had finally, *finally* sent Hailey a message. Seeing David Rainier's name on her phone took her breath away. It was a huge block of text, and her brain buzzed with possibilities even as she skimmed through it.

Hailey, I am sure you are aware that I have paid my Clarke & Straus tab. Rebekah's tab. I now consider this matter closed. I have no interest in continuing communication, and I will seek legal advice if you contact me again, either directly or through spurious accusations. I regret the consensual personal interaction between us, as do you, as evidenced by your previous voicemail. But that's precisely what it was: consensual. I can't help how my wife feels about it, any more than you could control your husband's reaction were he to find out. I trust this is the end of this matter. Good luck in all you do.

It was a clear threat: Leave me alone or I'll tell your husband. He was *irritated* by her; all he wanted was for Hailey to go away so he could get on with building his city, and that's what scared her the most. David Rainier was a jerk who had seduced her to prove a point to his wife, or maybe just to get laid, but the sickening feeling that she had been fighting for so long—that he had nothing to do with Sunshine Enterprises—was growing stronger by the minute. At the very least, it was impossible that David himself had been rifling through their house not forty-eight hours ago—did that make her feel better? With his money and his connections, he was a terrifying enough opponent, but without him in the picture, Sunshine Enterprises was almost otherworldly.

She studied Mack as he positioned the tree on the roof of the Cherokee. He was smiling, really smiling with his eyes and lots of teeth, and she should have been relieved to see it but . . . it wasn't fair. *He* had cashed those checks, he had burned down a goddamned *building* and hurt a child, and now look: he'd just about escaped scot-free, while Hailey had almost drowned in guilt, thinking she'd opened the door to this nightmare.

But she hadn't. There was no one else Hailey knew who would do this to them, who would send large amounts of money and bogus invoices and deranged threats. Mack was the dodgy one, the one descended from a con man, the one with no family, the one with mysterious benefactors like that old woman in Florida. Mack was the one who lusted after debutantes and had probably pissed off all kinds of rich people.

Lie down with dogs, Hailey's father had told her when he'd caught her in bed with that quarterback of ill repute, *and you'll get up with fleas.*

Too right. She checked the buckle on Gigi's car seat and slammed the car door shut, narrowly missing Mack's fingers.

"Hey!" he called out, but it wasn't because she had nearly maimed him. He had been peering into the back of the car. "Are the bungee cords in the back seat with the girls maybe?"

"Oh God," said Hailey. "Oh shit. I set them down."

"Set them down where?"

"On the kitchen counter."

He turned to look at her, and then he closed his eyes, and Hailey was surprised to see his mouth curl into a slow smile. He was laughing at her, or at both of them.

"Maybe they have some rope here they can sell us?" By the time she had finished her sentence, Mack had begun trotting back to the little hut where they had just paid forty-five bucks for the world's ugliest Christmas tree.

Mabel and Gigi were already aware of the issue when Mack reappeared empty-handed, and so both were more than ready to cry at the thought of going home with no tree. *Even this*, Hailey thought, *even this I can't get right*.

"We might have to come back," she was telling the girls gently, but Mack would not admit defeat.

"Ladies," he said to them, "Tree-y wants to ride inside the car with us. That's what he told me."

"Tree-y?" Hailey said as Mack opened up the back of the jeep. "*Tree-y*? Aren't you supposed to be a writer?"

"Shut up, and make room for Tree-y," Mack told her, and together they shoved the gangly tree in through the back of the car, until the top of it poked through the back seats. Then they kept on shoving, and pushing and twisting and bending, until Hailey finally had to climb into the back seat and pull Tree-y's armlike branches out over Mabel's and Gigi's laps.

"He's hugging us!" Mabel cried as Mack and Hailey, sweaty and laughing, shut the trunk and got into the front seats. "Look, Tree-y is hugging us!"

Mabel and Gigi, with their rosy cheeks and Santa hats and car seats literally *inside* the Christmas tree, could not have been happier that Hailey had messed up and forgotten the cords. The whole car was already covered in needles and probably sap too, but it smelled like pure Christmas.

"Everybody hug with Tree-y!" ordered Gigi, and Hailey felt Mack's arm reach across Tree-y's head between them, and wrap around her back. She twisted in her seat, and reached out her own hand through the tree toward Mabel's knees. Her other hand found its way over the top of Mack's shoulders and around the side of his neck, coming to rest between his warm skin and the smooth nylon of his coat. As they all leaned into Tree-y's prickly embrace, Hailey inhaled the pine scent, and with it she got a hint of Mack too—detergent and toothpaste and the books in his office and Gulliver and—just *him*.

"Tree-y likes this family," Gigi declared. "He said to *me* that he likes us very much."

"I do too," Hailey said, and in spite of everything and even though he didn't seem to notice, she kept one hand on the back of Mack's neck the whole way home.

✦

Because of his scrawny trunk, Tree-y leaned dangerously in his stand. They decorated him anyway, with all but the handful of ornaments that Mabel and Gigi took off into the study to play with. The downstairs playroom was a wasteland; Hailey still had the headache from the drills that had blasted up the concrete the day before. The section that Concrete Guy had excavated to get samples from could have been the Sahara for the amount of dust and silt that was spread around.

Mack was on the sofa drinking eggnog from the carton, and Hailey was pondering the best way to tell him about Rainier, the best way to let him know that she was not to blame. He had to get it right away, she knew, or she would kill him, no matter how good he smelled. If Mack didn't take over this weight she'd been carrying around with her for months, if they had Christmas pretending everything was just fine and Sunshine Enterprises somehow miraculously went away—and she wanted it to, she did—but then Hailey was still left in charge of the bills and the debt and . . . she would strangle him. She would. With the damn bungee cords she'd left on the kitchen counter.

His phone rang, and she went to get a drink while he answered it. She was still forming her rage into words when Mack began to shout.

"Who the fuck is this? *Who is this!*"

Then he was quiet.

He stayed that way for what felt like forever, listening. When Hailey said his name, he put his hand up to silence her.

"Yes." Mack said finally. "I heard you."

Hailey tried again, putting herself in his line of vision and mouthing *Who?* He shook his head and turned his back on her. He seemed to listen for a thousand years. He shook his head again and again.

"Yes, I understand. But you need to understand, I would never—"

The voice on the other end of the phone cut him off. Hailey stepped closer, slowly so that Mack would not back away, and she heard fragments of speech. The words sounded robotic.

"No," Mack said in a whisper. "No fucking way."

Then eventually he said, "Yes, I said that I heard you."

"No," he said, and then "Yes."

Whoever was on the other end of the line must have hung up because Mack simply slid the phone from his ear and stared at it.

"Who was it?" Hailey asked him, but he couldn't answer her.

39.

In criminology, they call the person who hires a hit man the instigator. This is unfair, if you ask me, because if someone wants a particular target dead, more often than not the target is the one who has set this chain of events in motion: maybe she got in the way of true love, maybe he was about to ruin a perfectly good business deal.

Fun fact: the most common reason for ordering a hit is to get rid of an unwanted spouse. (See previous example.) Usually this involves amateur hour on the dark web . . . some philandering housewife clicking around fantasizing about someone who will shoot fat, balding Robert, so she can bang the personal trainer in peace. Most people don't really have the stomach for it, or the determination, and they won't ever get all the way through the process.

But some do. Some will.

Be warned though, there are fraudsters out there who prey on just such disgruntled instigators. These contractors—these hit men—take a down payment, and then they don't follow through with the hit, or worse, they call the cops on you, and then they disappear back into the dark corners from whence they came.

You can also find a hit man offline, the old-fashioned way. The sketchiest person you know will ask the sketchiest person he knows, and so on and so forth. The trouble with this approach (and I speak from experience) is that somewhere down the chain, no matter how long it is, someone knows the guy who pulls the trigger personally. If he gets caught, the whole chain will sing like a choir of canaries, and this is how a serious instigator could end up on the wrong end of a conspiracy-to-commit-murder charge. The only way to deal with this situation is to take out the whole chain at the first sign of trouble. Which is excessive, in my opinion, and will usually result in the instigator having to find a whole new identity.

Practice has taught me that the best way to instigate (if indeed we must call it that) is this: you find a person or persons that would never, ever in a million years kill someone, and you set the conditions just right—because almost anyone will kill someone, if the conditions are just right.

Then you call this contractor you've chosen—your fledgling hit man—and you tell him to be in his car on Danekar Road in Richfield, Ohio, at 6:30 a.m. on the twenty-sixth of December, waiting. You even give him directions.

You tell him that a man will come by, jogging, in a neon-green jacket. This man runs every day at the same time, in all weathers, because he's training for a marathon. Danekar is a long, newish road with no houses on it yet, and thus none of those intrusive doorbell cameras. It leads to a trail through the woods that this man likes.

You tell your contractor that, traveling between fifty and sixty miles per hour, he should strike this neon-clad fitness fanatic with his car. It won't be difficult; all the contractor really has to do is drive in a straight line. You tell him exactly where to park while he's waiting for his target, and you warn him very clearly about doing any preliminary reconnaissance—that is the quickest path to the witness stand. You explain that, when the deed is done, the contractor should head directly home and park inside his garage. If there is damage to the hood or the windshield, he might want to think about waiting a while to get it fixed. You conclude by telling him that once this hit is complete, his balance is zero, his tab is closed, and you will never, ever contact him again.

Now, at this point in the conversation, your contractor will balk; they all do. That's when you point out that you've already paid him. You tell him that the authorities really might not like where that money he took came from, what it's tied to. You remind him of his penchant for burning down buildings and (almost) burning up teenagers. You reassure him that the target in this instance is an evil, evil man who deserves exactly what's coming to him.

Finally, you remind the contractor in painstaking detail of his attractive wife—his co-contractor—and his darling little daughters. Of his in-laws in Akron, and his mom all the way down there in Florida all alone. So vulnerable, all of them. Why, even this contractor's sister-in-law, his nieces and nephews, his young students, could be at risk, because this instigator, for one, isn't an amateur. This instigator might even have other contractors out there, just like him, with just as much to lose.

And they aren't all from fancy suburbs like Bratenahl, either, in case that matters.

40.

Mack

It was like a disease, like a cancer. There was nothing to go after head-on without destroying themselves in the process. Hailey had told him that this was not David Rainier, and Mack had to believe her—the prick wasn't even in the country, the prick was swanning around Switzerland. But who else had they ever come across that could be capable of the threats Mack had heard with his own ears? Who else had the time and the money to torture them this way? He hadn't even told Hailey the worst of it, how this weird, electronic voice—something straight out of a spy thriller, except *real*, except coming through right there in their family room—had talked about her parents and their plastic lawn junk, had used the full name of their babysitter, had dropped an address for Tilda's family, which Mack could only assume was correct.

All of them, any of them, could die because of you, the voice had said to him. *I could not be more serious.*

And Mack would be in no position to stop this from happening, because he and Hailey would be incarcerated, right from the word go. The money they'd taken would see to that: the voice had promised terrorism and human trafficking, it knew all about the account in Liberia and who else its account holder might have paid out to—drug dealers, arms dealers, people smugglers. Mack was pretty sure that he believed it; he had no reason not to. *Police raids*, the voice had said. *Swift and decisive action, let me tell you.*

How and why had this voice found them?

Hailey had a slightly different spin on a similar thought: "I told you to change your number," was the first thing she said to Mack once they'd absorbed the shock of the call. "Passwords aren't enough. This is *hacking*; we need to start all over. New devices, new phone numbers. I *told* you. God I wish Dennis would call me back. I'm sure he'd say that too."

"So now it's my fault? And you don't think this guy would have found some other way to tell us what he wants?" *Of course* Hailey had changed her number, had literally just taken possession of a new phone via UPS. Mack had refused; his compromised messages and emails were the least of his worries. Or they had been, until now.

All around him the machinery of Christmas was cranking on. In a repeat of Thanksgiving, Hailey wouldn't cancel her parents, which to Mack was pure craziness—Pam and Eddie would be walking into a war zone tomorrow, as far as he was concerned. But when the morning of the twenty-fourth dawned after another endless, sleepless night, he understood: Hailey had adopted a siege mentality, and their house was the Alamo, fortified with piles of wrapping paper and a hastily bought hunk of roast beef that looked way too small for the six of them.

"I told my dad to bring us a gun," she said to Mack quietly, while Mabel and Gigi, still in their pj's, were busy pressing sprinkles on a flaccid, uncut roll of store-bought cookie dough. "I told him about the break-in, and he's happy to do it."

"Did you tell him about the phone call?"

"No."

"What about the girls? We said we'd never let guns around the girls." But the words were empty; he wanted the gun as much as Hailey did. Maybe more. He wondered if Eddie would teach him how to fire it, or whether he would show Hailey instead.

It had snowed more overnight, and Mack found himself staring out windows, coffee cup in hand, looking for footprints around the house. (There weren't any, though he did notice that two of the window frames on the first floor were cracking, as were the walls around them. But let Simeon worry about that.)

Maybe Hailey had the right idea: If they were all barricaded in here, with new locks and a *gun*, how could anyone get to them? Then they could reassess, once Christmas had passed—and the twenty-sixth too. Then they could see where they stood, once they had disobeyed instructions, because there was no way, Mack realized, that this person was going to hunt down all their friends and family. It just wasn't possible; he'd never heard of such a thing, and he'd read a lot of crime novels. Hell, he *taught* a lot of them.

"Are you just going to stand around drinking coffee, or are you going to help me?" Hailey was trying to get rid of the concrete dust that had filtered through the air-conditioning vents; it coated the floors and the furniture in a fine white powder.

"I'm thinking," Mack told her. "And does a little dust really matter now? Who cares if the house is clean?"

He'd known before he opened his mouth that this would be a red flag to a bull; Hailey had not been happy about letting the cleaner go, even though she knew they couldn't afford it, even though Mack had promised to take over housekeeping duties since he wasn't working.

"It matters to me," she snapped. "I don't want my parents and my kids breathing this in. I think we have enough problems, don't you?"

You're reckless! is what she meant—Mack could read between the lines. He could sense the shift; she'd decided now that everything was his fault, when in reality they had no idea who was doing this to them, or why.

His phone rang, as if to chastise them for fighting. It was an Ohio number, but it wasn't in Mack's contacts. He said hello and then held his breath.

The voice was normal. A man's.

"Oh hey," it said. "I'm looking for Mrs. Evans, actually, but her number seems to be disconnected."

"Who's this?" Mack's words came out harsher than he'd intended, and the voice was taken aback.

"It's Ben Stales. Simeon gave me this number. I'm calling about the concrete sample."

"On Christmas Eve?"

"I don't know about you, buddy," said Ben Stales, his voice thick with contempt. "But it's a workday for me."

"Right. Sorry. Here's Hailey." Mack passed her his phone, and he did not wait around to hear the bad news. Instead, he went down to his stuffy, suffocating office.

Gulliver was in there, stretched out and frosted with cement particles. The door hadn't been closed, and the dust was still thick in the air. Mack clicked on his computer, and saw a new message from Sandy Hollow, from Tilda: Can you talk today? It was from two days ago.

Shit! He had forgotten to call his mother! For the second week in a row!

Are you working tomorrow? Mack wrote back. I could call her then, or on your first day back? Sorry, it's been wild around here.

He didn't know why he was apologizing to Tilda; it was his mother, and she had no idea he was calling anyway.

He brushed the dust from his desk with his hand, shook it from the yellowed picture of his ancestors and from the envelope with his father's death certificate, which had arrived from Florida, confirming what Mack already knew: Warner T. Evers (aka Warner T. Evans) had died in Daytona Beach, of natural causes.

He heard a rustle in the furnace room and followed Gulliver out to investigate. It was Hailey, crouching over the big hole in the floor by the drain, inspecting the pipes in the glare of the bare light bulb.

"I see it," she said into the phone, leaning back on her heels. "But how long will that take?"

Mack stood over her, and close up he could see that he was looking at steel beams, not pipes. Two feet below the basement floor there was a void, and the concrete inside it was stained a bright bloody red.

"What is *that*?" Mack's heart began to accelerate; his imagination went into overdrive. Where was everyone they knew at that moment? What if this had something to do with the break-in? What if—

"Okay, thanks," Hailey said. She didn't sound happy, but she didn't sound hysterical either, like she probably would if she were looking at a murder scene. "I'll see you on the twenty-sixth. Do you think I should call my lawyer and have him come? Right, right . . . One step at a time."

She handed Mack his phone over her shoulder, but she did not stand up. He waited, but she didn't say anything. Then her shoulders started to shake. Mack's heart, which had been reassured by the tone of Hailey's voice, sped up again.

"Hailey?" He knelt over her, felt her flinch when his hands touched her back. "Hailey, what is it?"

"Rust," she said.

"What?" His hands gripped her sharp narrow shoulders; he felt like he was hanging on for dear life.

"This red stain," she said, and he could see tears dripping off her jawbone. "It's rust. Iron."

"I don't think so," Mack told her. "Rust is like a brownish color." Even he knew this. "This looks more like"—he almost couldn't bring himself to say it—"blood."

"It's red like that because of salt. The concrete guy thinks the steel beams have been exposed to chemicals . . . to salt and acid."

"What? How?"

"He doesn't know. He's coming back after Christmas with another expert who can look at the metal."

"This happened in the construction process?"

"They don't know."

"Could it have been—"

"I don't know, Mack!" She got to her feet and backed away from him. "Stop asking me questions. I've told you everything he told me!"

Mack had a thousand more questions, like whether Simeon was just incompetent, whether this was a common thing Mack had just never heard of, but seeing Hailey cry twice in one week was more than he could take, so all he said was, "It'll be okay. It's just a house. They'll fix it."

"We can't afford to have them fix it! Pretty soon we won't even be able to pay the mortgage." Hailey was choking on sobs, and she looked just like Mabel when she cried, like a little girl. "I worked so fucking hard for this house, Mack. I loved this house! I *still* love it, even though all this terrible stuff is happening and the ceilings really are probably about to start falling down on our heads."

He didn't know what to say; to him the house was everything they'd done wrong. He probably should have cared more that it was falling apart, but all Mack wanted was his family back the way it was before they'd moved here, the family he'd created because he'd never had one of his own.

"And I know you hate it," Hailey went on, "and you hate me for building it. But I thought once we got here, once we had Christmases here and friends in the neighborhood, I thought . . . I thought you'd like it. And now everything's ruined." She kept right on crying—deep, ugly gasps that made him want to run from her.

"It's all going to be fine, and I don't hate this house," he told her, even though it probably wouldn't, and he really did, more and more with each passing day.

41.

Hailey

It was clear that Mack did not get it. How could the erosion of the materials that held their home together, the breaking down of the literal steel that kept their family anchored to the earth, how could that be *fine*? It was not lost on Hailey that this was the *second* time in Mack's life that buildings had crumbled around him, but when she pointed this out, he said she was nuts. His father was dead, and anyway, he hadn't been Don Corleone, Mack had kept repeating. But that wasn't what she was getting at: Mack's father may have been a low-life con, but Hailey was beginning to understand firsthand that victims of faulty construction might be very, *very* angry. Even decades later. So as soon as they got through Christmas, Hailey was going to call up this Irene Weigand herself and have a nice long talk. She would have thought of this sooner, if David Rainier hadn't blinded her to other possibilities.

Now she looked on as her own father, bundled up in a down jacket and a trapper's hat, demonstrated how to aim the 9mm pistol he'd just taken out of its carrying case.

"Now obviously this has no ammo in it," he said. "But if it did, it'd be a lot heavier. And now you aim it like so, line up that dominant eye, and remember that it's gonna kick back at you."

Hailey took the handgun from him. It was already heavier than she'd thought it would be, and cold in her hands. She held it up as Eddie had done.

"How do you load it?"

Her father just looked at her.

"What's wrong?"

Eddie Byers sighed and shifted his feet. He pushed Hailey's hand down gently until the gun faced the ground. "You keep it like that unless you're specifically aiming," he told her. "Even when it isn't loaded." He reached for a sip from the Coors Lite can he had perched on the patio step, even though it was only eleven thirty in the morning, and kept right on looking at her.

"*What?*"

"It's just . . . after the display I witnessed here on Thanksgiving, I'm a little more hesitant about all this than I normally would be."

Hailey laughed. "You're worried that Mack is going to shoot me?"

"I'm more worried about the other way around."

"Gee, thanks, Dad. He was the one bashing in doors with a golf club, if I remember correctly." *And worse. What would her dad say if he knew what Mack had done?*

"I'm serious. Are you two getting along better?"

"I guess," Hailey told him. "I don't have any plans to kill him, if that's what you're asking. I told you, that break-in scared me to death. It scared us both to death."

"I'm not surprised. This neighborhood . . ." He shook his head, and the flaps on his hat swung like elephant ears.

"*What?*" Hailey said again. "What's wrong with this neighborhood, exactly? You're telling me there's never been a break-in in Akron? How come you need so many guns then?"

"I just don't see the appeal of all this." He gestured out over the yard with the hand holding his beer. "You got these big huge houses up here, surrounded on all sides by— "

"By what Dad? Water?"

"By bad neighborhoods. Bad neighborhoods and a big ugly highway."

"You can't *say* that."

He took a last swig of his beer; he set the empty can down next to the gun case. "I can't say that? I can't say that the crime statistics are sky-high in East Cleveland, that you paid a whole lot of money to live somewhere where you can't safely walk down the street ten minutes from your house? God, it's like you're barricaded in here, except . . . except no one's ever in the gatehouse. And even if they were, is that how you should be living? I'm not surprised you were robbed; you're here rubbing your richness right in the face of desperate people."

"I'm not rubbing anything in anyone's face. It's . . . it's . . . Bratenahl is its own separate thing. It's on the other side of an interstate, for God's sake."

"All I'm saying is, I'd go insane, trapped in here like this. Marooned in your mansion. It's like *The Shining*. No wonder you're all crazy."

It's Christmas, Hailey told herself. *It's Christmas, and you're extra sensitive. Don't take the bait.*

"Please can you just show me how to put the bullets in?"

It was pretty straightforward, it turned out, and Hailey had already practiced it twice by the time the smoke alarm interrupted them. She burst back into the house to find the kitchen hazy and suffocating, and, when she opened the oven, Hailey saw that the breakfast casserole she had thrown together for brunch was black on the top. There was no one around; Mabel and Gigi were probably up in their rooms with their very recently delivered (guaranteed by 10PM on Christmas Eve for Prime Members!) presents, but where was her mother? Her mother was supposed to be watching the casserole.

"Mom?" Hailey called, but the house was quiet. "Mack?"

She grabbed a dishtowel and swung it frantically at the smoke detector until her father reached up over her head and turned it off.

"Where'd everybody go?" he said, and for some reason the calm way he asked the question freaked her out.

"Mack!" she yelled again. "Girls? Hello? Anybody?" She was basically screaming, and she didn't know why.

"Jesus Hailey, calm down," her father said at the exact same time her mother appeared in the doorway. Pammy was wearing yellow rubber gloves and holding a cleaning rag.

"What happened in here?"

"Casserole?!" Hailey said. "Remember? Breakfast?"

"Oh shoot! I . . . I was wiping down the dining room—there's so much dust I don't know how we're going to have dinner in there. Now, Lord knows I didn't want to use any cleaning fluid, but I do think that table needs something more than water to—"

"Didn't you hear the timer? Or the smoke alarm?"

"The girls have the music on in the other room and I guess I didn't—you don't have to *yell* at me, Hailey. It was just a mistake. I'll just scrape the top of that off—"

"Okay, sorry. No harm done." Hailey felt her father watching her. "But where's Mack?"

"He went downstairs a little while ago." Her parents' eyes met in disapproval, and in her head, Hailey agreed: Why was Mack holed up down there on Christmas morning? Even this shitty Christmas morning? *Especially* this shitty Christmas morning? Lucky for him her father had already packed the gun away.

"Honey, is this something you need?" Pammy opened a gloved hand to reveal a small black object about half the size of a sugar cube.

"What is it?"

"I don't know. I found it when I moved the stuff off your sideboard. I think it fell out of a plant. Could it belong to one of the girls? It looks like Lego."

Hailey held the thing up to the light: it was not Lego. It had a tiny round circle in the middle of one side.

A lens.

Hailey's feet were flying down the basement steps; her brain caught a snatch of her father saying "I'm telling you, Pam, something's not— " but she was focused on nothing but Mack.

"Look, look, *look* at this!" She threw open the door to his office. "I found a camera. My mom did. Please, *please* tell me this is something you got."

Mack was silent as he took it from her palm. He held it up, and her heart sank as she saw him find the lens and understand.

"Where was it?"

"In the dining room." Over his shoulder, she could see pictures of houses under construction and cross sections of beams on his computer screen.

"What are you doing?"

"I was just trying to see what could make the steel erode like that, whether it was common."

"Is it?" The Concrete Guy had already told her it was not.

"No."

They both looked at the tiny camera.

"I am trying," Hailey said very slowly, "not to completely lose my shit, but . . ."

"This is crazy." Mack scrambled to his feet. "There could be more of those, you know." He glanced around the room. "Anywhere in the house."

Hailey took the camera and picked at the black plastic with her fingernail. There were no buttons on it—it was too small for that—but she scratched at the lens. "Is it feeding back to someone? Could we find them that way?"

Mack reached out and closed his palm around the terrifying object. "The break-in . . . this could be what that was about. We need to see if there are more."

"That's going to take hours."

"So what, we sit here and have Christmas dinner while some nutcase—"

"No, no. I just . . ."

"You just what?"

"I think we take the iPad and go to the police." Hailey saw the fear rise in his face, but she pressed on. "I know it won't look great, but if we take the Sunshine Enterprises letters and the iPad and this . . . this . . . *spy* camera, maybe the police can at least help us understand what we are up against."

He gave in easily; or maybe he didn't even need convincing, maybe he had reached the same conclusion. "Okay," was all he said. "Agreed. Now? On Christmas?"

Hailey nodded. "I think so."

He drew a deep breath and opened his top desk drawer, then his gaze seemed to stall halfway to meeting Hailey's. "Did you take the letters? The statements?"

"Why would I take the statements?"

"Fuck," Mack whispered.

The pink iPad was still in there. Mack pulled it out and, with shaking fingers, powered it up.

They waited in silence until the screen blinked to life, and Mabel's and Gigi's sweet faces grinned out at them from a wholesome, child-friendly device with no trace of Sunshine Enterprises anywhere on it.

42.

Given its small size, Bratenahl has had more than its fair share of notable residents: the actress Margaret Hamilton, better known as the Wicked Witch of the West; James Salisbury, inventor of the Salisbury steak; Coburn Haskell, creator of the modern golf ball; a senator; a world-famous opera singer; and even a Kardashian and her basketball-star husband.

Eliot Ness too, legendary adversary of Al Capone, the one who sent America's favorite mobster down for tax evasion. (There's a strong lesson there about not leaving a paper trail, hey?)

After his big win against Capone in Chicago, Ness moved to Cleveland to become the city's public safety director. He lived for a time at 10229 Lake Shore Boulevard in Bratenahl, a 6,000-square-foot Tudor-style mansion with six bedrooms, three ballrooms, and a swimming pool set against the breathtaking vista of Lake Erie.

(Having been Untouchable, it should come as no surprise that Ness was only renting the place; he was a renter his whole life. Capone, once he'd finished his prison term, lived out his years in a 7,500-square-foot mansion in Palm Beach, which he owned outright. There's another lesson somewhere in there . . .)

When he got to Cleveland, Ness took over the investigation of an infamous case: between 1935 and 1938, a serial killer murdered and dismembered at least twelve people in East Cleveland. The Torso Murderer, as he (or she; let's be politically correct) came to be known, left body parts scattered all over the city. The victims came from the shantytowns that had grown up during the Depression, specifically one called Kingsbury Run. This Torso case proved to be an albatross for Ness; the murderer taunted him for years, sending him postcards and once leaving severed body parts in full view of his office window. This must've really struck a nerve (Get it?!) because toward the end of his investigation, Ness kind of lost his mind: he ordered his police force to storm Kingsbury Run, and then he had the whole shantytown burned to the ground. The killings stopped after that, but probably only because there was nobody left around to murder.

The Torso Murderer was never caught, and if you ask me, it's pretty clear that Ness failed because he abandoned the principles that had made his pursuit of Capone so successful. Investigation takes patience. It takes a calm head and long-term surveillance—a slow chipping away rather than grand reckless gestures. My father knew this: Do your digging, he used to say to his reporters, even if it's through a huge pile of shit. And I do, whether that means trolling through the furthest reaches of the internet (more results like these? Yes please!) or listening to hours and hours of whining about piss-stained floorboards. (That dog wouldn't last five minutes in any house of mine.) I know more about Mack and Hailey Evans than they know about themselves, and I have my father to thank for that—and Mack's father too, the dirty crook.

43.

Mack

I think we go anyway," Mack said. "In a way it's better without the rest of the stuff. We just take this camera, say someone's bugging our house, since the break-in or maybe before, and then we ask how can they help us."

And I don't go to prison—everyone's a winner, he did not say aloud.

"On Christmas Day?"

"I just *said* that, and you said yes. Why is it now ridiculous?"

"Because now all we have to show them is a tiny camera."

"We might have more than one," he told her. "If we look."

Hailey sighed the kind of sigh she reserved just for him, and then she waited, like she always did.

"Okay, so talk me through what to do," he said. "What do we do now, Hailey? The way I see it, we have Christmas dinner and play happy families until tomorrow, or we go to the police on Christmas Day and we try to explain this tiny black box, and why it couldn't wait twenty-four hours. I honestly don't know the answer, so you tell me."

"Why are you yelling at me? I don't know either."

"Hailey?" They could hear Eddie shuffling through the furnace room. "Holy hell," he muttered. "What a mess."

"We're in here, Dad," Hailey called, and to Mack she said, "Maybe we should tell my parents. See what they think."

But when Eddie appeared in the doorway, both of them were silent.

"That's a big hole you got out there," he said to them.

Eventually Mack nodded; he didn't trust himself to speak. He wasn't sure how much would come tumbling out.

"Okay, well. Brunch has been saved, so come on up."

This time Mack and Hailey both nodded, but neither moved.

Eddie's eyes moved over the computer screen, the tiny camera, Mack's dusty, can-strewn office. Then he gave a sigh identical to one of his daughter's and left the room.

✦

Going to the police did not come up again. In between cooking and new-toy assembling, Mack and Hailey spent the afternoon discreetly searching for more cameras. The most disturbing was the one Mack found in their bedroom, balanced atop the antique freestanding wardrobe that held the TV. It was in plain sight if you were tall enough and knew to look for it, and it was covered with a substantial layer of dust. Too much dust to have accumulated since the break-in.

"Oh my god," gasped Hailey when he showed her. "We could be naked all over the internet."

Mack was silent; he doubted there'd be enough content for a sex tape, certainly not in the last few months. The dust bothered him more than the thought of strangers watching him have sex with his own wife; someone had been spying on them for a long time. That made it weird, but then also maybe better: the police would focus on tracing the device the cameras were connected to, and they'd find this person, and then this would be over.

It felt like they'd just finished eating the smoke-flavored egg casserole when it was time to start on dinner. Something was festering between the four adults; Mack overheard a few whispered sidebars between Eddie and Pam, and terse exchanges between Hailey and Eddie, but around him everyone was silent. The beef was too small, the raw potatoes were discovered to have turned green, Hailey kept starting little jobs in the kitchen and then vanishing, and the afternoon dragged on.

"Where does she keep disappearing to?" Pammy finally asked in despair, as she tried to manage two timers going off at once.

Mack did not reply; he had just seen a missed call on his phone from the Sandy Hollow number. It had to be Tilda calling from his mother's room to let him know she was working today; there was no bill due yet, that much he knew, and they wouldn't be calling about that on Christmas anyway.

He messaged Tilda's cell, and his Facetime rang immediately. Mack heard Eddie mutter something unintelligible as he answered the phone and left the kitchen, but he ignored it. Mack sat down at the half-set dining room table and got ready to feel like the world's worst son. He could have done without this today, and it wasn't like what he did made any difference to his mother, did it?

"Merry Christmas, Mackie," beamed Tilda, and her cheery voice made the atmosphere in the house feel a thousand times worse. She was wearing earrings shaped like candy canes, and behind her, next to his mother's bed, was a miniature palm tree decorated with lights and baubles.

"Wow, that's a real Florida tree Mom's got there," Mack said, after the exaggerated pleasantries were over. "That's nice they do that."

"I did that," said Tilda. "I thought she should have some decorations."

"Oh gosh, thanks." Mack had detected the faintest trace of disapproval in her voice. "I'll pay you back; I really appreciate it. We've had a crazy couple of months— "

"No need. I'm happy to do it," said Tilda, but she didn't sound that happy; she sounded like she thought Mack was being neglectful, if he was interpreting it correctly. "Leonora's had a nice Christmas, I think. She's had some turkey, and some yams, and some pie. She got lots of Christmas cards too, which was nice."

Mack tried to keep the irritation from his face; he did not have the heart for this piece of theater right now. He could hear Hailey through the wall, rifling through the shelves in the study.

"Who'd she get cards from?" he asked with a sigh, because it was all he could think of to say. Irene Weigand was Leonora's only friend, and Mack was pretty sure she was Jewish.

"Well, now, let's see," and Mack couldn't suppress the eye roll as Tilda reached behind her to gather up the sizable collection displayed on Leonora's dresser. His mother looked more out of it than normal and did not follow Tilda's movements with her eyes, Mack noticed.

"There's a nice one from Franklin from down the hall," Tilda said. "And one from Marilyn in the office here."

She shuffled through them, rattling off names Mack did not recognize. He tuned her out until one came up that caught his eye: a burst of sunlight shining through snow-dusted trees.

"This one's from a company called Sunshine Enterprises," Tilda said, opening it. "I don't know what that is—"

Mack didn't hear the rest because he'd let the phone fall flat on the surface of the table.

"Mack? You there?"

"I'm here. Tilda, listen to me: Can you make sure that my mother doesn't have any new visitors? That no one—"

"Only Irene," said Tilda, misunderstanding him. "She's the one who suggested I try to call you. She's gonna be up north a bit more, and I think she wants to make sure you're being an attentive guardian in her absence." Tilda took a deep breath, and even with the adrenaline overwhelming him, Mack could feel a lecture coming. "Now, I know it seems like Leonora isn't aware of the festive season—"

"Tilda," Mack said, and he did not try to hide the panic in his voice. "I need you to make sure that no one visits my mom that you don't know."

"Pardon?"

"I need you to just make sure that no one gets in to visit her. Except Irene, of course. Actually, maybe not even Irene. It's . . . Sunshine Enterprises is—it's a company that's harassing me and Hailey. Really a lot. Threatening us. Is anyone in the office there today I can talk to about this?"

"No, Mack, it's a skeleton staff on Christmas. No one's—"

"Okay, I'll call back tomorrow." Hailey appeared in front of him in the dining room doorway, face ashen. "But can you tell the front desk today?"

"Yeah, of course. No visitors. You hear that, Leonora? No parties for a while!"

"Tilda, this is really important—"

"I understand." But she didn't sound frightened enough for Mack's liking.

"I'm going to go now," he said, his eyes closing on his mother's figure; so slight that she hardly made a bump in the bedspread. "I'll call tomorrow. I love you so much, Mom." He had just enough time to register the alarm that finally settled on Tilda's face before the call ended.

Mack spoke before Hailey could: "Have you talked to your sister today?"

"Not yet. It's only lunchtime in California."

Of course. Mack felt a rush of relief: Lyndsey and family had gone to her in-laws an hour or so outside LA. They would be safe there—though did he really believe they *weren't* safe at home in Dayton? Had Mack reached that point yet?

He saw Hailey begin to understand. "Why are you asking me about Lyndsey?"

"He threatened . . . the phone call mentioned my mom and your sister and—"

"And you didn't think to tell me that? My sister's safety didn't seem worth mentioning? I can't—"

"Call her," Mack said without raising his voice. "Call her and ask her if she got a card from Sunshine Enterprises. Wait—how long have they been away?"

"I don't remember." Hailey pulled her phone from her pocket. Mack watched as she dialed and waited. Lyndsey didn't pick up.

"Oh my god," Hailey said. "How could you not—"

She stopped, and Mack turned to find Pam and Eddie in the doorway behind him. Pammy was holding her purse, and Eddie's arms were piled high with their presents from Hailey and Mack.

"We're going to go," Eddie said. His tone gave Mack chills.

"What are you talking about? We haven't eaten dinner." But Hailey had to know what was coming; Mack certainly did.

"I didn't think anything could make me more uncomfortable than the Thanksgiving Day I spent here in this house, but you've topped it, the both of you." Eddie's face was red with fury. "I'm sorry if we are keeping you from something more important than Christmas with your family. I don't know what's going on here, but we've had enough. Mabel, Gigi," he called up the stairs. "Come kiss Grammie and Grandpa goodbye."

Pammy nodded to the room, her eyes brimming with tears.

"Dad, please," Hailey started in, and Mack was confident that she would be able to talk them into staying. Except it turned out that's not what she wanted; she was pointing to a small silver case in the pile of stuff Eddie was holding. "Please can you leave that?"

"Not a snowball's chance in hell," Eddie told her, and Mack realized that this must be the gun.

"Please. It's fine, we're just a little edgy. We'd feel so much safer with—"

"No, Hailey," her father said, and then he turned to Mack and dressed him down like a three-year-old: "First thing tomorrow, son, you call and get yourself a security system. Why you don't have one in a neighborhood like this is completely beyond me."

Eddie called out good night to the girls; he wasn't in a mood to wait. Pammy squeezed Mack's arm and gave Hailey the world's briefest hug, which in Pammy Byers's world was the equivalent, Mack knew, of slapping them both across the face.

He felt ashamed and exposed.

Especially the latter, without Eddie's gun. Not that he had the damnedest idea of how to fire it.

44.

Hailey

Mabel and Gigi could not have cared less that there was no Christmas dinner. At about seven they sat down at the counter, gnawed unsuccessfully on a few bites of the overcooked roast beef, wolfed down some of the potatoes dauphinoise that Pammy had made earlier, and went back to the Play-Doh ice cream truck and the hideous pink-haired "Jiggly Pet" that had been the favorite presents. Hailey had already had about twenty Play-Doh ice cream cones and had found one smashed into Gigi's bedroom carpet too—not that she had a single brain cell left with capacity to worry about bedroom carpet. She made no attempt to clean it up as she corralled the girls into bed.

Hailey and Mack stacked the dishes in the sink, and though Hailey knew they should keep looking for cameras—they had found four so far—she sank down onto the family room sofa. It felt like if she could just silence the steady buzz of fear in her head, she would know what to do.

Tomorrow had to be the police. With or without Mack. When you looked at it rationally, the decision was easy. She started with the relevant issue, which is what as a lawyer she had been trained to do, and the relevant issue here was that someone was threatening their family. That's all there was to this, if you set aside Mack's cashing of the checks, and Mack's criminal activity. Giving in to blackmail did nothing but embolden the blackmailer; Hailey had seen this play out in dozens of marriages, and why should it be any different in their situation?

Mack sank down in the Eames chair opposite her. "I guess we're not going anywhere tonight," he said, as if he could read her mind. "We can't very well leave the girls here alone."

"No." Hailey wondered if she should tell him to go ahead by himself, whether she could trust him to tell the whole story. Whether she *wanted* him to tell the whole story. "We could call them, though, just to get this harassment on record. In case anything happens."

The sentence hung in the air between them.

"If you think about it," Mack said after a minute, "the guy still hasn't actually *done* anything. He's still just threatening us."

"He broke into our house. He put *cameras* in our house. He . . . *tricked* you into committing . . . arson." Hailey felt she was being generous there. "I think that counts as something. You said yourself the phone call was insane."

"Yeah, but it's a far cry from . . . from actually hurting someone."

"Not such a far cry from sending those photos of you to the police. We need to get ahead of that. Waiting for someone to get hurt—someone else—doesn't sound like much of a strategy to me. This is escalating; you have to be able to see that."

Mack sighed, took off his glasses, and rubbed his eyes. Hailey had a flashback of him in the stacks in Perkins Library, grappling with an economics paper. She remembered being unable to fathom how he'd found the concepts so difficult; his brain just couldn't think that way, he told her. He'd dropped the course shortly after that, the only one they'd ever taken together. Now it felt like he was still that same Hunter S. Thompson–worshipping nineteen-year-old, for all the help he was bringing to this situation.

"We're going around in circles," he said finally. "But if we had any idea who was doing this—I mean, if it's not this David Rainier, are there other clients—"

"It's not David Rainier. There are no other clients."

"Okay. Then who else would do this?"

"Are we not going to talk about your father?"

He ignored her.

"This is someone with money to burn—forty-seven grand is not nothing to most people," Mack began, like he was opening a lecture. "Plus the cameras can't be cheap . . . and someone either paid for that hacking or really knows their way around a computer. You said that guy from your work just disappeared—"

"Dennis didn't disappear. I spoke to Liz in HR. She couldn't tell me much, but the gist was that he had burnout. Not exactly unheard of."

"But what if he doesn't have burnout? What if he's lying? He's a hacker, Hailey, you said—"

"Dennis does not have forty-seven grand in disposable income. I know what we pay him; the guy lives off Chipotle coupons. Besides, he has no reason to . . . Whoever is doing this *hates* us, Mack. On a deep and personal level."

"Some old associate of my father's does not hate us on a deep and personal level."

"What about one of his victims?" Hailey would not back down. Not now.

"It was a Florida real estate deal. It happened thirty-five years ago in God's waiting room—his victims have been dead for three decades! And why would they hate *me*, anyway?"

He kind of had her there, and Hailey was about to admit this until he added: "But plenty of people hate you."

It was such a simple statement, and yet it hurt so much.

Mack could clearly tell, because he backpedaled: "I just meant because of your job. Come on, there have to be a lot of angry husbands and wives. What about the Feldmans? The coffee lady?"

"What about Mackenzie Ewing?" Hailey said, before she could stop herself. She watched this land before she softened it just a touch: "What about one of your students?"

"You think a nineteen-year-old undergrad is bugging our house and threatening us?" Mack laughed. "At least the hacker has a job. Where would my students get forty-seven grand? I get that you want this to be my fault, but—"

"Mackenzie Ewing is a fucking debutante, Mack. You were partying with the Cleveland equivalent of Scarlett O'Hara, did you not know that? Didn't you google your little girlfriend? Her father is one of the largest donors Tech has. How can you not know that? What if it's a pissed-off parent doing this to us?"

"You know she wasn't my girlfriend. Why would you even say that, when you know it's not true?" His question was genuine, and it made Hailey feel even worse, which shouldn't have been possible.

"You'd absolutely love it if this were my fault, wouldn't you?" Mack said again as he got to his feet.

Hailey felt her pulse rise further; they might kill each other if they kept this up, but would he actually leave her here all alone in the house? She looked out through the huge family room windows into complete blackness and wondered how they could ever have survived this long without curtains.

Mack had only gone a few steps when his phone buzzed in his back pocket. He took one look at it, threw it toward Hailey, and ran for the stairs.

On the screen was a photo, almost too dark to make out, of Mabel on her bed sleeping, the hideous pink Jiggly Pet beside her.

Good luck tomorrow, read the caption. *So much is depending on you!*

45.

I'm not going to lie; I was a little annoyed about the cameras.

They cost me ten grand, believe it or not, and they'd survived the weekly maid service and the kids playing and the workmen crawling all through the place, but now, thanks to Grandma and her penchant for violent cleaning, I'm going to miss the season finale of my favorite show.

At least the one in Mabel's ceiling fan lasted long enough to provide supporting material for the pep talk that all my contractors need at the eleventh hour. And if the contorted faces and sweaty outstretched palms I got to watch live all day long are anything to go by, knowing they're being watched has made these Evanses scared. Really, really scared, and probably ripe for turning on each other.

I just wish I could be there to see it.

46.

Mack

Mack plucked the insect-like camera from Mabel's ceiling; it had been stuck to the inside of the sloped blade of the fan with some kind of adhesive. This time he didn't even look at it. He checked Mabel's room again, ransacking toys and books and the fucking crown moldings that had cost them thousands in carpentry costs. He tugged at the windows to be sure they were locked. Once he'd repeated the same process in Gigi's room, with a bewildered Hailey hissing whispers at him, he charged downstairs and out the front door. He shoved his feet in his snow boots and, instead of putting this spy camera with the others, threw it onto a plowed patch of the moonlit driveway and stamped on it. It was surprisingly robust, but he stamped and stamped until he could feel the hardness of the pavement radiate through his shin.

He knew Hailey was watching him, heard her cry his name from somewhere far away, mingled with the sound of Gulliver barking, but all he could think about was destroying this thing. This teeny, tiny, *minuscule* thing. He knelt and checked on it: it looked like the lens might have cracked—it was hard to tell for sure in the dark—but this was not enough for Mack. He put it back down, swapped legs, and stamped some more. He lost track of what Hailey was doing; she'd disappeared into the garage.

"Mack!"

He tried to angle his body to keep her away. He knew she was right to stop him, he was destroying evidence, he had lost his mind—

Hailey had a hammer in her hand.

Mack froze.

"Let me!" She squatted in the driveway, and he held Gulliver back as he watched her strike the tiny device with remarkable precision. It flattened like a pancake on her first go, but Hailey hit it again and again, even though the impacts must have reverberated through her bones like they had through Mack's. She let out some guttural blend of a scream and a growl with her final strike, and then everything was still.

"Holy shit," said Mack after a long minute. "You killed it." They stood over the splintered remnants of the camera like hunters around a felled deer. "I hope someone on the other end watched that live."

"Maybe it'll scare him away from us."

"It'll definitely scare him away from *you*," Mack told her. "I should have thought of that myself." He glanced at the tool in her hand, "except I would have had no idea where to find the hammer."

She fought the laugh. Her cheeks were flushed, and as she shook her head at him, he saw that the fury in her eyes had lessened. The ghost of a smile that followed dimmed the millions of permutations of worst-case scenario that had been playing out in Mack's head, and he had maybe two seconds of peace: someday this would all be behind them. Someday it would be a crazy story that would feel like it had happened to other people, and they might even laugh about it. If they were still speaking to each other.

Then Hailey whispered, "Why?"

Mack had no answer to that question either. He heard her try again: "I just don't understand . . . Do they really want us to kill someone?"

"Seems like it. The voice on the phone was pretty specific."

"Someone in Richfield."

Mack was silent. They had been over this part too, over and over and over again, both of them swearing they knew no one in the tiny Cleveland satellite too far south to be called a suburb. Richfield was basically farm country, scattered with a few fancy housing developments, from what Hailey could remember. They were scared to google it, which was ridiculous, when you thought about it, because it wasn't like Mack was ever in a million years going to drive there and kill someone, some nameless, faceless guy who liked to jog in the freezing cold.

"What if it's a hate crime?" said Hailey suddenly. "What if this man you're supposed to hit is—"

"Does it matter? I'm not actually going to kill anyone, am I? And neither are you."

He said this too loudly, saw Hailey glance over at the lights in the Sinclairs' windows.

"The voice on the phone said this person deserved it," Mack whispered. He hadn't told her this part, though he wasn't sure why.

"What does that mean? What could someone do to deserve being mowed down by a car?"

"There's no point in talking about it anymore." Mack tried not to think about the other secret he'd kept from her, the threat of more desperate people out there just like the two of them. "We're not going to do it."

Fresh snow began to fall around them, and Mack had just started to fixate on how wide open the front door was when he saw that it was glowing in a strange blue light.

47.

Hailey

Hailey's first thought was that someone had broken the etiquette about white Christmas lights. Then she saw that the blue beam that pulsed through the onslaught of snowflakes was coming from a police car parked on the other side of the fence that divided Magpie Court from the main road.

Mack headed straight for the boundary, and Gulliver tore after him. Hailey managed to grab the dog by the back of the plaid Christmas sweater that Pammy had given him, and then she followed Mack to the edge of the yard.

"Why aren't there any sirens?" Had the police come to them? For them?

"It looks like a roadblock," Mack said. "They've got someone pulled over."

Hailey pressed her face against the wrought-iron bars of the fence. "That seems crappy to do on Chris—"

"Betsy was right," Mack said, squinting. "It's that Allison woman. Betsy told me they've been trying to bust her."

"Bust her for what?" How on earth did Mack even know who Allison Murdoch was?

"Drinking and driving. She's apparently done it before."

They watched as a tall, thin policeman opened the driver's side door of a silver Mercedes G-Class. Then the silent scene exploded in front of them.

"Get out of the car!" The cop's voice made Hailey jump. "I said get the fuck out of the car!"

Allison Murdoch gave no discernible reply, and Hailey and Mack looked on as she was wrenched from the car and, not forty feet away from them, pushed to the ground, her hands pinned behind her back, her face pale against the darkness of the asphalt.

"He's going to hurt her," Mack said, and Hailey noticed that he stepped back from the fence, away from Allison and the cop.

"We have to do something," Hailey said, but in the softest whisper.

Allison sprang to life: "Get off me! Get away from me! Call my son! Call— " Her voice trailed off into an animal scream as the officer put his knee on her back. He pulled handcuffs from his side, and the size of him looming over Allison was too much for Hailey. She was sprinting along the fence toward the street when she heard the sirens, two separate cars that came from nowhere and blocked the road as they slid to a stop. Hailey stopped too, as soon as she saw that the cops that rushed out of these cars had their guns drawn. Her eyes went straight to Mack, who was edging his way along the fence toward her. The two of them met in the middle of the yard; Hailey knew they should go inside, should mind their own business.

The cops pulled Allison to her feet; she was wearing a Christmas sweater that said "Joy" across the front, and what looked to Hailey like bedroom slippers. A female officer pulled a bottle of vodka from the Mercedes and stood in front of Allison, who was then pushed down again to sit cross-legged on the frozen ground. The sirens drowned out the words, but Allison's mouth was going a million miles an hour, and she was shaking her head. Even from this distance, Hailey could see that she was crying.

"I'll bet she's sober now," said a voice, and Hailey had to stifle a scream. Betsy Wakefield stood behind them, shivering in the cold. "So awful."

Behind her, both Sinclairs stood in their driveway. Even one of the lawyers at the far end had come halfway down the street. A bitter thought snuck into Hailey's brain: Christmas brought out everyone's neighborly instincts.

"You were right," Mack was telling Betsy. "They must've been waiting for her. Man, why would she be out like this on Christmas?"

"She's just gone through a terrible divorce," Betsy said. "Pretty recently. She's just spiraled. It's so sad."

"Do you have her husband's number?" Hailey asked her. "Or her eldest's, maybe?"

"No. But they'll take her in no matter what we do. She doesn't even have a license anymore . . . Plus they'll want to make an example out of her so they can prove they aren't racist. Did you see the story on the news about how they only pull over Black drivers in Bratenahl?"

Hailey shook her head. They watched without comment while the cops bundled Allison into the back of a cruiser. And then, in a matter of a few minutes, the whole procession of police cars disappeared, leaving Allison's car stranded crookedly by the side of the street.

The tiny crowd of neighbors dispersed, but when Hailey started toward their own still-open front door, Mack didn't move. He stood staring out at the scene, and Hailey knew what he was thinking about even before he said it.

"That's the end of her life as she knows it," Mack whispered. "Just like that. She'll lose her kids, all her friends, her freedom . . . all at once."

"It sounds like it had been coming for a while," Hailey told him. "She must've had plenty of warnings. She could have just—"

"I can't go to jail," Mack pleaded with her, his voice breaking.

"You're not going to. Neither will Allison, probably. She'll get a slap on the wrist. But we need the police, Mack. This is so far out of control." Still, she had to agree that the image of the rushing blue figures with their guns and shouting made the prospect of ending up on the wrong side of dirty money and casual arson feel all too real.

"If that money really is linked to something like terrorism," Mack said, "it will make what just happened to that woman look like a fucking picnic."

"So what are you saying? That we kill someone to make it all go away?" Hailey was being sarcastic, but Mack did not smile, only gazed out across the street, and Hailey's stomach did a somersault. She stared at him, this man who had set a building on fire with someone inside it, and she realized he was watching something. Someone.

A figure stood under the streetlight opposite Allison's car. It saw Hailey and Mack and nodded at them. It was the old guy that Mack had befriended, once again caught in the act of patrolling his perimeter.

Mack was scowling at him. "What's he doing out here?"

"I'm sure he heard the commotion. Anyway, he's always out here. He walks around at night, I've seen him. He tried to talk to me about beach access." She thought of something then: "Did you throw away the shoes?"

"Of course I did. I put them in a dumpster yesterday." He stood, fixated, and Hailey realized she couldn't feel her toes in her thin ballet flats. She turned to go inside; Mack stayed where he was. "I mean, it's December. Why is the guy just standing there in the freezing cold in the middle of the night? He doesn't even have his dog. He's watching us."

"You're paranoid."

"He had all this computer equipment," Mack said.

When Hailey didn't reply, he doubled down. "I mean, he had mountains of tech—computers and gadgets . . . it could have been cameras, I wouldn't have noticed. He's obviously insanely rich. He knew our names, where we lived . . ."

"Why would an old man who hardly knows us do all this to us? To our children?"

"Why would anyone?"

Before she could stop him, Mack was charging down the driveway.

"Hey!" he shouted from next to the empty guard hut, and the figure across the street stilled, then started toward him.

"Mack, stop!" Hailey called, but not loudly enough. She saw the two men meet, watched their postures straighten. She wasn't close enough to hear them, and, shivering, she crept to the end of the driveway, Gulliver squirming and growling in her arms.

The man was shaking his head, Hailey saw as she rounded the corner by the guard hut. Her feet were soaked.

". . . out here snooping on everyone," she heard Mack say, and she had never heard him this confrontational. Mack dealt in wisecracks and sly insults; he held secret grudges and made faces behind the backs of people who cut in front of him in line or in traffic, but she had never, ever known him to pick a fight. Even when she wanted him to.

The guy looked surprised, Hailey thought, but not intimidated.

"Tell me how come you know so much about us," she heard Mack say as she got closer. "How'd you know which house was mine? Why—"

Mack was not tall, but he towered over his adversary. Still, the man was unflappable, which was more than Hailey could say for her husband. There was no mistaking the desperation in Mack's voice.

"I know it's you!" he shouted, and Hailey scanned the dark, empty street for someone to help her. "You knew that kid would be in there. You set me up!"

"Son," the man said, "I don't know what your problem is here—"

"He's drunk," Hailey lied, trying to drown out Mack's rant, to cover his tracks. "I'm so sorry." She dragged on Mack's arm as best she could without dropping Gulliver. "You'll have to excuse my husband's rudeness. But at least he's not driving, right?" She tried to laugh.

"Stop fucking with us!" Mack yelled, and as he lurched toward the man, Hailey fought him as hard as she could, felt his muscles tighten against her. He was going to hit this guy, he really was. He had completely separated from reality.

The guy seemed to sense this, and backed toward his own property, hand in the air. He ignored Hailey's apology and spoke directly to Mack. "Son," he said again, "when I decide to fuck with you, you'll damn well know it. Now listen to your pretty wife and get on back to that ugly house of yours. Merry Christmas."

The easy viciousness in his voice was so unlike the polite conversations Hailey had had with him that, for a second, she wondered whether . . . *no*. Mack might be losing it, but he wasn't going to take her with him.

48.

Mack

The light in the front hall was blinding; it dropped like a sheet over Mack's vision, the glare eclipsing everything in his house—bouncing from the floor, the walls, the mirrors, right into his eyes.

Mack couldn't breathe, couldn't speak, could think of nothing else but the image of Allison being bundled into that cruiser, her head disappearing inside, the slam of the door.

Then he thought of his girls: someone was going to hurt his girls.

It had to be him: Gerry Baptista, the man Hailey had just let walk away from him. The rich old bastard had slipped right through Mack's grasp. How could Hailey not see it? Should he go over there, to the guy's house? Rifle through his office? Punch him? Kill him?

Or it was his father. Of course it was his father. Mack burned with rage at all his father had done to him, to his mother—but how would he find a dead man?

David Rainier. Against all reason, against the laws of time and space, it could be the man who had fucked Mack's very own wife, then sailed off into the sunset on his yacht.

It was all those pricks, all around the world. Pushing him, daring him, *torturing* him. Driving him to acts he'd never, ever have committed without their voices in his ear. Trapping him. And he'd been stupid enough to walk right into it.

Why couldn't they have left Mack alone? Why couldn't he have lived his life like he wanted to, in his nice little house with his clever job and his wife who had, at one point, loved him? He hadn't asked for too much. He had never hurt anyone. Why *him*?

He bounded up the stairs; they had left the door open and unguarded. His girls . . . were his daughters okay? His heart would explode from his chest.

They were. His girls were in their beds, oblivious and safe.

But for how long?

How long would he wait while this thing circled outside? All these things? All these people the voice had mentioned, willing to do his job for him, willing to punish him for not doing it? Willing, maybe, to kill him or his family?

He paced. He checked the windows. At some point in the wee hours, he became aware of the floorboards—the ruined, splotchy floorboards stretching all through the house like a desert wasteland—and of Gulliver looking up at him, whining. Hailey was whining too, but her voice was a thousand miles away, and he could see, rather than feel, her hands grabbing at his arms, clasping his shoulders.

Then a piercing thought shot through the fog, and Mack frantically scanned the front hall—had anyone checked it? He tore both light fixtures from the walls on either side of the big mirror, sent them crashing to the floor. He turned the console table over, upended the porcelain umbrella stand. There were no cameras.

"Mack, *stop*!" Hailey wasn't whining anymore; she was pleading. "Please. I understand. But this isn't helping. We need to sleep for a little, so we can think. This isn't helping anyone," she said again.

"No," Mack agreed. "It isn't."

He knew then what he had to do. He grabbed his keys and bolted, ignoring the sound of Hailey's voice calling after him.

49.

Hailey

The Cherokee's headlights filled the garage as Hailey pounded on the driver's side window. She said Mack's name, but he wouldn't look at her. He put the key in the ignition and started the engine.

Hailey ran around the side of the car, slamming her hands on the glass so he would know where she was, so he wouldn't *run her over*—and then she stopped behind the rear windscreen. Her eyes met his in the rearview mirror, and he looked like a wild animal: cornered and ferocious.

"Get out of the way," Mack shouted at her. "I mean it."

"Where are you going?"

He shook his head, and she saw the motion of his right hand as he put the car in reverse.

"Mack! Stop it!"

"Move!" he shouted, and something in his voice made Hailey do it. He was past her and out of the garage in an instant. The Cherokee's tires spun on the icy driveway as he went to pull forward.

"This is not helping! Why can't you ever act like a grown-up?" she yelled after him, but he was too far gone to hear her.

50.

Mack

They were salting 77, a day late and a dollar short, Mack thought, because the road was already so iced over that the salt wouldn't do much good now. Still, Mack stuck close behind the salt truck all the way out of Cleveland, its cargo of tiny white crystals chipping away at his windscreen. He left the city's dark warehouses and plumed factory chimneys behind and slid down mostly empty, tire-strewn lanes until, after about forty minutes, he saw the sign for Richfield. He knew where he was going; it couldn't have been simpler.

Take 77, the voice on the phone had told him. *Go right off the first Richfield exit, right into the Deerfield Woods development, follow the main road right until it dead ends, and then you'll see it: Danekar Road.*

Was it just luck, then, that this unfortunate jogger lived maybe five actual turns away from Mack, tops? Or was this whole setup more about Mack, and less about wanting to kill this particular guy? Did it matter? Because somehow here Mack was, heading for the frontier of a housing development that looked pretty much like a bigger version of his own, minus the Great Lake. Deerfield Woods consisted of one long Deerfield Lane, lined on both sides with maybe twenty fully-grown houses, from what Mack could see. It was still dark, but he could make out big trees and mature hedges; he saw the shadows of Christmas decorations and the outlines of frosty basketball hoops and tree houses. He followed the road as it wound around to the right and the yards became scrubbier, newer. One house still had a dumpster out front; then a few empty lots down there was what looked like a French château whose roof hadn't been finished in time for winter. There were piles of lumber under tarps out front, freshly covered with snow.

Mack cut his lights and kept going.

51.

Hailey

For just a second, the initial shock of Mack's phone ringing gave way to relief: Hailey hadn't heard the car pull in, but he must be back now, safe if not sound.

Except that was impossible, because Hailey had been sitting on the steps, fretting at every tiny noise, for the last hour. So had Gulliver, in between bouts of chewing at his Christmas sweater, and there had been no headlights through the front windows, no tires on snow in the driveway. No barking. The ring came from the kitchen; Hailey found Mack's phone on the counter, vibrating angrily against the granite. Had he left it behind on purpose? To be untraceable?

No. She couldn't think like this.

The screen read Tilda/Sandy Hollow, and Hailey answered it just in time, with Gulliver's worried eyes staring up at her.

"Hello?" Her voice was hoarse.

"Oh, ah . . . Hailey? Is that Hailey Evans? I'm looking for Mack."

"Yes. Yes, this is Mack's phone. He's not here right now." Hailey briefly wondered whether she should have admitted this, but it was technically a working day, and even though it wasn't 7:00 a.m. yet, Mack could have been anywhere that early risers went: the gym, the office . . . any normal place.

The voice on the line was full of kindness. "Hailey, this is Tilda, from Sandy Hollow down in Jupiter . . . we met when you were here. I'm sorry for the early hour; is Mack due back anytime soon?"

"I'm not . . . He had something come up early this morning. He's not here," Hailey repeated; she was desperate to get off the phone and get back to listening for Mack. "Is anything wrong?"

"Well, I think it's best if I go ahead and let you know that his mother passed away this morning. Leonora died in her sleep, without any distress."

"What?"

"Leonora died this morning," Tilda said again. "I'm so sorry."

"When?"

"This morning."

"When this morning?"

A note of defensiveness crept into Tilda's voice: "Only just now, Mrs. Evans. I called Mack right away."

Hailey leaned over the counter. Mack's mother had died. This morning. Today. On this day.

Hailey tried to think of the questions she knew Mack would ask. "Were you with her?"

"No, I'm so sorry, but I wasn't. I started my shift not even half an hour ago, and they had just found her. I'm so very sorry. She was such a special lady. Are you okay? Will you have Mack call me?"

"Yes," Hailey said. "Yes, of course I will. Just as soon as he gets back."

She hung up, and the quiet that descended again had a disturbing new charge to it: with every fiber of her being, Hailey needed Mack to come back. But she also wanted him to stay away forever, so that she could protect him from this news that she would somehow have to deliver. Even in the black hole they were in, Mack would feel the loss of his mother so deeply that Hailey's own heart could sense what was coming, and the racing it had been prone to lately slowed to a pulsing ache.

Outside the window, it looked like the snow was being shoveled onto their house from above by some giant, invisible hand.

52.

Mack

The man who came jogging up Danekar Road was white. Middle-aged. Pretty thick around the middle for someone who was supposed to be such a devoted runner. It was barely light out, and Mack was tucked in a corner of the street (if you could call it that; Danekar was still mostly gravel, which actually made it more navigable in the snow), but the bright neon green of the man's jacket was unmistakable. Exactly as described.

Mack slid his eyes to the clock on the dashboard: 6:35 a.m.

Imagine being so disciplined, so *routine*, that hiring someone to kill you would be this easy. What if this guy had had too much to drink on Christmas Day, or too much to eat, or had stayed up late putting Christmas presents together, or . . . but here this man was. Mack disliked him instantly.

If anybody wanted to kill *Mack*, it would be a lot harder. They'd have to stake out at least three Starbucks, maybe make a contingency plan for gunning him down on the school run or behind his house while he hit golf balls. It would take a *village* to kill Mack. He spent a long minute fantasizing about this as the man got closer to him: things would be so much easier if someone could just put Mack Evans out of his misery. Hell, he even had some life insurance, so Hailey and the girls would be . . . *wait*. What if this man had life insurance too? That would make sense; that could be what this was all about. Maybe the man wanted to die, maybe this was suicide lite.

But why would the selfish bastard choose Mack then? Why do this to *him*?

The man's feet crunched on the gravel in time with Mack's thoughts: *Why, why, why*.

This dude was probably a murderer, Mack reasoned. The voice had assured him that this person had caused *unimaginable suffering*, so what did that mean? Was he a Mafia don, a child molester, a wife-beater? He could be any of those things or all of them, Mack felt in that moment.

The guy didn't run like someone who expected to die, either. He ran with the sureness of a person who wasn't thinking about stopping with every step, a style Mack envied. The man had a skullcap on, and woolly mittens that made Mack think of a child. If this selfish, murderous, perverted man-child noticed the Cherokee parked there—if it gave him a moment's pause to see a strange car out here in this deserted spot—he did not let on, and he didn't deviate from the route Mack had been assured that he would take: he jogged straight down the middle of the road, and then—just as the pounding in Mack's head began to whisper *Now! Now! Now!*—the man turned off to the left, into the woods.

Mack let him go, but he did not drive away. The man was coming back this way too—the voice on the phone had told him so.

Mack would wait.

53.

Hailey

Mabel and Gigi's fight over the Jiggly Pet ended as soon as they came into the kitchen and caught Hailey staring into space. At least there was that to be grateful for.

"Why are you crying, Mommy?" Gigi said, and this was the first Hailey knew of it. But yes, when she brushed her cheek, her hand came away wet.

It was surprising how much worse these two little faces could make her feel. If only the girls could have stayed in bed until Mack got back, until Hailey wasn't the only grown-up in the room. Should she tell them about their grandmother? She hadn't even told Mack.

It was eight thirty. He had been gone for almost three hours.

"Where's Daddy?" Mabel asked, and what could Hailey say?

She had turned to open the cereal cupboard when Gulliver snapped to attention, head toward the front window.

"He's here now," Hailey said over the barking, and she had possibly never been so relieved. The four of them went toward the front hall, Gulliver leading the charge, as if Mack had been away for a very long time. From the big window they watched the Cherokee's wheels spin as he turned into the driveway—or tried to: the snow had come down too fast even for all-wheel drive, and Magpie Lane had not been plowed yet. Hailey could hear the jeep's engine revving like crazy, and it occurred to her that if the tires suddenly found traction, Mack might end up flooring it right into the house.

Had he thought about this? Through the snow, Hailey could only make out the rough shape of him behind the wheel. He tried to reverse and pull forward again, but the front tires found the same track as before and spun out.

Mack kept trying, back and forth, snow and ice chips flying out from beneath his wheels. When Hailey opened the front door—she had to tell him to stop before he ended up in the living room—she could smell burning rubber. As she pulled on her boots, Mack flung open the car door and almost fell over as he stepped out. He let out something like a growl as he kicked at the snow packed in around the front tire, grunting and shouting. His movements were jerky, and he was more than loud enough for the neighbors to hear.

Gulliver shot past her, and Hailey's eyes followed the tip of his tail as he snaked through the deep snow toward the car. As she lurched after him, she saw that the front of the Cherokee was covered in salt particles. They stuck to the edges of the windscreen, and the front grill and bumper. Beneath them, on the side of the car closest to her, the metal had . . . *buckled*. The hood wasn't closed right, which gave Hailey an unwanted peek at the car's innards. The left front headlight was cracked.

Mack had hit something.

Hailey took a wobbly step back from the car. Gulliver was heading straight for the road, but she couldn't seem to make her legs work well enough to follow him.

Mack was sliding his way toward the back bumper. He almost went over, one knee hit the ground, but he righted himself, and then he shouted at her: "Get in and steer. I'll push." He gestured madly at the open garage, and then started pushing on the rear bumper.

"Now, Hailey," Mack yelled. "Please!" He was covered in sweat, steam rising from his damp clothes, and she could see the whites of his eyes.

When Hailey didn't move, Mack stopped pushing on the Cherokee.

"Please," he said again. His glasses were cracked, his sweatpants soaked to the knees. Hailey could see his bare hands trembling.

He had done it.

All feeling drained from Hailey's body. What was most conspicuously missing was disbelief, and that was because she had always known what was there in Mack. Beneath the grinning accidental golf champion, under the bespeckled academic with his silly, boyish drug habit and his talent for building Playmobil, was something primal and very, very angry. The river of misfortune that had run through his life, all the way back through his splintered family, had finally breached its dam. How could she be surprised that he had snapped—again. And yet . . .

Instinct was trying to take over, and Hailey's was to get as far away from Mack as possible. To run into the house, slam and bolt the door. Or to run, like Gulliver, as far and as fast down the street as her legs could carry her. But then her gaze found Gigi, just stepping out into the snow, and Mabel, still in the front window.

She squeezed her eyes shut and made the decision to give herself—and Mack—more time. She stepped through the snow to the garage and came out with the snow shovel, and a small spade that Mabel used to take to the sandbox in Lakewood Park. She thrust the small one at Mack and began hacking away at the snow around the left front tire with the wide lip of the big one. Mack followed her lead and started on the back wheels. As they worked, Hailey focused on not looking up at the dented bumper.

It did not take much clearing; a few minutes, and the tires found the traction they needed. Mack didn't even have to push as Hailey steered into the garage, narrowly missing Gulliver, who had also opted not to run. Hailey didn't even think to be careful of him getting under the car. She was too focused on her hands on the steering wheel, her fresh fingerprints on the leather.

As Mack closed the garage door, she turned off the ignition and sat, frozen and numb, in the driver's seat.

54.

There is an argument, to be sure, for leaving these sorts of things to the professionals, to the type of individual who can switch off any thoughts and feelings of his own and just get the job done. There have been studies—actual, academic studies—that conclude that even seasoned hit men make mistakes when they get too emotional. So you'd infer that, for a successful hit, one would want a cold, hard machine.

Far be it from me to argue with an academic, but I think you *want* that emotion. You just have to make sure that it's channeled properly, and most people, I find, are pretty focused about staying alive and out of prison.

It's about risk management, too, and trust me, when it comes to murder for hire, a first-timer is just what you want, every time. One and done, is the way I see it, because no matter how clean a professional hit man may be, no matter how meticulous he is, if he gets his hands dirty enough times, some of that grime will get stuck under his fingernails. Too many bodies buried under one patio, and the neighbors are bound to get a whiff of something nasty, metaphorically speaking. But lots and lots of patios, with just one body tucked away under each? That's a hell of a lot easier to manage. My method is better for the instigator, and better for the contractor, too. If everyone does their job right, it spreads the stink around.

If not, well . . . I'd tell you what happens if not, but then I'd have to kill you. (Or get someone else to do it. You know the drill.)

55.

Mack

Why was Hailey just sitting there? Gulliver was scratching up the side of the Cherokee, desperate to get to her, but she was just frozen there behind the wheel like a zombie. The least she could do on the worst day of Mack's life was to *move*.

He left her to it, and though he knew it was futile and always had been, Mack tried the interior door to the house, so he wouldn't have to open the garage again. And then, by some miracle, he suddenly found himself in his own back hall.

He laughed. He couldn't help it.

Gulliver scrambled to the threshold, utterly bewildered at this new portal into their home. After a minute even Hailey came to bear witness, appearing beside him like a specter.

"I don't believe it," Mack said. "I haven't tried it from this side since Thanksgiving, have you?"

Hailey didn't answer.

"What?"

She looked afraid, and so Mack was afraid too. Even more afraid than he had been two minutes ago. "Wha—aat?" he said again. He could hear his own syllables crescendo into hysteria.

"Why is the car smashed?" Hailey whispered, and Mack saw that she was looking past him. Gigi and Mabel were behind him.

"How are you here?" Gigi demanded from the kitchen doorway.

"What happened to the car, Mack?" Hailey asked again, and he moved back into the garage toward the Cherokee, around to the far side. For the first time he saw how bad the damage was.

"Shit," was all he could think to say.

"How did this get unbroken?" Mabel wanted to know, looking at the gashes on the kitchen side of the door. "Did you fix it, Daddy?"

Hailey pulled the broken, fixed door half closed on Mabel's question, and stood against it, between Mack and their daughters. That's when he realized: Hailey was afraid of *him*. Of Mack.

"Jesus," he said, finally understanding that she thought he was a murderer. "I didn't—" Mack saw small ankles behind Hailey's, little fingers trying to pull the door open. "I didn't do what you're thinking."

And she *did* think it, Mack could tell by the way she was looking at him, with fear yes, but with awe and curiosity too. She'd thought he would really kill for her. Mack turned this over in his mind; this was something. Maybe he *should* have killed for her, maybe he still would have to. But so far, he hadn't.

"I hit his mailbox," he told her. "I . . . I tried to talk to the guy. I don't know what I was thinking . . . I don't even know why I went there. I mean, I wanted to warn him, and I pulled up alongside and . . . I can't even remember what I said exactly. And he just freaked out."

"But the man is okay?"

"Yes. Yes, he's fine. He was just . . . scared. I tried to explain why I was there, but it . . . I mean, it's crazy, right? So I'm trying to follow him to explain, but obviously I'm in the car, and he's running away and it's icy and—"

"If the man is fine, why did you come back here like this?"

"Like what?"

"All freaked out!"

"Because *he* freaked out. And I sort of . . . I kind of chased him, I guess." Mack thought of the animal look in the man's eyes that had appeared as soon as the Cherokee had pulled up alongside him, as soon as Mack had opened his mouth. Mack had only said, "Can I talk to you for a minute?" and the guy was already a deer in headlights. Except there were no headlights: it was getting light by then, and the street that had been dark and deserted was suddenly as bright as the surface of the sun. That hadn't made the man feel any safer, though, so when Mack said—stupidly, he realized now—"I'm in kind of a weird situation," the guy had probably already decided he was nuts.

"You chased him?"

"I said *sort of* chased him." He did not tell Hailey that he'd driven into the snow-covered grass as he followed the guy, trying to explain, or about the terrible grinding noise the tires made that sent the man streaking across someone's lawn, stumbling through the snow. "Wait!" Mack had shouted, but the man had not. He disappeared into a patch of trees—he was smart enough, Mack had realized after a minute, not to lead some crazy stranger back to his house.

Still, Mack had not given up. He had held his nerve and waited at the end of the street for the guy to come out of the trees, hoping to catch him in his rearview mirror. If he could only get his address, Mack could find him, approach him some other way.

It had been a good strategy, and it had almost worked: on Deerfield Lane there was a little island of three houses adrift between the first beginnings of cross streets, and, emerging from cover once he thought Mack was gone, the man was definitely, *definitely* headed toward it, toward the house on the far end in particular. Then the man saw the Cherokee, and Mack saw that the man was on his cell phone, and they both panicked. The man turned and ran back across the street, the phone still to his ear, and Mack threw the car into reverse. He needed a street number for these houses, is what he was thinking. Just a street number, and he could google. Google and find this man's name. Call him. Write to him. Why hadn't Mack thought of this before he had scared the guy shitless?

Mack had reversed, in a sharp straight line. The tires behaved themselves, and then he was right next to an old-fashioned mailbox with the number 53 on it. Fifty-three Deerfield Lane, or maybe 55 or 57, would hold his salvation. Mack had rolled his window down and was reaching to open the mailbox—a name, he was thinking, maybe he could just get a name from a piece of mail—when again the man appeared in his rearview.

The guy was in the street behind him, looking right at Mack's license plate and speaking into his phone. "It's a black Cherokee," Mack had heard clearly through his open window, and then Mack had floored it, straight into the mailbox of the next house. He hadn't even felt the impact; he had reversed and shot off again down the road before a single thought had had time to pop into his brain.

Now, Mack was relieved to see Hailey digest an abbreviated, disorganized version of this without judgment.

"If he got the license plate, the police will be looking for the car."

"I guess so," said Mack. "Yeah."

"They'll come here. They'll follow it up if they think you were harassing him."

"I know." This is what had propelled Mack home at speed, despite the weather. That and the fact that his 6:30 a.m. deadline had passed, hours ago. How much did he believe that mattered?

"The guy's fine, so you haven't done anything wrong," Hailey said. "Although the police might be able to see the complaint from Tech. That was kind of harassment too."

Mack closed his eyes, rubbed his temples. "I just need to think about what to tell them."

But there was no time: Gulliver barked, then went careening into the house toward the front door. Outside the garage, they heard footsteps in the snow, and then voices.

56.

Hailey

They don't look like cops," Mack said, and even though she agreed, this did not make Hailey feel even a little bit better.

"Girls, can you go up to your room please?" Mabel and Gigi obeyed without questioning her, which was scary in itself, and then Hailey wondered if sending them off alone was the right thing to do.

"Go with them," Mack told her. "Whatever this is, I'll deal with it. Keep your phone on you."

Hailey obeyed too; she made it as far as the landing. Looking down from the window, she could see the tops of two heads outside the door, two big men in winter hats and bulky coats, not uniforms. The car that had been left at the end of the driveway was an unmarked van, the kind that she had warned Gigi and Mabel away from since their earliest consciousness.

"Mack," she called out, her stomach twisting. "Don't—"

He was already opening the door, and she strained to hear the muffled voices. He was letting them in, absolutely the wrong thing to do. Was their tone threatening? She couldn't decide, she—

"Now?" Mack's voice finally rose up the stairs; he had stepped back away from the door. He was in her sights now, through the bars of the banister, and she watched as he raked his hand through his hair. "I mean, I guess, why not? Now's as good a time as any, right?"

When he called out her name, it made Hailey jump: "Hailey? Can you come down?"

He was letting these men deeper into the house. Hailey hurried down the stairs, heart racing, and then she saw that one of the bundled-up figures was Ben, the Concrete Guy. Not a cop, and not someone even worse.

"I forgot you were coming." She fought to keep her voice from cracking. "I hope you had a good Christmas."

"I did, thanks. This is Bruce," said the Concrete Guy. "He's our steel expert. He just wants to take a look at those S-beams."

Hailey noticed that Mack put the deadbolt on the front door before he followed the three of them down the stairs. Then he went straight into his office.

She still, she realized as the men crouched over the crater in the floor, had not told him about his mother.

The Steel Man wasted no time. He climbed right into the hole and tucked himself in among the beams, illuminating splashes of bright red with his flashlight. Then he held up a hand, stained crimson.

"Yep," he said. "This is exactly what I thought from the pictures."

"Rust?" said Hailey.

"Rust. The steel is corroded. I shouldn't actually be touching this," he said. "It's acid, probably combined with salt, based on the color it's giving off."

The Concrete Guy passed him a cloth from his pocket.

Hailey could only sigh; her adrenaline was running dry. "How would acid get in our basement?"

The Steel Man shook his head. "I wouldn't like to speculate—"

"Had to be during the early construction process," the Concrete Guy said. "Once the foundation was poured, there would have been no access."

His voice was drowned out by the Steel Man scraping away at a beam with a small tool. The sound made Hailey want to scream.

"See, this is just dissolving under the friction," the Steel Man said once the scraping finally stopped. "Which means, I hate to tell you, that the house will eventually fail. Not tomorrow, not next week, but it will fail. I give it a year or so, tops."

"Fail?" Businesses failed, students failed, *houses* didn't fail. "How could this happen?"

Words failed too: neither man answered her.

"I need to understand." Hailey hoped Mack might hear her desperation and come out of his office. "How did acid get into our house? Did someone do this on purpose, is that what you are telling me?"

"Off the record," said Concrete Guy, "I think it had to be. You don't just have chemicals like this lying around on a construction site, so it's not like there was some kind of spill."

The Steel Man was nodding. "Vandalism is the only thing I can think of. Insurance'll investigate, for sure, but my guess is someone poured a salt solution all over your S-beams during the construction process."

"But *why*? Why would anyone—"

The familiarity of the question stole the oxygen from Hailey's lungs. "Did you say salt? Like saltwater?"

"You know," said the Concrete Guy, "this beachfront access argument around here is pretty heated. I just poured the foundation for one hell of a fence for somebody over on Lake Shore, and I know some folks used to be able to get down to the water this way, before they built your houses here. Maybe someone's got a bone to pick with this particular development. I'd check with your neighbors, see if they've had any issues that Simeon doesn't know about yet."

"Okay," Hailey said weakly, though she had the crushing feeling that she and Mack were all alone in this nightmare.

She went to him, after she'd closed the door on the two men and deadbolted it again. She stopped for a minute outside the office door. Which to tell him first, that someone had sabotaged their home, or that, not five hours ago, his mother had died?

"Mack?" she began, but the look on his face threw her. Had he checked his phone, somehow heard the news about his mother?

“I found the guy online,” he said quietly, turning in his chair so Hailey could see his computer screen. “I used his address and worked backward.”

“The guy you were supposed to run over?”

“Yeah.” With a shaking finger, Mack pointed to a photograph of a balding bespeckled man on his screen. “That’s him. I’m certain of it. Richard Ashman. He lives at 57 Deerfield Lane.”

“Him?” said Hailey, squinting at the picture of a beaming Richard Ashman in front of his place of business, surrounded by a group of his white-coated colleagues. “Why would anyone want to kill a dentist?”

57.

Life is full of disappointment, my father used to say, and then you die.

The death of my third marriage (read into that what you will) was a big disappointment. There had been real love there at one point, but the end, despite my careful preparations, was messy. By the time the whole thing was over with, I was a shell of my former self, and this time there were children involved. They caused me all sorts of problems, cost me thousands in therapy. It reached a point where it was either cut them loose too, or distract ourselves with a new adventure.

I began to look for somewhere we could all start over. Somewhere isolated and quiet and separate. Svalbard, Nova Scotia, Papua New Guinea—I did my homework like always. Eventually I found it: an undiscovered oasis hidden right in the heart of this fine country, with a fascinating history, nice views, and plenty of parking. Bratenahl ticked all my boxes (especially the "no one will ever think to look for us here" box), and so off we went.

But my father was right about disappointment. It will follow you everywhere, even to Cleveland. It found me again this morning when I discovered that my 9:00 a.m. root canal was to go ahead as scheduled. This particular root canal will be on the house, I've been assured, on account of the fact that six months ago Dr. Ashman stuck his drill into the wrong molar, completely destroying the last undamaged tooth I had left in my mouth. You can probably intimate how upsetting this was, given my reaction.

Anyway, here's another questionable Hemingway quote for you, Hailey Evans: "Never mistake motion for action."

Hailey and Mack have been flapping around, going through the motions, wasting my time and money. And yet Dr. Ashman lives to see another day, to grind up another perfectly good molar. It makes me angry, frankly, and the time has come to show these Evanses what action looks like.

58.

Mack

The way that Hailey knelt down in front of him, the way she leaned forward and met his eyes with such sadness, could have meant anything at this point, and yet what she said was not at all what Mack expected.

"Your mother." He felt her hands press into his knees. "Mack, your mother died this morning. Tilda called earlier. I'm so sorry."

Mack tipped dangerously sideways. He felt the earth move in the opposite direction; was he still on it? Did he have to be?

"Mack?"

He curled over, his head between his knees. Why couldn't Hailey ever just leave him alone? Why did she always have to say such awful things?

They can't stop the contractions. The baby is coming.

I'm just not sure that entertaining students is such a good idea right now.

We can't stay in this tiny house forever.

We don't have *ten thousand dollars a month.*

How could you just cash this without telling me?

"Oh my god," Mack said, sitting up again. "They killed her, didn't they? Sunshine Enterprises killed her, I know it."

"I don't think so." Hailey shook her head. "I thought that too, but Tilda said your mom died really early this morning. There's no way that—"

"Who died?" asked Mabel from the doorway. "Who died, Mommy?"

"Where's Gigi?" Mack was thinking of the hole in the floor, that it might swallow Gigi up. It felt like anything could happen.

"Upstairs," Mabel said, but as she spoke they heard feet padding through the furnace room, and then Gigi appeared. For a moment Mack just stared; she really was the spitting image of his mother.

"Daddy, who died?" Mabel tried again.

"My mom." Mack felt no sadness. How long would that last?

Mabel stilled for a minute, and then out of nowhere she began to howl. She went from zero to a hundred in a few short breaths. She cried so hard that she couldn't talk, while Hailey held her and smoothed the hair from her instantly drenched cheeks. Gigi looked on coldly—she did not share Mabel's devotion to a stranger, or maybe, Mack realized, she didn't know what death was—while Gulliver barked and barked. No one paid any attention to him.

"Grammie?" Mabel finally managed to squeak out.

"Oh no," Mack said, kneeling down beside her. "No Mabs, Grammie is *Mommy's* mommy. My mom, the one that lives in Florida, she's the one that died. Remember, I told you she's been sick for a long time?"

Mabel nodded, hiccupping. "Not Grammie?"

"No, not Grammie."

"Your mommy died of being sick for a long time?"

Mack looked at Hailey.

"She did," Hailey told Mabel, but really Mack. "She died right around six this morning, they told me, while you were still asleep, Mabel. She died peacefully."

"Six?" Mack said, trying to catch hold of one of the thoughts streaking through his brain. "Six a.m.? Not any later? Are you sure?"

"I'm pretty sure. I asked Tilda. She wasn't with her, but—"

"It can't be a coincidence, though, can it. Today? When the deadline—"

"What's a coincidence?" Gigi asked, and Mack had no more patience left. He scrambled to his feet. He felt like he was suffocating. He could hear Hailey whispering to his daughters as he brushed Gigi aside.

"I could have stopped this," he said when the girls had been shooed out. "I could've—"

"Could've what? Killed some innocent man?" Hailey's voice sounded calm, sure of itself. "Whoever is doing this to us is crazy. The house . . . Simeon's experts think someone poured acid on the foundations of the house when we were building it."

"What?"

"The beams have been coated in something . . . they thought maybe someone mad about the beach access tried to sabotage the development, they—"

"Hailey."

"What?"

"Sabotage on the beams. Bad construction." He didn't wait for her to catch up. "You were right. My father. Somebody knows about my father."

"It doesn't matter if I'm right," said Hailey. "The point is, this has been going on for months and months—*years*! Sunshine Enterprises, whoever the hell they are, aren't going to stop. Not even if you had killed this man, which we both know you were never, ever going to do."

She didn't know, of course.

Hailey would never know just how close Mack had come. Mack would never describe to her how the man—the dentist—had come back from his loop through the woods, had jogged back down Danekar Drive right into the path of the Cherokee. Mack would never explain to Hailey how he had sat there seething with hatred for this guy who was the whole reason Mack had to be out there at all. Mack loathed this jogger for probably being able to afford *his* soulless house, and for having a job he probably liked and a wife who could stand to be around him and maybe even a mother who could walk and talk. Also, there was someone out there who hated this guy enough to want him dead, which meant the guy must've been a prick of the highest order . . . Unless this prick wanted *himself* dead, in which case he was still a prick, and screw him, Mack would be happy to oblige. Mack's thoughts had circled round and round, tightening around him like a noose.

How could Hailey ever understand the temptation? The twisted thrill of just being able to move this situation forward, to show Sunshine Enterprises, whoever they were, that Mack Evans was crazy too, and not to be messed with? Mack could imagine the smack of the body on the windshield, the rush of disbelief he would feel at what he'd done. Would it numb the fear that had been humming in his nervous system for so long?—that had been the exact thought in Mack's head when he shifted the car into drive.

But then, about fifty yards in front of him, while Mack's foot was still firmly on the brake pedal, the man had slipped on a smooth patch of ice. Not just a stumble but a big, goofy slide that sent his mittened hands flailing out, his weight shifting backward, and almost landed him on his butt. It scared the guy, and Mack could read his lips as he righted himself: *Motherfucker*, the man said with a puff of air. *Fucking winter. Fuck!*

And for some reason—he didn't know what it was exactly—that outburst had brought Mack crashing back to reality, had saved the man's life without his ever knowing it.

Mack would never tell Hailey any of this.

She was talking, he realized now, and had been for a while.

"And even if someone *was* there waiting, would they have just instantly murdered your mother the second you didn't run the man over?" Mack saw her glance toward the door, to make sure the girls had gone upstairs. "In a staffed nursing home? I just don't believe it."

"I don't believe any of this," said Mack, stepping past her.

"Where are you going?"

"To get my phone. I have to call Tilda."

"It's here." Hailey took Mack's phone from her pocket. "But like I said, just keep an open mind."

Mack stopped in the doorway, his back to her. He hadn't heard a word she'd said.

"You weren't listening to me at all, were you?"

"I'm sorry. I—"

She turned him gently around to face her. "I was only saying that sometimes in the middle of terrible shit happening, something else terrible happens. And even though it feels like it's all connected, it isn't always. Sometimes in this fucked-up universe, terrible things just happen to happen to you all at once."

"Okay," said Mack as he took the phone from her. He couldn't quite bear to make eye contact. "I guess you could be right."

But nothing would ever convince him, even when the timing didn't line up, even when Tilda had assured him that there had been no visitors and no new staff, that everyone who had come into contact with Leonora in the days and hours before her death had been taking care of her for a long, long time, even then Mack still believed that his mother's death was connected to Sunshine Enterprises.

This overlap had to be a man-made occurrence; the universe could never have been so cruel on its own.

59.

Hailey

She couldn't bear to listen to Mack's conversation with Tilda. The desperate questions, the sad pauses, the stunted language of loss—it was a pit Hailey could not afford to fall into. She was standing in the dining room window, looking out at the driveway zigzagged with tire marks, when the landline rang. The unfamiliar sound coming up through the wall made her jump; she had to sprint down to Mack's office to find the handset.

It was Colin, from National City Bank. He wanted to talk about some unusual activity: an international wire transfer for—Colin lightly cleared his throat—ten million dollars had come through to Hailey and Mack's checking account in the last several hours, but it had been refused clearance on anti-money-laundering regulations. Hailey heard Colin take a deep breath, and then, like he was reading from a script, he assured her that this was standard practice for such a large amount. Colin would need them to come into the branch, if that might be possible, to arrange proper documentation for this payment and the smaller payments that had already been cleared from Sunshine Enterprises. Once this had been done, he said, they could ask the sender in—he coughed—Liberia to resend the money. By the time he'd finished, Colin had lost his polish and sounded as freaked out as Hailey felt. They set up a meeting for three o'clock the following day.

Hailey would have to tell Mack, and soon: she could hear his footsteps, the tap of Gulliver's nails behind him.

Mack came into the room holding out his phone, and for a minute she thought he wanted her to speak to Tilda. But no, he was showing her an email. His hand was shaking so badly that Hailey could barely focus her eyes on the screen. She caught the subject line first because it was in all caps: I WILL DESTROY YOU.

When she took the phone from him, she saw that the email had been *sent* from Mack's address.

He'd cc'd himself, too, but the primary addressee was Richard Ashman @ Ashman Dental.

"What is this?"

"An email from me that I didn't write," Mack said. "Someone's trying to set me up. Make it look like I have a motive to kill this guy."

"But Richard Ashman is fine." Hailey's voice cracked as her eyes flew over the rambling threats that Mack had supposedly sent to this man and his family. "You said he was fine."

"He was," Mack told her. "This morning he was. But I've . . . now he knows who I am. He called the police on me, so the police know who I am."

"So?"

"So now if anything happens to Richard Ashman—"

"Why would anything happen to him?" But even before she finished the sentence, Hailey had worked it out.

"The voice on the phone said there are others," Mack said in a whisper. "Others like us. That if I didn't do it, someone else would."

"Do you really believe that?"

"Yeah." Mack looked utterly defeated. "I do."

60.

Why must dentists, even the decent ones, put all that apparatus in your mouth, all the cotton and the clamps and those horrible sucky hoses, and then ramble on like you're out having a nice dinner together? *Isn't that mayor of ours something else?* Or, *Back again, hey? Can't get enough of me, can ya?* Try and get a word in edgewise, and you'll end up with a sliced gum or a chipped incisor.

Knowing that Dr. Ashman's reprieve is only temporary—I'll kill the bastard myself if I have to—is its own special reward for this morning's suffering. When he numbs me up, I'll hardly feel the needle at all. I'll just close my eyes and imagine the look on his face at the moment of impact.

Then, when Ashman really gets going, when he gets right down near my nerve where even the Novocaine can't keep the edge off the pain, I'll think of Mack and Hailey Evans and how they are about to get exactly what they deserve.

61.

Mack

I can't see a way forward. Can you?"

Please, he wanted to say, *please don't leave me alone in this*.

"If we had more time, we could try to find these people . . . or this person. At least confront them."

Even now, Mack knew, they didn't have the slightest idea as to the nature of what they were facing. One person? A roomful?

"I guess I go to the police and try to explain." Did he believe himself at all anymore?

"We should have done that a long time ago," Hailey said, wearily. "Now who would ever believe this? You'll end up in prison."

"Maybe that's where I belong."

"Don't say that." Hailey took his hand. "This is not your fault. I just—who could hate us so much?"

"I don't know." Mack's body felt like it weighed a thousand pounds. "We're not that bad, are we?"

For a minute she didn't answer, and he could sense her tallying the two of them up, flipping through their case file in her mind.

Then she said, "Yes. Yes, I think we might be pretty bad."

But she laughed, and Mack laughed too; he didn't know what else to do. The fear that she might just walk away would not let go of him; he kept waiting for the end, for the final fatal blow that only Hailey could deliver.

She read his mind: "You're not alone, okay? I know it feels like it will never stop. Like it could follow us everywhere."

It did feel like that, like Sunshine Enterprises would be burning down on them for the rest of their lives. Mack closed his eyes at the endlessness of it.

"Except what if it couldn't?" His eyes were open again; they settled on the photo of the pioneers. "What if it couldn't follow us everywhere?" He put his finger to his lips, then, from his Spotify, he turned on some Hendrix.

"What are you doing?"

He leaned forward to whisper in her ear—he had learned to be careful. "What if we run? What if we just disappear? All of us, all four of us."

"You're serious?" There was shock on her face and in the loudness of her voice. But Mack pressed on; he had made up his mind.

He kept his mouth on her ear. "My father did it. Remember? His only regret was that he left us behind. I won't do that. I need you. I need the girls. We could go together."

"Your father ended up in prison."

"So we disappear better. Run farther. If we stay, I'll end up in prison anyway. You might too, and then Mabel and Gigi would be alone."

She was quiet. She was actually considering it, Mack could tell. She was as crazy as he was, deep in the cracks where it mattered.

"What's here for us? Even if we fight this and win, what's left? A mountain of debt. A house that's falling down. Public humiliation. Two jobs in the toilet."

"My parents," Hailey said, and selfishly, the tears that slid down her cheeks brought Mack hope. She was thinking it through.

"We'd have to really disappear for a while, but then . . . Someday maybe . . . But your parents are in danger too. Maybe if we're gone, they won't be." Mack knew what he was asking of her, how hard it would be. But it was the only way he could think of to maybe save them all.

"How would we even do it?" Her voice had dropped, and Mack's heart quickened when she slid her cheek along his to bring her lips close to his ear. "I mean, can you really disappear in this world? With two kids?"

"I guess it depends on how quickly they start looking for us. The police, I mean. And Sunshine Enterprises." Mack thought the latter was probably the one they really had to worry about, the one most capable of finding them.

"Where would we go? They'd track the car." He could barely hear her now her words were so soft.

"So let them track it to the airport."

Hailey nodded—the tiniest brush of her hair on his cheek, but it meant everything. "We could buy the tickets in person. It's vacation season anyway, so it might not be that unusual. We could . . . we could say we're choosing where to go at the last minute. That we're travel influencers or something, and this is our thing."

"Then we get as far away from here as we can," Mack said. "One flight at a time."

Hailey was silent and still for what felt like an eternity; he knew she was arguing the case against herself.

Mack pulled her closer. "We're all we have left, Hailey," he told her, pressing his forehead against hers.

"You know it'll never work," she said, but then her arms were tight around his back, her whisper so close that it felt like it came from his own mouth: "But we need to hurry."

62.

Hailey

There was so much to think about.

None of it felt real; the stakes were too high.

The practicalities: Cash. Documents. (Thank God for Pammy and Eddie's anniversary in Cancun; the girls would never have had passports otherwise.)

Gulliver: His liquid eyes followed their every move, as if he knew they were deciding his fate. Could they take him? Would the airlines allow it, with no more than his piecemeal vet records and leftover tranquilizers? Would wherever they were going let him in? All they could do was try it; they could not risk a Google search.

What to pack: one suitcase each, clothes for warm weather. This was easy to decide, because they had a cover story to buy themselves some time: The Evans family were officially off to Florida to make arrangements for Mack's mother.

Hailey tested this first on Colin from the bank. He seemed all right with pushing the meeting back; if he was about to sic the feds on Mack and Hailey, he didn't let on. (But then he wouldn't, would he?)

Her parents were harder. Hailey pretended the tears on the phone were for poor Leonora, that her desperate *I love you so much* to Pam and Eddie was because, in the face of death, she now appreciated her own wonderful parents. (And she did, so much that she thought it might kill her. But the thought of their safety, and the possibility of them having to watch their daughter's life be destroyed in front of their eyes, made her ruthless.)

Mack and Hailey spread the story far and wide: messages to the firm, to Tech, to school and day care. Hailey even tipped off the Bratenahl grapevine, so that if the police came knocking, the neighbors would know exactly where to point them.

She stood at Betsy Wakefield's door, house key in hand. A babysitter answered; Hailey could hear cartoons and smell Kraft macaroni and cheese. It felt impossible that for other people, this was just a normal day.

"She'll be back in a few hours," the twentysomething sitter told Hailey when she asked for Betsy. "Maybe come again?"

"Well, you see we're off to Florida in a few minutes," Hailey said, and she felt a boost when one of Betsy's daughters appeared—a child was even more likely to pass on the story. "My mother-in-law died. Just this morning."

"I'm sorry for your loss," said the babysitter, as the Wakefield kid edged around her to get a look at Hailey.

"Thank you, yes. She'd been sick a long time. And, well, our trip is obviously last-minute, and I just wanted to leave a key for Betsy. Just in case anything goes wrong with the house while we are in Florida. Maybe she could check on it for us if we have to stay down there for longer than expected? We have to arrange the funeral and go through my mother-in-law's things . . . It could take a long time." While she spoke, Hailey kept an eye on Betsy's daughter. She was listening, taking it all in. This was good.

The sitter was hesitant, unsure as to whether she could agree to this on Betsy's behalf, but finally she nodded and reached out for the house key Hailey was holding.

It hurt to let go of it.

"I'll make sure Mrs. Wakefield gets this," the babysitter said, closing her palm around all of Hailey's hopes and dreams. "She'll be back soon. She's just at an appointment."

"She's at the dentist," Betsy's daughter chimed in. "She's *always* at the dentist."

Hailey wasn't listening, though; her eyes were on Mack, who had begun loading suitcases into the Cherokee. "Tell your mom I said we'll get together when I get back," she told the little girl, and she was already halfway down the Wakefields' front path when she finished her sentence: "Tell her we'll go for coffee."

63.

No one bothered to tell me they'd gone.

It was only when I found a random key on the windowsill by the front door that Arabella finally remembered to fill me in, to let me know I was supposed to be keeping an eye on their house.

(I can do that for you, Hailey, it's no trouble.)

The grandma in Florida died, apparently, but I know they aren't down there picking out hymns and a casket. There's no trace of them yet, not since they bought four plane tickets and a pet passport to São Paulo, but they'll pop up eventually. It's tough, building a whole new life, and most people slip up at some point.

Even me. Eighteen months ago, I tried to buy four acres to build my own piece of Bratenahl paradise. I had plans drawn up for a house, with a ninety-foot tower and views all the way to Canada. But just as I was about to close on the deal, the landowner figured out that he could make more money by carving up my plot into smaller ones. And then who should come along sniffing for a land grab? Mack and Hailey Evans and their crafty realtor, that's who. They outbid me by $47,000 for the prime lot—on the corner, view of the lake, best one in the development. I would have coughed up another couple of million to keep my estate intact, but I never even got the chance to counteroffer.

So, it had to be a longer game: two plots while I waited for the third to come available again. One horrible little gray house of my own, easy to build and easy to tear down when the identical monstrosity next door finally crumbles and I can wall off a decent chunk of land—though not quite the size of my original vision, thanks to the riffraff on the other side of the street. In the meantime, I'm tossed in among the neighborhood masses, forced to endure afternoon tennis matches and midmorning Botox parties. (I myself don't partake of the face poison, by the way. I just like to watch the needle go in.)

Amid that real estate clusterfuck, though, I really thought I had found myself a consolation prize: right from the beginning, right from the moment they first staked their plastic flamingo into the best plot of land left in Bratenahl, I recognized that Mack and Hailey Evans had bitten off more than they could chew. It's a most important quality in a potential contractor: Get 'em when they're starting out, my father used to say of his reporters, when they're hungry and desperate. Maybe Mack and Hailey were too desperate, maybe that was the problem. Maybe I should've known better than to choose a couple who were about to have the ceiling fall in on them—and not metaphorically, either.

Unlike my dad, though, I don't give up when the going gets tough. And even if I never find those Evanses, even if they do manage to keep running forever, I wasn't bluffing: As the good Dr. Ashman would tell you if he were still with us, there are plenty of others out there, just like them, with just the right amount to lose.

64.

Mack

The sight of the envelope, still white and crisp despite having been smashed into the PO box, sent Mack's heart racing. He set Gulliver down on the hot tiles and tugged away at their first real piece of mail in at least a year. He yanked the slim package from its too-tight surroundings, shredding both sides in the process. There was no return address on the back, and Mack's hands shook as he flipped it over. The sight of their innocuous, anonymous address carefully spelled out in familiar handwriting washed over his body like a wave.

The looping, orderly scroll belonged unmistakably to Pammy Byers, and Mack began to breathe again. They had been expecting this; he should have known. He had been on the furtive phone calls, had agreed with Hailey to compromise their secret (carefully!) for the sake of her parents' sanity. In his hands, Mack was holding one end of the thinnest of threads that connected the two of them to their old lives. He took a quick glance around the empty postal building, then slid his thumb along the end of the heavy envelope and tipped the contents out onto the dusty counter next to him.

There was a long note from Pammy that he didn't read, and a couple of flat pieces of metal on a string—some kind of wind chime, by the looks of it. There were three packets of grape Kool-Aid, which any interested customs guy would definitely have thought was poorly disguised cocaine. Mack took another furtive look around before he turned his attention to the last of the Pammy Byers booty: a copy of *Cleveland Social* magazine.

The glossy cover photo of the brilliant autumn trees on Lake Erie's southern edge filled him with a mixture of revulsion and nostalgia. September was the Bratenahl Issue, and Mack couldn't decide whether Pammy had sent it out of desperate hope, or utter madness. The landscape was a world away from his current surroundings. Had he ever lived there, really?

He had tried it on, for sure. He had never wanted it like Hailey did, but still, he had accepted fresh towels from the Shoreby pool attendant and signed on to pay school bills higher than the GDP of a small country. In the end, though, it was Bratenahl that didn't want Mack. It had chewed him up and spat him out, and that was okay. He was fine with it, and now here he was in the tropics, with the warm sun on his back. Right then he resolved for the millionth time to write that novel: he would be a Hemingway for the twenty-first century, one with a pen name, whose true identity would only be discovered upon his death, leaving a legacy for future generations who could come and visit the tiny apartment where he wrote his masterpiece . . . More importantly, of course, Mack had his family around him, and they were all safe, and that's what mattered.

From time to time he did wonder, though—especially right then as his eyes lingered on the ad for Cleveland Tech on the back cover of the magazine—from time to time he did think of his students, and what they had made of his daring escape. Whether they would have thought him foolish, or brave.

He hoped it was the latter.

65.

Hailey

It was thrilling to hear the shrieks and murmurs that drifted out from the playground. The tone of the girls' voices was the same, but increasingly, Hailey had no idea what they were saying. Their brains were young and elastic and they gobbled up vocabulary in a way that Hailey could not; they had racked up so many friends and produced so much laughter that it was as if they'd been here forever. Hailey less so, but she would keep trying: she had her good old-fashioned flash cards and the Duolingo app and whole afternoons of soap operas that she mined for the smallest nuggets of understanding. She would put in the work, and soon the four of them would be as good as local. After that, who knew?

Actually, Hailey did: She would find a job. Maybe teach. Maybe Mack could too.

She shifted her feet on the ground; it was so hot her flip-flops were melting into the cement. She called the girls over and applied a fresh layer of sunscream, much to the amusement of two locals on a neighboring bench. The school on the other side of the playground was small but popular, and in an out-of-the-way neighborhood with a reasonably camouflaging international population. They had been lucky to get two spaces, the school administrator had told them.

Gigi squirmed, slipped through Hailey's hands, and took off running with only one arm lotioned. Hailey wiped the excess cream on her shorts and brushed the sweat from her forehead.

Maybe not teaching. Maybe somehow, in some crafty, unofficial capacity, Hailey could get back to law. Or real estate. She'd be good at the contracts, once she learned the language, and that way she could get an early lead on a house, something with more room than they had now. Maybe even a pool.

The sweat was running down her back.

Mack would disapprove, she knew. He was wary of too many connections, and the only job he seemed interested in was giving golf lessons to European tourists. Not exactly high aspirations, but they matched his outfit: he was wearing an old Hard Rock Café T-shirt and knock-off Crocs as he made his way toward her now, a big white envelope under one arm and Gulliver tucked into the other.

Hailey wept at the sight of the purple Kool-Aid packets, and she read her mother's letter over and over until the sun started going down. When they got home, they hung the delicate wind chime (which when assembled turned out to be a cardinal, the state bird of Ohio) on the scraggly tree outside the apartment door, and they talked about how they would see Grammie and Grandpa again before too long. Gigi and even Mabel were forgetting; this kind of conversation no longer made them sad.

When they were all fed and watered and the girls were tucked in, Hailey sat in one of the plastic balcony chairs with a glass of cold wine and the copy of *Cleveland Social.* She felt a firm, hard nothing inside as she flipped through the pages of Bratenahl real estate. The two towers looked ugly to her now, the lake a murky brown even in the good photos.

Toward the end of the issue though, her heart fluttered to life: between the pages, she found a Marc's receipt that Pammy had obviously intended as a bookmark. It flagged an article about Magpie Court. Hailey read it in less than a minute.

"Mack," she called, and he came out holding the wine bottle. "Have you seen this?"

He had not; he read it at an infuriatingly slow pace and then *reread* it.

"Well," he said finally. "I guess that's the epilogue to our Bratenahl experiment."

"It's like we never existed there. Literally. We've been wiped off the map." Hailey closed her eyes, tried one last time to conjure up the view of Lake Erie from their bedroom. It wouldn't come; the house was like a mirage that vanished before her eyes. Had it ever really existed? She thought of the handprints they'd left in the cement under the front porch, imagined them swept away and turned back to dust.

"You know who I feel sorry for?" Mack said as he switched out the lights to keep the mosquitoes away and came to sit down next to Hailey. "Betsy Wakefield. Wonder where she ended up?"

CLEVELAND SOCIAL

September 20**

THE BRATENAHL ISSUE

Magpie Megamansion

Local council members have faced heavy criticism from housing officials after approving a new plan to reverse-develop a controversial group of cluster homes. The northern half of Magpie Court, which currently consists of five homes on six lots, has been purchased by a mystery buyer with plans to tear down at least two existing homes and build a 25,000-square-foot compound that would become one of the largest single-family dwellings in Bratenahl.

Dunlop & McConnell LLP, the architecture firm behind the new design, refused to comment on the buyer's identity, but said

that construction on the neighborhood's newest estate will begin next summer. Though questions have been raised about the social consciousness of reducing housing stock and nothing has yet been revealed about how this will affect residents' beach access, one thing's for sure: the view will be spectacular!

Acknowledgments

A huge thank-you goes to Steph Thwaites at Curtis Brown, my agent and friend, the sharpest and sweetest tiger in this business. Thank you for believing in me and in this book, and for having the uncanny ability to make one small suggestion that pulls a whole novel together. Another big hug of gratitude goes to Christy Fletcher at UTA, my American guardian angel. It's been an absolute joy to get to know you. Many thanks too to Leah Valaydon and Claire Yoo for expert guidance.

Cicely Aspinall at HQ and Sarah Stein at Harper have made this book much richer than it was when we started; I have felt so safe in your expert hands. Thanks also to Emily Griffin for taking a chance on this debut, and to Seema Mitra at HQ for stepping in so brilliantly. Huge thanks to Jackie Quaranto and Francesca von Krauland for keeping me on the straight and narrow.

Thank you to Miranda Ottewell for the meticulous and fascinating copyedits, right down to Mabel's jelly plastic shoes.

The gorgeous cover was designed by Robin Bilardello and adapted for the UK by Stephanie Heathcote, and thank you to the production team at Harper for helping to make this idea in my head into an actual physical object: Lydia Weaver, Jocelyn Larnick and Elina Cohen. My extreme gratitude goes also to Stephanie Mendoza and Sam Lubash at Harper and Isabel Williams and Sophie Rosewell at HQ, for shouting about this novel from the rooftops. I'd never heard of Bratenahl when I started work on this novel, and a lot of what's in these pages is my fictional version of the place. But the history is mostly real, and I do owe a debt to the Bratenahl Historical Society website, as well as *Bygone Bratenahl* by William Beckenbach and *A Place Apart: The History of Bratenahl, Ohio* by Diana Tittle for background on this fascinating little strip of a suburb. Thanks also to Erin Johnson for real estate advice.

The wonderful folks at Curtis Brown Creative—Anna Davis, Jack Hadley, Abby Parsons, Jennifer Kerslake, Lyndsey Ng, Danni Georgiou, and Ruby Gaffney—have kept me in the black while I was writing this; working for CBC has been one of the highlights of my career.

Thank you to Susan Quick, for thirty years of friendship and for always being an encouraging reader; and to her mini-me Olivia, too, who snuck in a very early and age-inappropriate read.

Thanks to the rest of my sisterhood too, for love and support: Pri Anand, Shirit Kedar, Helen Cutt, Zoe Coyle-Beeche, I'm so lucky to have you. Also to Nicky Worthington and Treacle and Emily Reddy and Skye, for long calming walks and endless cups of coffee.

Also much love and many treats go to Howie, who would never, *ever* pee in the house and who has been my faithful companion while I wrote this.

Barbara Pearson, I won the mother-in-law lottery when I married your son. Thanks for your unending support and careful reads.

My wonderful little sister, Alexandra Wright, and my brother-in-law, Andy Wright, gave me much information on all things Cleveland; thanks, guys, for being my boots on the ground.

Thank you to my parents John and Karla Schott, for everything—ideas, reads, support, shoulders to cry on, inspiration, encouragement, love. There are no better parents in this world.

To my children Ava and Johnny, your creativity and brilliance inspires me every day and your fearlessness makes me brave. Thank you for being you.

And finally, to Chris, my better half, my best friend, the Mack to my Hailey (or the Hailey to my Mack?). Thank you for believing in me. If you wanted one, I would get you a toe.

About the Author

LAUREN SCHOTT is a freelance editor and ghostwriter with more than twenty-five years of experience in book and magazine publishing. A graduate of Duke University, she was born and raised in Akron, Ohio, but now lives in Henley-on-Thames, England, with her family. *Very Slowly All at Once* is her first novel for adults.